6/18/16

Alternative Reports

Headlines scream "atrosity."
Newscasts ~~blurt~~ shout the same.
But why should prose or poetry
Be ~~featured in that~~ game?
Why cannot words extol - instead
The wonders so alive
That they don't focus on the ~~dead~~
But ~~rather~~ what should thrive?

The spheric opal moon last night
Spread jewels upon the ~~tide~~ sea;
It ~~aired~~ roses so fragrant, bright
Sent senses on a ride.
A ~~host of children on the lawn~~
~~rose and in smiles~~ greet the dawn,
As neighbors rose to greet the dawn,
~~To greet the morning sun. It~~

Let headlines tout diversity
And newscasts ply airwaves
With deeds of ~~common~~ hope and courtesy.
That's what the public craves.

WHAT THE OWL SAW

A Rex Nickels Mystery

Edward Phillips
Arthur Rogers

ISBN: 1497352924
ISBN 13: 9781497352926
Library of Congress Control Number: 2014905251
CreateSpace Independent Publishing Platform
North Charleston, South Carolina

For Mary Louise and Synthia Ann, our Muses

CHAPTER ONE

"**F**eathers? You're tellin' me you think the death may have been caused by bird feathers?" Captain Fred Wunderlich was in no mood for fooling around at this hour on Monday morning, after being rousted by a six thirty a.m. call from headquarters. Wunderlich, veteran investigator of the Redwood City Police Department, stood amidst a beehive of activity in Union Cemetery talking to Nick Nakamura, County Medical Examiner. The entrance to the cemetery and a good part of the Woodside Road frontage were occupied by patrol cars, unmarked cars with "E" license plates, and County Health Department vehicles. The focus of attention was centered around what was left of the monument to the men of San Mateo County who had given their all in the Civil War to preserve the Union. Vandals had stolen the life size statue of the uniformed soldier that once stood there, and years later had returned and smashed the replacement statue into pieces. Only the granite plinth now remained intact. Propped up against this structure was a dead male clad only in a clear plastic raincoat, by now discreetly shrouded by a police blanket.

"Can't rule it out, Captain. Part of the evidence found on the body," replied Nakamura, hiding a mischievous smile. "Pulling your leg a bit. Actually we did find a single white feather lodged in the left nostril. May or may not be of significance. Not much else that we can see at this point. No wounds, no marks to speak of other than some blueness around his lips. We need to run a blood test to see if there are any drugs present, or any effects of disease. Weird case—maybe the guy was some kind of geek who ate live birds, though I will say that I don't see avian remains around the scene." Nakamura enjoyed irritating Wunderlich with little absurdities.

"Hummppf," Wunderlich muttered. "I'm told the body was discovered this morning by a birdwatcher who happened to be prowling around the cemetery premises. Looking for unusual birds, I bet. Well, he sure found one here. A one-feather bird. Okay, here's Sergeant Rooney now. Bud, you were the first detail on the scene, right?"

"Yes, Captain. Call came into dispatch at six twenty three this morning, from a fellow who identified himself as Earl T. Crow. Said he was calling from a pay phone on El Camino near Woodside Road. Described himself as a birdwatcher who often visited Union Cemetery early mornings. We arrived here at six thirty seven, just about a half hour ago. Crow was here. He'd come back after going away to find a phone. We got his statement and saw no reason to detain him at this time. We found the body where you see it, no clothes, no wallet, no ID, no watch, no rings or other jewelry. And nothing more from a search of the perimeter. Just the plastic raincoat, with the words 'If you see k...' scrawled on it in what appears to be lipstick. It was all smeary after the 'k', like someone was in a hurry. The victim looks to be mid-forties, Caucasian, good health (till now), no dentures or other traceable dental work. Probably not used to hard labor—smooth hands."

"What about prints?"

"We've taken the victim's prints. And there were some latents on the raincoat and partials in the smeared lipstick that didn't get entirely wiped off. We got those too. I've just dispatched a man to the station house to get the prints sent off for some identification. We should have a response in two or three days. Oh, and I've just checked in by radio with our office and the Sheriff's department. We've got no missing person report that fits the victim's description. But it's still early. Possibly the victim has not been missed by anyone yet. The day's just starting."

"Nick," Wunderlich asked, "do we have any fix on the time of death?"

"At this point my guess would be he passed about six hours ago, say between one and two a.m. We'll be able to pinpoint this a little better after we do some testing back at the morgue," said Nakamura.

"Okay, then. A little early for any kind of conclusions. I have a gut sense of some kind of drug-related revenge action, be it big-time or small-time. But, Bud, let's just keep an eye on Mr. Crow. And Nick, will you be able to identify the source of the feather?"

"Not me, but the county has an ornithologist on retainer, mostly working in the county parks. I'll send a sample over to her after the lab has a look at the body."

"Also, Bud, as soon as you get back downtown, write up a press release for my approval. We better get something out. You can see, out there on the road, all the morning rush hour traffic, slowing down to get a peek at what's going on in here. With everything that's happened to this monument, people are wondering 'what now?' I'll wager nothing ever like this before. A lot of public curiosity brewing. If only they knew! Well, that all you got, Nick?" Wunderlich asked. "Any guesses as to what did this guy in? Other than maybe bein' kissed to death?"

"A possibility. Very insightful of you, Captain Wunderlich."

"Think nothing of it, Examiner Nakamura."

CHAPTER TWO

Feathers. If there was anything he hated more than feathers, he couldn't bring it to mind, Rex mused as he banged the sofa cushions against the door jamb. The resulting dust and grit made a small cloud, and one little white feather worked its way through the upholstery and floated to the floor of his office. He plopped the two seat cushions back into place, stained side down. Then he gave the back pillows several whomps against the woodwork. Despite the pounding, the hair oil stains remained, so that the green fabric of each billow kept a distinctly gray element.

The last time Sheila came in here about her alimony being late, Rex recalled, she bitched about my dusty couch and her damned allergies so much, she gave me a headache. I'm not giving her the chance again. Dumb broad, I don't know why in hell I married her in the first place. Big knockers, I guess. And her telling me the rabbit died, when it didn't really. Now I'd as soon shoot the old sow as look at her.

Rex made his way over to the small table next to his desk. With a grunt he reached out for the old Sunbeam Coffeemaster he and Sheila had kept on the kitchen counter before their divorce.

"Coffee...need...coffee," he murmured. "I guess I do miss that part about being hitched to old Sheila. She sure made good tasting fresh coffee. Mine's never any good. Wonder how she made the coffee that way? She always said the secret was to use bottled water, because it kept the pot clean. I don't know if she was lying or not, 'cause I can never get it the same."

Rex poured what was left of yesterday's coffee into the trash can, and followed it with the used-up grounds. He measured out two scoops of fresh Folgers and propelled them into the Coffeemaster's empty, if not cleaned, basket with unnecessary force, punctuating his actions with words.

"Lyin'..." he said with the first scoop..."broad," he said with the second. He filled the machine with water from a plastic bottle which he had filled at the drinking fountain in the hallway the day before, and turned on the coffee maker. "Now where's my frigging coffee cup?"

Rex found his coffee cup under part of the morning newspaper. Barely glancing at the headlines on his way to the obituaries, he tossed the front page at the nearest horizontal surface. The cup still had some damp brown residue from the last coffee it had held, and Rex stared at it for a moment, thinking of the time and effort it would take to go down the hall and rinse it out. Something in the paper caught his eye, and it gave him an excuse not to make the trip and to use the cup as it was. As he wiped the cup with the clean part of his previously-used handkerchief, he studied the small headline below the fold. It read...

Dead Man Found in Cemetery

Authorities were called to Union Cemetery in Redwood City early Monday morning, when a birdwatcher discovered the body of a man propped up in a seated position at the base of the Union Soldier Monument. Police said it was that of a white male in his mid-forties and that he was wearing only a clear plastic raincoat...

"Well, Jeezus Christ on a crutch!" Rex exclaimed. "What else do you find in a cemetery if it's not dead people? Uh, let's see what else it says..."

...with the message "IF YOU SEE K..." written in red lipstick across the coat's front. The end of the message was smeared and unreadable. Captain Fred Wunderlich,

Redwood City Police spokesman, said they had yet to iden-
tify the body and there was no immediately apparent cause
of death.

Rex glanced at his 1970 wall calendar. Today is Tuesday, March 17, he noted. "The body was found yesterday morning. Sounds like something that happened Sunday night sometime."

Rex felt a mild interest in the event. Union Cemetery was nearby. He knew several white males roughly in their mid-forties and he certainly remembered a woman named Kay. He smiled to himself when he thought of her. These facts alone didn't arouse in Rex a great deal of curiosity, but there was something about the article that just wouldn't let go. What the hell is it, I can't remem...hey, I have a clear plastic raincoat, and I haven't seen it in a long time. He had an uneasy feeling. Well...lots of people lose plastic raincoats. I mean, they're so cheap, who gives a shit, he concluded.

Rex tried to dismiss the whole thing as just another one of those tragic incidents that happen somewhere every day, but don't really relate to him. Still, the uneasiness just wouldn't leave him.

I wonder what my dad would think. Damn, I wish he were here. Nothin' ever got by Rufus Nickels, nothin'! "Well, Dad ain't here to ask, Rex my friend, so let's take it up with Doctor Jack," Rex said aloud as he opened the bottom drawer of his antique roll top desk. He pulled a fifth of whiskey from the drawer and made room for it amid the clutter on his desk. He looked at his empty coffee cup and, unwilling to wait for the coffee which only moments before he craved so much, hooked his finger over its edge and drew the cup up into his beefy hand. With his index finger still over the edge, he poured himself a shot of whiskey, pouring until he felt liquid touch his fingernail. He swirled the whiskey around and around, and resting the cup on the arm of his office chair, watched as it continued to circle in a miniature whirlpool. Then he snatched the cup to his face and downed his drink in a single, continuous motion.

"O.K, Jack, enlighten me. Talk to me about raincoats. Clear plastic ones."

Rex dropped onto the sofa, cup still in hand, reached back for a pillow, and rested the back of his head. He closed his eyelids, hoping the healing effects of "Doctor Jack" would clear his clouded brain and. bring to memory the fate of his raincoat, but nothing came to him. It was very quiet in his office and nothing gave signs of human existence save the gurgle and splash emanating from the Coffeemaster and the seductive aroma of the coffee as it brewed.

Suddenly his reverie was interrupted by a thumping in the hallway, and a more than anxious knocking at the door. As he pulled up from the sofa, Rex gave one of those guttural utterances overweight men over forty and two hundred pounds express when getting up from soft upholstery, and cripped his way toward the door. Another knock! This one with more authority and anger. "Just a minute...juuust a minute! I got only two speeds, and the other one's slower than this one!" He pulled the door open, and there stood a familiar face sporting an unfamiliar expression.

"Sheila! What do you want? I'm caught up on your blood-sucking alimony! Wha...?" Rex managed to get out.

"Can it, Sexy Rexy! You know what I want!" she sneered. "Hand it over now and avoid much bigger trouble later!"

"What are you talking about? Hand over what?" defended Rex.

"I don't have time to waste flappin' my gums. Just get it!" his statuesque ex-wife screeched.

First one office door and then another cracked open down the hallway as nearby office workers peeked out to see what the ruckus was about. This wasn't the first assault on civility they had witnessed from Sheila Sneaker, as she now called herself. A full-figured woman, she usually came dressed in a cocktail dress about a half-size too small, in four-inch high heels and with her hair pulled back in a bun secured with a red Chinese comb. This time she wore a big white silk gardenia in her hair and her dress was now a whole size too small.

Most important, instead of her usual plaid collapsible umbrella, she carried a chrome-plated .45 caliber pistol, which she pointed at Rex Nickels' nose. The cracks in the doors in the hallway became very small.

The fluorescent overhead lights reflected off the pistol and into Rex's eyes, making him blink.

"Gawd damn, Sheila! What in the name of Sam Spade are you doing with that thing? Put it back in your purse and calm down before you bust a bra strap or kill someone."

"Rex Nickels, you either get 'em and give 'em to me, or I'm goin' to show you I know how to use this thing." She adjusted the aim of the gun to the middle of his forehead. "And one more crack about my bra straps or any other part of my underwear or my anatomy and you will need a new head. Just one 'tit joke', one little 'tit joke', and you are history, slime ball. Now get 'em!"

"Gawd *damn*, woman! I swear I don't know what the hell you're talking about." Rex shouted in a shaky voice.

Sheila shifted the muzzle of the .45 and pointed it downward at an angle that put the fear of God into Rex. He began to sense that she meant business.

"Shit! Can't you tell I really don't know what it is you want? If I knew—I don't care what it is—giving it to you would be far better than getting my pecker shot off! Can't you see that?"

"All right, Rexy Boy, I dunno why I'm explaining this to you— because you already know—but I need that little bottle of pills you fished out of my bag when you came by my place yesterday with the check. You didn't think I saw you going through my purse when I left the room to get my receipt book, but I did. The phone rang just when I was goin' to nail you for it, but by the time I got off, you'd left. I checked and my pills were gone, and so was my lipstick."

"For crying out loud, Sheila, why would I want your damn lipstick? Or your medicine? I was looking for my lighter that you borrowed last time," said Rex, trying to explain, trying to calm her down.

"I can't find either of them anywhere, so you must have taken 'em. I know you've got 'em and either I leave here with 'em—or you stay here dickless—or maybe worse!"

Rex stood wide-eyed for a moment. Could anything be worse?

"Easy does it, Sheila. Eeeasy, now. Come on in and we'll look for them, together. I'm sure that I made a mistake. They must be here somewhere, I'm sure. Alright? Just come on in and put down the gun."

"I'll put the gun down, all right, down your pants! Back up, Rex. Eeeasy like," she said, mocking his words. She forced Rex to walk backwards into his office, her gun still pointed at him. She never was very good in heels, and her anger made her even more unsteady as she crossed the threshold.

Ca-wham! The .45 roared as Sheila's ankle folded to one side and jerked her off balance. The doorway and its occupant disappeared in the smoke, and the acrid smell of gunpowder filled the air. Her left shoe remained stuck in the crack between the hallway's ceramic tile and the cheap office carpet. Sheila crashed onto Rex, flattening him amidst screams from both of them.

Stunned, Rex couldn't feel anything, at first, except considerable pressure from Sheila. He felt no pain anywhere, particularly in his groin. Maybe it doesn't hurt because it isn't there, he thought. His hands were at his sides, normally within easy reach of the anatomical member in question, but now his arms were pinned by the overflow of hips from above. He couldn't move.

"Get the hell off of me, Sheila, I can't breathe and I got to see if it is still there!"

Sheila had the wind knocked out of her and was wheezing deeply trying to get a breath. She could not speak.

"Move!" Rex shouted out grimly. He made his hand into a fist which he was able to rotate and free up his arm a little. He could then open his hand again and push up on her hip. Fortunately, his hand found the point of her hip bone which gave him enough leverage to roll her over and off of him. He checked.

"It's still there. You didn't shoot it off, you dumb jerk," Rex sighed with relief and relaxed his body back onto the office carpet.

"Oh, Rex honey!" she gasped, struggling to catch her breath. She had risen to her hands and knees, her breasts hanging prominently near his face. "I'm...sorry! I was just shittin' you. I tripped on the carpet and the thing went off. You're okay, aren't you baby?"

"Yeah, I'm okay. Just shook up. Scared the hell outta me." He hunched up on his elbows. They both scanned the room. The glass air deflector at the window sill was shattered. The Jack Daniels bottle stood intact amidst the shards. "Well, ol' J. D. came through okay. All is not lost. Thank you, Jesus."

Rex managed to work his way to a standing position and headed unsteadily for the window. "We both need a good slug after that." He retrieved his cup from beside the sofa, and found a cloudy glass in a bottom desk drawer. He poured a few ounces in each vessel, considered, and poured a bit more in his cup. He handed the Old Fashioned glass to Sheila, who was still on the floor, now sitting with her back against the sofa.

"Thanks, hon. I can use that. Really, Rex, I'm sorry!"

"Hon?—hon you say! Geeze! Well, it's okay, I guess it's okay. Now what about this stuff that's supposed to be missing from your purse that brought this mess on. What's in the bottle that's so frigging all-fired important that you come after me with a gun? Huh?"

Sheila stared down at the pattern of light and shadow cast on the carpet by the half-open blinds. She thought maybe Rex hadn't taken the bottle after all and maybe he really didn't know the contents. "Oh...it, well...well, it's sort of personal, but...well, they are birth control pills, and why I might need them is none of your goddamn business."

"What the hell would I do with them, huh?" Rex was incredulous, but couldn't contain the start of a small giggle.

"I'm sorry. I guess I was acting a little...desperate."

"A little desperate! You lugged that chrome piece all the way down here to make me return some stinking birth control pills that are worthless to me? Come on old gal, get a grip on yourself. Try some reality for a change. You don't need those damn things anyway, old as you are."

"I've got your reality all right," and Sheila was about to attack Rex once more when they were interrupted by a harsh rapping on the frosted glass pane of the office door.

"Police! We're coming in!"

CHAPTER THREE

Earlier that same Tuesday, the morning sun brought a glow to the billowing drapes that covered the open windows in the bedroom of Owen "The Colonel" Owens at his richly- appointed house at the Hillandale Stables compound. The slight wind that filled the fine silk curtains carried on it the freshness of the air, perfumed, on days when the breeze was from the east, with the slight fragrance of horse manure from the stables nearby. Owens loved that smell, elusive though it now was, because it reminded him of just how far he had come from his penniless days cleaning stables. Now he owned the stables, but the smell was just the same.

And, he thought, there is a world of difference in *getting* to smell manure, and *having* to smell it. He squinted at the alarm clock, saw that it was only six thirty a.m. and decided to close his eyes and sleep another fifteen minutes. Just a little extra snooze. The fatigue of travel and his late arrival the night before turned his little snooze into another four hours or so of much needed sleep. He awoke at ten forty a.m., fully alert and refreshed. Not concerned that he might have overslept, he quickly got out of bed and showered, ready for his day.

As he dressed, he thought of the past two days in Kentucky, the ceremony to initiate yet another honorary Kentucky Colonel like himself, and the bumpy flight back from Blue Grass Airport in Lexington to San Francisco International late yesterday afternoon. And then the long trip from the airport to his place here near the ocean outside San Gregorio.

Ah, my friend Kato and his limo service, he thought. Sure is convenient not to have to make that drive myself any more. That view of the coast and the ocean at sunset, and then the beautiful moon over Half Moon Bay. I kind of wish I had stopped at the beach at Half Moon and just looked, but then that would have put me in here after eleven, which is way past my bed time. I was bushed. I'll have to do Half Moon some other day.

But that was yesterday and this was today and time to attend to matters at hand. Always a fitness advocate, he forced himself to report to his workout room downstairs, in spite of the stiffness in his legs and back. After his blood pressure pills and the required stretches, he mounted his treadmill and began. Once into the rhythm of it, he pushed the yellow and green incline button on his treadmill, as he jogged along in this continuing morning ritual. As it tilted a few degrees upward, the machine squeaked a bit louder in response, and its whine increased as it competed with the sound of his Adidases on the rubber conveyor belt beneath his feet. Maintaining his speed at a manageable 2.5 miles per hour, he grabbed the television remote from the pocket holder under the handle grip and clicked on the morning news.

"Let's see what they've done to my California while I was gone," he said.

Good late morning to everyone and welcome to the "Seven at Eleven" news, brought to you, of course, by the Seventh Heaven convenience store in your neighborhood. The "Seven at Eleven" up-to-date news comes to you seven days a week, morning, evening and night. "Ahead of the rest and still the best." I'm Norbert Swisher. Nan ☐*bu and I will be bringing you the news. Good morning, Nan. What are the top stories for today?*

Good morning to you, Swish. There has been a bizarre incident that has residents of one Bay Area neighborhood wondering if they should go outside or not. It seems an elephant is missing from a nearby zoo. The San Francisco 49ers got a big surprise yesterday, and Peninsula authorities still have questions about how an unburied body turned up in a cemetery. On the international front, rioting has erupted in an east African country. Now, back to you, Swish, for more details on the local news.

Thanks Nan, we will see you later in the broadcast with the weather for the Bay Area and beyond. In Oakland, a six-year-old female elephant named Kimi is somehow missing from the zoo. Zoo personnel report that Kimi has not been seen since feeding time last night. Channel 7 viewers may remember another Oakland elephant, Effie, who gained some fame about twelve years ago for her harmonica-playing artistry. When Kimi came to the zoo as an infant, she was taken under the wing, or perhaps trunk, of the adult Effie. Since Effie was sent to Busch gardens four years ago Kimi has never been happy. They do say that elephants never forget. No word on whether Effie was able to teach harmonica to Kimi. We'll stay on top of this story in our later newscasts. Skipping across the Bay, the focus is on the cemetery in Redwood City, where the body of a man, apparently murdered, was found early Monday. Authorities have still not identified the body, which was found propped against the base of the old Union war monument wearing a clear plastic raincoat with something written on it in lipstick. Our reporter was not able to determine from an interview with police Captain Wunderlich if fingerprints or any other form of identification were found. At this time, no cause of death has been determined. We will keep you updated as more information is made available. And next, Willie Pisantelli, with why Cliff Harris will not be playing with the Niners next season.

Thanks, Swish. Well, better get out your raincoats and umbrellas today, this morning, at least. Brief showers are expected until noon and then it is due to be clear and breezy the rest of the afternoon....

"Well, that's enough of that," muttered Owens, clicking off the TV. "Looks like someone has done something for a change. Clear and breezy, my ass. Sounds to me like what the dead guy was dressed in was clear and breezy for sure."

After twenty-five of his scheduled thirty minutes were up, Owens hit the OFF switch and stopped the treadmill. "Whoweee! I've had enough of this exercise crap for one day. I wanna look at the morning paper and get the details," he said aloud. As he got off of the treadmill and found his towel, he noticed that the rash on his elbow was coming back and that it itched like crazy.

"Twilee," he called. "Or Amber. Whichever one of you can hear me."

From the kitchen he heard a duet of lilting voices call back. "Yes, Kerny."

"Will one of you get me the morning Tribune?" said Owen, "and bring me that little bottle of anti-itch spray. It's in the medicine cabinet in the guest bath."

By the time he had wiped the sweat from his face, wrapped the towel around his neck and done his cooling-down stretches, two long-legged young women in short tennis dresses came into the work-out room with the morning paper and a small spray bottle.

"Here's your Trib," chirped Amber, a true redhead with bangs. "I couldn't find the anti-itch stuff. All that was in there was this thing of Binaca mouth spray. Will that help?"

"No, it won't, bubblehead. That stuff is for bad breath. I may need that too, but right now I need something for this damn itch. Just never mind. I would have sworn it was in there. Thanks for the paper."

"Anything else, boss man?" said Twilee, cocking her head in a provocative way. Her voice seemed an octave too low for such a pert, but well-endowed, blonde. It was a strange companion for the ponytail which she flipped frequently for emphasis. "Coffee?" she asked. "Or tea? Or me?" she giggled.

"Or us?" interjected Amber. "Any other itches?"

Owen paused at the questions, and almost gave an answer that would certainly have postponed his reading the paper. He could still feel his heart beating under his tee shirt at a pretty high rate from his workout, so he decided that reading about the details of the murder should take precedent over lust. He was, after all, seventy-seven, even if he tried to perform otherwise as often as possible.

"That is an offer hard to refuse, my little chickadees, but I have other priorities this morning, not the least of which is reading the newspaper. So, fly off! But not before one of you brings me my coffee."

Wagging their tails behind them, they left Colonel Owen "Kerny" Owens to his reading and headed for the kitchen.

He unfolded the Redwood City Tribune and on the front page found the headline he was looking for and scanned the article below.

Dead Man Found in Cemetery

...Union Cemetery...Monday morning...nude body of a man propped up...in a seated position at the base...statue of the...Monument. ... white male in his mid-forties...wearing... clear plastic raincoat...with message "IF YOU SEE K"...red lipstick across the coat's front....Police...had yet to identify the bod...and no...apparent cause of death.

Well, well, well. So we see what really happened, Owens mused to himself. Ha! A clear plastic raincoat. That's more like it...nude? Except for a raincoat? A see-thru raincoat? Buck-nekkid is what that is. Aloud, Owens read again, "If you see k..."

"Oh! But I thought coffee was all you wanted, Kerny. Would you like something else? Should I call Amber?" came a voice from behind him. It was Twilee, holding a small tray with a cup of steaming coffee. She had startled him, and he turned the newspaper page over swiftly. Her low voice always was a curiosity to him, at times it was even an aphrodisiac. This time it was an unwelcome surprise.

"Not funny. Put it on the table and you two go swim or sunbathe or something. And don't scare me like that again. I'm not paying you to give me a heart attack, not that way anyhow. Go on, and make sure Amber goes with you. I need some privacy."

He took his coffee and stood by the window looking at the terrace and pool outside. He saw the girls emerge from the house and head for the pool where they removed most of what little they had on, anointed each other with sun tan lotion, and came to rest on reclining benches to sun themselves. Assured that he was alone and had complete privacy, he picked up the phone and punched in Red Ramsey's line.

"Red. Saw something on TV about a body in the cemetery at Redwood City," he said. "Could it be that something was taken care of while I was gone? And lipstick messages may not be new, but where did the raincoat gimmick come from, anyway?"

There was a long pause at the other end of the line, and Owens said, "Hello? Red? Are you there?"

"I'm here, Colonel," replied Rod "Red" Ramsey, his major-domo and confidante, "and I don't have the slightest idea what you're talking about, except I do recall something about lipstick writing and your late wife."

"Oh really? Well, first of all, you better just take some steel wool and wipe your ass-for- brain clean of any recollection of my late wife. And secondly, you better catch up on your newspaper reading. I did."

CHAPTER FOUR

The door to Rex's office flew full open, revealing a pair of uniformed officers—one crouched with arms fully extended, both hands clutching a pistol. The partner stood a bit to the side, his weapon pointing upward.

"Someone in the building reported gunfire from this office. Now I want both of you to go stand in front of the desk. Hold your hands up where I can see them. I'm Officer Richard Dailey, this is my partner Officer Rodriguez. Maybe you can tell me what's going on here, other than a pretty wild party," said Dailey as he took in the coffee cup and the Old Fashioned glass, along with the chrome-plated .45 that lay discarded by the sofa.

Rex recognized Officer Dailey from previous dealings with the police. He held up both hands in mock surrender and with a big smile said, "Whoa, there Dick. Don't you recognize me? I'm Rex Nickels. We worked together on that case last year when the mayor's car turned up missing. Captain Wunderlich was really pleased with your performance as I recall."

"Oh, yeah! It's you, is it? Put your gun away, Rodriguez, this guy's okay." Both officers holstered their guns and relaxed. "What is going on here, anyway?"

"Just a little accident. I was showing my wife, er, ex-wife, Sheila here, how to load this .45 I got her for self-protection, and it went off. Scared the hell out of both of us. I'm sorry you were called on a false alarm. I know you have a lot to do."

"You have that right. The department has classes on firearms if you want to attend. Just call the station and they can tell you all about if you are interested."

"Thanks. Maybe we should do that. Looks like I have a mess to clean up here first," said Rex.

"Let's go Rod. We have done all we can here for Redwood City," and the officers tipped their caps to Sheila as they headed for the door.

"Tell Captain Wunderlich hello from me," said Rex.

•••

Rex waited till the door closed behind the cops. "Okay, Sweetie, you're outa here! And stay away. I don't need any more of this kind of trouble." Against foul-mouthed protests, Rex was able to put Sheila back together with her shoes, purse and .45, and get her out of the door. Exhausted, Rex shuffled to the sofa where he collapsed in relief, finally able to catch his breath and think. When things finally returned to a semblance of normal, he decided to renew his conversation with his friend Jack Daniels.

"Where were we, my friend, when we were so rudely interrupted, which is to put it mildly. Ah, yes, the raincoats. You were about to enlighten me about raincoats," said Rex as he reached for his coffee cup and the bottle just within reach on the corner of his desk. "I'm here to listen."

The whiskey spoke to Rex in its own way, and as he enjoyed its renewing properties, the thought occurred to him that his raincoat, which he bought to wear when washing his car, was probably in the trunk of the car, small as it was. So that was the answer to that. Still, the news article wouldn't go away.

"It's not about my raincoat, is it Jack? Nah, it's about something else. Something I can't put my finger on. Come on friend, turn on the light." And Rex freshened his cup.

"The cemetery? What a weird place to dump a body. Whatever it is you are trying to tell me, Jack, it has to do with the cemetery.

This is an itch I cannot scratch," and Rex heaved himself up off of the couch and straightened his clothes as best as he could under the circumstances, for they were never really straight. "Maybe if I called over there and talked to someone they might let something slip that will satisfy my curiosity. We don't get a lot of murders here in Red City, and I just want to be in on the know. Maybe I am just curious for no good reason and I don't have to explain it.

He went to the phone and dialed 411. "Give me the number of the Union Cemetery, please. Yes, of course in Redwood City."

•••

Sheila was in high dudgeon and about to prance down the hall and out of the building when she remembered what she had come for. She turned to go back into the office and just as she was about to turn the knob on the door she heard Rex's voice, calling Information.

Now what in the name of my sainted Uncle Feeny is that dumb bastard calling the cemetery for? thought Sheila. She got as close to the obscure glass in the door as her anatomy would permit and listened to Rex.

"Two two seven, four eight nine two. Hold it while I get a something to write with," muttered Rex.

"Why didn't the son of a bitch get that before he dialed," Sheila almost said aloud.

"Okay, I got it. Now give it to me again," said Rex to the operator.

Not on your life, liver dick, thought Sheila. You got the last I'm gonna' give you and that was a long time ago."

"Okay, I'm ready now." He managed to write the number on the shirt cuff he had rolled down for this very purpose. "Two two seven, four eight nine two...bye."

Jamming his pudgy index finger into the holes on the telephone, Rex dialed the number. In the hall, Sheila began to tap the toe of her 7-1/2 AAA pump on the hall floor in impatience. She could hear the rotary dial's ratchety click as it returned to zero after each number. She thought he would never get the damned number dialed. Particularly when his finger slipped and he had to start over again. She quickly pulled her head back when she heard a door open down the hall. A small, meek-looking accountant walked past her and down the stairs, wondering to himself why such a woman was pressing her breasts against the window pane of an office door.

"Hello? This Union Cemetery? Yeah. Okay-dokay. I was wondering...oh, my name is Rex Nickels...yes, like the money...I was wondering if you know more about the body they found there in your graveyard." Sheila continued to listen in her same position.

"What do ya mean you can't say? Either you know something or you don't. Who am I? I just told you. I am Rex Nickels. What I failed to mention is that I am Rex Nickels, Private Eye. I'm THAT Rex Nickels," said Rex, straightening up his posture a bit. "I thought you guys might need a little help over there and it sounds as if I may be right. Let me talk to your boss, whoever he is."

"Oh, he can't come to the phone? Well, crap. Good friggin' bye!" Rex slammed the receiver onto its cradle.

"They just don't know how curious Rex Nickels can get, do they, JD? Well, they are about to find out, 'cause I'm goin' over there," and he started for the door.

As he turned from the desk he saw the imprint of Sheila on the glass of the door. "Bitch" he muttered to himself. He grabbed his scuffed, peeling briefcase and headed toward the window, trying to avoid the splintered air deflector at the window so Sheila wouldn't hear a telltale crunch of shoes on broken glass.

Rex scampered over the window sill, congratulating himself on his foresight. When he had leased the space upstairs in the Young's Drug Building, he had passed up better-lighted, street-side quarters in favor of a room on the back with fire escape access. The catwalk gave him a short route to a corridor window, around a corner from where Sheila was lurking. He passed through it into the corridor to the first door on the left, then down the stairs to the ground level. Avoiding the terrazzo-floored lobby, he ducked out the alley door. A few steps brought him to Main Street. He needed to get to his house and car without running into Sheila, so he walked quickly away.

When he got to his house he approached it cautiously, but did not see Sheila's car or other indication of her presence. At the end of his driveway waited his beloved 1962 Corvair Monza Spyder convertible. First he opened the trunk and, sure enough, there was his once clear plastic raincoat, now slightly grey and black with mildew and in a wrinkled ball where he had left it.

Well, that clears that up. The sucker isn't wearing anything from my wardrobe, Rex smirked, shutting the trunk. Then, he patted the front fender of the Monza, got in and drove to Main Street, then to Woodside Road and the Union Cemetery. At the cemetery entrance Rex found that the police blocked all access. Pulling up to the curb he spotted Patrolman Gary Geary, an old pal. "Hey, Geary! What's up? Can I get a look at the crime scene?"

"No can do, Rex," Geary replied, with arms crossed over his chest. "Nothing to see, anyway. Work pretty much wrapped up yesterday. Body and evidence all carted away. My job is to keep looky-lous away. Been a lot of those all morning. Captain Wunderlich is in charge. You best see him down at headquarters."

"Yeah, I just might do that," said Rex in a huff. He wasn't used to police rebuffs. He sped off.

CHAPTER FIVE

Sensing a prolonged silence in the office, Sheila opened the door, expecting to see Rex with his feet on the desk. No Rex, just a breeze from the open window ruffling papers on the desk. Shee-it! I forgot about his escape route. He's at the graveyard by now, and I'm not going to catch up with him with this broken heel.

She took the stairs to the ground floor, exited onto Broadway and hobbled into the Break-Thyme Cafe next door. She took a seat in a coral Naugahyde booth by the window, and scanned the mimeod list of daily specials. She would need some fuel to help her work out details of her "Get Rex" strategy.

Sheila was flat out hungry. She didn't know exactly what kind of hungry she was, until she studied the menu and saw that the special for the day was "Chili Three Ways-Peoria Style". That's the kind of hungry I am, she thought, I'm hungry three ways. I'm hungry for love, I'm hungry for money and I am hungry for food. Mostly food. The ongoing and constant test of the tensile strength of the fabric of her blouse confirmed that. She loved chili, but "Peoria style" made her wonder if it "would play in Peoria," as the old saw went. "Peoria Style, my ass," she said aloud, just as there was a lull in the buzz of conversation in the crowded cafe.

All heard her, but only one person responded, the one person who was a stranger in this part of town. It was Jud Periwinkle, biker. He sat at the end of the counter, isolated in space, time and intellect from the other patrons. When he heard Sheila's comment, his slouched, bent over posture, suddenly straightened to attention. He looked over the deep fryer, straight through the pass-through, to the kitchen beyond, and belched.

"Ah'm from Peoria," he said, trying to act the tough redneck. It was a flat statement, as if it held great meaning that required no definition. There was a collective intake of breath as everyone in the cafe sat transfixed. Everyone, that is, except Sheila who really didn't give a rat's fanny what she said or who heard it.

"Well, that ought to make a lot of Peeorians happy," announced Sheila, and she giggled.

"Ah'm from Peoria, and my name is Judson Kayne Periwinkle. People call me Kayne."

Sheila twisted around on the Naugahyde beneath her, producing the squeal of flesh moving on plastic under great pressure, and spoke across the room to Jud Periwinkle. "You said your name was Kay. Why, that sounds like a girl's name to me."

"Ah said people call me Kayne," Jud replied, each word increasing in volume. "And jest who the fuck do you think you are to be talkin' to me like that?" With that he kicked the under-counter with the steel toe of his boot and spun around to face Sheila. As she was half-turned on the Naugahyde bench, he could see her in profile, which left no doubt as to her gender.

"Bitch!" he spat.

What happened next surprised everyone in the cafe, including Jud. With the surprising economy of motion that some large-breasted women seem to possess, Sheila reached into her hand bag, pulled out her .45 and leveled it at the top of Jud's nose before he could inhale from his last expletive. He wasn't sure what he was looking at, but he had a pretty good idea. To be sure he got down from his stool and started toward her. Finally he figured it out and started to retreat.

"Freeze, you dumb sucker," said Sheila in a voice that could stop the devil in his tracks. "I have been called a bitch by one too many idiots today, and you are the last friggin' straw. Now get your tattooed ass out of this cafe and out of my sight. And if you don't think I won't pull this trigger, just imagine what that blue barbed wire tattoo around your skinny neck will look like with a big red hole in it."

Judson Kayne Periwinkle understood exactly what she said. In need of no more convincing, he set the speed record for leaving a cafe and disappearing around a corner.

"Bye, bye, Kay sweetie," hooted Sheila as the glass door shut behind him, and she eased the .45 back into her purse, the safety still on. "Relax folks, I'm ready for my 'Chili Three Ways' now that that bumbledick is headed back to Peoria. He'll be in good company, believe me. I've been there."

There was a collective exhalation of breath from the relieved cafe patrons, punctuated by the prolonged squeal of Sheila's behind moving across the Naugahyde as she re-positioned herself for feeding.

Outside, Jud found his old 1963 Triumph motorcycle where he had hidden it next to the Dempster Dumpster behind the cafe. He sat down in the alley next to his bike, totally dejected. That bitch and her gun. She scares me...I am so mixed up...I said my name was Periwinkle, but that my friends call me Kayne...shit, that ain't true...I don't have no friends...Periwinkle is only my dance name...it's a private name for...oh shit...my 'Periwinkle skirt'! He quickly checked the saddlebags to see if they had been disturbed. He could feel the skirt in one of them. Confused but reassured his secret was still intact, he put his head between his knees and softly began to sob.

CHAPTER SIX

I just ain't worth shit. Jud looked up at the sky as if asking God to maybe disagree. It wasn't a prayer or a lament, but a statement of a conclusion he had come to. Lettin' a broad like her scare me out of there like that. I shudda' stood up to her. Damn, damn, DAMN! He pounded the seat on the motorcycle. I'm such a chicken-shit jerk.

Judson Kayne didn't know how long he had been sitting in the alley, with his arms folded around his knees. His tears dried and he was thinking of nothing in particular when he noticed his watch. "Almost two o'clock. Oh, shit! Red will have my butt if I'm not there when I said would be."

Jud jumped up, got on the Triumph and hit the kick starter five times with no result. Finally, the engine coughed to a start and after a couple of throaty revs, he took off like a bat out of hell, trailing a rooster tail of dirt and alley debris in his wake. He cut left onto Jefferson Street and sped the half block to Broadway. He saw a stop sign and stopped quickly, seeing a cop across the street. "Not today, sucker," he said under his breath, and carefully turned right onto Broadway, following as many traffic laws as he could remember. A check in his mirror confirmed he wasn't being followed and he took Broadway west until he could turn back south onto El Camino Real, "The Big Cam", Jud had heard the bikers call it. After a mile on the Big Cam he connected with Woodside Road. He sped past the Union cemetery and continued on in light traffic past the Alameda and Menlo Country Club into the town of Woodside. Through the rustic village he was forced to slow for the narrow road and reduced speed limit. After King's Mountain Road he was able to gain speed as he passed long stretches of wooden fences and horse setups.

Clueless to the dangers, Jud thrilled to the speed and the attention the bike drew to him from the cars he passed on the road. It made him feel in control and important. He felt like 'somebody'. After racing past the former Folger Ranch, he made a sharp right turn on Woodside Road at its juncture with Portola Road.

At this point began a biker's dream, a sharply ascending, twisty road through a redwood forest, with occasional views opening out toward the Stanford campus on his left and the bay far beyond. The twisted road continued for four or five miles to the little crossroads settlement of Skylonda. Here, he could see biker groups gathered at a couple of roadside cafes, even though it was a weekday.

Man, this is a cool place for a guy to be. A cat just could wander around, relate to the studs, and inspect the machines, polish his biker talk, maybe do a little weed.

But he didn't stop. Instead he continued on, picking up speed, glancing at the speedometer each time he advanced the throttle, as he headed for La Honda, a small village nestled amidst emerald green hills. When he hit 55, he leaned back and began to feel good. The wind in his face washed away his humiliation, and he changed lanes and passed cars with abandon at reckless speeds for such a twisting, hilly road. He really didn't care.

Then it started to rain, just a light mist, but enough to make the roadway slippery. Even Jud had sense enough to slow down. When he did, his clothes began to get wet and he wished he had his raincoat. He hadn't had time to get a new one and didn't think about it until just now. He saw a bus stop turnout ahead and pulled off the road when he came to it. The sheltered bench was a good place to stay dry until the rain let up. Unfortunately, the roof overhang wasn't enough cover both him and his bike.

"I know it won't really hurt, but I hate to see you get wet," he said to the motorcycle, as he got up, removed the saddlebags and returned to the bench. He was alone at the bus stop, and at this time of day, with school in session, probably would remain so for a while. So, he opened one of the saddle bags and took out his Periwinkle skirt and draped it over the bike. At least it covered the seat and the motor and Grandma Rosebud wouldn't care since she was about to give it to Goodwill anyway when he asked her if he could have it. The skirt always reminded him of Grandma and when he was younger and she told him stories. One of his favorites was the one about how she got her nickname Rosebud from a sled in a movie, and how his father got their new name Kayne from the same flick. Jud had always wanted to see it, but Grandma wouldn't take him. Said it was too scary.

Remembering story time with Grandma always had a settling effect on Jud and as he waited for the rain to stop, Jud began to think about the past three days and what had happened, particularly on Sunday night. "I didn't mean to hurt you, Daddy," he said aloud, softly. Tears came to his eyes. "I just wanted you to wake up. But you wouldn't wake up. I didn't know what to do. So I went to get Aunt Kay to help."

Jud began to cry, and his voice choked with sobs. He absently studied the rain until he regained his voice, then said, loudly as if Earnest were present and conscious, "Aunt Kay came back with me and we tried to wake you up. I grabbed the rain coat and shook you. Then Kay slapped your face to get you to wake up. But you didn't do anything. Kay told me to stop shaking you, that I would hurt you. But I didn't stop. I'm sorry. I am so sorry. I should have stopped sooner." And once again Jud broke down.

The rain began to subside, and Jud finally ended his introspection, this time in a hoarse whisper, "We didn't mean to hurt you. We didn't. We didn't. Honest Daddy, we didn't."

In all, the rain lasted less than ten minutes, and when it was over Jud got back on the road again. At first he was preoccupied with the events of Sunday night, but nothing stayed on his scattered mind very long and he was quickly back to his reckless and mindless riding.

Very soon, Jud slowed down a bit for La Honda. Then, the road, now leveling and straightening, passed through more redwoods and crossed La Honda Creek, and a little further, San Gregorio Creek. It wasn't long before the road flattened out as it entered a wide valley, following San Gregorio Creek. The grass was at its greenest March brilliance. Jud zoomed past eucalyptus windbreaks, wood and wire fences, houses, and barns, hardly noticing them. In the distance some large agricultural spreads and an enclosing ridge could be seen behind a light veil of marine air, but Jud was oblivious to the beauty of the view. Within ten minutes, he spotted the sign for Bear Gulch Road, and turned off there. After following the road for the next half mile, he saw the entry to the ranch at last.

"There it is!" he exclaimed as if there were another person along, and pointed to the open gate with the sign overhead reading "Hillandale Stables est. 1960", painted in green script on a white background. The gate was open at this time of day for truck deliveries, so Jud zoomed past the gateposts without hesitation onto the graveled lane that led to a cluster of white buildings on a nearby rise. He ignored the speed bump in the road and was airborne for the first twenty feet. He bounced high when he hit the bump, wobbling in mid flight. But he managed to stay on the bike until he landed with a thud in a cloud of dust and the tires flattened out under the impact. But dumb luck was with Judson Kayne, and he and the Triumph remained upright, the tires resumed their normal shape, and he drove on as if nothing out of the ordinary had occurred.

He followed the tree-lined drive up to where it circled in front of the assortment of buildings that composed the Hillandale Stables establishment. Facing the compound, Jud could see a rambling house on his left, another large house in front of him, and stables and other farm buildings on his right, along with another small house. With barely a pause, he pulled the bike to his right and headed for the stables. He disengaged the clutch as he rolled into a parking area in front of the stable, revving the engine to get the maximum acoustic effect to announce his arrival. He cut the engine. No one was in sight, so he parked his bike.

Rod "Red" Ramsey heard the cycle coming as soon as it passed the gate, and he stood just out of sight in the open end of the stable. He could see the parking lot through the small cracks in the siding on the barn, but could not be seen. He watched as Jud walked around and around, looking for someone to meet him, and he enjoyed Jud's growing discomfort and confusion. Jud looked at his watch and then Red looked at his, and realized it was two forty five, the time that he said he would be there. Just as Jud looked as if he were about to come looking for him, Red figured maybe it was time to make his presence known. The last thing he wanted to do was have the punk yellin' out his name and spookin' the horses any more than his noisy arrival already had.

"Hey there boy!" he called as he ambled toward the parking lot. "Glad you could make it. Let me put it to you straight. You've missed almost two days' work without any good reason that I can think of or know about. Ordinarily, I'd fire your ass for that, or anyone else's ass for that matter. But because you're 'special', you still have a job. Now, did you have somethin' you want to say to me?"

"Uh, hi Red." stammered Jud. "I can explain."

"You damn well better, hear me, Mr. Kayne? If this shit shovelin' is too good for you, I'm friggin' sorry." Red Ramsey sneered in his belittling way.

"It's about Sunday night," said Jud softly.

Red reached out and carefully placed his hand on Jud's forearm. "What about Sunday night?"

"Uh," Jud started to cry a little. "Uh, it's about Earnest. Earnest Kayne."

Red looked at Jud and thoughts came quickly. This kid's name is Kayne. He's talking about Earnest. Could he be Earnest's kid? Does he look like Earnest? Why did he mention Sunday night? Does he know anything?

"What are you saying about Earnest Kayne?" Red asked.

"He's dead. Earnest is dead. He was my...friend, and he's dead. I found out and I got drunk. I'm sorry I missed work." Tears were streaming down Judson Kayne's face. He desperately wanted not to be there.

"Well, I'm sorry about your friend," Red said and thought to himself, Gotta be careful, mustn't show I know anything about Earnest, or Sunday night. But how does he know? The cops haven't announced any identification yet. Then he said to Jud, "How did it happen? When? How did you hear about it?"

Jud moaned. "Oh, I just know...I just feel like shit." He was weeping again.

"Listen, numbskull, I am sorry about your friend bein' dead. But you gotta pull yourself together. There's work to do here. Get busy, and get your mind off of it."

"Okay, I'll try," Jud sniffled. "Can I go now?"

"Yeah, you can go," Red said, pulling out a pack of Tarletons. "Say, you got a light there?" And he pointed at the slight bulge in Jud's shirt pocket.

"Sure," said Jud, and without thinking reached into the shirt pocket and pulled out a tube of lipstick.

"Oh, shit," he said when he saw his mistake, and he quickly stuffed the lipstick back in, fumbling and almost dropping it as he did so. "Here," he said as he extracted his lighter from his pants pocket and extended it toward Red's waiting Tarleton.

"Thanks," said Red as he cupped his hand and took a deep drag on the cigarette, looking up with narrowed eyes to stare at Jud as he did. "Now get outta' my sight. And get your ass busy. There are stalls to be mucked out and I don't want to see you till they are all done."

And Jud returned to the Triumph motorcycle to collect his saddlebags and headed for his bunk in the back of the tack room. By the time he reached it his tears for his father were forgotten, and his main concern had become how to get his Periwinkle skirt dried without being noticed.

CHAPTER SEVEN

As was his morning custom, William Dale II turned on the television at seven o'clock. He sat in the den of his tastefully furnished house on Selby Lane in the town of Atherton, just across the city limit line from Redwood City and barely three miles from Palo Alto to the south, where his office was located.

Although only seven or eight blocks from the middle class neighborhoods surrounding Union Cemetery, Selby Lane was miles apart socially, and architecturally as well. Carefully treading the line between ostentation and false humility, the Dale residence was not overtly a mansion nor was it an oversized bungalow. When Dale had it built for his new wife Kay in 1965, he had put her in charge of managing its design and construction. He was confident of her management skills from when she had worked for him, and he was comfortable in a role on the sidelines. He did, however, keep his hand in on decisions regarding the overall configuration of the house, with a keen eye to function and his reputation in the neighborhood. The modest two story front façade belied the existence of an elaborate sub-grade level where there was a large game room and a wine cellar on the grand scale. On the main floor his den adjoined and mirrored that of his wife, in plan if not in décor. The layout was such that they could have their privacy with the touch of a button that controlled a hidden wall that rolled out and made two rooms from one. By the same token, they had the option of having as much togetherness as desired by reversing the process.

On this particular Wednesday morning, there was just one room, and Dale had just settled in his favorite leather chair for his cup of hot, freshly ground and brewed Brazilian coffee when he was startled by the news coming from the television. He folded the morning paper and watched the screen.

Good morning to everyone and welcome to the "Seven at Seven" newscast, brought to you by the Seven Seas Seafood restaurant nearest you. Channel 7 comes to you seven days a week, morning, evening and night. "Ahead of the rest and still the best." I'm Norbert Swisher and I will be your host as usual, along with Nan □bu, who is here now with today's headline stories. Good morning, Nan.

Good morning to you, Swish. On the international front there is still rioting in Africa and strife in Iran. Now we're going to go live to Oakland, where our East Bay bureau reporter, Ted Ace, has breaking news on the missing elephant.

Thanks, Nan. We're here alongside Highway 13, the Earl Warren Freeway, near Golf Links Road, not far from the Oakland Zoo entrance. Kimi was discovered by passing commuters early this morning, grazing in the tall grass at the edge of the shoulder of the freeway. There, we have her on camera now, along with a couple of keepers who we're told are trying the arrange transportation back to the safety of the zoo. Now the big story shifts to how to untangle the traffic mess left over from all the rush hour drivers who stopped for pictures or just slowed to gape. We've got solid lines of cars stretching to Berkeley north of here to Castro Valley and Hayward to the south. We'll have more on this on our "Seven at Eleven" newscast later this morning. Back to you, Nan.

Thanks Ted. I understand there is an important announcement coming, so, back to you Swish for that important bulletin.

Thanks Nan, we will see you later in the broadcast with more on the international scene and the weather. But now for the latest Peninsula news. Redwood City authorities have released the name of the deceased man found early Monday at the base of the old Union Soldier Monument in Union Cemetery. Police identified the white male as Earnest Franken Kayne, age 45, a pharmacist from Stockton. As outlined earlier, he has been described as being naked except for a clear plastic raincoat, on which a message was written, apparently in lipstick, although that has not been confirmed as of yet. The content of the message was the basis for a possible inquiry into the whereabouts of someone or something whose name began with the letter 'K'. A police spokesman said the County Medical Examiner's office has yet to determine the cause of death. We will keep you posted on any new information related to this case as soon as it becomes available.

"Earnest Kayne!" said Dale under his breath. "Why, that's Kay's half brother." Getting up from his chair, he called out "Kay!" and headed up to their bedroom to tell her the news.

CHAPTER EIGHT

Rex had come to his office a little early this Wednesday morning. He needed to clean the place up after the debacle with Sheila the day before. Mostly he wanted to get back to business as usual. Nothing like a fresh start in a tidy office to put the insults and frustrations of yesterday behind him. After he notified the building manager about the need to replace the air deflector in the window, and after he swept the floor and picked up the flotsam and jetsam of the previous month that covered most of the hard surfaces of the establishment, he felt much better about life in general. Although the tops of tables and file cabinets were once again visible, his desk was not. A great deal of the flotsam and jetsam had ended up there in a tall, ragged stack. The morning paper, unread, was at the very top of the stack. Rex vowed to tackle the pile after he had finished cleaning the office cups and glasses. He took them, along with the Coffeemaster and made a trip to the janitor's closet in the hall, where he gave everything at least a good hot rinse, if not a thorough washing.

"That's enough K.P. for a while," he said aloud when he got back into the office with his still damp china and the coffee maker, now filled with fresh water for a new brew. "Maybe my mother wouldn't be exactly proud of this place, but it passes my inspection."

Rex put everything where at least he thought it belonged, found the Folgers and put the Coffeemaster to work once more.

Phew, he thought as he sat down at his desk. That's enough exercise for today. He stared at the stack of paper on the desk and waited for his mid-morning coffee. He was reaching for the newspaper at the top of the stack of papers when the phone rang.

"Nickels Investigative Services. Rex Nickels here. How can I help you?" he said in a more-pleasant-than-usual voice.

"Iss dis Rex Nickels, Private Eye? Iss that correct?" a slightly German-accented voice queried.

"That's what I said. Yes, ma'am. That's me. *Und wer bist du?*" Rex said on a hunch, surprising himself that he remembered all the way back to MP training.

"*Oh, du sprichst Deutsch?*" The caller sounded genuinely surprised.

"*Nein, Nicht viel mehr als das. Wer sind Sie? In Englischer sprache, bitte?*" he said in a lowering voice as his German ran out. "Please speak in English."

"I am Hulda. Hulda Stern-Franken. I am in need of the services of a private investigator. I got your name and number from an acquaintance of mine," said the low female voice on the other end of the line.

"I am a private investigator. Exactly who was it that gave you my name and number?"

"Actually, it was from Christopher Sherwood who said he got it from a Mr. Alan Poole-Gass."

"Well I may not know Sherwood, but I do know Poole-Gass. How can I help you?"

"My son was killed on Sunday night. I want you to find who did it." said Hulda Stern-Franken.

"I am terribly sorry to hear that. But what about the police? As much as I'd like to help you out, isn't finding murderers what the police do? Have you called them?" Rex was cautious, although he wanted the work.

"There are things that the police don't need to know. All they need to do is to find the killer. These other things are not for them to know."

"And me? Am I going to learn these things? I can't work for you if you keep secrets that I need to know to do my job. Call it company policy. And I won't do anything illegal. Now, what is going on? More important, who's your son?"

"My son is Earnest Kayne. He was found in the cemetery, Monday morning." Hulda's voice began to break. "Will you help me?"

"Oohhh. That was your son. I read about it in the paper yesterday. I didn't know that they had identified the...that is, I didn't know an identification had been made."

"Yesterday afternoon, they found out it was Earnest. I saw it on the news this morning and it is in the morning paper."

As Rex reached for the morning Tribune at the top of the pile on his desk, he said, "Oh, sorry, I haven't had time to look at either." And he quickly scanned the headline as they talked.

Man Found in Cemetery Identified

Authorities here have identified the man found dead in Union Cemetery on Monday as 45 year-old Earnest Kayne from the city of Stockton where he was a pharmacist. Police spokesman Sergeant Bud Rooney said that Kayne was not married, but had a son, Judson Kayne, who has not been located. "Normally, we don't release the name of the deceased until next of kin have been notified, but in this case..."

"Are you going to help? Will you work on this for me?" Hulda was insistent.

Rex stopped reading and returned to the phone conversation. "That depends. Probably yes, but I need to meet you and talk some more, and find out more about these 'things' you referred to before I agree to anything. Can you come to my office tomorrow, at say ten o'clock? And by the way, just to save time, I do require a retainer, and as I told you before, I won't do anything illegal."

"I have to be back home in Pleasanton tomorrow at ten. But I can come today? I am in Redwood City at the bank now and I can come whenever you say. If I can save a trip back tomorrow, I'd like to."

"Which bank?" Rex asked, pretty much guessing why the grieving mother might just be visiting a bank two days after her son was found dead. He was thinking maybe...a will. But if the guy was from Stockton, why would he bank in Red City, unless there was a joint account of some private nature to check on.

"Sequoia National, just down the street from you on Broadway," was the answer.

Rex learned the value of playing one's cards close to the chest when he was in the Army, and he hadn't forgotten. He didn't want to appear too eager or show his interest in the case, which of course had been re-awaked from its defeat the day before. "I have an appointment in about five minutes which shouldn't last more than that. Let's say nine fifteen."

"I will be there," said Hulda.

"Second floor, back. Stairs in front are quickest."

And the phone call ended. Rex really had nothing to do for the next twenty minutes, so he decided to take a closer look at the newspaper. He skipped through what he had read before and then finished the article.

...Kayne was found naked under a see-through plastic rain-coat, which had a message written on the front, possibly with a lipstick, although police have yet to confirm that. The message referred to a person or thing whose name began with the letter "K". A Police spokesman said they have yet to determine the cause of death...

Other than the name not much of it was new to Rex and he headed for the obituaries. As he flipped the page, an article on the back of the paper caught his eye.

Local Professor Awarded Bird Medal

The Allday Avian Conservatory has announced today that Earl T. Crow has been awarded its annual Gold Medal for his research on the habits of Strix varia or the barred owl, known more commonly as a hoot owl. Crow, third from the left in the picture above, was given the award, the conservatory said, due to his 'unflagging interest in and pursuit of

Strix varia, and his transcription of the calls of the bird and the meanings that can now be attributed to those calls. "His research," the citation reads, "will greatly help in preservation efforts to keep this bird off of the endangered species list." Robert Strouse, president of the Conservatory, said in an interview that the popularity of the owl's soft and fluffy chest feathers for use in pillows and comforters has recently alarmed ornithologists across the globe, fearing a harvest of the birds for commercial purposes. "The nocturnal call of Strix varia, 'Hoot/hoo, hoo, too-HOO; hoo, hoo, too-HOO, ooo', has a combination of frequencies yet to be clearly differentiated in the laboratory," said Strouse. "Crow's recordings will greatly help in the untangling of this mystery." When approached for a comment about the award, Crow, currently an Adjunct Professor of Ornithology at Foothill College, declined, preferring "to keep to myself and my owls," he said.

"Well, I'll be damned," exclaimed Rex. "If I'm not mistaken, that's the guy who discovered the body. Where is that paper from yesterday?" He spied it half way down the pile and thought if he jerked it out quickly, like the old trick of removing a tablecloth with place settings on it, he wouldn't disturb the pile. It didn't work. Papers and magazines and the general composite of flotsam and jetsam went everywhere, the last hitting the floor just as there was a knock on the door.

"Who is it?" he called, not really needing to ask as he charged around gathering the fallen treasures up in his arms and then stuffing them in the knee space beneath his desk.

"It is Hulda Stern-Franken," a voice said.

"Oh, come on in, by all means, Frau Stern-Franken," and he opened the door.

"That is Fraulein, if you don't mind. I will explain in due time."

Rex was speechless. In front of him stood one of the most beautiful women he had ever seen. The low, determined voice didn't go with the figure he saw. Her 5'4" body was perfectly proportioned, and her miniskirt revealed muscular and virtually unblemished legs. She flashed a serious but beautiful smile with perfect teeth and blue eyes framed in a page boy cut of silver blonde hair. "Pert" was the adjective that came to his mind, along with disbelief. He calculated that if her son was 46, how could she have a son that old? She looks 35.

"Eh, yeah, sure," he said, trying not to gulp or stare. "Please come over and have a seat." He pulled up a wooden chair to be next to his desk and went around to his own chair, realizing when he did, that there was no place for his feet under the desk. So he sat side saddle, with his arm on the desk and tried to look casual and still businesslike.

"I want you to find this killer. The person who killed my Earnest," said Hulda quietly and with steel in her voice.

"That I know. What I don't know is why you aren't talking to my friend Fred Wunderlich in the police department. You say there are 'things' he doesn't need to know. Why don't we start with these 'things'?" As struck as Rex was by her looks, and he had done the math quickly in his head and figured she had to be in her sixties, he was getting into a murder case and he was determined to stay on point, at least for now. "Suppose you tell me about yourself. Your accent is slight, but I take it from our phone conversation that you are German. At least you speak it."

And so, flashing a smile that had worked on people for sixty some years, Hulda Stern-Franken told her story.

Hulda told how she had come to the United States as a child acrobat with a touring German circus in 1913. That she, six at the time, along with her family, was stranded here when WW I broke out, and never returned to Europe. A few years after the war, in 1924, they joined the Feld traveling circus, which was eventually booked to perform in Palo Alto as part of a circuit. To save money, the performers were housed on Stanford University's campus.

"There was room there for the elephants, and they were welcome," Hulda giggled as she thought back, her voice returning to a teenager's pitch.

It was there, at Stanford, in the cafeteria, that she met Bradley Sherman, who worked there. Met him and fell in love at seventeen.

"I was easy prey for Brad...and in love and...inexperienced, shall we say. I got pregnant on our second date and learned too quickly about young men and their promises of love. That is how Earnest came into being. Bradley refused to marry me, saying he didn't love me enough. Well, that is an old story, now isn't?"

"I guess," said Rex, getting more uncomfortable by the minute. "The jerk!"

"Not so bad a jerk, though. Even though he got married in a few years, he supported both of us until Earnest was eighteen. But it was a secret from everyone. If I were to tell, he said the support would end. He provided us with a nice house in Pleasanton, and I still live there. He even helped a bit with Earnest's education. I got over the hurt a long time ago. And I think he loved me all that time, a little bit anyway. Brad called me 'Rosebud' instead of Hulda and later Jud started calling me Grandma Rosebud. When Earnest reached eighteen, Brad helped to legally change both of our names to Kayne. Something to do with an Orson Wells movie he saw. I don't go to a lot of movies, so I never understood all of what that meant. But I have paid for the money I got with my loneliness at times, and no one likes living with a secret."

"No they don't. So this is what you didn't want to tell the cops? That Earnest was illegitimate? That's not a big bad secret that would get you into trouble." Rex was growing skeptical.

"Bradley Sherman was Earnest's father, but he was also the father of Kay Sherman, who you may have heard of as Kay Sherman Dale, socialite. As I said, I was sworn to secrecy by Brad for all those years, and I did as I promised. Kay Sherman Dale only found out when Brad told her as he was dying. Kay's mother doesn't know and Brad wanted it so she will never know. She will never hear it from me, or Kay Dale, I am sure. Mrs. Dale has been really nice to me about it all. In particular, she has befriended my poor Judson, my grandson, Earnest's boy. He turned out to be a problem child."

Of course Rex had heard of her, long before she became the socialite Mrs. Dale. The mention of her name in this context gave him a little jolt, even though he had thought of her when he first read about the body in the cemetery. But he kept his reaction to himself and simply said, "I think we are about to get to the part you want to keep from the police. Is that right?"

"Yes. And it is my fault, I'm afraid," and Hulda's voice became very conspiratorial. "As I said, Bradley provided for us all those years. But there was a limit, even though he had a good paying job. He had a family to support, and he did what he could do without being discovered, and I understood that. So I have had to have an outside income. You don't think that looking like this and dressing this way when you are sixty three is easy or free, do you?"

"You aren't telling me you are a...?" began Rex.

"No, I am not, and I don't appreciate the compliment."

"Well, what did you do for extra money?" Rex was not easily put off.

"When I was younger I was a fashion model, and that led to becoming a fashion consultant. It was more glamour than real money. Most people think being a fashion consultant means a high income. The truth is different. So I became a farmer. In my own house. I think the Latin for it would be something like *cannibis sativa agricultura*."

"Pot!" exclaimed Rex. "Well, I'll be a turkey's neck at Thanksgiving," and he laughed a big hearty laugh. "Pot? You grow pot?"

"It may be funny to you, but it isn't to me and wouldn't be to the police if they found out. I changed my name back to Stern-Franken when Earnest left home, so it will take some time for them to connect me to Earnest. And I need that time. Time to close down the farm, for one thing."

"How do you grow pot for all these years in peaceful little Pleasanton without getting caught? In your basement, or something?" Rex was incredulous as well as suspicious.

"That is about right. Not a basement, but a well-insulated, properly-lit, climate-controlled attic, that no one except me and a few hippies know about."

"And I'll bet one of those hippies is poor Judson, your grandson. Did Earnest know?"

"Of course he did, and it is to his everlasting discredit that he told Jud. As a result, *die grossmutter* is his source for his means of escape. I only allow it to go on to keep him out of more trouble trying to buy the stuff."

Rex held up his hand with his palm toward Hulda to indicate he had heard enough.

"I have a hearing problem, and I don't think I ever heard you tell me about farming or a second income. Let's leave it at that. Since I didn't hear that, then nothing you have told me about involves me in anything illegal, which I said from the beginning I won't get into. You have come here to hire me and I will agree to try to find Earnest's killer for two reasons. One, because I am curious about the case. Two, and the main one, you are willing to pay to find out who did it. And it must be clear that I am going to work with the authorities, and whoever it is gets turned over to them, not you. I will not lie on your behalf to the police and if you lie to me about anything at all, it's over. Do we understand each other?"

"Yes, *Mein Herr*, I think we do. What are your fees going to be, and what are the terms?"

Rex looked at her as she batted her eyes and the corners of her mouth turned into a come-hither smile and thought, "This is the best lookin' broad I've ever had business with when I wasn't the one payin'."

"It's simple," he said. "A thousand a week, in advance. And every week thereafter until I find the person. Upon arrest and indictment, another thousand. That way, you trust me to do the work before I do it; I don't have to trust you to pay me after I have done it. Once a week, at the least, I will give you a report of what I have learned. Remember, you are paying for information services here. Not hanging Sheetrock. As for terms, you have heard them all. Oh yes, you cover all my out of ordinary expenses and payment is to be in cash for which I will give you a receipt, in both cases."

'Very well. I didn't come to bargain. I sense from the looks of this place that you are bargained out, anyway." She reached into her purse and pulled out a roll of bills. "Hundreds okay?"

"They spend the same. Sure." And he reached in the desk drawer for his receipt book and wrote the promised document. As he gave it to her, eyeing the roll of bills still in her hand, he said, "Now I know why you were at the bank".

"No, you really don't," she said and stood to leave. "When do you start, and where, if I may ask?"

"Tomorrow morning, first thing. And it will be at the library, where they keep all the information, I'm told."

"I look forward to learning of your progress."

"Me too," said Rex. "Me too."

CHAPTER NINE

Four of the five buttons on the phone at Dale II's desk were lit up, and of these, three were blinking when the buzzer on the intercom line sounded, and that light began to blink also.

"Hold on a minute, Ralph, Linda is buzzing me. Won't take a minute. I'll be right back," said Dale as he punched one button to hold and another to see what Linda wanted.

"Sorry to bother you, sir, but it is Mrs. Dale and she said she had to talk with you, that it is urgent. I told her you were on the phone but she said to interrupt you." Linda sounded stressed.

"That's all right. I'll take the call," Dale sighed, and punched the blinking button on the confidential line. "Good morning, dear. What is it? Is it about Earnest? Sorry I had to wake you with that news and then leave like I did. I had to get here to get a scheduled call. Did you want to talk about it?"

"No, I really can't talk about it just now. After you left this morning, I just went to pieces."

"I didn't know you were that close to him."

"I wasn't, but, well you know. He was my brother after all. It just hit me all of a sudden," said Kay, her voice wavering.

"I am really sorry. What can I do to help?" Dale said, but in such a way that his lack of sincerity and enthusiasm was intentionally transparent.

"Nothing really. I know you are terribly busy. I called to tell you that I am going out to the farm for a while. Maybe a little ride on old Posey out there in the country will clear my head. I'll touch base with you later." The waver in Kay's voice was absent now.

"Hold on a minute, Kay, let me get this other line," said Dale and put her on hold and connected with Ralph.

"Hey Ralph, I need a few more minutes. Domestic matter. Be right with you," and he punched the button which connected him with Kay again.

"That sounds like a good idea, if you think it will help. I had wanted for us to take Ralph and Wanda out to dinner tonight. Can you make it back in time, do you think?"

"Oh, please. Can you cancel that? I am just not up to it. I doubt if I could get home and have time to shower and dress, but even if I did, I just don't feel like talking. Please understand." Kay found her waver once more.

"Well, dear, I understand. I can't very well call it off, but I can say there is a change of plans and make it an all men's evening." Dale was relieved. He was up to his neck with lawyers and the stock acquisition he had been working on for months, and he really didn't need a distraction just now. "Don't worry about it, Kay. You sound like you really need to get away, I can tell. Take your time."

"I don't know exactly when I'll be back," said Kay.

"Well, not to worry. Just be careful if it is after dark. I will probably be pretty late getting in myself, if I know Ralph. He is a real talker and a night owl. And I need to close this deal with him as soon as I can. Take care and I love you." Dale was sincere with his closing comment.

"I love you too," responded Kay, with a combination of resignation and relief.

"Hello, Ralph?" said Dale as he punched the phone buttons once more. "Ralph, how about we batch it tonight? Just you and I. Kay's coming down with something, she just told me, and you said before that you hadn't talked to Wanda yet. Maybe we can get this thing off of dead center if it is just the two of us."

"Yes, and a good bottle of *La Tache* Pinot Noir, say 1961." Ralph was setting high stakes early for the evening's forthcoming negotiations.

"Sounds good. I'll see you at Perot's at seven," said Dale.

"Make it seven thirty. I need to wind things up here first, so I have a clear mind for our chat. Ciao."

"Ciao?" said Dale to himself He shook his head and punched into another blinking line for yet another call.

CHAPTER TEN

Rex knew he should get some exercise, as his belt was running out of notches. It was a pleasant evening and he felt better than usual, so after he got home and had some left-over lasagna and a beer, he put on his old sneakers and headed out for some walk-and-think time. Normally not a contemplative person, Rex was in a thoughtful mood on this particular evening, and wanted a little peace and quiet while he reviewed the unfolding events. As he walked, he lined up what he knew, thinking of the half pieces of information, the pieces that fit and those that didn't. It wasn't long before his walking reverie brought him to his office building, and he was startled that he had come so far. It occurred to him that perhaps his friend Jack was still in the office, and maybe he could help shed light on Rex's thoughts. He slowly made it up the stairs to his floor and let himself into the office where he had spent most of the day already. As his eyes scanned the room for his bottle of Jack Daniels, the flashing light on the answering machine caught his eye. He went over and punched it into action. He heard the beep and then a woman's voice came on.

"Rex Nickels, this is a voice from your past. I used to be Kay Sherman, but I got married and I am now Kay Dale. Maybe you know that already."

"Where do you think I have been, on the moon?" said Rex to the machine. "Of course I know who you are. How could I forget?"

48

"Anyway," the voice continued, "You said to me one time to call you if I ever needed anything. Well, I need you. I mean your services as a private investigator, or maybe it's better to say I need your help. I can't explain any more of it on the phone right now. I had hoped to catch you there at your office. I got this number from the ad in the Yellow Pages. Information said your home number was unlisted. Please don't try to call me. I will call again later." Then the phone clicked off.

"Well, you never know in this business, you never know." And Rex sidled up to his friend Jack and took a quick nip before heading home, this time to stay.

Jack, it turned out, had a brother staying at Rex's house, named Jack II, and Jack II became Rex's companion for the evening. After he kicked off his sneakers, using the toe on one foot against the heel of the other, and put on some pants with elastic in the waist, Rex settled down in his favorite easy chair with Jack II in one hand and a glass in the other, and began to think.

His memory traveled back to that terrific three weeks he'd had with Kay Sherman. My, God, that was ten years ago. I was—what?—thirty-three and she must have been about twenty-nine or thirty, he said to himself. Was she a number. I wonder what she wants now. Hope it is not what she wanted ten years ago. I can't keep up the pace like that anymore. She liked the horses. She sure did. I spent a lot of time and money on horses then, and I won that one big bet and got my picture in the paper. Forty-five hundred bucks! She saw my picture and called me. That's how we tied up together again. Three weeks. Horses and sex, constant for three weeks without a let-up. Then it was over. Like the end of a horse race. Oh, shit, at least we crossed the finish line at the same time. Nose to nose. Dead heat. And he smiled at his own joke.

He took a big swig of whiskey and his bleary mind poked farther back in history. It was when he was in the Army, stationed at The Presidio. I was one squared-away MP in those days. I didn't give no shit and I didn't take no shit—from nobody! Then that damn USO dance at Stanford. That's where we met. That bastard

sergeant Brileau put me in charge of all those G.I.s that we bused
to the dance for those sorority girls. I thought for sure I'd lose my
stripes. But, hell, I was tough. I did all right. They behaved. I saw
to that. Then she walked over to me, and said something, and I
said something, and all I could think of was getting in her pants
and I could tell she felt the same way. Bammo! Just like that, in a
minute, we were on the back seat of that G.I. bus.... Rex stopped
thinking about exactly what happened and tried to remember
just how good it felt, and his faced relaxed and his smile grew
larger and larger as he drifted off into the memory of wild, young,
and uncomplicated sex.

● ● ●

William Dale was very, very tired. As he drove up to the auto-
matic gate at the front of his driveway on Selby Lane, he fumbled
with the remote operator and almost ran into the fence before he
got the car stopped and the device pointed in the right direction.
Finally, he got the gate open, his Mercedes through it, and navi-
gated his way up the drive and to the garage, which he opened
with the same remote, this time aimed correctly. It barely registered with him that neither Kay's Thunderbird nor the station
wagon were there, but he was so tired, and a little high, that it was
all he could do to get out of the car, unlock the door to the house
and turn off the burglar alarm when he got inside. His focus was
to get his clothes off and into bed, fast. As he passed by the study
on his way to the stair, however, his eye caught the blinking light
on the answering machine on the hall table.

"What now?" He let out an irritated sigh. He clicked the
machine on.

"Hi Bill. It's me." Kay's voice came on. "I have decided to
spend the night here at the farm. I had a great ride, but it lasted
longer than I thought it would. It is too late to drive in now, the
way I feel. Since you are so busy with that Pataglio contract, you
probably won't have time for a lot of chit-chat anyhow, so I may

stay here most of tomorrow too. It depends on how I feel then. At any rate, I'll be back home tomorrow afternoon, four or five at the latest. Hope you close the deal."

As the message ended, a disembodied voice said, "Wednesday, five sixteen p.m."

CHAPTER ELEVEN

Thursday morning, after a restorative dose of coffee with a bit of JD stirred in, Rex went over in his mind his plan of action. As he had told Hulda Stern-Franken, for whom he was now working, he planned to start his investigation at the library. He was mainly concerned with this Earnest Kayne character, but he still had Kay Sherman in mind. He thought he might check a little on her while he was at it. Couldn't hurt.

These were his thoughts as he left his house on foot—it was not far to the library. He strolled over to Middlefield and Jefferson, and from there to the Redwood City Library, a graying structure of mediocre WPA design that had, with the wisdom of the city fathers and dollars from the Roosevelt administration, regrettably replaced the beloved old Carnegie Library over there on Broadway. He found the periodicals desk at the back of the main floor in a high ceilinged room with suspended, flickering fluorescent lights. In the center of the room was a battered oak desk, probably a survivor from Carnegie days, piled to eye-level with yellowing newspapers and moldering cardboard boxes of microfilm reels. Rex knew from experience that behind that barricade of newsprint and acetate he would find Rosemarie Budner, the reference librarian, known popularly as "Rosie".

"Oh, it's you. Rex the Wonder," snarled Rosie, peering over horn-rimmed half-glasses. "Let me guess. You're after the late

Mr. Earnest Franken Kayne, I'll bet. And my next guess is that you also want information on Mr. William Dale the second, God only knows why. Don't think you're my first visitor today asking questions about those two."

Rex was caught off guard by her opening remarks, but rallied quickly, quick enough to respond with a broad gesture and a smile as he smacked his forehead with the palm of his hand and said lightly, "Wow! I've heard you were a mind-reader, Rosie, but that takes the cake! However..." and he rolled his eyes and brought his voice to a more serious tone, "your guess..."

"What about my guess?"

"Your guess, Rosie dear, would only be half right. As a matter of fact, it is Mrs. William Dale II, not her husband that I am interested in."

"*Mrs.* William Dale? Of course. Kay Dale. I should have known," smirked Rosie.

"I am here mainly to inquire about what the newspapers may have said in the past about one Earnest Kayne. You know, the guy they found dead in the cemetery Monday morning. And while I am here, I just thought I might as well see what you have on Mrs. Dale for some other research I am doing. Save me a trip later."

Rex, standing with his hands in his pockets in what he thought was a devil-may-care posture in front of Rosie, tried to act casual about the fact that he was making an inquiry about Kay Dale.

"I'm sure a lot of folks might find Mrs. Dale an interesting person, though. Who was it, some student writing a term paper on the town's social history? The Dale family goes way back, you know," queried Rex.

"No, it was not a student, as if it is any of your business, Rexy. Why do you want to know, are you writing a book?" Rosie smirked up at Rex.

"Might be, might be" said Rex, returning the smirk.

"Then make it a mystery," said Rosie.

"Come on Rosie, I don't have time for high school humor anymore. Who was your previous visitor?"

"Oh all right. I guess a library is for information. It was a little short guy named Abe Willing. Here, he left a card. See... 'Abel N. Willing, Sales 415-633-2468.' Said to call him Abe, though. A little too friendly for a stranger, if you ask me."

Rex, having seen the phone number on Willing's card, tried to write it on a note pad in his pocket. He had heard of some famous reporter that knew how to do that, so he was trying to learn how to do it too and he struggled with the pencil stub. He wanted to jot down the number without seeming too obvious.

"Uh, never heard of him. So what was he interested in concerning Mr. William Dale, Madam Librarian?"

"I haven't the slightest idea, Mr. Private Investigator. He asked for information on both Kayne and Mr. Dale, and I had to go to the back and get the files. Dale's was in the Business section and it is more current and closer so I got it first. After I gave him the folder of material on Mr. Dale, I told him I would have to go back further in the stacks and look for whatever we had on Mr. Kayne. He was reading the Dale stuff when I went to the stacks and when I got back he was gone. But the folder was still here. That was about ten minutes ago. You want to look at it?" said Rosie as she gathered up the folder on William Dale. "Otherwise, I'll put it back where it belongs."

"Nah, said Rex. "Not right now. If I need it I know where to come and who to see."

Rosie gave him one of her dismissive looks and said, "And I didn't find anything on Mr. Kayne. He was from Stockton, you know—we don't archive the Stockton paper. And apparently he never made the news around here. Till now that is."

Rex sidled around the stacked barrier of research resources, and leaned close into the face of the reference librarian.

"Rosie my sweet, you always read me like a book ... or maybe like the Sunday edition. I need information on Mr. Kayne, and I also happen to have, as I said ... a passing interest in the estimable Mrs. Dale. Just ... a mild curiosity about an old acquaintance, a slight acquaintance. Research of a possible coincidence. Maybe you could be an angel and fetch me whatever files you have on the lady.

Rosie muttered something unintelligible, which, as Rex knew from experience, was bound to be profane, as she eased out of her chair and disappeared into the labyrinth of archives that filled the dim space beyond her desk. Rex fidgeted and paced for a bit. He tried to relax on the oak bench opposite Rosie's work area. Rex wouldn't have known the bench's origins, but, had he asked, Rosie could have told him it was a Gustave Stickley piece, part of the original furnishings installed when the Carnegie Building was completed in 1905. Rosie hadn't been at her post that long, but she had weathered successive waves of modernization and been able to assert her claim to keeping one of the last surviving examples of the good stuff in her part of the library, her domain.

In a surprisingly short time, Rosie re-appeared with several file folders stuffed with newspaper clippings. The Redwood City Library, as a matter of economy as well as tradition, clung to its old tried and true ways of obtaining and keeping things, and files of stories and pictures clipped from newspapers were still lovingly maintained and updated by local journalism students from San Mateo and Foothill colleges.

"Okay, Rexy, this is what we have. I re-checked, still not a thing on Earnest Franken Kayne. Mrs. Kathleen Dale is different. She is one of the area's bigger social lionesses—not a Jackie O, mind ya, but someone who's managed to push her name and face into print over the years. And the answer is 'No,' you're not going to be able to treat me good enough to reveal any more about my prior visitor than I already have. And," she added slyly, "you know how tidy I am—you're not going to find any footprints in this file but mine. You can go through the file here, or I can let you use the conference room across the hall."

Rex shrugged. Although his butt was uncomfortable on the old oak, it wasn't uncomfortable enough to make him get up the energy to move. "Naw, I'll stay here," he said, taking the files from Rosie. He started leafing through the clips.

Kathleen Emily Sherman Engaged to William Dale II.

The handsome couple married with all the trappings.

Mrs. Dale and other ladies at the Peninsula Symphony opening night.

Mrs. Kay Dale with the Mayor at the Children's Hospital Ball.

✓ *Mrs. Dale (in shorts, left) presenting the trophy to the junior women's doubles champion.*

Mrs. Dale with her architect in the kitchen of her Atherton home, promoting a charity house tour.

Mrs. William Dale II and other members of the Stanford Art Museum Board at the opening of the blockbuster traveling exhibition, "Unknown Treasures of Peoria."

And so on. Maybe a few times a year, her name and picture would appear. As Rosie said, "no Jackie O", but a lioness of sorts by the standards of the society section, lately and boldly renamed the *Living Top*s section.

As he was going through the clippings, Rex thought maybe this was not the productive effort he had conjured up out on the street. He was doing research on an old flame, not on a murder victim. Still, he was intrigued by what she had become. Kay was pictured with but a few men, not what he would have expected from what he knew about her. But this was a squeaky-clean town, if you believed the Tribune. And her husband was very well known.

Rex flipped through the rest of the clippings. At the bottom of the stack his eye stopped his hand at a story about last year's Grossmont Stakes, accompanying a group photo shot in the winner's circle at Bay Meadows. Mr. and Mrs. William Dale with Colonel Owen Owens, co-owners of Hillandale Stables, Rod "Red" Ramsey, trainer, Butch Kennedy, jockey, and the Stakes winner, Princess Khey.

"Well, all right, all right!" laughed Rex, "A lot of females are named Kay, and some of them are nags, some are princesses."

CHAPTER TWELVE

Rex Nickels arrived at Hillandale Stables as the sun was directly overhead, and shadows gave no hint of direction. He leaned on the white railing that enclosed the workout track and reflected on the scene before him and the events that had taken place. The unmistakable aroma coming from a nearby manure pile got his attention.

I shoulda parked in the parking lot, then I wouldn't have to smell that shit. But then, no one knows I am over here, and they won't bother me as long as they don't spot me or my car back off of the road there, he thought, as he dipped his finger into his coffee to see if it was still warm. He wrapped his hand around the paper cup and put his nose near the cup's edge to let the aroma from the coffee envelop his face and permeate his senses.

It was proving to be an aromatic day.

He spied a black furry caterpillar inching its way along the top rail of the track. He was about to smash it flat when he thought of Sheila's cousin Vinnie from Peoria, and how his eyebrows grow in a single line across his face, just like that damned caterpillar. And of his job at the roofing company when he was a kid, and when Vinnie came to work there and just sat around all day reading the racing form, and the guy who asked about it once too often and accidentally 'fell' off the roof when...I'm thinkin' too damn much.

And Rex Nickels, private detective, drank deep from his paper coffee cup, emptying it, then crumpled the cup in his beefy fist in a quick, single squeeze.

"If you are thinkin 'bout throwing that on the track, you might want to think about it some more," said a voice behind him.

Rex spun around and instinctively reached for his shoulder holster, which was empty.

"This what you're looking for?" said Red Ramsey, and held up a snubnosed .38 special. "You left it in your car. I turned the radio off for ya, too. Good way to run down a battery."

"Where did you come from?" said Rex in a panic.

"Peoria, originally," said Ramsey with a smirk. "Doesn't everyone?"

"Look asshole, don't get cute. I mean just now. Where did you come from? How did you sneak up on me without me knowin'? And who the hell are you, anyhow?" Rex blurted out.

"You aren't in a real good position to be callin' people nasty names, considering that I'm the one with the chrome," said Red, and lowered the gun came down and pointed it at Rex's belly.

"I know who you are!" exclaimed Rex as he put two and two together. "You're Rod 'Red' Ramsey! I saw you at the library. In the picture with the rich folks and their horse. Beautiful horse. Beautiful legs, that horse. You are the trainer."

"And you would be?" Red's question was a flat statement, with just a touch of menace.

"Me? I am someone who just loves horses. And betting." Rex was thinking fast, making it up as he went along.

"And?" Red kept the gun aimed at Rex's belt buckle.

"Well... say, could you lower that? I'm not real comfortable looking at it from this end," said Rex with his palms up and extended.

Red had been around enough to know when to ease up, and so he did, knowing that he was quick enough and tough enough to take this guy barehanded if he had to.

"All right, but keep the hands where I can see them." And he lowered the gun to his side. "Go on. Tell me what you are doing here."

"I like to place a few bets now and then, and I have been reading about a Princess Khey and what a phenomenal filly she is. I heard Willie Pissanteli say on the television that she's one of the finest pieces of horse flesh that God ever made. Out of Kiss Me Sweet and Prince Sashay. Just happened to have some business in San Gregorio and dropped over here on the outside chance I could see her in the flesh. Maybe up close. I always like to see things up close before I bet on them."

"That all sounds pretty fancy. I still don't know who you are or what business you are in," said Red.

"I'm in investments," Rex returned.

"Who isn't? So, you were on your way to the stock exchange in San Gregorio and just happened to be in the neighborhood and thought you'd drop by, eh?" And Ramsey chuckled without mirth. "Come on, who the fuck do you think you're talking to?" and the gun in Red's hand came up again to point at Rex's belly.

But Rex Nickels, although overweight and a little wheezy, was surprisingly quick, and as fast as a mongoose on a cobra he backhanded the .38 to one side, grabbed Red's arm with his free hand, and within two seconds had Red in a choke hold, gasping for air.

"I think I'm talking to a guy whose mouth is faster than his trigger finger," said Rex from behind him into Red's ear, which was close enough for him to bite. "Let go of the gun, tough guy."

And Red did, after which Rex gave him a big push, which enabled Rex to retrieve the gun while Red was stumbling to catch his balance and his breath. Then Rex did a strange thing. He put the gun into his shoulder holster and gave his clothes a brush as if to tidy them, signaling that this kind of confrontation was not a big deal at all to him.

"MP. U.S. Army. Some things you never forget," Rex said with a small, satisfied smile. "Let's play nice, huh?"

Realizing that Rex had the upper hand and was likely to keep it, Red moved to the fence and leaned on it with his elbows. He turned his head to Rex and said in a low voice. "Okay. You win. What do you want?"

Rex followed suit and took a place at the rail, but at a discreet distance. He looked around and then past Red to the far end of the track and said, "This is a nice spread you have here. I don't suppose that horse in the pasture is Princess Khey, by chance?"

"As a matter of fact it is. I just let her out to run a bit."

"I sure wish I could see her up close."

"Well, you can't. I'm not about to chase her for you. She is supposed to be having a workout, but the stable boy showed up missing today and I just let her out to run off some energy. She'll come back for some oats eventually. But even if she were here, I couldn't let you get very close. Farm rules. Damn little punk!" Red was getting angry. "If Jud had shown up, none of this would be happening."

"Who?"

"Jud. Punk!"

"And Jud is?" asked Rex.

"Judson Kayne. Some stable bum that Mrs. Dale brought in from Stockton. She wanted me to give him a job, so I hired him to muck the stalls. Sometimes, I let him walk the horses. Strange dude. Rides a motorcycle and carries weird stuff in his pockets. Last time I saw him, I asked him for a light and when he went to get his lighter, a tube of lipstick fell out of his pocket. He really did a dance getting it back in. He finally found his lighter, the dumb butt. Uh, speaking of lights, you don't happen to have one, do you?" said Red, pulling a pack of Marlboros and tapping out a cigarette.

"As a matter of fact, I do," said Rex, and handed Red a pack of matches.

●●●

Returning from Hillandale Stables, nursing the Corvair Monza as it struggled up the grades to La Honda, Rex took stock of recent events.

Okay, Rex, my man, Sexy Rexy. What the hell have we got here?

A body, naked as a jay bird, except he's wearing a see-through raincoat;

A body sitting up against the base which held the Civil War trooper, destroyed by vandals, twice;

Some kinda' message in lipstick on the raincoat, something about "K.";

Sheila comes bustin' into my office with a gun looking for some friggin' pills;

The body turns out to be some guy from out in Stockton, name of Earnest Kayne, who ends up dead in Redwood City;

Earnest Kayne's mother, Hulda FrankenStern, or Stern-Franken, hires me to find the killer;

A message on my answering machine from Kay Sherman, now Dale, nothing to do with old times' sake, but sounding like she's in some kind of serious trouble;

Fact that Kay has a history with Red Ramsey and Colonel Owen Owens, and they're all big in thoroughbreds—raising and racing;

That strange lad, Judson, who works for Ramsey at the stables, is some kind of nephew of Lady Dale; related to the victim… well, his son…and grandson of Hulda Stern—whatever;

Red Ramsey is a son of a bitch from the word go. Needs to be watched. He's up to something. Or maybe he's just a shit;

Meanwhile, some guy named Abel N. Willing has been asking questions about William Dale and the late Mr. Kayne;

Seems like there's gotta be something that connects all this. My former 'special' friend Kay could be at the center. And what does she want with me? Is it all about horses? Who in the name of Seabiscuit is Abel N. Willing?"

As the Corvair finally attained the summit along Skyline Drive, Rex called out loud, "Whoa! Looks like it's time to check in with my good buddy Captain Wunderlich. See what he knows. He doesn't need to know what I know, not right now anyway. But I may need to know what he knows."

Rex pressed on downhill toward Redwood City's police headquarters, muttering silent prayers that the brakes would get him safely to Middlefield Road.

CHAPTER THIRTEEN

Back in Redwood City, Rex searched for a free parking space near police headquarters, but he was out of luck.

Well, hell, I don't live near downtown for nothing. I'll just scoot over and leave the Monza at my house and stroll back to the cop shop.

As he pulled into his driveway, a rumbling from his stomach told Rex that it was after two p.m. and he hadn't stopped for lunch today. He let himself in through the kitchen door and went straight to the fridge. Slim pickings. A pizza slice left from God knows when, a couple of shriveled franks and a can of Acme beer. In the cupboard, he sorted through what was there; half a box of Cheerios, a few Ritz crackers, and a packet of spaghetti, but no sauce.

Bummer! There really are times when I miss Sheila's domestic talents. Well, okay, I can make it on cold pizza and beer. I've enjoyed worse meals. Later I'll go around to El Charro and get me some frozen margaritas and an enchilada dinner with all the trimmings.

After lunch Rex walked the few blocks to police headquarters. He exchanged crude pleasantries with the desk officer, who buzzed him through into the detective bureau. He found Captain Wunderlich's office and rapped three times on the glass in the open office door.

Fred Wunderlich, a burly, balding former redhead, turned to see Rex and rose from his desk with a mock grimace. "Nickels, my man, come on in! How's the P.I. racket treating you these days?"

"Been doing pretty well. As long as folks around here keep up their indiscreet behavior, and their spouses keep up their suspicions, I'll make a living. What's new on the crime front?"

Wunderlich grinned. "Oh, we've been busy. Hippies and drugs, drugs and hippies. A lot of that element right there in your neighborhood, I'm sure you know. But the big deal in the shop is the body in the cemetery."

Rex managed an air of puzzlement. "Oh? I guess I haven't heard anything about that. What's the story?"

Amazed, Wunderlich replied, "What? Are you telling me you haven't seen the TV or newspapers? They've been full of it all week!"

"To tell the truth, between being up to my eyeballs in my case work, and my regular carousing, I haven't been paying much attention to the news. Tell me about it."

"Well, long story short, a male corpse was found in the Union Cemetery early Monday morning. And I don't mean one of the regular residents. Guy propped up on the base of the old statue. No clothing, or I.D., or anything, except for a clear plastic raincoat. With some fingerprints on it. But we do have a make on the victim. Earnest Kayne, resident of Stockton, a pharmacist there."

Rex's eyes got big. "No kidding! Sounds like you got some weird stuff going on! What do you think he was doing in Redwood City? Any local connections?"

"No contacts we know of yet, but, we just dug up the fact that he was registered at the Catalina Motel, down El Camino, on Sunday night. No record of any phone calls from the motel. That's about it so far."

"Amazing. Well Fred, good luck on the investigation. That old cemetery! What a hot bed, so to speak, of strange doings, what with the destruction of the soldier statue and all the other vandalism. Oh, by the way, while I'm here, a name came up in one of my divorce cases. Wonder if you would recognize it. Have you ever heard of Abel N. Willing?"

Wunderlich responded quickly. "Oh, sure! We know Abe well. He works as an investigator for the State Horse Racing Board. Home base is the San Francisco office. Mainly assigned to Bay Meadows. Why? Has he been fooling around with one of the local housewives?"

"Oh, no, no. Nothing like that! It was just that he might have some information I'd be interested in. So, thanks. Now I'll know where to find him. Okay, Freddy, keep up the good work in the public service. I'll watch for more news on the plastic raincoat caper. Gotta be moving on now. I'll see you again soon."

CHAPTER FOURTEEN

It was Friday, six thirty a.m. The Dale residence on Selby Lane was usually quiet at this time of morning, but not this quiet. It was the kind of silence that wakes a person, particularly if he is not in the place he normally spends the night. William Dale woke with a start and found he was in his recliner where he had apparently fallen asleep the night before. He was still in the business suit pants and white shirt from the day before, his tie loose around his neck and his shoes on the floor beside the chair where he had kicked them off. There was an empty martini glass on the table beside him. His head finally cleared and he fully realized that it was the morning after the closing of the Pataglio deal and he hadn't been to bed at all.

"Kay," he said. "Kay?" He called louder as he got up and went from room to room on the first floor. "Kay, are you up?"

He took the stairs two at a time and went to their bedroom and saw quickly that the bed hadn't been slept in. He searched the entire upstairs, put on some tennis shoes from his closet and then went down the back stairs that led through the pantry and eventually to the game room and wine cellar on the lower level. After he had searched both the ground floor and the lower level, finally it became clear that she wasn't home and probably hadn't come home yesterday at all, let alone spent the night there. He checked the garage and the driveways, just to be certain, and her car was not there. He went to the kitchen and called their house at the Hillandale Stables complex. There was no answer after ten rings so he hung up and re-dialed, letting it ring more than ten times, to no avail, before giving up.

It was not in Dale's nature to panic, as some men might have. Instead, he sat down at the desk in his downstairs study, folded hands in front of him, calmed himself and tried to think of the logical thing to do. He organized a plan of action in his head. Item number one was to call the house at Hillandale and see if Kay was there. He had done that and she wasn't, at least she didn't answer the phone. Next then would be to call Owen at the farm and ask him if he had seen her, either yesterday afternoon or this morning.

"No," he murmured aloud, "on second thought, I will call Red Ramsey instead. Owen won't be up yet, and Red knows everything that goes on down there anyway." Using the Rolodex on his credenza, Dale quickly found the number and called it, using the grey Princess extension phone Kay had given him for his birthday.

"Red, this is Bill. Sorry to call so early, but it is important."

"Hi, Bill. It's okay. I start at six," said Red Ramsey from the phone in his office at Hillandale Stables. "What do you need?"

"It's about my wife, Kay. Have you seen her?" asked Dale.

"Not since Wednesday around noon. She came out here to see Princess Khey and then took old Posey out for a spin. Said she needed to get out in the country, have herself a good ride. She seemed a little upset, so I had young Kayne ride with her. Posey may be old but she gets nervous if her rider is nervous. And Mrs. Dale was a tad jittery it seemed to me. I didn't want to take a chance, if you know what I mean."

"What about yesterday and last night? Did you see her then?"

"No, but then I was in and out all day," answered Red carefully.

"This morning? Have you seen her this morning? Do you think she is at the farm, maybe?" said Dale, growing more concerned.

"I don't think so. It's foggy out here, so if anyone was there and up, I would see lights on. But it is early. Do you want me to go over there and look in? Say, the light just went on in the Colonel's bedroom. He must have seen my line light up on his phone. I'll ask him. And I can check over here and ask young Kayne what he knows. He should be up and working in the stable by now."

"Yes, please do all that, and call me back. Right away."

"You bet!" And with that, Red hung up and headed out on his search of the property for Kay.

Within fifteen minutes Red had circumnavigated the building compound of the ranch. First, he searched he stables themselves where there was no one except the horses, and they were unattended and manure was collecting in the stalls. Princess Khey was in her special stall as she should have been, along side of Peoria Heights. Posey was there too, along with the rest of the horses. He checked the adjacent tack room and workers' quarters behind them. No one was there, nor any sign of anyone. Then he made his way to the Dale's house at the west side of the compound. It wasn't locked but he knocked on several doors and windows before he went in. No one was there either. Lastly, he went to Colonel Owens's house. He let himself in and called up the spiral staircase in a muted tone, just in case Owens wasn't up or had gone back to bed.

"Colonel? You up? It's me, Red."

"Yeah, I'm up," said the Colonel, coming to the top of the stairs as he cinched up the sash on his silk dressing gown. "What in the hell is going on? Who in the fuck is calling here at this god forsaken time of the day?"

"Bill Dale. Why are you up so early? Did that little blinking phone light wake you?"

"I had to take a leak, if you must know. I saw the light then. What does he want?" The Colonel was irritated, but businesslike.

"It seems as if Mrs. Dale didn't make it home last night. He wants to know if we have seen her."

"Well, have we?" asked Owens, coming down the stairs.

"Unless you have, no. I checked all around. The stables, the tack room and I even went through their house. She's not here. The last time I saw her, she and that Kayne kid were going out for a ride with old Posey, and that was around noon on Wednesday."

"What about the kid. Did you ask him if he'd seen her?"

"He's not around either."

"What about Princess Khey? Is she there?"

"Yeah. She's in her stall where she should be. Posey and the other horses are there too, but the stalls haven't been cleaned. And since the kid is gone, I need to let her out, right now. Damn, I don't know how long she's been in there."

"Okay, okay," said the Colonel in a low voice, taking charge. "You do that. We can't let anything happen to that horse. Meanwhile, I will call Dale. And keep it quiet around here. No need to wake the ladies and have to deal with them with everything else we have on our plate."

Red rolled his eyes at the mention of the women he called 'the bimbos', and simply nodded and left the house.

Owens went to a phone and called William Dale.

The door to the guest bedroom, which had been open just wide enough for two faces pressed together, side by side, closed quietly, and Twilee and Amber carefully retreated within, unnoticed but not uninformed.

"One of us needs that Binaca," said Amber.

•••

While William Dale was waiting to hear from Red Ramsey, he kept to his ordered way of doing things. He called his private number at his office, knowing that Linda, his secretary, would retrieve the message from the answering machine when she came in at eight o'clock.

"Linda, this is Bill. Something has come up that is very serious, so listen carefully. I don't know where Kay is. She didn't come home last night and she is not at Bear Gulch. What you can do for me is this. First, clear my calendar for today. Think up some plausible reason for postponing whatever I have on tap. Do not, under any circumstances, tell anyone about Kay until we learn more. If the police contact you, say as little as possible, but tell the truth. But if reporters from either the newspaper or TV try to get any information from you, don't say a word. If I call you or you need to call me, be sure you are on the private line. Of course, if it is Kay, I know you will get in touch immediately. If someone other than Kay wants to reach me, take a number and I will call them. I don't have any reason at this point to suspect kidnapping, but I can't rule it out either. We just have to be very, very careful. I have to get off now. I am expecting a call from Red Ramsey at the farm. I'll call you later."

Dale no sooner put the phone down than it rang. "Hello, Red?" he said.

"No, this is Owen. Red is in the stable tending to Princess Khey and the other horses. He told me about the situation. Where in the hell do you suppose she is?"

"I don't know. She was here when I left for work on Wednesday morning and then I talked to her from the office later. I got home late that night—big deal with Ralph Pataglio that I will tell you about when we have time—and I found a message on the machine that she was spending the night at the our house out there, but that she would be home late yesterday afternoon. Yesterday was a bear of a day with the lawyers closing the Pataglio deal and I didn't think about calling her and she didn't call me. I phoned her late in the day and when she didn't answer I wound things up at the office and came home to see what was up. I was really drained, had just one martini to relax, and conked out in my chair while I was waiting for her. I woke up this morning still in the damn chair, in my clothes. I looked all around, called the villa and she wasn't at either place. That's when I called Red. I figured you would still be asleep."

"Well, I wasn't. I was up to take a pee when I saw the phone blink on Red's line. If I'd known it was you I would have picked up and saved you all this time of explaining it twice."

"Where's Red?" Dale wanted to know. "He was supposed to call me." Dale was accustomed to having calls returned in person.

"I'm calling instead. He said he looked everywhere here; stable, tack room, this house, and even your villa. She's not here.

Pure and simple. Last anyone saw of her was Wednesday noon when she went riding on Posey. The Kayne kid was with her. And, incidentally, he hasn't shown up for work since Wednesday. We don't know where he is either. I don't know what that means, if anything. He hasn't set any records out here for reliability, I can tell you."

"Oh, really?" Dale said, and the way he said it sounded odd to Owens. "Jud's gone too?"

"Yes. So?" answered Owens carefully, sensing something.

"I need to tell you something, Colonel. Something very confidential. Something that not very many people know. When I tell you, it is important that this information doesn't become public knowledge any more than can be helped. Can you promise me your absolute discretion?" Dale said with the savvy of a keen businessman.

"Is it legal?" Owens had his own business acumen.

"Yes, of course. That is not the issue." Dale waited a moment and then said, "Judson Kayne is Kay's nephew."

"What the hell! How could that be?"

"It seems that Kay's father, Brad Sherman, had more than one family. He fathered a child out of wedlock before he married Kay's mother. It was some German circus entertainer he had a fling with. He supported that woman and her child for years on the side, in secret. Her name was Hulda Stern-Franken. For the sake of the kid, he had her change their last name to Kayne."

"Kayne! Oh shit. Keep going," said Owens, but he sensed something strange was coming.

"The kid grew up to be our friend, Earnest Kayne, the father of the Judson Kayne who works for you, and the recent corpus delecti found holding up a monument in a cemetery."

"I think I may have heard it rumored that Earnest Kayne was Jud's father, but I had no idea Earnest was Kay's brother."

"Half brother," corrected Dale.

"Whatever, this little fact complicates a lot of things, doesn't it? How long have you known?"

"Not that it is anyone's business but my wife's and mine, but the answer is that I have known as long as she has. She found out when her father died two years ago and she told me about it right away. It is not a problem with us. At least it hasn't been. Now, not only my reputation, but Kay's is liable to be shadowed by this."

"You bet your ass it is a problem, Mr. Dale, probably more than you want know. We will all be in hot water if this goes beyond your step brother-in-law getting discovered murdered with only his raincoat on. It will be more than just a shadow. Mr. Dale, I think we need to talk."

CHAPTER FIFTEEN

"Were you followed?" asked Colonel Owen Owens, looking over Red's shoulder at the parked cars scattered around the Bay Meadows Race Course parking lot.

"No." said Rod "Red" Ramsey, verging on truculence.

"Why the attitude?" Owens took a lot off of Ramsey, because he needed him and because Ramsey knew everything. Almost everything.

"Twenty five miles seems like a hell of a long way to come just to talk about something I could have walked over to your living room and discussed. Bein' away from the stables this long makes me nervous. And as you know the stable boy didn't show up today."

"Well, that's too damn bad. I was in Red City at the courthouse earlier and happened to run into our friend Abe Willing coming out of the library. I stopped to talk. I always try to chat and be friendly with those that have some control in my life. You might try that sometime."

Red gave Owens one of those "screw-you-get-on-with-it" looks. "Control? I thought you had it rigged so that no one had control over you."

"Almost no one. Except the damn State Horse Racing Board... and their little busybody, Mr. Abel Willing." Owens squinted his eyes and looked off in thought.

"So?"

"So, our little chit-chat more or less scared the shit out of me, to be honest. And you know me well enough that you know I wouldn't say that if it weren't true. Although there was no way he knew what I was thinking. Everything was hunky dory when we finished. As soon as he was out of sight I phoned you."

"Pay phone?"

"God damn it Red! Cut the shit. Of course it was a pay phone. And I made sure he couldn't see me." He paused and looked Red in the eye. "Let's not forget who works for who, my friend," Owens said softly, back in control.

"Well, what was it that is so scary? And why meet here at the track?"

"The demise of one Earnest Kayne was the center of our conversation. He was sly about bringing it up, but I could tell he was more than casually interested, even though he tried to disguise it. He brought your name into it in an offhanded way, but I let it pass. But I got the impression he might pay you a call at the farm."

"Do you think he knows anything?"

"I think he thinks he is on to something, whether he actually is or is not. I can't take a chance on him talking to you and us not having our stories straight. I needed to meet you and take care of that ahead of time. Somewhere that he wouldn't think of. For all I know he was headed for the farm right after he left me. I needed to meet you away from there. And what better place to avoid a State Horse Racing Board snoop than at a race track?" Owens said sardonically, with an evil little grin, his lower teeth showing.

"And, if he or anyone else should happen to see us out here together, well..."

"We are just checking out the condition of the track," Owens finished the thought.

"Good thinking. All the talk about having the Breeder's Cup here next year and you being the president of the CTBA, it is only natural for you to make an early evaluation of the track with your head trainer," smirked Ramsey. "So, our ass is covered. What is the big worry?"

"It's about Earnest's little visit to the farm last Saturday."

"Do you think he knows about it?"

"Willing? I couldn't tell, exactly. I doubt if he knows. But he did make an offhand remark about people no longer having a pharmacist that makes house calls. I asked him what he meant and his answer was strange. At least to me. You could take it either way."

"What was it?" asked Ramsey, getting a bit anxious.

"Hold on. Let's get out of this parking lot and take a look at the track. That is why we are here, remember." Owens put his hand on Red's shoulder and guided him toward the track, pointing at different features of the establishment with his other hand as they walked. Owens continued. "Abel said that it was his understanding, from his 'sources', that Earnest Kayne was suspected of doing business outside of the pharmacy where he works. And I said, 'Sources?' Then he looked at me sort of eyeball-to-eyeball and said with dead seriousness, 'In my business, Mr. Owens, one develops friendships, professional friendships. One of mine that has grown over the years is with certain people in the Stockton Police Department.'"

Red was listening very, very carefully now. "Go on."

"Well, it seems that the narcotics squad there in Stockton, has had Earnest Kayne on their radar screen for some time now. His house was frequented by a known druggie, some weird wannabe biker named Periwinkle. A little surveillance, visual and audio, revealed that Earnest Kayne made more than a few trips to Pleasanton, some with Periwinkle along, to see someone called Rosebud."

"This seems like a lot of information from an investigator like Willing," said Ramsey.

"He needed to talk. Like I told you, you have to befriend people who can possibly mess up your life. I caught Abel in a talkative mood and I was a good listener. Okay? So, he went on to say that the Stockton cops finally did their homework and found out that Periwinkle was Earnest's son and that his real name is Judson Kayne, and Rosebud turned out to be the kid's grandmother, not a drug connection. The kid actually lives in Stockton in his father's house. He just doesn't live there very often. Once they got all that straightened out, they lost interest in the older Kayne and considered the kid just another pot-smoking punk with a motorcycle. Abe said he still isn't sure about the trips to the grandma's house. But the narcs were keeping their eye out for Periwinkle, and if and when he showed up, Willing's friends in the department there kept him informed about both Kaynes. When one showed up dead, well, shall we say Willing got very interested in some things. One of which is that the Kayne kid works for us at the stables."

"I know the punk smokes weed, hell, he reeks of it half the time. But he is so dumb, he couldn't find his ass with both hands. I can't see him sellin' the stuff. Not to his grandmother."

As they leaned on the track rail, two horses passed by at a slow trot, out with their trainers for a workout. One horse was 20 yards ahead of the other, and the combination of the sound of their hoofs and their rhythmic breathing and saddle noises made it impossible for their riders to hear or understand what Owens and Ramsey were saying. Nonetheless, the Colonel and Red were silent until the horses were around the turn and well out of earshot. They remained quiet for several contemplative minutes, staring at the horses as they reached the far side of the track. Finally, Ramsey spoke.

"Did any horse's names come up? In any way? Odds, handicaps, things like that," he said quietly. "Any hint of it?"

"No, none at all," answered Owens."

"Well, thank God for that. That is one activity of ours that doesn't need attention, or we could be in deep shit. We have to do everything we can to keep Willing from having the slightest idea about our 'activities' in other places."

Owens nodded in agreement. "But the thing the worries me the most is that Willing went from a chatty mood to such a business-like one, and that he told me so much. And he was looking at me closely to see if I reacted physically to any of it. You know, facial twitch, forehead pulse, flush face—things like that. I think he may be a little sharper that we have given him credit for."

"And?"

"And he got nothing. I didn't get to where I am without a very tough poker face." Then Owens' eyes grew narrow and steely. "But he told me a lot about himself by that look. He said to me with that look that he knew what he was doing, that he was after something, and that he intended to get it. I wouldn't put it past him to have followed Earnest when he came out to the farm on Saturday and he was fishing to see if I knew about it."

"I was there Saturday and saw Earnest drive in," said Red. "I was up at the high pasture checkin' fences and could see both gates from where I was. He came in from La Honda and went past the back gate, up Bear Gulch then doubled back to the gate. He went into the stable and was out of there in less than five minutes. He got in his car and took the San Gregorio way out. I'm positive he wasn't followed. I watched for it." Red was ever cautious, and took pride in his thoroughness. "He did what he came for and left."

"I wouldn't know about that," said Owens.

"You were out of town. How could you?"

●●●

When he got back to Hillandale, Owens was in no mood to talk with anybody. The sun had gone down and he was tired of driving. As he walked into his house the phone was ringing and he was determined not to answer it. But, after the fifth ring he gave in, and with a sigh of resignation, picked up the receiver.

"Owens here," he said gruffly.

"Owen, this is Bill Dale. You said we needed to talk. I agree. So what have you got on your mind. And this is the special line, in case you wanted to know."

"Well, first of all, has she shown up yet?" asked Owens.

"No. But that can't be why you wanted to talk."

"Well, it sort of is. I have been thinking about that stuff you told me on the phone this morning, and, you know, all things considered, it might be better if we kept the fact that she and the kid are missing to ourselves. You don't need the publicity just now. I'm sure she will show up and when she does there will be a lot of questions. And maybe we don't want the public to know the answers. Why don't you give it another day?"

"That is an interesting point of view. Whether I agree with your thinking or not, it is too late. I filed a missing persons report with the police about two hours ago. She is my wife and I am worried as hell about her. The news people will pick up on it very quickly, and that is bound to help. Now, is that all you wanted to talk to me about?"

"There are some other things, maybe. They can wait. Good luck and keep me posted. Good night Mr. Dale."

"Good night, *Colonel*."

CHAPTER SIXTEEN

A good Saturday evening to everyone and welcome to the "Seven at Seven" weekend newscast, brought to you by Seven Sweet Seasons bakery cafes of San Mateo. Channel 7 comes to you seven days a week, morning, evening and night. "Ahead of the rest and still the best." I am your host, Norbert Swisher, and along with Nan ⬚bu, will, as usual, be bringing you the news of the day tonight. Nan will be with us later with the weather and an update on the international front. As we reported last night, Redwood City is in the headlines again. Friday's police report indicates that Mrs. Kay Dale, wife of well-known businessman William Dale II, has been reported missing. Dale told police he hasn't seen his wife since he left for work at seven fifteen a.m. on Wednesday. In a possibly related event, Judson Kayne, a stable hand at the Dale's horse farm, Hillandale Stables near San Gregorio, has also been reported missing. Owen Owens, co-owner of the farm, and Rod Ramsey, the farm manager, said they have not seen or heard from Kayne since Wednesday around noon. Redwood City Police spokesman Fred Wunderlich said in a prepared statement that they are considering both cases separately at this time but that he is not ruling out that they may be connected. He said he was in close contact with the San Mateo Sheriff's office concerning the matter. When asked if these disappearances could be connected

*to the 'plastic raincoat' murder at Redwood City's Union
Cemetery. Captain Wunderlich declined to comment.*

Wunderlich was at home in his den. With the rest of the
household settled for the night, he watched the news
at 11. After hearing the up-to-date media interpretation of the
case, or cases, of the missing socialite and the stable hand, he was
restless. Not yet ready to go to bed, he switched off the TV. He
crossed the room to his home desk and typewriter, took a seat and
composed a status report on the ongoing police investigation of
Earnest Kayne.

<u>*INTERNAL POLICE DEPARTMENT USE ONLY*</u>
<u>*NOT FOR RELEASE TO THE PUBLIC*</u>
<u>*OR MEMBERS OF THE PRESS*</u>

<u>Subject</u>: Earnest Kayne, born 1925, Pleasanton, CA. Raised by
single mother,
Hulda Stern-Franken Kayne, age 63, currently residing
in Pleasanton, CA.

<u>Subject education</u>: Pleasanton public schools.
University of California, Davis: Chemistry major,
1942-43. Joined Navy, worked as pharmacist's mate,
Mare Island Navy Base. After WWII, earned degree
in pharmacy, College of the Pacific, Stockton, CA,
1950.

<u>Family</u>: Married Marilyn Judson 1944. Divorced
1955. Son Judson Perry Kayne, born 1945. Ex-wife
Marilyn is currently a nurse at Kaiser Hospital,
Oakland, and resides in that city. She had custody of
Judson until he was 17 and finished high school in
1962. Judson then sent to live with father in Stockton.
Judson Kayne reported to be living intermittently
away from father's home. No evidence of permanent
employment; said to have had a series of odd jobs,
mostly involving horses for which he is believed to

have an affinity. Currently is working as a stable hand at Hillandale Stables, near San Gregorio, CA.

Career: Established pharmacy business 1952 with partner, Douglas McCreary. Business bought out by drug chain in 1962. Kayne continued to work for the new firm until the time of his death.

Police reports: Fall, 1969 Stockton. Suspected Earnest Kayne of involvement in illicit drug trade. However, evidence actually was found to implicate son Judson Kayne, who was thought to be selling marijuana; later cleared of charges. Investigation of local lodging revealed that subject checked into Catalina Motel on El Camino Real, Redwood City, 0.5 miles from Union Cemetery at 4:00 p.m. Sunday, April 15. Registration indicates Kayne drove 1969 Oldsmobile Cutlass, dark blue. No report of such a vehicle being stolen or abandoned. About 4:30 subject was observed by motel manager talking in the parking lot with a large, red-haired male; the two men left the premises in subject's Oldsmobile. He did not return. Manager states that there was no evidence that the room had been slept in.

END OF REPORT

CHAPTER SEVENTEEN

Sunday mornings held no special religious meaning for Rex, other than not being able to listen to his favorite music because the station that featured country western music broadcast only evangelical church services and preachers asking for money until noon on Sundays. That never ceased to aggravate him, and he tried to compensate by finding something noisy to do around the house that would have made listening to any program impossible. It was on these occasions that Rex, normally not a quiet person, seemed to be able to make very little noise, whatever it was that he set about to do. In desperation, he found his sweeper, the old Hoover that Sheila left him in the divorce, and decided to vacuum the living room carpet, a relatively new experience for him. He noticed that the cord was frayed when he plugged it in, which he considered of no consequence until he turned the sweeper on and the cord began to give off intermittent sparks matched by the motor going on and off in the same rhythm.

Now I know why she gave in on letting me have this. The sucker is broke. Or worse, maybe she thought I would get electrocuted, and she would get everything, along with getting rid of me. Well, it won't work, bitch, and with that Rex jerked the cord from the wall amidst a shower of sparks and took the vacuum outside and threw it into the trash heap in his back yard.

"You always win, don't you Sheila?" he muttered.

He heard the phone ringing as he came back into the house. "What do you want now, Sheila, you mean old sow. Lose something else? I need to get my damn phone number changed," Rex hollered loudly into the empty house.

He picked up the phone and, in his anger and presuming the caller to be Sheila, yelled into it.

"Yeah. What the hell is it this time? Don't you know it is Sunday?"

"Hello?" came a disconcerted female voice, not Sheila's.

"Oh. I thought it was someone else. Who is this?" Rex calmed down quickly.

"I'm sorry to bother you on Sunday. This is Kay Dale. Kay Sherman Dale."

Rex was silent.

"Hello, hello? Is this Rex, Rex Nickels?" asked Kay.

"Yeah, it is. Long time, huh? I got your message. Why all the mystery? And how the hell did you get this number? Did Sheila put it in the paper or something?" Rex's manners slipped and gave way to some left over irritation with Sheila.

"I have to talk to you, Rex. I need your help," said Kay in a quavering voice.

"Yeah. That's what you said on your message. So, talk. I'm here to listen, as the saying goes." Rex tried to lighten up and improve his etiquette.

"I don't want to on the phone. And I need to keep this call short. Can we meet somewhere and talk?"

"Yes. But first I want to know how you got my number? It is supposed to be unlisted." Rex gathered his professional caution.

"Well, you are a private investigator, aren't you? Then you know that there are ways to find out what unlisted numbers are. But I don't have time to banter. I will explain the number thing later. I just need to meet you and talk. Please?"

The notes of sincerity and need struck a sympathetic chord in Rex and he replied. "Okay.

We can talk. Where do you want to meet? And when?"

"The Queen Bee Cafe in San Mateo. It is just across from the train station on B Street," said Kay.

"Yeah, I know it. When?"

"Today sometime, if that's possible," said Kay.

"I think they open at noon on Sundays," said Rex. "How about two o'clock?"

"Yes, I can make it by then," she said.

"How far do you have to come?" asked Rex. "You didn't say where you are calling from."

"No, I didn't," said Kay and she hung up.

●●●

After Kay's call, Rex replaced the receiver on the cradle and sat for moment in thought. It was now about ten thirty. He was to meet Kay at two o'clock and the drive to San Mateo would take no more than thirty minutes. So, what to do for three hours? He couldn't sweep anymore because he had trashed the vacuum sweeper, so he decided to use the time to make himself look presentable. He took a quick bath and carefully shaved. He got dressed then, after considering several choices of outfit. He applied a little Vitalis to his head and carefully brushed his hair. All ready to go, he checked his watch and saw that he still had two and a quarter hours before he had to be there.

So Rex decided to retreat into his regular Sunday routine of coffee, cereal, toast and newspaper. But he was distracted all the while by his anticipation of today's meeting and by his memories of Kay. It had been twenty years since their first meeting and ten since their "interlude", as Kay used to refer to it.

Time seemed to creep by, and shortly after noon he began to feel that his attire was not smart enough, so he changed to a different assemblage to get more of a Sunday casual look. This time it was simply slacks, sports shirt and jacket. He tried to find his blue, button-down short-sleeve shirt, but couldn't, so he settled for the plaid one. And he added a little Old Spice aftershave for good measure. The mirror finally told him he would pass muster. He gathered his wallet, sunglasses and keys and exited his kitchen door at twelve forty-five p.m. sharp.

He fired up the Corvair and set out for an attempted leisurely trip up El Camino Real, through San Carlos, Belmont, into San Mateo, past the Bay Meadows track, on past Highway 92 and Central Park to Third Street. By the time he got that far, it was still only one thirty. Okay, he said to himself, I'll go ahead and park and just be early.

Rex found a parking space just around the corner from the Queen Bee Cafe. "Free parking on Sunday" the sign read. The cafe was far from filled. It was not a champagne brunch sort of place. Rex seated himself, as instructed by a sign at the entrance, choosing a booth toward the rear, removed from most of the other patrons scattered across the room. He ordered coffee when the waitress asked and spent some time perusing the menu. The waitress had just finished re-filling his cup when Rex saw a woman in dark clothes and sun glasses with a black scarf wrapped tightly around her head.

She stopped at his booth and said, "Hello, Rex."

"Kay?" Rex stammered as he awkwardly rose and sidled out of the booth simultaneously. "I was thinking you might be Jackie O.! Long time no see. Why the get-up?"

"I'm trying to be as invisible as possible. Maybe I overdid it a bit," Kay said with a small smile. "I have some friends around San Mateo that I wouldn't want to see me just now—though I doubt that any of them would be having Sunday brunch at this place."

Rex motioned for Kay to take a seat opposite his in the booth and they both sat down.

"Yeah, I can see that," said Rex, not knowing exactly what to say.

"It has been a long time," said Kay as she removed her sunglasses and loosened her head scarf.

"Ten years or so," said Rex with a very personal smile.

The conversation stalled until Kay picked it up. "Well, now, I thought I was running early, but I find you've beaten me here. Good! We shouldn't waste any time."

To that, Rex responded, "What the hell, since we only meet every ten years, seems like all we got is time! Anyhow, it's really good to see you, Kay. Or however much of you I can see. Well, first, should we order?"

As Rex beckoned the waitress, Kay removed the scarf entirely and tossed her hair to give it back its volume.

Kay responded, "I don't think I'll have anything to eat. Just some coffee. But you should go ahead and have something."

Rex ordered coffee for Kay and a slice of apple pie for himself.

"Now then," Rex said. "You're the one who called this meeting. It feels like a great mystery story, complete with disguises and secret meetings. And memories. Oh, by the way, I'm sorry I was short with you on the phone before. So spill it. What's up?"

Kay took out a cigarette. Rex lit it for her.

Kay exhaled, glanced around the room and balanced her cigarette on the ashtray. Looking into Rex's eyes for the first time, she began. "Rex, thank you for seeing me. The memories are nice, but right now I badly need help from someone I can trust. There are so few people I can really rely on. Of course my husband is one, but I believe he's just not in a position to help me in my current situation. The thing is, I know I can rely on you to keep things confidential. I know you have been discreet about our past...uh... association. I am relying on you to be even more discreet now."

Rex was relieved that he hadn't been entirely cut off by her "memories are nice, BUT" comment. He tried to look cool and nodded, "Go on."

"Rex, I'm just so afraid. It's very hard for me to express. There are evil forces in my life—maybe that sounds too biblical—there were and are people doing bad things that threaten my husband's, and my, business, our reputation and even our existence. I'm saying our lives may be at stake. Also, I've recently become attached to my nephew Judson and I'm concerned for his well-being."

Rex interrupted. "Wait! You're talking about the cemetery murder, aren't you? This Jud Kayne who's missing from your farm is your nephew? Is he related to Earnest Kayne? His son, maybe? That would mean that Earnest was your, what? Brother-in-law, or..."

"Earnest Kayne was my half brother. He had a different mother and was born before I was, but I only learned of his existence at the time of my father's death two years ago. I first met Earnest, and his son Jud, shortly after that. It was at Earnest's house in Stockton. Earnest acted a bit strange and Jud seemed to be a young man who had yet to find himself. I had no further contact with them until a few months ago when Jud came to me and asked if I could help him get a job so he could get away from Earnest. I felt sorry for him and managed to get him hired on as a stable boy at Hillandale, our horse farm out at San Gregorio. He could stay out there and get away from his father. His only interests seem to have been in horses and motorcycles, and I couldn't help him with the latter."

"Amazing!" Rex interjected, carefully painting a picture of himself as one just hearing this information, when in fact he already knew most of what she was telling him. "Then does this mean that you could be the Kay in 'if you see K...' that was written on the raincoat?"

"I don't know about that. But...yes, I will say to you that I may be involved."

"How?" Rex's curiosity was guarded and keen. "And what is this 'evil forces' stuff? And who is threatening you and how is your life at stake?"

Kay managed a tear and said in a small, reluctant voice, "It's Hillandale, the people out there. Red Ramsey, the trainer, and Owen Owens, my husband's partner in the farm. For a long time I have felt there was something fishy going on with the horses, and Owens wins at the track more than the average person. He makes a lot of money betting, whether it is win or lose."

"Why does that make him someone to be afraid of?" Rex asked. "Gambling is not evil, even if it is crooked. It isn't a violent activity."

"Owens started out life back in the Midwest somewhere with nothing. Somehow he managed to get to college where he got to know my late father-in-law. They had some business together out here, part of which ended up in the Hillandale Corporation. He married rich, divorced rich and then did it again. That's where he got started with his money. The third wife is why I am frightened. She was the widow of a banker when he married her and four years later she was found dead behind the horse paddock on the farm he used to own. They never did figure out what she died from and—this is the where it gets frightening—the letter K was scrawled on the stall of one of the horses there. In lipstick. In the past I have been out there riding, and on several occasions I saw Ramsey talking to some people I don't know. When I asked him about it, he was evasive to the point of being surly. Since the death of my half brother, well, I feel responsible for Jud being out there, and I am concerned about his safety. I may have put him in danger. I know he doesn't get along with Red Ramsey."

"Who does get along with Mr. Friendly?" Rex asked rhetorically.

"I got Jud away from Hillandale and he is with me. I'm not going to tell you more than that now. My main concern at this moment is to avoid having to face public questioning, both of me and of Jud. We need to let this play out, while we stay under cover for at least a little while more. Jud and I have been staying at a motel in Hayward, just near the other end of the San Mateo Bridge. But now we're both in the news on TV, and in the papers all over the Bay Area, as being missing. Let's get to the point. I want help in finding a safe place where we can hide out. I can't really run far away. Money is a bit of a problem. Any use of credit cards for air travel, gasoline, or lodging could be tracked. I have a little cash to get by on for a while, but not enough for real travel or accommodations. I would certainly promise to reimburse you for any costs of helping me, Rex."

"Wait." Rex took a deep breath. "Okay. I think I understand your dilemma, even though you may not be leveling with me on the details, or who or what you're so afraid of. I can see your fear, and...hell, I don't know why...I've always had a feeling for you these last twenty years. I guess I do want to help you. But not on commission. I can't do that. Reimbursable expenses only. This is strictly off the record, my helping you. If you are in some legal mess, I don't need any of it to rub off on me. You're worried about your business and your rep...well so am I. I gotta' be careful." He hesitated.

"Oh, Rex, what are we going to do?" Kay said, holding back another quaver.

Rex looked intensely at Kay and she parried with the best helpless look she could muster. Then he stared off at nothing in particular and thought as clearly as he could about what he was about to say. Kay held to her silence, using it almost as a tool in getting her way.

"Oh, what the hell. I've got a wild, crazy idea," Rex finally said. "I think I can set this up, discreetly, let's say. My ex-wife Sheila, she lives in a nice house up in the hills above Redwood City. I lived there once too, when we were married. She got it in the divorce. Fairly isolated there, woodsy, houses kinda' far apart. Doubt if any of your friends live in that neighborhood. Not the ones that don't come in here, for sure. There would be plenty of room there for you and Jud, and you both could lie low. Sheila would do it for me. I'm sure." Rex wasn't all that sure, but Kay's lingering spell provided him with some unfounded confidence.

"Oh, Rex, thank you," Kay said with a big show of relief and a demure little smile. "You are a life saver! How can I ever thank you?"

"I haven't closed the deal yet. I'll need a little time. Go back to the motel in Hayward for tonight and I'll work it out. Give me the number at the motel. I'll call you later. I think we'll be able to get you settled tomorrow. But I hope you've packed some...ahem... brighter clothes? I'd like to get a better look at you."

"Well, maybe later. Till then, I'll be waiting for your call," and Kay gave Rex her best little "come hither" smile.

CHAPTER EIGHTEEN

When Kay returned to her Cadillac Eldorado station wagon, she got in, sank into the seat, and took a deep, deep breath. Determined to put some order to her circumstance, she went back over what had happened.

Well, that worked out pretty well, she thought with relief. She ran her fingers across the rosewood dash, momentarily enjoying the sensation of luxury it gave her. She pushed the button that made the seat recline, lowered the windows with other buttons and put her head into a comfortable position against the headrest. The dash was now out of reach, but the seat next to her wasn't, and she placed her palm there, feeling the imported Spanish suede she had ordered installed, and enjoying the sense of exclusiveness it gave her. She propped her sunglasses on the end of her nose and closed her eyes. She was exhausted and very much needed to stop and collect herself. The spring breeze and the quiet of the Sunday afternoon served to calm her nerves and she relaxed and began to compose her thoughts.

When did it start? Probably when I went to meet Earnest Kayne and that poor wretch Judson walked in and I started paying them to be quiet. It had worked for a while, but I should have known better, she thought. The kid was a mess, and I couldn't resist his need. And besides, they were related, and I felt an obligation to help. That thought took me back to sorority days in Psi Psi

Psi and our big charity fund-raising dance with the U.S.O. That's how I met Rex Nickels, she mused, and what a meeting that was.

She smiled openly at the memory. Thirty minutes in a school bus can teach you a lot. Good old Rex, yeah. He was good then, very good. And at that time ten years ago, he was still good, but a little older. Now he is good *old* Rex. He doesn't realize it and I am not telling him any different. He sure has bailed me out with a place to stay, though. And he hasn't the slightest idea what I've been through with Jud. He knows that Earnest is dead, that's all over the news. He must suspect some connection with Jud and Earnest's death. But he sure hasn't asked me very many questions. Amazing what the right kind of smile will do. It would be a lot different if he didn't think I was special, and I intend for it to stay that way. But I need to keep him away from Jud.

Kay's thoughts shifted to Jud. She shifted her weight in the seat as she became more focused. Jud seems to have to talk about everything he knows. Cooped up at that motel with him made me his captive audience. If he tells Rex that he was at Hillandale when Earnest paid a visit out there last Saturday, and that he saw Earnest go into the stable, or that he had overheard Red talking to Earnest on the phone several times before that, well, the fat will be in the fire. He promised not to tell anyone that stuff after he told me, but I don't know about that kid, I just don't know.

Well! Enough meditation for today. She raised the seat back and adjusted her sunglasses. As she started the car she glanced at the clock. Damn, she thought, I've left him over in Hayward way too long. I need to get back before he finds someone else for a listening post.

CHAPTER NINETEEN

Rex was on high anxiety alert as he set out for Sheila's house. He left the convertible top up and hunched tensely over the wheel as he left his driveway. Soon, however, as he drove into the hills, beyond the buttoned-up uniformity of the neighborhoods along the Alameda, he relaxed a bit and entered the much more laid-back vicinity of Vista Drive. He remembered how he had enjoyed life here for those ten or so years he was married to Sheila when they had lived here together in the house she now had on her own. He always enjoyed the sense of freedom he felt along the narrow twisty roads with no curbs or sidewalks to hem one in. He admired the variety of the houses, built over several decades, with vacant lots scattered among them. No formal lawns or hedges, but a landscape of native oaks and redwoods. Folks here had more pickups and sports cars than sedans. Folks like Rex and Sheila, actually. A little less proper, a little off-beat. One could imagine cannabis plants thriving in some of the hidden ravines.

As Rex reached Sheila's street, his apprehension returned. The reverie ended and he had to face the fact that his mission, to convince Sheila to do something he knew she would be dead set against, was about to commence.

I think I'd rather storm hell with a pitcher of ice water than to try to get her to take that kid in. Damn, why did I ever tell Kay I could do this? She got me in a weak moment and I had to be the damn knight that came to the rescue. Guess she still has what you might call a 'groinal' effect on me. Once again, Sexy Rexy, you've let your dick do your thinkin' for you.

"Oh, Rex, what are we going to do?" Kay had said. Well, Rex had a pretty good idea what they could do, but had resisted the temptation, not wanting to wear out his welcome at the Queen Bee. Instead, he stayed on the straight, and now very narrow, path that led him to Sheila's driveway and what at one time was his parking space. Taking care not to slam the car door, he walked up the porch steps and rapped politely with the door knocker.

"Who is it?" called Sheila from within.

"Me," yelled Rex.

"Hold on, whoever you are. I'm not decent," she yelled back.

"I know that. It's common knowledge," Rex was tempted to say, but didn't. No need to pour fuel on the fire he was about to face. "It's me, Rex," he called instead. "Take your time. I'm in no hurry."

Finally, the knob on the door twisted and the door opened just enough for her to see out.

"What in the..."

"Cool it sweetie, I need your help," Rex said softly. "I have something to tell you."

"Did you find my pills?" she said as the door came full open, revealing a barefoot Sheila in a dressing gown fastened in front with a safety pin and at the waist with a two inch wide oriental sash. She was clearly not expecting company.

"Not exactly." Rex put his foot carefully across the threshold as he said it. "Can I come in, please? I will pay your alimony early this month, if you just talk to me. And not out here on the porch, either."

"Got your goddamn checkbook with you?"

"Yes. But no check until we've talked. I'm not that desperate to hear your voice, however lovely it may sound."

"Screw you, Rex."

"Been there, done that," said Rex and he took his foot out of the door and turned to leave.

"Hold on, Rexy. Come on in. We can talk. With you talk is just like your aftershave, it's cheap and usually doesn't help any."

The prospect of an early alimony payment had softened Sheila, as Rex knew it would.

"You may think it is cheap, but it isn't cheap for your old Rexy. An early payment, that is what I said. But not until after we talk. Not until after you listen. Got it?" Rex knew better than to negotiate any further with the shifty Sheila.

"You write the fuckin' check and then we talk," she pushed back.

"I'll tell you what, Angel Mouth, I'll write the check, all right, but I won't give it to you until you sit your fat ass down on the couch over there and listen, *for a change*, to what I have to say."

As much vulgarity and temper as Sheila had in her, she had a good head for figures and a thirst for money. Thus she contained herself and sat down. "I'm here to listen, as they say," said Sheila, and Rex was taken aback. It hadn't been six hours since he had used the same flip comment with Kay. Now it came the other way, and scattered his thoughts momentarily. During this lull, Sheila managed to shift herself around on the couch in such a way that her dressing gown with its sash and pin was challenged, and it threatened to spill its contents into her lap. Distraction is the better part of negotiation.

"I'm going to say a name, Sheila, and then I am going to look at my watch. I will give you one minute, to the second, to yell, scream, holler, or use any other means of expression, with whatever foul language that you wish, and then you have to stop. I don't care how vile it is, and believe me I know how good you are at vile language, and no matter how mad you are, you have to stop at one minute. If you don't, the deal's off and I walk. Got it?"

"What's the name?"

"I said, 'got it?'"

"Yes, shit head, I got it. Give me the name."

"Judson Kayne. Sometimes he calls himself Periwinkle."

"*Judson Kayne*. That little shit-head. 'Ahm from PAYorya and Ah yam tougher than a piece of limp spaghetti.' The little fart.

The little chicken-shit punk! I almost shot the little turd walloper last Tuesday when he interrupted my lunch at the Break-Thyme. 'Mah name is Judson Kayne Periwinkle but mah frens call me Kayne,' my ass. Periwinkle tinkle is what he is. What in the name of Tricky Dick Nixon are you doin' with that piece of excrement? Huh? *Huh*? You gone queer on me?" Sheila was livid, as Rex knew she would be. But she had surprised him.

"Excrement?" Rex exclaimed. "Where in the hell did that come from?" He had never heard Sheila utter an expletive that wasn't a dirty word.

"Probably from a dog's butt, you idiot," Sheila was turning red in the face now, and the top half of her breasts were the same color as her face. "His kind just make me sick. Pot-smokin' wannabe biker pussy!"

Rex waved the check he had written and looked at his watch. "How much time have I got?"

"A little less than fifteen seconds, so you better finish the thought and wind it up." It was hard for Rex not to laugh.

"I'll finish the thought all right, you sarcastic son of a bitch," yelled Sheila and she heaved forward to get up from the couch, and with a rrripp and a plop she made it to a standing position, with her dressing gown and its sash gathered at her waist, her gender defining protuberances jiggling gently back and forth in their newfound freedom.

For one single, magic moment, neither spoke nor moved. Then Rex, seeking a place for his eyes to focus other than at Sheila's half naked body, looked at his watch.

"Time's up!" he called, louder than necessary.

"Whaddaya staring at, owl face?" said Sheila as she rearranged herself, trying for some sense of modesty. "Like you ain't never seen 'em before, or anything like 'em?"

"Well, yes, but, no, not really like that, to tell the truth," said Rex, recalling his experience the previous week on the floor of his office.

As Sheila pulled her gown back in place and plunked herself down again on the couch, Rex regrouped and leaned forward, back to the matter at hand. "I have another person to ask you about, and this one you can't unload on. It is Kay Dale. Ever heard of her?"

"Of course I've heard of her. Is there anyone in this town that hasn't? She's hoity toity high society stuff. What has she got to do with Candyass Perrywinky, is he her closet lover or a secret bastard son or something?" Sheila could have been making an innocent wild comment or she could be smarter than she let on, and Rex knew her well enough to know she might be on to something. Sheila might be a lot of things, but dumb wasn't one of them.

"As a matter of fact, it is a secret. Or it was. He is her nephew. Her half brother's son."

"No shit?" Sheila was flabbergasted. "How in hell did that come about?"

"I will tell you some time when I don't have anything better to do. For now, the two of them have a problem, and I promised to help."

"I have this sneaking suspicion that I am part of Sexy Rexy's solution to Winkle and Tinkle's little problem. Spill it, you bastard."

"They need a place to stay." Rex just put it out there.

"And?"

"And since you are all alone in this spacious three bedroom house, and it has an extra half bathroom, I thought..."

"You thought wrong, mister big deal maker," Sheila interrupted. "No way in hell. Unh unh, no way, Sexaay Rexaaay!"

Rex anticipated this reaction and was ready with a counter move. "Of course there would have been compensation for your trouble, but if you aren't interested..."

"On the other hand, my wardrobe could stand some enhancement. I am willing to reconsider. Depending on the compensation." Sheila put her hands on her hips and paused for effect. "How much you offerin', Mr. High Roller?"

"How about half of what the alimony is? That is more than fair," Rex said.

"Fair? Fair, my ass. Come on Rex, you know better than to try that crap with me. Just leave. I ain't interested in runnin' a flop house for your screwed-up friends."

"Too bad. I thought I could rely on you to help me. Here's your check like I promised. See ya'." Rex handed her his check and headed for the door. He got as far as putting his hand on the knob when he hesitated and said over his shoulder. "How about equal to the alimony but at the end of the month?"

"How about in advance, per week?" Sheila replied, victory in her voice and a smile on her face for the first time.

"End of each week, or no deal. I have to be sure you don't drive them away or squeal on them."

"Squeal?"

"That's what I said. Squeal. One word to anyone that they are here, and you don't get paid. Is that understood?" Rex was closing the door on the deal without closing the one on the house. "Have the two back bedrooms cleaned out and the beds fresh-made by eight tomorrow morning. I'll have them over here by then. And keep your damn mouth shut."

Rex left the house on Vista Drive, put the top down on his car and drove off feeling good.

"We did it, Monza. We did it!" he crowed.

● ● ●

Rex returned to his house and was, as usual, hungry. He grabbed an Acme beer from the fridge, took a swig, then put some left-over pizza into a frying pan to warm and sat down by his phone. And let out a big sigh and belched. It was the end of a big day and he still had things to do. He was now faced with how to get Kay and Jud moved out of their motel in Hayward and across the bridge to Sheila's in Redwood City without a lot of exposure. He had told Sheila eight a.m., but as he thought about it driving home he decided to make it later. Traffic at eight o'clock on a Monday morning was bound to be heavy and he didn't want to deal with that in addition to everything else.

He started by phoning Sheila. "Sheila, this is Rex."

"Yes, what now?" Sheila was a little irritated and out of breath from being outside and having to hurry in to catch the phone.

"We won't be there until ten o'clock. Less traffic that way. Be sure the garage has enough room to park her car. It's a big station wagon, so move any junk you have in there out of the way so we can park it there. And make room for a motorcycle too."

"Why in hell does she get my garage? Did you think covered parking comes with the room? Let her or the kid move all that shit, I will be getting the rooms ready."

"Sheila, please don't fight me on this. The point of them being there is to, well, you know, hide out for a while. That station wagon of hers sitting out front of your place would be like a big billboard, to say nothing of his old motorcycle. So just cooperate. And no, I won't pay you more."

"All right, mother-fucking Mister Detective," said Sheila as she hung up.

Docking the moon lander in outer space has got to be easier than this, thought Rex. I need to call Kay. Where in the hell is that slip of paper she gave me? Unable to find it in an accessible pocket, and unwilling to look in another room or go out to the car and check there, he simply called information for the number of the Bayside Motel in Hayward. When he got the motel desk on the phone, he was told that there was no guest there named Dale or Kayne. Using an old P.I. trick, he then told the desk clerk he was an investigator calling in an official capacity and that his badge number was 1970302 if he wanted to call in and check. Rex, saying they may be wanted, described Kay and Jud to the young man, who then said that he must be referring to Mrs. Friendly from Peoria and her son in Rooms 119 and 120.

"Please connect me to Mrs. Friendly's room. Tell her that it is the real estate agent."

After a few minutes on hold, he was put through to Kay. "Hello, who is this?" she said.

"It's me," said Rex, confident she would recognize his voice, which she did.

"Oh, you have some news about the house we discussed earlier?" Kay was quick to catch on.

"Yes. The current owner can't show it at eight. That is too early. Since I have to drive you there anyway, why don't I just meet you there at the motel about nine and we can talk. I should have a fixed time when we can see it by then. When is check-out?"

"Noon, I believe."

"Good. We will have plenty of time for a cup of coffee and some conversation, I'm sure."

"Yes, real nice of you to buy my breakfast," said Kay.

"See you at nine, then."

CHAPTER TWENTY

Fred Wunderlich answered his phone at the Redwood City police headquarters. It was nine thirty on Monday, a week after the discovery of the body in Union Cemetery.

"Captain, Mr. Willing is holding for you on line one."

Wunderlich pressed the blinking button. "Well, good morning, Abel! So you got my message from the weekend?"

"Yes, hello, Fred. You're right, we do have things to talk about. I'm up here at Bay Meadows now, just about to leave. What do you say I drive down and see you about ten o'clock?"

"By all means. I'll see you then," Wunderlich said, ringing off.

At ten sharp, Willing was shown into Wunderlich's office.

"Great to see you, Abel," Wunderlich said, shaking Willing's hand. "Have a seat. You know, of course, that I'm working on this homicide at the cemetery here. The more of this that I try to piece together, the more I find some very big names popping up, folks that are connected with the racing business."

Willing replied, "Yes, I've been aware of some of that, but go on."

"First, we know the victim is Earnest Kayne. He was a pharmacist in Stockton. Well, he's not such a big name, but his son, Judson, happens to work at Hillandale Stables, which, of course, is owned by Owen Owens and William and Kay Dale. Now we learn that Mrs. Dale and Judson Kayne are listed as missing persons, separately or possibly together. The Stockton police tell us

100

that there's been some suspicion of drug trafficking on the part of young Kayne, and maybe his father, but there have never been any charges."

"Right," Willing responded. "I'm up on the Kaynes' suspected involvement with drugs. Earnest was a reasonably good pharmacist with a strong background in chemistry. I've had my eye on him. You may be interested to know that Earnest Kayne made the long trip out to Hillandale, a week ago Saturday. Now, maybe it was just to visit his son. That boy's been pretty much a loser. He's known for his connections to dealers of pot, LSD, various pills. Also reputed to be an okay stable hand and a good worker with the horses. Hard to figure, though, how he got from little ranchettes in the San Joaquin valley to a prestigious outfit like Hillandale. It gives one cause to wonder. In any case, it now seems that by last Tuesday night, the boy was long gone from San Gregorio. My big interest, on behalf of the State Horse Racing Board, would be if any of this stuff sticks to the stable owners, Owens and the Dales. And I am also currently observing Red Ramsey, the trainer and manager out there. As you've noted, there are big players here, and if any of them are up to anything shady, anything hinting at doping or race-fixing, my office is officially interested. So, the news this last weekend that Mrs. Dale and the stable boy seem to have taken off somewhere last Tuesday or Wednesday, it got my attention. That's only a few days after the kid's father was found dead and naked in a raincoat. Suffice it to say, I think there's more to the story than an updated Lady Chatterley."

"Oh, uh, well, I guess I don't remember that case," muttered Wunderlich. "But I do agree with your analysis. And, our information from the manager of the Catalina Motel, where Earnest Kayne stayed, or at least, was registered, Saturday night last, is that Earnest was seen talking to a big red-haired guy. From what we now know, that could have been Red Ramsey."

Willing offered, "I can get you a photo of Ramsey. Maybe the motel manager can I.D. him."

Wunderlich said, "Then you really think all of this case really revolves around some horse-doping scheme? Do you think Earnest was the supplier?"

"He could be, but I don't know if he had the technical knowledge that would be required to develop drugs that would evade detection. If this is what our conjecture makes it out to be, I would think that a superior scientific mind or technical mind or team of minds is more likely. Kayne could be the middle man. Of course, this looks like a high stakes enterprise. The operational brain would probably be in the money group, in this case Owens and Dale. Dale seems to be a straight arrow, sort of a gentleman farmer, but Owens is a really top guy in racing circles, nationally. It may be too big a risk for Owens to get into any kind of shady business. Another possibility is that this has some mob backing. Still, we have to think about this rash of coincidences, as surprising as it may be that some society type like Mrs. Dale disappears at the same time that a druggy stable hand takes off."

Wunderlich responded, "Yes, there's always the mob element to consider. It wouldn't be the first time some outsider messed around in Redwood City. We're not immune here. And also, Earnest was not especially liked in Stockton, in particular by a former partner, or by his former wife, who lives in Oakland. Not that any of them are suspects, but we need to be open to other scenarios, not just the pursuit of the big name group."

"I agree," said Willing.

"Meanwhile, we have circulated a description of Kay Dale and the Cadillac she was seen driving. Checking airports and train and bus stations. Also watching her bank to see if she attempts to make a withdrawal of cash. Our only picture of the kid is from DMV, showing a beard, which it seems does not exist now. And we have a description of his old Triumph bike."

"Fred," Abel interjected, "You haven't said anything about the cause of death. Any news on that front?" He was getting a little beyond a racing investigation with the question, so he was careful how he said it.

Wunderlich made a snort of exasperation. "No, unfortunately. The medical examiner is still working on it. There was a preliminary notion that death resulted from suffocation, but they're apparently still doing tests and promise a report shortly. And all we've got physical evidence-wise is the plastic raincoat we found him in, the lipstick that's smeared on the raincoat and some fingerprints. Should have had the fingerprint I.D.'s back by now, but we don't have that either."

"Well, Fred, I need to get back to work on other evil doings in the racing world. I'll get you that photo of Ramsey over to you later today. I hope it helps identify the guy seen with Earnest just before the event."

"Oh, say, Abel, before you go, your name came up the other day. We have a local P.I. in town, small time. Actually his father was a former chief of police. The guy's involved mostly in divorce cases and such. Name of Rex Nickels. Anyway, he happened to ask me if I knew who you were. Any chance you know him, or of him?"

"No," said Willing. "I can't say I've ever heard of him. But, I'll have to remember that name. Rex Nickels. Just in case I ever run into him."

CHAPTER TWENTY-ONE

All of these phone calls were making Rex a little nervous. He knew where he himself got a lot of information, and it wasn't the message board at the Laundromat. He could write a book on phone tapping, he just didn't want anyone to read it but himself. When he got to the motel in Hayward, it was just after nine o'clock on Monday morning. Those customers who were traveling had left, and those that were staying mostly weren't up, so there was little activity in the parking lot when he pulled in. He waited and checked his rear view mirror to see if he was followed or if there were cars on the street that passed more than once. When he felt he was alone, he quickly found Room 119 with Kay at the door, waiting.

"Hi. You certainly are prompt," said Kay.

Rex smiled, but was all business. "Where's Jud?"

"He's in his room. I think he is still asleep. I'll get him," and Kay started for the door that connected their rooms.

"No, hold on for a minute. I want us to get some things straight about today and this deal I have set up. We don't have a great deal of time, so have a seat and let me do this one-two-three. When we are done, we'll get Jud in here and tell him the things he needs to know."

"I feel like I am talking to an MP I knew a long time ago at a dance at Stanford." Kay never missed a chance to wedge Rex's emotions against his reason. This time it didn't work.

Rex continued as before. "Here are my rules:

One: Where I am taking you is not free. I am committed to pay quite a bit for it. I assume you will reimburse me, and in a timely manner, in cash.

Two: You will have to pay for your food and drink. Sheila will get what you want and you will also reimburse her in a timely manner, also in cash.

Three: I assume you have a bank account where you can cash a check, a big check, and that you have your checkbook with you and we can do this today.

Four: Neither of you can leave the house once we get you there and settled. If you need something, Sheila will go after it for you. You can't be seen in anyway. Not on the porch or through the windows. See to it that Jud understands that.

Five: You will have your own room as will Jud. You will share a bathroom with Sheila, Jud will have the half bath. If and when he wants to shower, he will have to negotiate with you and Sheila.

Six: Do your best to get along with Sheila. That is asking a lot, I know. I couldn't do it but you have to. So get ready to be patient. She is a tough case. Just know that going in.

Seven and last: No pot, no drugs of any kind by either of you. Do any, and the deal is over and you are on the street. I have a license to keep, and no trust fund if I lose it."

"You can bring in Sleeping Beauty, now. When he gets in here, you can tell him all of what I just said, except for the money stuff. That is just between you and me. Do we understand each other?"

Kathleen Sherman Dale wasn't really used to being talked to that way, and she had to consider whether she would take it off of this guy or not. Finally, giving Rex a hard and level look, she said, "Okay, I agree, Sergeant," and she went after Jud.

After Jud came in and was awake enough to take in information, always a marginal state at best, Kay relayed what Rex had told her.

Jud's only response was, "Do I have to stay in my room?"

"That you will have to work out with Sheila and Kay," said Rex. "Now get your shit together and let's get out of here. Kay, are you packed?"

"Yes. I have a lot of things in the car from when I left last week. I got everything else ready before you got here. My stuff is by the door."

"Good. Give me your keys and we will get your things into your car while you check out." He raised his voice, "Step to it Judson," handing him the keys and pointing to Kay's luggage. "Give me a hand."

As they loaded Kay's car, he continued. "You are going to ride your bike and follow me. Kay will follow you. She is checking out now and when she gets back, I'll give you both directions in case we get separated in traffic. While we are alone, you and I need to get something straight." Rex motioned for Jud to sit down.

"And what would that be, *sir*?" smirked Jud.

Rex walked over to Jud and grabbed him by the shirt collar with one beefy hand and lifted him straight up in the air, drawing him close enough to his face that Jud was enveloped in coffee breath when Rex spoke. "Listen, ass-wipe, you have no idea how much trouble you have caused me in the past two days, and how pissed off I can be. If it weren't for Mrs. Dale, I wouldn't be here. You are just along for the ride. So don't give me any shit or I'll dump you like yesterday's French fries. And if you think I am unfriendly, wait till you get to where I am taking you. Has Kay told you whose house you'll be staying at?" With that he released Jud who plunked wide-eyed back into the chair.

"She said it was the house of a woman named Sheila. And that I had to behave myself and act right." Jud was suddenly eleven years old again.

"Here is some new information for you. Sheila happens to be the woman that kicked you out of the Break-Thyme Cafe last week, mister biker tough guy."

"Oh, no!"

"Oh, yes, my friend. I'm not real interested what happened there and I have patched it up with her on your behalf. Put it behind you. But be careful what you say to her, or she'll have your head in a minute. You aren't one of her favorite people."

"That bitch," muttered Jud, his head down.

Rex was about to slap Jud on the ear when Kay appeared at the door. "You ready?" she asked.

"Yes, I think so. But first, here is the plan. I am driving that Monza convertible out there. I will go first and you two will follow. Jud will ride his bike and follow me, and Kay, you will follow him. I will put the top down on my car so you can see me if I need to give any directions. Now listen, cowboy, don't do anything fancy with your little motor scooter. Just drive it straight. If we get separated in traffic, and either of you can't find me, go to the corner of Whipple and El Camino Real and wait there. We will be going across the bridge on 92 clear to 101 and then south toward Redwood City. Take the Whipple Avenue exit and go about five blocks to El Camino Real and cross it and wait for everyone else. Once we are all there, it shouldn't be hard to follow me the rest of the way. If at any time we are followed by the cops or they try to stop us, keep going and separate. I will occupy the cops. Meet me at the same place, but at noon. Got that, Lone Ranger? The Big Cam and Whipple. Don't forget it."

He handed Kay her keys and motioned Jud to stand up. Then he looked at his watch. "Nine thirty. Perfect timing. Let's go."

CHAPTER TWENTY-TWO

As it turned out, there was no need for the contingency directions, and the little caravan made the trip to Whipple and El Camino and then up to Vista Drive without incident. Sheila was waiting for them on the porch and when they got to the foot of the driveway she pressed the button on the remote. The garage door opened, looking like a crocodile saying hello. Rex drove past the driveway and motioned for the others to drive up to the garage. They followed his directions and paused before the open door. Then he backed up and turned in to follow them. He stopped beside Sheila's two door Toyota Corona, which was parked outside of the garage, got out, and with his best MP gestures motioned first Kay and then Jud into the garage.

"By God, it is clean!" Rex said to himself in wonder. "Not only is there room in there, but it is clean. I wonder what has come over Sheila?"

When all of the engines were shut off and Jud and Kay were out of the garage, Rex motioned for Sheila to hit the remote again and close the door.

"Okay, everyone in," said Rex, herding the group into the house and checking the street in both directions. "Introductions when we are inside."

The whole procedure took less than two minutes and Vista Drive resumed its spring morning quiet.

It was quiet inside also. But a different kind of quiet, an awkward, vacant silence. Rex continued his military persona, and not knowing what to do next, they followed his directions like sheep. Considering the quirky, explosive, and calculating personalities involved, that was remarkable.

"Why don't we all go in the living room and get introduced?" he said.

"This way," said Sheila, and like a good hostess she directed the party to the living room where they all sat, albeit with little ease.

Rex remained standing, almost at the parade rest position, and addressed the troops. "This is Sheila, who is providing you two with a place to stay. Sheila, this is Mrs. Kathleen Dale, and this is Judson Kayne, who I believe you know."

The immediate and inevitable tension between Sheila and Jud was quickly broken by Kathleen, who smiled warmly at Sheila and said, "Please call me Kay. It is so nice to meet you and be here at your lovely house."

"It is good to have you here in my home and I hope you will be comfortable here. Rex has told me so many wonderful things about you."

I have? Rex said to himself. I must have missed it.

Rex could see Kay working her stuff on Sheila and he loved it. Kay knew how to bring out the best in people, and she had found a heretofore unknown side of Sheila. Some would call it a touch of class.

"I have gone over the rules with Kay and Jud this morning and with Sheila last night, so I don't need to repeat them this morning. But you three need to talk about what I said to be sure you all understand what is expected of you. Now there is a bit of unfinished business that I have to attend to downtown, so I am going to leave you so you can discuss the ground rules. Remember, it is important that you two are not seen here. You can get your luggage through the garage door to the kitchen, so there is no need to go out. Kay, could I see you for a second in the kitchen?"

When they were out of earshot from the rest, Kay asked, "What is it?"

"I think you know, since you have your purse. Your checkbook. You said you had it. If you would be so kind to write me a nice check—payable to 'Cash', and call your banker to explain that I am coming, I will leave you to your fate here and take care of business. There is a wall phone over there. Here is the amount," he said, and he patted his pockets for a slip of paper. He found one, and it had her phone number written on it. Oh, that's where that was, he thought, as he turned it over and wrote out the amount that would more than cover what he expected would be coming in the way of expense.

Kay wrote the check, and Rex waited while she called her bank. She got through to her personal banker, a vice-president named Lester Moore, and explained that she needed some cash money for a very personal reason and that she was sending a messenger to the bank to get it this morning. She cleverly implied that there was a medical procedure that she wanted to keep from her husband "until the time is right" and the reason she had been reported missing was tied to that, and a lack of communication with her husband over her disappearance. She asked the banker to keep her confidence in the matter.

He asked a question to which Kay replied, "Hershey Bar" and then after another moment, she hung up.

"What's with the 'Hershey Bar'?" queried Rex, as he returned to his role as an investigator.

"It's a code word to signal him that this is not a kidnapping and that I am okay."

"How do I know it isn't a code word that says you are not okay?"

"You don't. But why would I do that? I'm the one who is hiding, not you. And this is all legal."

"You're right, but I will feel better when I have the cash. Well, I need to get out of here.

See if you can make peace in there and try to keep Junior in his cage. Messenger, huh. And that was Lester Moore I am supposed to see?"

"Mr. Moore," said Kay, with a hint of satisfaction in her voice.

They returned to the living room, where Rex said goodbye to everyone and asked Sheila to follow him to the door. When they got there, he said, "I need to borrow your car. I don't really want to be spotted where I am going."

"What is so all-fired important that you can't be seen in your own car?"

"It's about your money, that's all you need to know. Can I have the keys? We need to get this over with." Rex made a real effort at being civil.

"Okay, big shot. There they are on the hook behind the door. That way I don't lose 'em when I'm home." Sheila was proud of herself.

Rex took the keys and left. Her car was next to his and before he got in, he went to his car and retrieved from the glove compartment a fake moustache, a small bottle of gum arabic to stick it on, and an Oakland A's baseball cap. He kept these items in his car for occasions such as this. With the cap, a pair of oversized sunglasses, and without his sports coat, he looked pretty much as one would expect a messenger to look. That he also looked like a typical bank robber went through his mind as he got into Sheila's Toyota and flipped the visor mirror down to apply his moustache. It was tricky getting it straight, but he did his best, and with a sigh of resignation tossed the bottle of gum arabic onto the floor of the car.

"Damn thing still isn't straight, but what the hell," he said as he looked in the mirror. He flipped the visor up and drove off.

●●●

His trip to the bank in downtown Redwood City was efficient and uneventful, but as he turned onto Broadway at the bank's corner, he passed a white Ford Crown Victoria 4 door with prominent blackwall tires and no wheel covers parked at the curb. He had already turned when he recognized it as an unmarked police car. Instead of stopping at the bank, he went to the next corner and turned left and noted another car identical to the first, parked on that street. Both cars had occupants in civilian clothes who had a line of vision to the bank, and both cars were for all intents and purposes out of sight and innocuous to all but the most astute observer.

"Uh, oh," said Rex. "Things are getting dicey. Could be unmarked traffic guys. Could be. Then maybe, something else. They use uniformed guys for speed traps. Let's just see what we can see," and Rex found a parking spot on Broadway in the next block from the bank and took in the scene. Within a few minutes he spotted a guy leaning against a building reading a newspaper and smoking a cigarette. He did a double take when he recognized him. He couldn't call his name, but he remembered where he knew him. It was the Redwood City Police Firearms Center, and he had been next to him in a class for long-range pistol shooting. As he remembered, the guy was pretty good too. But Rex reminded himself he was no slouch either.

Wow, these guys are about as subtle as a bag of hammers, thought Rex. How long did it take me to spot 'em, four minutes at the most? Well, that takes care of Clark Gable for today, and he peeled off the moustache, wincing.

Still need some cash. Don't want the wheels to come off too soon, things are working so well. Rex drove to his own bank where he took three hundred dollars out of his savings account and put half into his checking account and half in his shirt pocket. This should take care of Sheila for a week or so, he thought, but if this goes longer, I'll have to get something quick from Kay. I'm not financing this past today.

Forty five minutes after he left, he was back on Vista Drive.

Not knowing what to expect when he walked into the living room, he was pleasantly surprised to find Kay and Sheila laughing together.

"Well, you two seem to be enjoying each other. May I share in the joke?"

"Oh, it's just something we found we have in common. Girl talk," giggled Sheila.

It came to Rex's mind that the only thing they could have in common was him, and he hoped their laughter had nothing to do with any part of his anatomy. But he wouldn't put it past either of them.

"Where's Jud?"

"In the bedroom, watching TV," she said. "He is a very nervous young man, but we had a little talk and he and I are okay with things. He needs someone to talk to, I think. For now, I took the TV out of the kitchen and put it in his room. It seems he loves daytime soap operas. That will take him into the afternoon. After that, well, we have to figure out something else for him to do. He's like a four year old as far as attention span goes." All at once Sheila had become Earth Mother.

Go figure, said Rex to himself. Must be something about Kay that brings out the best in people. Me included, at one time anyway. He said to both women, "Well, whatever he is, I think it's a good idea to keep track of the keys to his motorcycle. We can't have him taking off in the middle of the night to go smoke something, just to settle his nerves."

"Way ahead of you, Rexy," grinned Sheila, as she held up a short chain holding a bottle opener, a whistle, a little spoon, tiny wrenches and about ten keys of one kind or another. "His is one of these, and I convinced him he wouldn't be needing them."

With that, she dropped the chain and its contents into the pockets of her stylish denim "let's go bake bread" housedress. It wasn't until then that Rex noticed that her hair was arranged in a ponytail with a ribbon around it. She looked, for the first time in a long time, cute.

Rex motioned for Kay to follow him to the kitchen again and she did.

"How did it go? Did Lester cooperate?" Kay opened the discussion.

"As a matter of fact, he didn't. The place was staked out like John Dillinger was on his way for a visit. Hershey Bar, huh!" Rex was past even being skeptical.

"Rex, I had no way..." Kay started.

Rex cut her off. "I need some money from you Kay. You can't take money out of the bank with the cops watching it like they are. So what other ideas have you got?"

"Can't you take an I.O.U?" Kay was trying, but not getting a lot sympathy from him.

"No." Rex looked at her and let the tension build.

Kay opened her Louis Vuitton purse, reached to the bottom and produced a broach with intricately carved gold work circling a cluster of pearls, rubies and sapphires, with a single three carat diamond in the middle. She let it take its effect on Rex.

"Wow!" he said. "I don't think you'll need that."

"When I decided I needed to be away for a while, I stopped by the house in the middle of the day and got some things together for my absence. You've seen my luggage."

"Yes, I had to help move it. Pretty fancy stuff. And the broach?"

"I thought I might need something to pay my way, particularly if things don't work out. So I went through our jewelry safe and got a couple of rings and bracelets, and this. I picked something that won't be missed, if someone starts nosing around. I have a lot of rings and four or five broaches. I love broaches and they are very similar. And all are worth a great deal of money."

"It seems you have cost Mr. Dale a lot in the short time you've been married."

"He's got a lot. And besides, they didn't all come from him. I had a life before William Dale II, you know."

"Yeah, I know," said Rex, finally realizing that he had never had a place at the table, however much she hinted that he did. He got back to business. "I see it has a patriotic theme. Rubies, pearls and sapphires. Red, white and blue. Never saw that before. How much is it worth?"

"This was a gift from a young French friend, and as such, is private to me. It is not on the insurance list and has never been appraised. But, I would say no less than twelve to twenty thousand."

"That ought to buy Sheila a bra or two." Rex said. "So how does it fit in to you paying my bills? They don't take diamonds at Safeway."

"Here, you take it as security. If I haven't gotten some cash to you by the middle of next month, you have my permission to sell it."

"What will Lucky Pierre think of that?" Rex could not resist.

"Lucky Pierre got unlucky a long time ago," said Kay, thinking of how they parted.

"Okay, I'll take it, but on the condition that if it's fake, I am out of this deal altogether. You see, I will have it appraised. Maybe not insured, but I will know what it's worth by the end of tomorrow."

"Is that all, then?" Kay said, the charm gone from her voice.

"Yes," he said, and they joined the Sheila in the living room.

Rex finally felt he could ease up. He had been successful in his mission.

"The moon lander has docked," he said aloud as he headed for the door. "Bye, ladies."

"Wait," cried Sheila with a note of alarm. "The A's cap!"

"Oh, yeah, that," said Rex as he turned the bill backwards.

"Go Giants," he called from the porch. They all had a good laugh as he left.

CHAPTER TWENTY-THREE

He was in his own car at last, and on the drive back home from Sheila's house. Rex felt relieved that he finally got his brood settled. As he pulled into his driveway, he also felt the need for more relief in the form of food. He quickly found his way in and went directly to his old Kelvinator and found a beer and enough leftover Spam for a Spam and Velveeta sandwich, which he quickly put together along with some mayo and pickles he kept on hand for just such occasions. That and a jot of Tabasco sauce.

"No damn lettuce or mustard. And this is the last beer. I am out of essentials. I need to get to the store. This bread is starting to turn bluish green," he said as he trimmed the spots off.

Rex found his favorite spot on the couch in the familiar indentation his regular use had created. He sat back and ate his sandwich, washing it down with beer. Both were finished within six minutes.

But he just couldn't settle. He belched a deep, satisfying, Rex Nickels belch, but it didn't bring the comfort it usually did, and Rex grew more and more restless. Finally he blurted, "The hell with it!" and left the house. Believing that maybe walking would clear his head, he set out on foot for the brief walk to his office.

Need to check the mail and messages, he convinced himself as he ambled along, although he really didn't need a reason. By the time he got to his office, he was once again ready to think clearly. Although disappointed at finding no messages or mail, he was relaxed at last and, tilting his chair back and putting his feet up on the desk, he went over his situation.

It looks as if I have gotten myself involved in something. Or Kay got me involved, to tell the truth. So Kay's scared shitless of Owen Owens, who's her husband's partner in the horse business, and of Ramsey, who seems to work mostly for Owens. Real scared, like she thinks Owens and Ramsey are responsible for the death of Earnest, who turns out to be her half-brother, and like they're not gonna' stop there! So she runs off with her nephew, to protect him as well as herself. She's told me a lot but something tells me she's not really opening up. Anyway, I said I would help her, and I will if I can. But if she's not the killer...(hell, of course she's not)... then she needs to come clean and spill what she knows.

He paused and gathered himself for another attack on the mystery, looking out the window momentarily at the single cloud in the sky.

Maybe her problem is what the kid knows? I don't know if my promise to Kay extends to Jud or not, for crissakes. He works for Ramsey. Who is he loyal to? Ramsey? His father? His Aunt Kay? I need to find a way to get with that kid and find out how he's involved, what he knows.

And then there's that guy Abel N. Willing.

Rex thought about his visit to the library and Rosie Budner's showing him the guy's card and the phone number on the pad in his pocket.

Hey, I never did look at that, he said to himself, and reached into his side pants pocket and brought out a bent up little note-book. On it was scrawled "Abel N. Willing, Sales 1-415-633-2468," barely readable. Sales? Humph. Sales, my ass. He must be on to something. Surely he knows Ramsey and Owens through racing connections. Why was he researching Dale in the library? Will he talk to me or is he too much in bed with the cops? It seems to me Ramsey is the best bet for the "Bad Guy." Not that Owens is the "Good Guy," but he probably wouldn't get his own hands dirty. What if all this has nothing to do with racing? Then could it be Kayne's wife? Or the son? Some domestic game of vengeance, maybe? Or some other problem in Stockton, like some prescription screw-up that resulted in death and revenge? I wonder how can I get close to Jud and get him to talk about his family, or about what he may have seen or heard at the stables? Well, Rex better get to work, this is a big assignment.

With that, he stood up, stretched and scratched himself where it itched from sitting down.

The only definite connection of Kayne to Redwood City, he mulled to himself as he left the office, is the Catalina Motel. Why was he staying there? Was it to visit Kay, who lives close by? I think I'll just get my butt over there and see what the manager has to offer in the way of information. After that, I can stop at 7-Eleven on the way back to stock up on groceries.

CHAPTER TWENTY-FOUR

The Catalina Motel was located on a deep site with narrow frontage, on the west side of El Camino Real. It was about a quarter mile south of the Union Cemetery, and incidentally, a short distance north of the intersection of El Camino Real and Selby Lane. But unlike the genteel, leafy, exurban character that El Camino takes on just before Selby Lane at the Atherton town limit, the motel was located on a flashy commercial strip of highway, with service stations, drive-ins, small food and liquor stores, outsized neon signs and parking lots. The biggest sign, flanked by a pair of towering palm trees, was at The Catalina.

Rex steered the Chevy Monza convertible to the porte-cochere in front of the small lobby. The building stretched back in what appeared to be an endless two-level line of doors and windows, with a narrow, railed catwalk for access to the upper rooms. The procession of rooms overlooked a corresponding length of divot-ted asphalt with only a scattering of cars on this weekday mid afternoon.

The afternoon breeze was picking up, bringing in a hint of fog from the north. Rex decided it was time to close the Monza's top. After completing the struggle with the uncooperative steel struts and canvas and securing all latches, Rex walked into the glass-fronted lobby.

"Cool wheels!" murmured a male voice from behind the front desk.

Rex saw a young man, with a very dark complexion, wrinkled white shirt, black clip-on tie. Rex responded, "Thank you! I try to keep her in good shape. That's why I was taking a little time to close her up. It looks like some fog or even rain might be coming in. My name's Rex Nickels, here's my card. Not looking for a room at this time, but I am interested in some information. Would you be the manager?"

The young man smiled and said, "Yes, that is, I'm the assistant manager. My uncle is actually the manager and the owner of the property. My name's Roy Patel, as you see on my name badge. And I see by your card you're a private investigator. Well, we do get P.I.'s coming in here for one reason or another. I take it your reason is to ask some questions. I'll certainly help you if I can."

Rex explained, "I happen to represent a close member of the family of the man whose body was found over in the Union Cemetery a week ago. According to news accounts, the gentleman was a guest of yours, at least for the night before he was discovered in the early morning hours. My client is grieving severely, and craves any kind of insight into what might have happened leading up to the death. Is there anything you might have observed, or heard, that might help bring some comfort to my client?"

"As I said, I'd like to help, Mr. Nickels", Patel answered. "But I've already given a statement to the police. I've answered a lot of press inquiries. I've talked to my maids and so have the police. I don't really know of anything that hasn't already been made public."

"Look, Mr. Patel, I've been in the P.I. game a long time. I know that not everything that goes to the police gets to the press. I don't even know for sure that the police know everything you know. I'm just looking for some extra tidbit that can help my client deal with the tragedy. I'm authorized by my client to make it worth your while."

Patel raised his eyebrows and said, "Oh, Mr. Nickels, you may not understand that we run a totally clean operation here. Respectfully, I'm somewhat offended that you would suggest that I might take some reward for information. My uncle would drum me out of the family. However, I will confide, in all honesty, there is one bit of information that the police were given that I've not seen in the press...but I'm still reluctant; a reward would be very troublesome for me if it got back to my uncle."

"I respect your sense of family solidarity and your sincerity. But, it's my understanding that, in the hospitality industry, it's customary for hosts and employees to receive some form of, uh, remuneration, or, let's say, gratuity...I think, maybe, where your family came from? Isn't there a word like 'back-sis' or something that sounds like that?"

Patel smiled, "Oh, you mean 'baksheesh'! Oh, but no. That's about charitable giving. Like, where your family comes from, they put something in the collection plate, no?"

"Yes, that's precisely what I mean. I have in my pocket an empty white envelope, into which I would really like to place two new twenty dollar bills, and then place the whole thing into that ashtray on your desk there, for you to pass along to your favorite charity. That is, if you will confide in me what you told the police that you did not tell the press."

Patel responded, "Then I think we understand each other, Mr. Nickels. May I call you Rex? All of that would be possible if I were to find five new twenties in the offering."

"You drive a hard bargain, Roy. Done! So give!"

"I reported to the police that Mr. Kayne checked in early Saturday afternoon and left in his car soon afterward. I didn't see him any more on Saturday or that night, but I know from the maid his bed was slept in and made up on Sunday. The next time I saw him was Sunday afternoon about four thirty, and I have no idea what he was doing earlier in the day. On Sunday I observed, from here at the desk, Mr. Kayne talking, out in the parking lot, near his Oldsmobile, to a large gentleman with bright red hair. The conversation was very animated and increasingly loud. Suddenly they stopped, made some gestures toward the car, nodded to each other, and then got into the car, Mr. Kayne in the driver's seat. They drove out of the lot, made a left turn and headed up El Camino. And that's the last I saw of Mr. Kayne."

"And you didn't hear what they were saying in the parking lot?"

"No. Musak was on in here, and I can't read lips. Besides they weren't facing this way."

"And you don't have any idea who the redhead was?"

"No, I hadn't seen him around here. He was tall, maybe six foot, two inches. Big, not fat. Maybe about your age. I can't tell about American types. He was wearing a plaid shirt with jeans— and boots."

"Okay, Roy," Rex concluded. "You've been a lot of help, truly generous. Now, just because I've been very generous and charitable with, uh, 'back-seats', can you tell me if you have any thoughts on where those two guys were headed when they drove out of here?"

Patel paused, thoughtfully. "I have the feeling that they wanted to continue their conversation. It was the time of day when guests ask me if there's a nice bar nearby. I usually suggest El Flamingo Real, just up beyond Woodside Road. If I think the guests want something that's a little higher class, I'll send them to one of a couple of spots on Woodside Road, up toward the Alameda. They would be the Pulgas Patio and the Redwood Retreat. But of course these guys didn't ask me. So it kind of depends on how well they knew the area."

"Thanks for the leads, Roy. You're a true gentleman. You have my card, if you think of anything else, give me a ring. More charity may flow."

"Thanks so much, Rex. Your contribution will be put to good service. And remember, if you have need for a room, we have fine ones, some suites, a pool. We could work out an afternoon rate, if that would be your desire. Goodbye now, Mr. Nickels."

CHAPTER TWENTY-FIVE

"**I** gotta' piss," Jud said as he burst out of the bedroom, making both Sheila and Kay jump. "Where's the pisser?"

"If you mean the bathroom, it's that door on your right," said Sheila. "And put the seat down when you're through."

"You'll be lucky if he puts it up when he starts," sighed Kay.

Jud didn't exactly slam the guest bathroom door, but he made sure everyone could hear that it was shut.

"And as long as you're in my house, clean up your mouth," Sheila yelled after him, her old self emerging. "They may use that kind of language in Peoria, but you aren't in Peoria anymore." Her Earth Mother image had slipped a bit but she softened back into it as she finished her sentence.

None could deny that the toilet had been flushed, as it could be heard midway through its progress when Jud emerged, drying his just rinsed hands on his shirt front.

"I'm not from Peoria," Jud said flatly, standing in the open doorway. "I don't even know where Peoria is at. I just said that."

"Why?" Sheila's question was genuine.

"Aw, I don't know. I heard a lot of tough guys come from there. Guys you don't want to mess with. The cool guys I hang with sometimes tell a lot of boss stories about 'em." Jud felt and looked awkward, just standing there in the company of two older women. And he was especially wary of Sheila, whose change from the person who humiliated him in the cafe to Earth Mother had further addled his already confused brain.

"Why don't you just come on into the living room and sit with us a bit? We talked a lot at the motel, but it is more comfortable here," offered Kay.

"I was watching the soaps. I need to get back. I just caught the tail end of 'The Edge of Night', and 'Days of Our Lives' is about to start," Jud muttered as he started back to the bedroom.

"I just love 'Days'," said Sheila as warmly as she could. "Stay here with us and we can all see it together. Will that be all right with you, Kay?"

"Certainly. It is one of my favorites." Kay made it a point never to watch soap operas, saying to her friends that soap was for washing and opera was something she supported financially and attended whenever she had the chance. But now, in this circumstance, was not the time for that speech and these people wouldn't know the difference. So she smiled, showed her teeth and lied through them.

Jud came into the room reluctantly, and the three of them arranged themselves in front of the television. Sheila turned on the set, and the picture soon came up, tuned fortuitously to the channel for "Days of Our Lives", which was just starting. "Like sands through the hourglass, so are the days of our lives," a voice intoned, and after the credits rolled, the episode began.

Sheila was not lying about watching soap operas, and in truth this was her favorite show. Had the others not been there, this is what she would be doing.

"I can't wait to see what Victor does today. I just love that character," said Sheila.

"I have been a Tom Horton fan since I was a teenager," said Kay, "and Macdonald Carey is one of my favorite actors." Although she had never seen the show, Kay had seen Carey's name in the credits, and knew him from the movie "John Paul Jones" where he played Patrick Henry. She had seen it on one of her dates with Rex Nickels during what she called "the interlude." And she had met Macdonald Carey once at a charity fund raiser, and remembered his voice. "That's his voice you just heard."

"Really?" Jud was impressed. "It is? How did you know that?"

"I met him once."

"No, kidding. Wow. I watch this show all the time. Now I'll know." Jud was registering about eleven on the age scale again.

The three occupied themselves with watching television until half way through "General Hospital", when one of the interns under Dr. Hardy accidentally caused the near-death of a patient with severe asthma by administering the wrong throat spray. Both Kay and Jud suddenly became very uncomfortable, and Jud became more and more agitated. When Sheila shot a puzzled glance at her, Kay attempted an explanation for Jud's behavior.

"When we were at the motel, we saw someone in the parking lot who was having an asthma attack and Jud told me he had asthma when he was a little kid. The memory of not being able to breathe still scares him," Kay said to Sheila.

Then to Jud, "Why don't you take a break from these two old ladies here, and watch the TV in your room. I think 'Let's Make A Deal' is on and there is 'Speed Racer'. You told me yesterday that you liked both of those."

"'Let's Make A Deal' is friggin' over, and 'Speed Racer' is for little kids," Jud whined.

"Well, I'm sure you can find something. You must calm down, Judson," Kay said.

"I gotta' get outta' this friggin' place," said Jud with a desperate tone, and headed for the mantel over the fake fireplace where he had last seen the key to his Triumph.

"Just what are you going to do, my young friend?" asked Sheila, who had anticipated his move. She stood at the front door of the house, dangling his key ring in front of her.

"I think maybe you should follow my advice to watch TV in your room, Jud," warned Kay. "You know how those shows calm you down. You told me that. So just go into the bedroom and settle. Okay?"

It was more than a request or a suggestion, and Jud had come to depend on Kay, since she seemed so steady. He returned to the bedroom and shut the door. In a moment, the television could be heard.

"I guess we don't need to watch any more soap operas. We seem to have one of our own," said Sheila as she turned off the set and dropped onto the couch.

After a few pregnant moments and a couple of false starts, the two women got their conversation going again, and soon this unlikely and mismatched pair found something in common to discuss. They began talking about their mothers, and how they first made cookies with them.

"A gingerbread man, with raisin eyes," remembered Kay.

"No sh...er, no kidding! Me and my mom too. Only for eyes, we used..."

At that moment, the phone rang, interrupting the reverie.

"I wonder who the hell that could be. Must be Rex. Wonder what favor he wants from me now," said Sheila as she picked up the phone. "Hello? Oh, Susanne. Hold a sec." she put her hand over the receiver and said to Kay, "It's Susanne Shepard, my next door neighbor."

"Susanne, I'm back. What's up?...Oh, shit! No, don't call the police. It's okay. It's my nephew, and he is a little crazy sometimes. Thanks, I'll come over later and explain. Bye."

Sheila put the phone down and, followed by Kay, made a bee line for Jud's bedroom.

"Shee...it", she said as she opened the door. "Well, can you believe that," and both women looked at the open window and the curtains moving gently in the breeze.

"What...?" Kay was mystified.

"The sucker climbed out the window. Susanne saw him. Then the little turd hot-wired my car and took off. She saw it all. That's when she called me, the nosey old bitch. She's a pain in the ass most of the time, and she snoops. Good thing she was doing it this time or we wouldn't know."

"What good does it do us to know now?" said Kay in a non-socialite narrow voice. "He's gone."

"And so is my goddamned fuckin' car." Sheila's time as a hearth-based mom was over.

CHAPTER TWENTY-SIX

Rex turned the Monza around in the Catalina parking lot, and, before exiting, briefly reviewed the bars recommended by Patel. If the red-headed guy Patel saw was indeed Ramsey, he would know his way around these parts. Regardless of the described rural clothing, he might favor the spots that were noted as "higher class", which happened to be located along the route he might travel to get back and forth to the farm. So Rex decided to start with the Pulgas Patio, pretty close to the Town of Woodside. Then he would track back to the Redwood Retreat, and if necessary, El Flamingo Real.

The Pulgas Patio sat near the edge of Woodside Road and Rex pulled into the parking lot behind the building. The rear entry to the bar went through a brick patio partially covered with vines on trellises. A handful of patrons were drinking at outdoor tables.

Inside, a padded-leather bar stretched along part of one wall, and the usual assortment of tables and booths filled the rest of the rather small space, which was occupied by customers. The barman was leaning forward, talking to a young couple seated on stools. When he saw Rex enter, he straightened up, turned and said, "Welcome stranger! What can we do you for?"

"How about a small draft beer?" suggested Rex with a smile.

"Sure thing. We got Anchor Steam."

"My favorite!" Rex nodded.

With a bit of a flourish, the bar man presented the glass of amber brew with its head of froth. The stitching on his shirt identified him as "Bud".

Rex took a sip and smiled with satisfaction. "Say, Bud, I'd like to ask you something. I'm wondering if you were on duty about this time on Sunday afternoon a week ago?"

Bud paused, and then replied, "Well, yeah, I guess I was. But why do you ask?"

Rex handed Bud a business card and said, "I'm doing a little bit of investigating. I'm trying to catch up with a couple of guys who may have stopped in here at that time. They were probably having a heated argument, so you may have noticed them. Guys maybe in their late forties, one with red hair and dressed in jeans and plaid."

"No," said the barman, "doesn't ring any bells for me. Here, let's ask Janice, she was taking care of the patio last Sunday." He beckoned to a tall brunette, who came over to the bar, and he relayed Rex's question to her.

"Oh no, I'm sure." Janice said. "It was funny for that late on an afternoon. No men at all. Just a couple of parties of ladies at the tables outside. More like the crowd we see on weekdays after lunch."

Rex thanked the bar staff for their efforts. He paid up, took a few more sips of beer, then, with his glass not fully drained, he took his leave and headed back down Woodside Road.

The Redwood Retreat was on the opposite side of the road, about halfway back toward El Camino. Unlike the Pulgas Patio, the Retreat had parking in front, no outdoor seating, and as it turned out, no draft beer. Otherwise the two watering holes were almost carbon copies, as Rex realized when he walked in. He was greeted by a hostess, in a low-cut black sheath dress, who said her name was Maria. Rex observed that Maria, although just a bit slight to do justice to the dress, had a sweet, open face.

Rex reprised his routine from the Pulgas Patio, only this time he asked for a bottle of Heineken's. When Maria returned with his order, she responded to his query. "Yeah, sure, I remember those guys! Especially the red-headed one. They came in very up-tight, very tense. Not much talking. I put them at a table back in the corner. They looked like they weren't interested in a lot of socialization. They had a couple of drinks each. They never got real loud, but there was some pounding of fists on the table, and quite a few four-letter words were exchanged."

"Do you recall what time they came in?" Rex asked.

"It was just about five, maybe a little before. Then a little after six they ordered a third round, and they asked me where would be a good place nearby to get a steak dinner. They wanted some place that wasn't a formal, dress-up scene. I suggested the El Flamingo Real, over on El Camino. They left pretty soon after, didn't finish the last drink. Didn't leave much of a tip, either."

Rex put a generous tip for Maria on the table, again left a par-tially full glass of beer, and exited for the El Flamingo Real.

"The Flamingo", as it was commonly known to patrons, was a rare local survivor from an architectural era called "streamlined moderne". A curving stucco front with lots of glass was set off by a thin blade of a tower bearing the business name plus a many-times life-sized image of a flamingo in pink neon. Parallel strips of pink neon tubing ran around the parapets. The building sat well back from the street, with an asphalt parking surface fanning out front, a vestige of its early life as a drive-in restaurant where car-side deliveries were made by pretty girls on roller skates. As a local resident in his boyhood, Rex knew The Flamingo well through most of the years of both of its lives. The interior, as now constituted, was mostly a lounge bar with dark materials, and low level lighting. And smoke of course. Lots of smoke.

The restaurant operation was secondary by 1970, a menu limited to steaks, burgers, the occasional chicken, with gener-ous servings of fries and onion rings and with iceberg lettuce and Roquefort as a specialty. Dining patrons mostly occupied a cres-cent of booths that followed the curved line of front windows.

The Flamingo was moderately popular in the afternoons and evenings; that is, no waiting for a place. There were a few empty spots among the booths, at the cocktail tables and the bar. The central location of the bar allowed a sweeping view of the drinking area, so Rex proceeded directly there. Two bartenders, a man and a woman, were working on drink orders. Rex caught the eye of the man, whom he took to be the senior of the two. Seeing that the bar served Acme on tap, he ordered a short one. When the beer was delivered Rex presented his card and his inquiry to the bartender.

This time he was able to say confidently, "I have it on very good authority that these guys were here about half-past six, Sunday night a week ago."

The bar man, Barney, shrugged. "You see how it is right now. We have a lot of folks, a lot of turnover. If your guys came for dinner, they would probably have been seated in a booth. Some of the booths are pretty much outside of my field of vision. You see the blonde waitress other there? Cissy? She was working last Sunday. When she comes over to the bar for an order, you can ask her if she remembers your guys."

Rex sipped his beer and kept his eye on Cissy as she moved around her booths and tables. He was somewhat distracted by her bottom. Finally she approached the waiter station at the bar.

Rex addressed her. "Cissy, Barney says I should talk to you. My name is Rex. I'm a private investigator checking up on a couple of men who I know were here last Sunday at this time. Two guys, late forties, one with red hair. They had been seen having an argument in another bar, and they came over here for steaks."

"Uh, I'm sorry, uh, Rex," Cissy answered. "I can't recollect anybody like that. I do remember it was pretty busy here that Sunday, a lot more so than tonight."

Rex felt a tap on his arm. He turned to see an older man, slender, with white hair, a little stooped. The type Rex would call a codger.

"Pardon me, sir," the man said to Rex. "I overheard. I remember the gentlemen you describe. I was here last Sunday night."

"You don't say!" Rex blurted. "Tell me, please. Can I buy you a drink? Let's sit down. My name is Rex Nickels. Here's my card."

"Well, I'm pleased to meet you, Mr. Nickels. My name is Arthur Jimson. And thanks, I think I will. I'd like to have an Old Fashioned. Well...to tell the story, I was sitting in the next booth to those fellows, with a couple of my friends. We were all chewing the fat, like old guys do. And I could hear them in the next booth talking pretty loudly. I couldn't really make out what they were saying, though. You can see I wear a hearing aid. From the tone I got the feeling that one was unhappy about the price of something. There were a lot of dirty words. I could hear those." Mr. Jimson's drink was delivered to the table. "Cheers, and thanks," Jimson interjected.

"So...to continue, the shorter one went to the restroom and while he was gone, the red-headed one went to the bar for some fresh drinks. It was odd, because there was a very nice waitress on duty. He brought the glasses back to the table and when the other one got back they seemed to make a toast or something. The short one got drunk real fast and they almost came to blows and then they left. Didn't even have anything to eat.

"My group was about ready to leave and the argument sort of took the edge off the evening anyway, so we left right after they did. It turned out that we were parked in the same area as they were. It was almost dark by then, just a few lights in the parking lot. But I could see the two fellows sort of wrestling with each other, next to a car. It was fairly new, appeared to be some GM model, not sure which, like a hardtop coupe. The big man, the redhead, suddenly swung his left arm around and landed a punch in the jaw of the other one. The other man just slumped against the car. The redhead propped him up and managed to get the passenger door open, shoved him inside, ran around and got in the driver's seat, then took off like a bat and almost sideswiped one of my friends as he passed us. He raced out to El Camino and headed south, in the direction of Woodside Road."

Rex was thrilled to finally get some solid information. "Ah, Mr. Jimson, I can't thank you enough! I would just like to ask, is there anything else you can remember that you heard or saw in the bar or in the parking lot?"

"Oh, yes. I think I did hear the one man call the other 'Red', which was pretty obvious. And when their car sped past us in the lot, I caught a glimpse of something on the license plate frame. It looked like a big RX, you know, like the symbol they use for prescriptions?"

Rex gulped down the last of his short one, shook Jimson's hand, and left the building.

CHAPTER TWENTY-SEVEN

The house on Maple Street never looked better to Rex as he pulled up in his Corvair and parked in his driveway. He was just about drained. As much as he liked drinking, he didn't like going from bar to bar, asking questions, pretending to have drunk a lot when he really had drunk very little, staying sharp mentally, staying on top of the situation everywhere he went. Bars and drinking were supposed to be for fun, not fact finding. He had learned some things he needed to know. But he had had enough for one day. He just wanted to get into the house and put on some pants that weren't too tight and get himself a beer. A nice, ice cold Acme beer in a bottle.

He had no sooner shut the door when he saw the blinking light on his home answering machine.

"Shit and double shit. Whose tits are in a wringer now?" Rex cursed his way across the room to the machine. He hesitated... maybe he should just pretend he didn't hear it or hadn't gotten home till late. But Rex wouldn't be a detective, private or otherwise, if he weren't basically curious, some might even say nosy. So he stopped and listened.

"Rex, that little low-life slime ball mother-effing jerk is gone." Sheila didn't bother to announce who was calling and Rex didn't need to wonder who it was.

"Gone? *Gone?*" Rex was incredulous as he spoke to the machine. "I put him there with you so he would *not* be gone!"

And he collapsed onto the nearest chair, muttering to himself. What the hell happened? I thought he was shut up in the bedroom watching cartoons or something.

He dialed her number. "Sheila? What's going on?" he said and exhaled a tired breath.

"The window. The little shit went out the back window."

"But that's a seven foot drop to the ground on that side of the house. Is he hurt?"

"Maybe he flew, the little pot head. You remember old nosy Susanne next door. She was snooping as usual and saw him crawl out and drop to the ground. Then he came around the house and got my car and took off like a bat out of hell." Sheila was furious.

"I thought we hid the keys."

"We did. The sucker hot-wired it and was gone in thirty seconds."

"Any idea where he went?"

"Not a clue, Sherlock. And Scarlet O'Hara in there is about to come apart at the seams. You better get your ass back over here. Pronto, Rexy."

"I'm on my way," he said, not bothering to say good-bye. He hung up, re-traced his steps to the door, got in the car and headed back to Vista Drive, tapping his last few ounces of strength and mental focus.

When Rex pulled his car into Sheila's driveway she was standing at the front door, waiting for him, still in her Mother Hubbard dress.

Well, isn't that homey, thought Rex. Next she will tell me that dinner is on the table and that she has a cake in the oven. He thought a moment and said aloud, "Naah."

"Where the fuck have you been all evening and what in the hell have you been up to?" she said. Sheila might look like a 60's earth mother, but she didn't sound like one now.

"Nothing, nothing at all. And where I have been is my business. What is going on?"

"Hot news, my inquisitive friend. The little turd walloper just phoned."

"You just never let up, do you Sheila?"

"Not when it comes to that little two-timing pissant."

"Okay! Out with it. I didn't drive all the way back here to listen to your foul mouth. What did he say? And try to be civil. Remember, I am paying you for this."

"I'll tell you what he said, if you can just keep your damn pants on till we get inside." She turned, and they both entered the house.

They found Kay sitting on the edge of the couch, crying. Real tears. Her eyes were red and full of fear as she looked up at Rex. The woman was distraught.

"So? What did Jud say?" Rex asked.

"I don't know where he is or what he has been doing, but he sounded a lot calmer than he was when he was here. Probably went off and found some grass to smoke. He didn't sound real high, though. Pretty hard to tell with a weirdo like that."

"Did he tell you where he was?" asked Rex.

"No, Dick Tracy. I just got through telling you that. Listen up! I tried to get it out of him and then Kay tried, but he clammed up. That's when she started to bawl. I got back on the phone then and he told me that he left my car at the Red City train station. Then the little..."

"Sheila...," Rex warned.

"...tyke hung up. Without so much as a 'go fu...'"

"Sheila, put a lid on it." Rex snapped. Both she and Rex knew he could talk to her like that because she was on his payroll. But there was still tension in the air. "We have to concentrate on find- ing Jud and getting him back under our protection, and I use that last word guardedly." Rex was more than just a little put out that Sheila had let Jud get loose, and it showed. "Did he give any kind of hint at all as to where he was headed?"

"Not in the slightest. Kay and I were talking about it while waiting forever for you to get here, and we came up with nothin'. Or more like too many somethin's. From that station he could be headed for San Francisco or San Jose, or even take a bus back to Hayward, though I don't know why he would go back to Hayward after all the trouble it took to get him away from there," said Sheila.

Kay added, "He could go to Stockton or just about anywhere the bus goes. He could also get to the airport from that station. But he has hardly any money. I gave him a ten dollar bill to buy some cigarettes at the motel and he never gave me the change. As far as I know, that is all the money he's got. Certainly not enough to fly anywhere."

"Not in a plane, anyway," sniped Sheila.

"He's probably holed up somewhere with his biker friends, if they really exist," Kay offered. "He boasted about them when we talked in Hayward, but there was so much braggadocio in the way he talked, it was hard to know what to believe. I am so worried." Kay's voice got shaky again. Then she paused and looked at the others, saying "Oh my! I don't know why I didn't think of that earlier."

"Think of what?" asked Rex.

"His mother. You don't suppose he went to his mother's house, do you?" said Kay.

"Mother. Yes, I guess he has to have a mother. Good point. Do you know her or where she lives?" Rex's professional instincts went on full alert.

"She is Earnest's ex-wife and she is a nurse at a hospital over in Oakland." Kay reported. "Her name is Marilyn. I don't know if she changed her last name or not. Jud talked about her being a nurse when we were at the motel. But he said they didn't see much of each other, that she made him nervous, that she tried to control his life. I doubt he would go there."

"Did he say what hospital?"

"I think I heard him say it was Kaiser. I'm not sure," answered Kay. "Why?"

"No reason," Rex said.

"Rexy has a bad habit of being tedious. Don't worry about it," sighed Sheila, getting impatient.

Rex clapped his hands softly together to signal the end of the conversation, stating, "Well, he's gone and we have to face the fact that there's nothing we can do about it, not tonight anyway. He's wanted as a suspect by the cops, and he knows that, so he is not only hiding from us, but them as well. He may be on the moon for all I know."

And with that, Rex checked out for the night. He thought of nothing as he left Sheila's and headed home for what he desperately hoped was the last time that day.

CHAPTER TWENTY-EIGHT

Jud hung up the pay phone before Sheila could ask him any more questions. She ought to be grateful that I told her where her junky old car is, the bitch! He headed up Broadway on foot, away from the train station and away from bossy women. He came to El Camino Real and stood for a few minutes, hands in his pockets, staring at nothing in particular, trying to decide what to do. The automobile traffic on "Big Cam", with cars like big insects with headlight eyes, whizzed by, and frightened him. As soon as possible, he crossed El Camino to follow Broadway westward. Then he saw the school grounds that looked like a large park, and the big Mission-styled school buildings. Through the darkness he thought he heard shouting and singing and he could see lights through the trees.

I ain't got nuthin' else to do, so I might as well see what's goin' on, he thought, and headed toward the lights and noise.

"All we are saying is give peace a chance..." he could hear a crowd singing as he got closer. Soon he came to a large number of people surrounding a lighted tennis court where there was a band and people with bullhorns making speeches. These speeches were followed with the singing, and chants of "Hell no, we won't go!" Some present tried to sing "God Bless America" but were shouted down. Jud stopped at the edge of the crowd and as he took it all in he noticed a number of motorcycles parked together and several tattooed men and women with headbands and leather vests standing by themselves nearby. They were neither chanting nor singing, just watching.

He approached this group of bikers cautiously, and finally worked up the nerve to ask one of them, "Hey man, know where I can score some weed?"

"Do I know you, punk?" was his answer.

"Hey Ricky, be nice. He just wants a date with you that's all," laughed one of the bikers.

The group began to form a circle around Jud, and it finally dawned on him that he shouldn't be there. He started to shake.

"Hey, look at that. He wants to dance," chided one of the women, and they all laughed and started to shake their butts in derision. "I'm Sara. Come boogie with me, Pussywillow. Shake it with me." And the small crowd hooted.

"He's mine," said a man next to the one that Jud had approached. It was clear from his tone that he was the alpha dog in the pack. There was an edge in the air.

"Hey, wait a minute. I know this guy," said Little Victor, a short, swarthy young man with acne scars. "He got busted with me in that phony raid over in Stockton last month."

"You didn't get busted, jerk-off. They didn't find anything is what you told us," said Rick.

"Yeah, some shit-head tipped the cops off about the deal, but they got there too early and didn't have nuttin'. We were just sit-tin' there on the front porch, waitin' for the delivery with some other cats, when the fuzz showed. This cat was there, waitin' like the rest of us. I remember because when the cops came, one of them thought this guy lived in that house, thought his name was Kayne. But this guy whined his way out of it, convinced them his name was Perry Winkle."

Some of the bikers laughed.

"I ain't never heard the sissy name 'Tinkle'," teased Lugwrench Lewis.

"That's winkle, Periwinkle" said Jud, "One name. Periwinkle." Tears came to his eyes and started to roll down his cheeks.

"Winkle, winkle, little tinkle, winkie, tinkey, little stinkey, winkie tinkey doo!" chanted Sara, and she clapped her hands in rhythm with the words. The rest of the bikers joined her and danced around Jud, getting closer and closer to him, ridiculing and threatening him.

All at once Jud screamed, "That's not my name! Periwinkle ain't my name. My name is Kayne! I gotta' get away!"

And before anyone could stop him he darted out of the circle of bikers and headed into the darkness of the trees that were between them and the main demonstration.

"That little fart! Get him! Vic. Wrench. Go after him," ordered the alpha man. "The little shit. No one runs off from Rick Parish that way."

But Lugwrench, Little Victor and those that joined them in the chase soon lost sight of Jud as he ran through the trees and into the crowd. They gave up the chase, but not without the flurry of expletives that was a major portion of their expressive but limited vocabulary.

Jud worked his way around the circle of demonstrators and, out of breath, spotted a school bus at the edge of the trees. He crawled under it out of sight of his pursuers. Only when he heard their curses fade did he feel safe to come out. Looking around to make sure no lingering bikers were near, he emerged into the open. All he could see were six or seven scruffy looking people, and as his eyes adjusted he realized that he knew most of them.

The lights from the tennis court illuminated one side of the bus, and its psychedelic décor was familiar and he knew that he was away from danger and in the presence of a group of people who were at least acquaintances, if not friends.

"Hey dude," said one of them, "what are you runnin' from? The Man?"

"From the bikers. Those bastards. They're after me for some reason. I gotta' get away," said Jud, looking from one face to another. "Don't I know you guys?"

"Yeah. From the Round-Up. Hey everyone. It's Periwinkle from the Round-Up, the man with the sweet grass. How's it goin', man?"

"Not so hot. You're Frodo, aren't you? Yeah, and there's Jack and Jill, and...I can't remember the rest. Some of you are new. You guys got any weed? I am really stressed, man."

"Every time we see you, you are stressed, man. What's goin' down?" asked a bearded young hippie.

"Peace brothers, peace. Give him some peace. Come rest your soul with us, son." The speaker was a man who looked to be the oldest there, perhaps thirty or maybe forty years old. He affected a shaved head with a red mark on his forehead and wore a robe with lots of beads. And he raised a hand with strange markings on it and made an odd gesture that was more of an "X" than a cross.

"Are you a...a ...preacher or somethin'?" asked Jud.

"Yeah, he's the Saint of Mary. Mary Juana," said Jill. "We love him, and he loves us. We help him with the weeds in his garden."

"And he owns the bus," added Jack with a slight sardonic smile.

"Come and join us in a joint. Sit here, enjoy the music," invited The Saint.

Suddenly, someone yelled "God damn, look at that!" and they all looked toward the tennis court, where they could see the smoke and fire from a burning American flag. "Things are heatin' up. This ought to be good. Watch those right wingers now! Come on, let's join the party!" All of them started toward the ongoing melee but stopped short when sirens were heard and the flashing red and blue lights of police cars were seen coming from the other side of the crowd.

"Whoa, brethren. Maybe we better go to another service. They don't have our kind of people at this one," said The Saint. "This chariot is leaving."

"What about us sistren?" asked Jill aggressively.

"You also," said The Saint with a rueful smile.

They all piled into the painted school bus and as they did, Frodo looked back at Jud and said, "Ain't you comin', Periwinkle?"

"You betcha," cried Jud happily, and joined the hippies in their school bus as it left the park. Left it to the bikers, the flag burners, the peaceniks, the wingers, the bullhorns and the gawkers to worship there in their own way.

As they turned out onto Broadway, someone asked, "Where we goin', oh Holy One?" It was said with neither mockery nor respect, but some of each.

"The Round-Up Saloon seems to be the den of iniquity of choice. Methinks there might be some communion plants there. What say ye?" The Saint replied with his self-deprecating humor, which even a Harvard education hadn't diminished.

"Hear, hear!" they all cheered, even Jud, as if their approval were needed.

It was a short trip down Broadway to Main Street and the seedy bar that was their destination, and they were there before anyone even had time to roll any smokes, let alone light up. When they got to the Round-Up, The Saint pulled around behind it, in the alley, and parked by the gate. Finding it locked, and motioning the crew to stop talking and exit the bus without slamming the doors and to be as quiet as possible, he led them around to the front of the establishment where they entered and resumed their normal chatter as they walked the length of the bar to the rear.

Behind the bar, watching their every move, was the owner of the Round-Up Saloon, the no-nonsense Donna Ellen "LaDonnie" Mobley. As they passed out the back door to the bar patio, nothing was said, but The Saint raised his fingers and made the same odd gesture to her as he had to Jud—more of an "X" than a cross.

They made themselves comfortable at their usual picnic table in the courtyard, a small area decorated with a western ranch corral in mind, wood rail fence, lassos and all. The saddles placed there originally had long since disappeared. It was a good place to drink beer and smoke marijuana and do other illegal things that hurt no one, and they all felt comfortable there. Jud, with the consumption of various substances, relaxed, and answered the others' questions. He appealed to their sympathies with his plight of injustices done to him and his serious need to get away and hide.

As it got later into the evening, the conversation slowed, and finally, The Saint stood up and announced to his flock. "Fellow travelers, let's go somewhere we can spend the night. The holy bus told me earlier it liked Half Moon Bay in general and the old Blue Sky Motel on Highway 1 in particular. Do we agree with the bus?"

All nodded yes in a quietly intoxicated way, and Frodo opened his mouth to call for the check. The Saint motioned him to be still, and signaled his flock to follow him over the fence and depart in the bus.

To their surprise, out of the bar, charging like a wounded moose, came LaDonnie Mobley.

"Where in the blazin' hell do you turkeys think you are going?"

A tall, muscular, one-time professional woman wrestler, she stood in the doorway like Atlas holding the world, waving the bar tab in her hand. Everyone froze.

"Are Charlie Brown, Lucy, Linus and the rest of you 'Peanuts' people going to pay up or do I call the black & white?"

"Don't forget Pig Pen here," said Frodo, pointing at Jud.

"Don't I wish I could. Damn hippie pot smokin' candy ass. And that goes for all the rest of you, too. Pay up, or pay the price. And do it now. I want to go home." LaDonnie not only looked like a drill sergeant, she sounded like one. She stood tapping her foot, her hand held out.

"Hey, go easy on the guy." said Jill. "He's broke and got a lot of shit on his head right now. Have some sympathy for Pig Pen for a change, Okay?"

"If he wants sympathy tell him to look in the dictionary between shit and syphilis. I'm fresh out." LaDonnie sneered, wiggling her fingers against her thumb for her money.

The Saint took the bill and paid her and she unlocked the back gate for them as they headed for the bus. "Thanks and take your time coming back," she called after them.

They then piled into the bus, took seats and passed a couple of joints around as they headed west to Half Moon Bay and the Blue Sky Motel. Jud knew at last that he could spend the night in hiding with friends, and he could get as stoned as he wanted to.

CHAPTER TWENTY-NINE

"**B**ath." If there was anything he loved more than a bath, he couldn't bring it to mind, Rex thought as he awoke on Tuesday morning. "Not even JD or food. Nothing else this morning but a bath," Rex muttered and rolled out of bed.

After a restless, sweaty night, his mind a jumble of pieces of information, he wanted a bath in the worst way, a steaming hot, soapy one. His tired, achy body needed a good cleansing soak, and his brain needed to relax and come to zero for a while. He opened the tub's faucets, and when the water was just the right mix of hot and cold, he slipped in and put his back against the cold porcelain, feeling it warm as the tub filled. The addition of the considerable mass of Rex's body raised the water level almost immediately to the top of his chest, and when it got to his chin, he stretched out his legs and with his toes shut off the water.

One of Rex's secret and very private joys in life was taking a bubble bath, and today was no exception. He reached over to the top of the adjacent toilet and grabbed his bottle of "Bullwinkle Bubble Bath" and put just the right amount of it into the bathwater. He turned on the faucets again for a short burst of new water to get things frothing just the way he liked it, and soon there was a four inch layer of foam in the tub with only Rex's toes and head in sight amidst the rising steam. He was surrounded by silence as he shut the water off and closed his eyes.

It was a steamy morning.

He drifted off to sleep for five minutes or so and would have slept longer but some foam went up his nose and he woke up with a snort and sat straight up in the tub.

"Well, it was nice while it lasted," he said aloud and reached his hands out for a towel on a nearby rack and dried his hands. "And I am ready to get some work done."

By scooting up from his semi-prone position he could reach the small table next to the tub where lay a pencil and a note pad. Rex called this set-up his office-at-sea, a device he used many times to clear his head and order his thoughts. He was just able to reach over the edge of the tub and put his forearm on the table to write notes to himself.

Good thing I am left-handed, or this wouldn't work, he thought. Or I'd have to move to a house with a tub pointed the right direction. Or learn to write under water.

And so, being of clear mind and clean body, he began to think about the murder of Earnest Kayne and the people who might be involved.

He started by making a list down the left side of his note paper.
1) Rod "Red" Ramsey
2) Judson Kayne
3) Owen Owens
4) William Dale
5) Kayne's ex-wife?
And if I am objective, I have to include ...
6) Abel Willing
and ...
7) Kay Sherman Dale—although I'm sure neither one had anything to do with this.

He put down the pencil and lay back in thought, his hands behind his head. Seven. Huh. My "Magnificent Seven". Now that was a movie! And, Steve McQueen, boy, there's an actor. wonder what he would do with this list. He's never been a P.I. They ought to do a movie with him as one. He was such a tough cop in "Bullitt", he ought to try this end of it once. Seven, seven. Seven, eleven. Which reminds me. Groceries. Back to business, Rexy. Back to what you are being paid to do. For once, Rex's mind didn't focus on food or booze. He was all business now, all investigator business.

He went back to the notepad and wrote "SUSPECT" at the top of a page and beside it "MOTIVE"

Let's start with Ramsey. Numero uno. Rod "Red" Ramsey. Would that be Rodney? Need to check that. And Rex flipped a page on the note pad and jotted down "THINGS TO CHECK ON", followed by, "Red Ramsey's real name".

Motive? Rex pondered. Can't see any here. He works for Owens at Kay's horse farm. Saw him in the picture at the library. Horse trainer and tough guy. At least he thinks he's tough. Victim's son Jud works for Ramsey at that horse farm. Ramsey dislikes him but has to keep him on because Kay put the kid there. Said that Jud was carrying lipstick. I wonder if that's true. Or was Red putting me on? Then the damn TV news report quotes Ramsey as being the last to see Jud and Kay and that was Wednesday. At least that is what Ramsey said. Is he lyin' there too? Still can't see a motive. He really hates Jud, but that's not a reason to kill his father. And did he know that Earnest Kayne was Jud's father? My gut says there is a connection between this guy and the victim, but I can't put my finger on it.

For having such big, bulky fingers, Rex was exceptionally deft with a pencil, and he quickly turned his thoughts into clearly written notes for future reference.

What Rex liked best about working in his office-at-sea was being able to stop and submerge himself periodically, which he now did, almost forcing the water level over the edge of the tub. Noting this, when he arose again, he let some water out of the tub and turned on the hot water to get the water temperature back to its therapeutic state .

"Ahhhhh..." he exhaled, relishing in this ritual that was his personal baptism. And then he got back to work.

Who's next? He consulted his list.

Judson Kayne. AKA Periwinkle. What a case that guy is. He is a loose cannon if there ever was one. So is there motive here? To kill his own father? That could be. It is not unheard of for someone to kill one of their parents. And what is this with him carrying lipstick around. The message on the raincoat was written in lipstick. I wonder if Wunderlich knows about that lipstick that Ramsey claims he saw fall out of Jud's pocket. And the fingerprints on the raincoat. What if they are his? That would pretty well nail him. At least as the prime suspect.

On the other hand he is such a weakling. All puff and no dragon. He smokes a lot of pot, but I've never known that to be something that makes people weird enough to kill.

Goes by the name of Periwinkle sometimes? That's strange. Needs to get away from the Dale's farm for some reason, and looks like he went to Kay for help. Not illogical since she sort of mother-henned him to get him away from his father. But why didn't he just go to live with his mother if he didn't like it with dear old Dad? I think that I'd better find her and pay a visit. Yes I do need to do that. Meanwhile, let's just list him as a "possible".

Rex made his notes accordingly under "THINGS TO CHECK ON", underlining find and visit Jud's mother.

The water in the tub was getting close to room temperature, and the foam of the bubble bath had virtually disappeared, so Rex decided it was about time to either get out or let the water drain, refill the tub with hot water and start his bath anew. He decided to do both and stepped out and pulled the plug. Before he put on his terrycloth bathrobe, he caught a glimpse of himself in bathroom mirror and realized how much his skin resembled a prune. He then thought better of the continued bath and, wrapped in his robe, sat on the toilet lid and continued his review of suspects while the tub emptied itself with a gurgle.

"Owen Owens, you are up at bat," Rex called out, consulting his list. Motive? Well, nothing pops to mind right off, but he is Red's boss and makes a lot of money off the horses, Kay said. And she is afraid of the two because she thinks they are evil forces.

Like I told her, gambling wouldn't make him an evil force. But the three wives with one dead of unknown causes sure turns on the red lights on my dashboard. And here comes lipstick again. Can't have been Jud's, too long ago. Probably no connection, but the single letter "K" being left at two murder scenes is hard to ignore. Then, we don't know for sure if wife number three was murdered. Linked or not? Let's just put it down and see what comes out of it as we go along. And once more he wrote his concise thoughts in neat, clear writing on the pad.

Hummm. And Kay is scared of Ramsey and Owens enough to go AWOL and asks me to hide her. Hummm, mused Rex, and added another item to his notes.

Let me see who is batting cleanup on this list. Here we go. It's William Dale, the second baseman. Little Billy Dale. Big bucks. When the wife gets her picture in the paper and lists her name as Mrs. So & So and uses the husband's name, particularly a woman like Kay, then you know they are rich. With Owens, Billy owns the farm where everyone else works. Owns the horses that everyone is betting on. And his father was a college buddy and partner of Owen Owens. That's an interesting tie-in. Since he's known Owens all his life, it must be hard to be innocent of Owens's dealings. Motive? There has to be something really big, bigger than I can imagine, to make this guy a killer. Something really big with a lot of money involved. His reputation round town says he is a cool customer, and makes tons of money because he is always so calm. Not a likely suspect, unless...something big. Blackmail maybe? What would it be? List him as "not very likely, but...."

And the next in the batter's box is the ex-wife herself. The late victim's former wife, not the late wife of another suspect. Don't want to get these all these ex-wives mixed up. This one is alive, I presume. Talk about motive. From what I've been hearing about this guy Kayne, it wouldn't take much for his ex-wife to want to do him in. Maybe divorce wasn't enough, maybe he was hassling her and she just put a cap on it. Wouldn't be the first time. Well, she's on the list already under Jud's column, but I need to know more about her. And from her.

The terrycloth robe didn't offer much padding against the hard toilet seat lid, and Rex could feel its texture imprinting his bare butt. It was time to get some clothes on and finish the list over a cup of coffee and maybe a Danish at the Formica top table in his dining room.

He rooted through his dresser drawer trying to find some Jockey shorts. Damn boxers. Hate the damn things and that's all I can find in here. Sheila gave these to me years ago and I never wear 'em.

Finally he located a pair of Jockey shorts and a tee shirt and put them on. He couldn't find the slacks he wore the day before, and muttered "the hell with it" and went into the kitchen wearing just his underwear. He was impatient to get back on track with his assessments, and quickly poured yesterday's coffee into a pan and set it on the range. By the time he found a Danish that was still soft, the coffee was hot, boiling as a matter of fact, but his breakfast was ready, and he sat down at the table, ready to complete his task.

"Hoo-wee, this plastic seat is cold!" he exclaimed. Tough, Rex, get to it, he told himself and took a bite of the pastry.

Where was I? Here we go. Abe Willing. Abel N. Willing. Yeah, I'll bet. Fred said he was an agent with the State Horse Racing Board. He sure is interested in this case. Now why? Why is a Racing Board agent interested in a murder case? Why? Why? Why? No reason on the surface. So, there must be something else going on here. Rex's nose is smelling something. And it is not just this damned burned coffee. Rex stood up, momentarily bringing the chrome and plastic dinette chair with him as it stuck to the back of his legs. Released by gravity, it bounced an inch or two on its rubber crutch tips before it settled on the dining room floor.

That leaves Kay Sherman Dale for last. The best way to rule her out is to make her the number one suspect and then objectively list the reasons and then challenge each one. Can I find a motive here? Rex decided to stand and avoid sticking to the chair again, which tended to break his concentration. He stood behind the chair and spoke aloud as he added to his notes.

"One: Blackmail. Let's start with that. Earnest Kayne was blackmailing her. Ramsey and Owens are tied up with something crooked at the farm with the horses and Kay either found out about it from Jud or was a part of it. Kay was paying Earnest hush money and he got greedy and threatened to involve William Dale in a public accusation.

"Two: Shame. When Kay took Jud under her wing, she gradually found out things about her half-brother that would have damaged her society image if people learned they were related.

"Three: Indignation. Jud revealed to her how his father was treating him and had continually abused and ridiculed him. Something happened between Jud and Earnest that was the last straw and she killed Earnest to save Jud. That's a little thin, though.

"Four: Can't think of a fourth."

So I have Kay up on three counts for motive: blackmail, shame, and indignation. Oh, crap. Kay's not a killer. None of these things carry any weight. She would tell her husband if anyone tried to blackmail her, she's got more balls than to be that worried about social pressure, and she is too ambitious to throw it all away just for the sake of justice and bump someone off.

Of the seven I'd have to rank Ramsey at the top with Owens a close second. Then Jud tied with the ex-wife for the next slot followed by William Dale and then Willing with Kay last, if at all. I shouldn't even have put Willing on the list.

Rex closed up the note pad and retreated to his bedroom to put on some pants. He found those from last night hanging on the bedroom door knob, and put them on, sucking it in a little to get them buttoned. A shirt was hanging under the pants, and it passed the sniff test and so he put it on. He was about to put on his socks when he remembered that he was out of Desenex for his athlete's foot, and that he needed to go to the drug store and get some. That's when it hit him.

Drug store—pharmacy! And with that he smacked himself on the forehead. Well, it sure took you long enough. Rex expanded on his thoughts. Kayne was a pharmacist and that means drugs. And drugs mean a lot of different things to different people. Horse racing and drugs. Betting and horse racing. God only knows what they mean to poor Jud. But his thing is street drugs, not drug store drugs like our victim dispensed. I wonder what, other than aspirin, he had access to. I thought earlier that there was something out there that wasn't coming to mind. Maybe this is it. Stockton, it said in the paper. That is where Kayne worked as a pharmacist. The local cops have probably contacted their fuzz buddies in Stockton, but there's always the possibility that they've missed some personal angle. I need to get over there and sniff things out. I need to know more about who were friends of Earnest Kayne (if he had any) and who were his enemies. Better write it down with the other shit.

He took the socks and went back to his table and the chair he used earlier. He pulled it away from the table and sat down.

Can't stick to it with my pants on, he thought as he pulled on his socks. He turned to his note pad and the page with "THINGS TO CHECK ON", and saw his note to "find and visit Jud's mother". Yeah, looks like I've got my marching orders, all right. Now if I can just find my shoes.

He looked under the table and there they were, right where he had kicked them off last night when he got home and had his snack.

CHAPTER THIRTY

Last night at Sheila's, Rex had talked to Kay about Jud and his background, and he learned the name of Jud's mother, Marilyn Kayne, and that she worked as a nurse at the Kaiser Hospital in Oakland.

After his bubble bath Rex telephoned the Kaiser Hospital in Oakland and, eventually, he was connected with the nursing administration office. He left a message for Marilyn Kayne, explaining that he was a friend of Kay Dale's and that he had information about Marilyn's son. He suggested that she call to arrange a meeting.

To his surprise, Rex's phone rang thirty minutes later. "Mr. Nickels, this is Marilyn Kayne. I know that my ex-husband has been killed, and I know that Jud and his Aunt Kay are somehow missing. Can you tell me anything I don't know from the news?"

"Hello, Mrs. Kayne. Thanks for calling back." He decided to fib a little, no need to explain that Jud has slipped his protective custody. Not yet. "Jud is all right, he's in good hands with Kay. I've arranged for them to stay at the home of a friend of mine in Redwood City. I'm a private investigator."

A pause. "Well," said Marilyn, "maybe all that beats Jud sleeping under a bridge, which Lord knows he's done before. Why are he and Kay hiding? Did they have anything to do with Earnest's death?"

"I'm sure they didn't," replied Rex, again not being up-front regarding his own thoughts. "I think they're spooked by the whole thing and the press interest, and need a little time to reckon with what's happened."

Marilyn asked, "What can I do for you? I've already been interviewed by the Redwood City police. If you don't have any specific information for me about Jud's whereabouts or condition, I'm not sure we really have anything to talk about, Mr. Nickels."

"I can't say more over the phone. I would like to drive over and meet with you. I can be a little more specific about events as I see them, including Jud, and I hope you can give me some insight that will allow me to help Jud in some way. And, incidentally, to help Kay too, who's an old friend of mine."

"Maybe there's no harm in meeting. I've been estranged from Jud for a long time but he's still my son and now he's fatherless. Do you think you could get over to Oakland by around noon today? I could meet you during my lunch break."

Rex calculated. "It's about ten thirty now. I don't see why I couldn't get there by noon. Where can we meet?"

Marilyn gave Rex the address of Sammy's, a hamburger joint on Piedmont Avenue, a couple of blocks from the hospital, with directions on how to get there, and said goodbye.

Rex found his sport coat and put on a tie, making himself a little spiffier than he ordinarily would in his daily routine. He set off in the Monza, top up for freeway driving, found his way to 101, and proceeded northward to the turnoff to the San Mateo-Hayward Bridge. He was a little reluctant to take this route, as he was unsure about how he would connect to get to Oakland. He was more familiar with the way through San Francisco and the Bay Bridge. But this was what Marilyn recommended, so he thought it best to comply. As it turned out he needn't have worried. On the opposite shore, the bridge route continued as a freeway, and after a short distance a big green sign directed him to Oakland. He negotiated a tight curving ramp and found himself on Freeway 17, "The Nimitz".

Rex pressed on in the tight traffic. "Lordy," he blurted out loud, "I've never seem so many trucks. Thank God I put the top up—a little less diesel to breathe." The rush carried him past exits for Hayward, San Leandro, the Oakland Airport and a bunch of numbered Oakland streets. Then he could see the tall buildings getting closer and a sign announcing Oak Street. Recalling this name from Marilyn's directions, he took the exit. He released a loud sigh. It was wonderful to leave the freeway madness behind. With Marilyn's directions in mind, Rex drove coolly up Oak Street and along the shore of Lake Merritt, eventually reaching MacArthur Boulevard. With the tall, all-aluminum tower of Kaiser Hospital in view, he made a right on Piedmont Avenue and found Sammy's, the designated meeting spot. He was at the end of his trip, finally, and was delighted to find free parking behind the place.

He entered the joint and surveyed the clientele. It appeared to be roughly split between neighborhood old-timers and youngish folks in medical attire—blues, greens, whites, or simply I.D. badges. Several of the "whites" were attractive women of a certain degree of maturity. He liked the looks of a blonde wearing white slacks and shoes with a light blue sweater, seated alone, and he took a step in her direction. But on the next step he had eye-contact with an auburn-tressed female, also alone, in similar attire, but with a lime-colored jacket. She tentatively raised a hand. Rex walked over to her table.

"Marilyn?" he inquired.

"I thought you might be Rex. Maybe because you weren't wearing an I.D. and you looked under 60. Please sit down," Marilyn said, offering her hand in greeting.

They ordered their choices of burgers and drinks, his with fries, hers with none. Marilyn opened the conversation. "So tell me what's up with Jud. You say he's staying somewhere with Kay?"

Rex figured he had to own up. "Well, he was, I had it all set up. But he went sorta stir crazy and ran off. Truth is, we're not sure where he is right now. He has connections with a local biker community, and we think he might have hooked up with them. But we have his bike under lock and key, and I don't think he will be able to stand being without it. I take it he hasn't tried to contact you?"

"No, but I wouldn't really expect it. He flew my coop, right after barely graduating from Oakland Tech seven years ago. He thought he would do better, have a freer, easier life with his father out in Stockton. Not that that worked out so well—I think he's been more or less on the road for more time than he has been with Earnest. And I think you're right about his attachment to his bike. So I'm not going to worry too much for now—I expect you and Kay will see him again soon.

"Jud calls me once or twice a year," Marilyn continued. "He's come back to my place a couple of times for a few days. I know about Earnest's surprise relationship with Kay Dale and her father. I haven't met Kay—would you say she cares for Jud? Can she help straighten out his life?"

Rex smiled. "That would be like trying to straighten a pretzel. But yes, I do think she wants to help him, and probably will be able to once they've worked their way through the current mess."

Marilyn made a little shrug, took a sip of her coffee, and responded. "So, okay. Why are they hiding out? Are they suspects in Earnest's death? Earnest was a son of a bitch, a failure as a husband and father. But it's hard to imagine his son, or even his half-sister, doing him in. Incidentally, I was on duty at the hospital here on the night of his death. The Redwood City police have taken my statement and verified it. Why don't Kay and Jud come forward and tell what they know, if anything?"

Rex nodded, "I agree that they need to speak up. That's assuming they are innocent, which I can't help but believe. I plan to push in that direction, soon as we get Jud back in the flock. So now, you've made clear your high regard for Earnest. What else should I know?"

"Maybe you need to know that he was the same self-serving bastard as a business partner to Doug McCreary that he was as a family man. I think it would be worth your while to talk to him out in Stockton. I'll give you the address and phone number."

Rex and Marilyn finished their meal with a little light small talk. She gave him the contact information for McCreary and general directions on how to get to Stockton and to McCreary's location. In the end Marilyn said to Rex, "Please keep me posted on Jud, will you? And, for what it's worth, I think you're probably a good guy. I wouldn't mind looking into that idea a little more. I hope we get to meet again."

Rex was caught a little off-guard by these last words. He could only mumble. "Well, yeah, uh, me too. Yeah, I'll sure be in touch. Well, then, thanks for everything. I've got to be off."

Marilyn walked with Rex to his car (which, to his pleasure, she admired) and pointing, she said, "Take Forty-first here five blocks to the signal light, turn right and keep going till you come to the tunnel under the Oakland Hills. After that, you're on your way to Stockton. Just follow Highways 24 and 4. It's something like fifty miles. Have a good trip. And let me know how it goes."

As he was following her directions to Stockton, he regained his composure and, reflecting on his encounter with Marilyn, thought to himself, That was something. Not what I expected! How much did I really learn? Maybe I told more than I got back? I wonder.

CHAPTER THIRTY-ONE

Coming out of the tunnel from Oakland, Rex was astounded by the emerald green hills, steeper and greener than any he had seen out toward San Gregorio. As he proceeded he could see modern houses clinging to the hillsides. He passed Walnut Creek, which appeared to be a prosperous little city he hadn't been aware of. Further along, where he turned off onto Highway 4, he saw another burgeoning suburb, Concord. And that wasn't all. Soon there was Pittsburg, Antioch, then Brentwood, all with active construction of housing tracts. Past Antioch the highway was reduced to two lanes. The flatness of the landscape and the straightness of the roads told him he was now in the San Joaquin Valley, no longer in the hilly, waterside Bay Area.

At lunch, Marilyn Kayne had told him that when he arrived in Stockton, he should stay on Highway 4 until he came to California Street, then turn north and travel about a mile to St. Joseph's Hospital. Across the street, at the corner of Chestnut Street, he would find the small pharmacy run by Doug McCreary, the former partner of Earnest.

Rex got to Stockton by about three thirty in the afternoon and found the shop as directed. Unfortunately, he discovered he had to pay a meter to get parked. Entering the small store, which really was a basic pharmaceutical dispensary, not the all-purpose drugstore that was becoming the norm, Rex saw behind the counter a pleasant looking, sandy-haired man of about his own age. As luck would have it, the man wore a name tag, "Douglas J. McCreary, Pharmacist". Rex introduced himself, offered his card, explained that he was seeking background information on Earnest Kayne, and that he had been referred by Marilyn Kayne.

McCreary came from behind the counter and gestured toward a small customer waiting area. He offered Rex a chair and turned another around and sat facing Rex. McCreary paused in thought, then shrugged.

"I'll try to help you out. Marilyn was a good friend in the old days. Of course I saw the news on TV. But you're behind the police, you know, they've already interviewed me, asked me where I was that night. In fact I was at a church board meeting, so there are plenty of solid, godly folks who'll vouch for me.

"Earnest and I were in pharmacy school together, here in town, at UOP, the University of the Pacific. Smart guy, he already had a degree in chemistry. We set up shop together here in Stockton, after we graduated from UOP. I borrowed from my parents, and he was able to use money that Marilyn had socked away. They married young, and after she completed her nurses' training, she worked hard to support him while he got his pharmacy degree and license. We did well and prospered for several years. The medical industry was booming in this town as elsewhere, and we got our share. The time came when we got an irresistible offer from one of the big new drug chains, the ones with the big-box stores."

Rex nodded. "I appreciate everything you're telling me. Please go on."

McCreary continued, his mouth set in a thin line, "To make a long story short, I pretty much let Earnest handle the negotiations with the chain people. I thought both he and I were going to end up in fat city. Well, I guess he did. Didn't work out so well for me." McCreary's hands gripped the arms of his chair and he let out a rush of breath. He continued in an agitated voice. "Fact is, he plain screwed me out of a big interest in the business. Legal counsel hasn't been much help to me. So here I sit." He glanced away momentarily and shifted in the chair, more relaxed. "But in

160

the long run I can't complain. I've been able to build up this little shop in a great location across from a big hospital. I'm independent, and I think that's better than he came out of it. So, I do think Earnest was a shit-head, and I don't miss him now he's dead. But I wouldn't have wished him that kind of harm."

"Thanks so much for being frank with me," Rex said. "I wonder if I could get you to comment on his private life. I've met his son, Jud. I think he's maybe basically good, but maybe not too bright, and very confused. I've also met with Marilyn. I'd say she's very solid and probably tried her best to be a good mother to Jud."

"Oh yes," McCreary replied. "I agree. I'm sure Marilyn tried hard as a mother, and she was a single mother for most of the time. My wife and I saw Earnest and Marilyn socially in the early days, during and after college. It became apparent he was making life pretty miserable for her. He didn't pay much attention to Jud. Then after high school the kid came here to live with Earnest. But he was in and out, still not getting much fatherly attention. Ran with bad crowds, supposedly got mixed up in some drug deals. To his credit he was able to get work caring for horses at spreads around the area here. So he's not all bad. I don't even think he's as dumb as he might appear. Well, too bad. Now it looks like the kid's a suspect? He's on the lam? I don't think he had much use for his father. I didn't either. But I couldn't have killed him, and I don't think Jud would have any more than I would. It's a sad case. I hope things work out for Jud."

Again, Rex thanked McCreary for his time and frankness. He asked to be called if anything else relevant came to mind. McCreary agreed he would, showing he still held Rex's card. They said goodbye and Rex left the store.

Rex was on his way back to Redwood City by four thirty. He was glad he wouldn't have to spend the night in the Central Valley, and figured he should be home by seven or so. It had been a busy day, many miles covered. But he felt he had gained some insights into Jud's family life, and he was curiously happy to have met Marilyn.

CHAPTER THIRTY-TWO

Rex went out on his front porch to get the morning Tribune, yawned and scratched his backside as he bent over to get the paper. As he came up he realized he was in his underwear and in plain sight of anyone nearby. A quick scan of the street assured him he was alone and with a sigh of relief he went back in to read the news. Once inside, he finished his scratch. Then he sat down at the dining room table with a freshly brewed cup of coffee and began to read. Below the fold on the front page of the paper was a headline that caught his attention.

Violence At Peace Rally

Flag burned, demonstrators jailed, later released

Redwood City police were called to the Sequoia High School campus Monday night about 10:30 PM when a peace rally being held on one of the school's tennis courts turned violent. Protestors against the war in Vietnam were making speeches and singing songs without incident when an American flag was set on fire and fistfights broke out among members of the crowd that had gathered for the event. "Those hippies have no respect. They are cowards and don't want to fight for their freedom," said a man with a bandage on his head, who declined to identify himself. "They just want to kill our babies," screamed activist Sarah Robustout as she was being escorted to a police car.

Police Captain Fred Wunderlich said, "People just let themselves get out of control. As soon as we got them all to the station, and calmed down and identified, they were released on their promises that they all go home." Asked if he knew who was responsible for setting the flag on fire, Wunderlich said it could have been any one of a number of people, some of whom were seen departing just as the police arrived at the campus. "There were some folks that must have decided to leave early, and I wish we could have questioned them, but we needed to stop the fighting first."

When asked for further information about those that left early, Wunderlich would only say that some were bikers who went west, and others were observed in a bus with psychedelic markings all over it that was seen heading toward El Camino Real, but was not further observed as to direction of travel. "That's all the spotlights on the cruisers could pick up through the trees. There are a lot of bikers and a lot of hippies around here, so God only knows which ones they were. I sure don't. But I aim to find out."

"Yeah, Fred, and you probably will. Bet you never thought you'd be chasin' hippies in buses and hoods on motorcycles when you signed up. But there it is. Wish I could help," Rex said to the paper. There may be a lot of hippies, but I haven't seen that many around here with school bus all painted up in the 'psychedelic' style everyone talks about. Pretty hard to hide one of those on the street, it would seem to me. Fred will figure that out quick enough, and start lookin' and askin'. Which is what I ought to do about young Judson Kayne. I need to start lookin' 'n' askin', he thought.

Rex began to shift away from his morning paper mood to his investigative persona, and the wheels started to turn. Maybe Fred and I have more in common than being ugly. Maybe we are looking for the same thing. Or maybe we should be looking in the same place for different things. Judson Kayne Periwinkle. Hmmm.

Wannabe biker. Smokes a lot of Mary. No one knows where he is. Probably he doesn't know where he is. But between the two, between bikers and potheads, he's less likely to try to be with Hell's Angels types than he is with Timothy Leary types. Okay. That narrows it to Wunderlich looking for a psychedelic school bus and I am looking for a pothead that might be somewhere near one of those.

So, Rex, find where the school bus parks. Find the school bus, find the kid. That's my path. Who would I know that would know where those people park their cars, where they park their asses. Same place: that' the working theory here. Hmm. Rosie Budner probably knows, but won't tell me. Abe Willing I'm sure knows, but I can't ask him. Same with Wunderlich. Can't tip them that I am involved with anything Kayne. Kay might have heard something from Jud at the motel, but all she could come up with was his mother in Oakland. Sheila! She has always known more than I expected her to. A bitch at times, but a smart bitch. I can't think of anyone else. Why not her?

Rex dialed her number and his hunch paid off.

"Glad you are at least smart enough to call Mama when your brain runs dry. What do I know about hippie hangouts and psychedelic school buses? More than I want to. You remember 'The Big LaDonn', the lady wrestler we used to watch on TV? Remember her tattoos?"

"Who could forget tattoos like that? What a pair!" quipped Rex.

"Look, smart ass, do you want my help or not?"

"Yeah, go on. Just joking. The fist in the middle of her chest was pretty scary".

"I always thought it looked like it was holding up her bra, or coming out of her wrestling suit to smash somebody," said Sheila, thinking back.

"Get to the point, Sheila."

"Well, one time when I was getting my hair fixed, the woman next to me and I got to talking about 'The Big LaDonn' and her tattoos, and I asked where does a broad like that get a tattoo? Especially where she has it? 'She owns a bar about three blocks from here,' the stylist said. 'She gets her hair cut here about three times a year. Tough woman. The name of her place is some something Saloon. I went there once, but there were a lot of strange-acting hippies out front and this weird school bus with strange painting on the sides, and I didn't stop.' "

Rex's antenna was on full alert. "So she didn't go into the bar and ask about her tattoos?"

"I just told you, no!" said Sheila. "I don't blame her. That wrestler, she's a weird woman. All those muscles. And my hair dresser is like me, we can't stand druggies, and she said it looked like they must hang out there, around the tattooed lady's bar. She said it looked like nothing but trouble. So, no. She didn't go in and didn't talk to her. Now is that all, Sherlock? I've told you what I know."

"That's enough for me. Except, what street did your stylist say that bar is on?" asked Rex.

"I think it was on Main, pretty close to Broadway. You gonna' get a friggin' tattoo?"

"I just want to see if Jud has been around there, that's all. I think he may be with some hippies. Thanks for the info." And he hung up and headed out looking for a bar on Main, near Broadway, with the name "Saloon" on it.

It really wasn't that hard to find the bar. The name "The Round-Up Saloon" was apparent from the red neon sign over the door, although time and lack of attention had taken their toll and it now read " he ound-Up S loon". But that, combined with the presence of two long- haired young men in tie-dyed shirts and pants with frayed cuffs leaning against the front of the building, was enough to convince Rex that he had the right place. He parked a few doors down, in front of a used furniture store, and for once wished he didn't drive a convertible. He locked its doors anyway, knowing that the fabric top was an easy target for mischief. He drew himself up as much as he could to his full height and walked his old MP walk to the saloon door. The hippies looked him up and down, took drags on their cigarettes and turned away in fake disinterest. Rex, for his part, tried his best to look like a cop and make them as uncomfortable as possible.

Once inside, it took a minute for his eyes to adjust to the darkness. Most of the illumination came from the various beer signs above the bar and scattered on the walls. There was no one behind the bar and no customers at the bar or the wood tables. He was alone with the smells of stale beer and cigarettes, body odors and marijuana smoke that were permanently impregnated into the ceiling, floors and walls of the room. A beaded curtain near a back corner of the room rattled and parted as a large woman wearing workout sweats and black Buddy Holly eyeglasses appeared.

"I don't start serving until ten o'clock," said the woman, eyeing Rex suspiciously.

"And I don't start drinking until after noon. I didn't come here for that," replied Rex evenly.

"Are you a cop? New? Where are the regular guys? They were here just last week. I'm within regulations. What the hell do you want?" she demanded in a less than solicitous tone.

"Whoa, lady. Just want some information about a young man I am looking for. That's all."

"What kind of information?" said the woman, "And who are you with anyway and what is your name?"

"You ask a lot of questions at the same time, don't you? Relax, I'm not a cop. My name is Rex Nickels. I'm a private investigator." Rex tried a little friendliness, because she was obviously hostile, and returning the hostility wouldn't help him find Jud. Not with someone so obviously into the tough gal role.

"Here's my card."

"If you are what you say you are, I guess it's okay. But make it quick. I have things to do.Have a seat," she said, and motioned to one of the dingy tables nearby. She joined him saying, "I'm LaDonnie Mobley. I own this place. Who are you looking for and why? And why here?"

"The 'who' is a young guy who goes by Jud Kayne, or Jud Periwinkle. A hippie type who can't quite figure out whether he is...ah, he...what he is. Loves to ride a motorcycle and works with horses off and on. As to why I am looking for him, let's just say that's not important to this conversation. And as to why I am looking here, well, it's kind of complicated."

"Complicated? Do I look dumb? Go on, but speak slowly," LaDonnie said sarcastically.

"My ex, Sheila, talked to her hairdresser who said she drove by here once and saw some hippies hanging around in front with their painted-up school bus. I don't know much about what hippies do or where they go, so I thought I might as well start here and see what I can find out. It's as simple as that. Can you help me?" Rex continued to play the role of the innocent, open- faced searcher. And it worked, to a degree.

"We have some hippie, as you call them, customers in here. I don't really care who comes in as long as they pay their tab. There is a bunch that comes in. I call 'em the Peanuts bunch. Seem to be led by a guy they call 'The Saint' who drives an old school bus that was yellow a long time ago. Now it has psychedelic painting all over it. They always go out back and sit at the picnic table out there. They smoke a lot of grass, so I prefer they stay out there. I always have to watch them when it comes time to leave. They were in here Monday and tried to leave without payin', the shitheads."

"Was one of them kind of skinny and whiney?" asked Rex, trying to find a description that didn't include the word 'effeminate'.

"Oh, you mean the one they call Pig Pen?"

"I don't know. Could be."

The name seemed to stir up something in LaDonnie. "There is one who's always as nervous as a whore in church. Damn hippie pot smokin' candy ass. They called him Pig Pen last night, but I have heard him called Winkie, or Periwinkle before too. Always looking for sympathy. Last night especially."

Rex knew that this must be Jud and that his non-confrontational strategy with the woman wrestler turned bar owner had paid off. "Where do you think they went from here?"

"How in the fuck would I know? Or care? I got 'em to pay, and they went off to God-knows-where in that stupid school bus of theirs."

"No idea? They didn't say anything that you might have overheard?" Rex was pushing it.

"That's all you're gonna' get. I have to get back to work," LaDonnie said and stood up, towering over Rex even though she was three feet away. And she quickly strode across the room and was through the beaded curtain before Rex could get out of his chair.

"Thanks," Rex blurted, and managed to head for the exit, a little stunned at her quick departure.

Just before he reached the door, the curtain parted and LaDonnie peered out and said, "The old Sequoia Hotel. I've heard they hang out there sometimes. You might try that." And she was gone.

When Rex reached the street, the hippies who had been there were gone too. His Monza was where he left it, untouched. Rex got in and drove off and said out loud, "That broad has a big problem about something I don't even want to know about, but she did give me some clues."

CHAPTER THIRTY-THREE

When he left the Round-Up, Rex had the intention of following up with a visit to the Sequoia Hotel, just down the street. But there was no immediate hurry, and he was still a little antsy about the health of the Monza if it were left parked on the street in the vicinity of Main and Broadway. So he drove few blocks back to the relative security of his own driveway, left the car, and strolled up to the Break-Thyme Cafe. After grabbing a bowl of Chili Three Ways-Peoria Style (extra onions) and a bottle of Acme, Rex walked across Broadway to the once-proud, still-fabled Sequoia.

The three-story building wrapped the southwest corner of the Broadway and Main intersection. With its projecting classical cornice, it was the largest and most imposing building this side of the Court House. The arched, classical entry faced the corner, and the curved wall above was decorated with a design of redwoods rendered in still-brilliant terra-cotta. Above the roof a steel framework held rusty letters that proclaimed "HOTEL $3 up". Rex knew the building well from his vantage as an across-the-street tenant. He had been around town since he was a kid, and he was aware that the establishment had seen better days. It just hadn't been able to keep up with the newer hostelries, now located along El Camino or 101, with ample parking and plumbing that worked.

In the sparsely furnished lobby Rex found Scruff Barnes behind the reception desk, leafing through the Racing Form. Scruff was the manager, daytime clerk, house detective and part owner of the hotel, as well as being a top-floor resident. Rex was acquainted with Scruff from the neighborhood. He had a reputation for knowing what was happening in Redwood City and could be counted upon to be aware of any vulnerabilities or shenanigans attributable to county supervisors, city councilmen, police and sheriff's officers, and other local officials.

"Good morning, Rex! Welcome to the Western Waldorf," called Scruff with a grin. "How's the investigation biz?"

Rex shook Scruff's hand across the desk. A good, firm shake, not like some hippies he'd met. The man's lined face had about a week's growth of reddish beard, and his hazel eyes made strong contact with Rex's. "Actually, things are popping, for a change," Rex responded to the query. "I came over to ask you about some local characters who may have some connection with a case I'm working on. Earlier I was at the Round-Up talking to LaDonnie Mobley. She said you'd probably know something of the comings and goings of these kids — she calls them the Peanuts Bunch."

"Ah, LaDonnie, my good friend and neighbor." Scruff said. "Known her forever, we go way back. Tougher than an old boot, but a good heart. She recently took over the Round-Up and seems to be getting it squared away after some rough times there. The Peanuts Bunch? I haven't heard that, but I bet I know who she means. The kids in the painted-up old bus. I see them around all the time. Maybe as many as a dozen of them, all skinny, long dirty hair, jeans, beads. Mostly boys, some girls, though it's pretty hard to tell which is which. I see them here on the sidewalk, sometimes making music with guitars, recorders, drums, castanets and such. They wander in sometimes.

"Maybe I'll let them stay in the lobby a while if it's cold or rainy. But I'm not going to rent them rooms—I have too much past experience with kids overcrowding and trashing the rooms

170

and wrecking the plumbing. Plus I think most of them are under-age, especially the girls. So I keep my distance. I don't like them to park the bus out front—could give the place a bad name—so sometimes I have to shoo them away."

Rex asked, "What about the police—do they give the kids any trouble?"

Barnes shook his head. "No—they treat 'em pretty much as I do. They want to see them keep moving, no congregating, and keeping the bus from cluttering the streets, particularly in the business district."

"LaDonnie told me they had a leader?" said Rex. "An older guy, called him The Saint?"

"Oh, yeah. That's right, The Saint," Barnes confirmed. "Tall, dark guy, fortyish, with a beard and a shaved head. He looks reasonably clean and groomed, but is usually dressed in a sort of kaftan—you know like an Arab or something. I've met him. A smart guy. I guess you'd call him spiritual, kind of priest-like. A little phony in ways, though. I've let him stay here a few times, but making sure he doesn't have any of the kids with him. I don't know where he stays most of the time—maybe in the bus. I haven't peeked inside—I'm too squeamish. I think maybe he has a steadying influence on the kids," Barnes smiled. "I suspect he smokes pot with the kids. But on the other hand, I don't think any of the gang is on hard stuff. Anyway, The Saint's clearly in charge. And so far as I can see, there must be some turnover in the kids—often I see new faces, and I miss some that I've come to recognize." Barnes lifted his hands in a broad gesture. "I like to think that means that they've gone back to their homes."

Rex commented, "Sounds like you have some respect for what they're doing."

"Well," Scruff said, scratching his chin, "you got to give a little consideration to the times. I'm sure some kids have bad situations at home, and they could fall into worse company. They have their own little community going on the bus."

Rex inquired, "I wonder if you ever noticed a kid that LaDonnie said was called Pig Pen or sometimes Winkie—kind of nervous, girly-like?"

"You know, that could fit a number of them. I haven't heard those names. But, yeah, I have seen one that acts a little sissy-fied. I think he's pretty new to the bunch. Yeah, I think I've heard him called Periwinkle. Is that who you're looking for in your investigation?"

"That would be him. Any idea where they are now—have you seen the bus today or any stray kids?"

Scruff replied, "I think I heard them talking about taking a ride out to the coast, a little outing, like. Maybe Half Moon Bay or thereabouts—maybe San Gregorio."

Rex thanked Scruff profusely and promised to buy him a drink at the Round-Up the next time they crossed paths.

CHAPTER THIRTY-FOUR

Rex headed over to his house after taking leave of Scruff. He ducked inside to get the car keys and use the facility, but carefully avoided looking at the answering machine for fear there would be a message from Sheila.

Once relieved, he locked the house, fired up the Monza, and headed out, top down, for the trip to the ocean. He reminisced about his recent trip through the redwoods to San Gregorio, but decided he needed to get out to Half Moon Bay pronto. He figured the kids on the bus would have gotten there in the wee hours of Tuesday morning, so they would have about a 36 hour lead on him. Sensing at this time of day the freeways would be drivable, he picked up Highway101 near downtown, headed up to San Mateo, looped on to Highway 92 and up and over the hills. After crossing Interstate 280. Highway 92 dropped to two lanes and made its way across a narrow isthmus between the upper and lower Crystal Springs Reservoirs. These bodies stored the San Francisco water supply, after the water had passed through giant pipes from the Sierra Nevada, almost 200 miles to the east.

Rex always shuddered a bit as he recalled that this valley marked the location of the San Andreas Fault, and its lurking potential for creating earthquake havoc. A few minutes later Rex crossed Skyline Boulevard, at the spine of the peninsula, and began his gradual descent to sea level.

The highway curved back and forth between loaf-shaped green hills which afforded little sense of approach to the ocean. But suddenly the topography leveled out, and the scene was dominated by shades of blue, white, and gray, with no discernible line between water and sky. The place he came to was little more than a scattering of low buildings, mostly light stucco, stretched thinly along a few streets parallel to the beach. This town, Half Moon Bay, was actually the southern-most of a chain of settlements that stretched about seven miles along the namesake bay and Pillar Point harbor. Rex had only passing familiarity with the area, but he knew that most of the accommodations were modest and scattered. Half Moon Bay and its neighbors constituted an extended beach town, but the area had never become a real tourist mecca, the kind with high-rise hotels and condominiums. Ocean views were grand and plentiful, but the water was cold, the surf rough, and the beaches rocky. And there were sharks of course.

Where 92 met Highway 1, known locally as Cabrillo Highway, Rex hesitated and flipped a mental coin, which somehow came up heads, prompting him to turn right and head north toward Point Montara on the first leg of his search. Through the hamlets of El Granada, Princeton, Moss Beach and Montara, he noted a dozen or so motels along with two camp grounds that might attract the Peanuts Bunch, but no signs of their bus.

Among the motels with campgrounds surveyed by Rex in passing was the Blue Sky Motel, a mile north of Half Moon Bay. Had Rex stopped and inquired, he might have learned that The Saint and the gang had spent last night, Tuesday night, in the camp site to the rear of the motel. They had checked out before noon on Wednesday because the site was previously booked by a bunch of surfers for the next three nights. The Saint's people had actually arrived at the coast about two o'clock on Tuesday morning. They had been able to crash until sun-up on a secluded beach, without being rousted.

Headed back down the highway toward Half Moon Bay, Rex spotted a dock-side cafe at Pillar Point Harbor, and he decided he needed coffee and maybe a slice of pie just to keep him going. Having been served those restoratives with a smile, he was relaxing, enjoying the view of Pillar Point through the cafe's big windows, when a bus lumbered up to the side of the adjacent gas station. Not the "Peanuts" bus, not that brightly decorated, but its turquoise paint was quirky enough to pique Rex's interest. Clearly it was no longer a school bus or any kind of public conveyance.

A man with long hair wrapped with a bandana got out of the bus, raised the hood and appeared to be doing some repairs. Rex paid for his coffee and pie and wandered over.

"Nice rig you got there. Must be good for getting away to the beach with all your stuff."

"Yup," came the reply. "She gets me and my buddies around up and down the coast, wherever the big waves are. How-do. They call me Angel, don't ask why. Old crate's been overheating a bit. Maybe I need a new thermostat."

"Angel, eh? Happy to meet you. My Name's Rex. So, do you stay overnight in the bus?" Rex asked. "Can you just park at the beaches or do you pull in and stay at a motel or some place?"

Angel shifted his bandana a bit to catch some sweat on his forehead. "We always try to get free parking, but sometimes we get rousted by the rangers. Then we might go to a campground if there's one nearby. In these parts we like to stop at a campground down near the south end of Half Moon. Hudson's it's called—don't know why—it's run by a guy name of Gonzales. But they take care of us okay, and it don't cost much."

Rex nodded. "Sounds good," he said. "I'll remember that when I'm camping. You know, your name being Angel, that's a funny coincidence. I happen to know a guy named The Saint. Gets around with a bunch of kids in a bus kinda like yours, older vehicle, not in such good shape, painted with all kinds of colors and symbols. You ever run into those guys?"

Angel grinned. "Yeah, yeah, I know The Saint. You know, we hang out at the same beaches and places. A few times we've been at Hudson's at the same time. Good guy, smart as heck. Good pal to those kids."

Rex then said a fast goodbye to his new friend Angel, got in his car and hustled on down the highway till he spotted a small sign announcing Hudson's Campground by the side of the road, just south of the main part of the town of Half Moon Bay. He turned the Monza into a rutted gravel driveway, and stopped at an Airstream with the word Office painted by the door.

A youngish woman in jeans and tank top stepped out of the trailer and approached Rex's car. "Help ya?"

Rex asked, "Mr. Gonzales around?"

The woman told Rex that Gonzales, her husband, had run into town on some errands, and should be back soon. She said if he was looking for a place to camp, they were full. He might have to look for a motel.

Rex explained that his friend Angel had told him about the campground, and that he was trying to catch up with their mutual friend, The Saint, who Angel said had stopped here before. He described the bus and the general make-up of the Peanuts Gang.

"Well, don't that beat all? They were just here a couple of hours ago! Had to turn them away. We got no space for the next few days. Too bad. The waves are coming in big and all the surfers are gathering. So we had to say no to The Saint and his friends. They headed on down toward San Gregorio. But I don't know what kinda luck they're gonna find there, either."

"Thanks," said Rex, and headed on down Highway 1, dipping into a few by-ways and checking the state beaches at San Gregorio and Pomponio. The afternoon was waning. Hell, he thought, I'm not gonna chase them all the way to Santa Cruz. They could be anywhere by now. He pointed the Monza back toward San Gregorio and called it a day.

CHAPTER THIRTY-FIVE

"**H**ey, Saint, when are we going to stop? I'm tired of riding," yelled Frodo from the back of the bus.

"Peace, brother. And patience. That goes for all of us," replied The Saint over his shoulder as he pulled onto a roadside parking area on a bluff overlooking the ocean and stopped the school bus. "I believe it is time we counseled."

"Where are we gonna' stop for the night? I'm hungry and I'm getting strung out," whined Charlie Brown.

"Yeah, we need some weed," said Frodo.

"It's getting late," said a muffled voice from the back.

"Peace brothers and sisters, peace. Come on out of the bus and let us sit in our peace circle and look out at the water. Come, come."

The Saint herded the little band of "free people" out of the bus and to a nearby spot where all could sit, yoga style and see the ocean and the horizon line.

Once seated, he stood before them with his robe blowing in the breeze, its beads softly rattling, and as he had done with them many times raised the hand with strange markings on it and made his odd gesture that was more of an X than a cross.

"X marks the spot for what? We can't stay here. Lookin' at endless water ain't gonna' help us eat," complained Linus.

"You said the Holy Bus wanted to go to the Blue Sky Motel, and we stayed there last night, just like you said, Saint," Charlie Brown chipped in.

"And they are full up for tonight. And so is everywhere else, my friends." The Saint tried to calm the restless group. "Even the camp grounds are full."

"Tell us the truth. You always say to believe in the truth," said Lucy.

"Yeah, the truth!" called Jack and Jill in unison.

There was silence for a few minutes while The Saint looked out to sea. Then, with a sigh, he turned back to his "free people" and said quietly, "I don't know where else to go."

"Ask the Holy Bus. Maybe it knows," cracked Frodo, and everyone giggled nervously.

"I know where," a quiet voice said. It was Judson Kayne. "We can go to my place."

"Oh sure, like you have a place, man. Anywhere," smirked Frodo, and everyone chuckled.

"And where would that be, Pig Pen?" asked The Saint with a mixture of relief and apprehension.

"It's not far from here. It is my family's farm. It is where I work, sometimes. With the horses," Jud answered.

"You mean you have a job?" Frodo was incredulous.

"Like I said. I work with the horses there. Some are thorough-breds. It's not far from here. On the road to La Honda, just past San Gregorio."

"Well, back in the bus, my fine group of friends. We have a destination. At last!" said The Saint, and they a scrambled into their psychedelic transport.

"Ah yes, the Holy Bus," muttered Jack.

Jud sat just behind the driver's seat so he could direct The Saint as he drove the bus.

"Where to, Pig Pen? You said the road to La Honda?" asked The Saint.

"Yes, we passed it on our way here. It was on the left. And please don't call me Pig Pen. My name is Judson."

"Okay, Judson," replied The Saint. "Can I make that just Jud?"

"Judson" was his answer.

Someone called out, "What about food? I'm still hungry and getting hungrier."

"We can stop off in San Gregorio and get some groceries. Before we get there, someone needs to take up a collection," said The Saint as he headed back north for the turn off onto La Honda Road.

•••

Red Ramsey had put the last horse up in the stable for the night when he saw something strange coming up the drive to Hillandale Farms. It was an old school bus painted with crazy designs in garish colors. The sight brought on a mixture of rage and curiosity that led Ramsey to the end of the drive where he stood with his hands raised in front of him, signaling the intruder to go no further.

"What the hell do you want? You hippies ain't welcome here!" he yelled so everyone could hear him, even though the bus had stopped within three feet of where he stood blocking the roadway.

Red could see The Saint though the windshield giving his strange hand signal, which only served to confuse and anger Red even more. Then the bus doors opened and Jud stepped out.

"What the hell?" Red shouted. "Are you one of them, or did you just hitch a ride or something?"

"We need a place to camp for the night, Red," said Jud.

"Shit, we? Then you are one of them."

"They're my friends. We just need a place to stay. I didn't think Aunt Kay would mind," said Jud, pulling a little rank, and coming closer to Red so their conversation would be less audible. As he did, The Saint appeared on the steps to the bus, repeating his sign.

"Who is the Jesus guy that keeps giving me the finger?" Red's eyes narrowed.

"Oh, that's just The Saint. It's his bus, I think, and he's sort of the leader. I am not really a member or anything, but they are friends I hang out with once in a while, and they did me a favor last week. And he's not giving you the finger. I think that means peace or something like that."

"So the favor they did was to hide you out from the cops, huh," Red was quick to figure out that part. "What are you running from, anyway? Everyone's been looking for you. And your aunt as well."

"Come on, Red," Jud almost whispered, "let us come on in. Just one night. In the pasture."

Red weighed the situation and figured that he had little to lose and maybe a lot to gain by letting them stay. If nothing else, it would keep the focus on Jud and Kay. And he would report them being there in the morning, after they had gone, saying he didn't know they spent the night.

"Okay, shit-for-brains," he said quietly. "You and the potheads can stay. But only if you don't set any fires and you leave the toilet in the stalls clean. And if you leave first thing in the morning and tell anyone that asks that I didn't know you were here. And park that friggin' psycho bus behind the barn where no one can see it from the road. Got all that?"

"Thanks, Red. And would you do me one more favor? And not ask why?" Jud was going out on a limb, but he felt he had to.

"Haven't I friggin' done enough?" Red said, and then thought about Kay being his boss and Jud's aunt. "What is it?"

"Call me Judson. When I go back over there, just say, 'It's a deal,' or 'Go on in.' Something like that. But be sure that you call me Judson loud enough that they can hear."

"Oh, shit yes." And Red couldn't help laughing, and he put his hand on Jud's shoulder and gave it a squeeze. A hard squeeze that hurt. Then he politely pushed Jud toward the bus where his friends were, saying loudly, "That's a deal, Mister Judson, just leave the place like you found it." And Red turned around and walked to his house, muttering obscenities all the way.

As Jud followed The Saint back into the bus, the group let out a whoop, and Frodo said, "Mister Judson, wow!"

The Saint started up the bus, and Jud directed him to the far pasture and the old equipment shed behind the stables and the paddock. There, they would be out of sight from everyone except some unlikely traveler on Bear Gulch Road and anyone who might be at the Dale or Owens houses on the farm. But no one was there.

CHAPTER THIRTY-SIX

As he headed back north and came to the San Gregorio turn-off, Rex hesitated, mulling his options.

I know the coast is full up with surfers, he thought, so it will be hard to find lodging. But I don't want to drive all the way back through Half Moon Bay and San Mateo. Me and Monza are both dog-tired. I sure as hell don't want to fight the curves up through La Honda in the dark of night. Let's just see if there's a room here in San Gregorio.

With that objective in mind, he turned right at the turnoff onto La Honda Road and headed into the center of San Gregorio, a handful of wild-west type buildings, and swung into the rutted parking area of the general store/post office.

An elevated, covered porch spanned the front of the store. Above that was a stucco parapet, arched in a sort of "Alamo" design. San Gregorio General Store was displayed in painted letters on a board above the porch roof. On the porch were a mixed assortment of chairs and benches, mostly of the metal lawn variety, a couple of newspaper boxes, a Goodwill donation box, and a community billboard full of colorful posters. At the left end, just in front of the porch, was a single gas pump with no brand name.

Rex exited his car, went up the steps and entered through a screen door. His entry stretched the spring, which made the screen door slap against its frame as soon as Rex had passed through. The interior of the general store looked like it had once been a warehouse of some kind—a lofty timbered ceiling, a few hanging lights, a couple of rows of grocery shelving, a meat display case, a beverage case, and a frozen food box. A few tables and chairs for eating. Another space which reached back into the depths of the building seemed to have displays of work clothing along with hardware items, big and small.

Rex saw a mustachioed man stepping from behind the meat case, and called out "Howdy, pod'ner!"

The mustachioed man cracked a lopsided smile. "Howdy pod'ner? Where in the world did you wander in from? The Sierra Madre or central casting? Welcome to San Gregorio, Dear Sir. My name is Greg, believe it or not."

Rex shook Greg's hand. "Howdy...I mean how do you do? I may have gotten a little carried away with the ranchland atmosphere. I'm Rex Nickels, over from Redwood City. I don't usually say 'pod'ner'."

"Well, different strokes," Greg smiled. "So how can I help you this evening?"

"The thing is, I'm kinda stranded out here at the coast with no place to stay, and I don't want to drive back over to the Bay Area tonight. Is there any place around where I could bunk for one night?"

Greg smiled again. "You may be in luck, pod'ner, as far as a bunk is concerned. There's a little one-room cottage out back. A bed and some furniture. We keep it clean. No private bath, mind you, but it's just a few steps from the store's bathroom which has a shower. I can let you have it for, let's say, $20 for the night."

Rex also smiled. "Sounds a little like off-highway robbery, but as they say, any port in a storm. I'll take it. Got anything to eat here?"

"Got the full menu of sandwiches. I think there's some soup left. All the beer or soda pop you can drink."

"And Jack Daniels?"

"Got one fifth left. Can't drink it in the store but you can take it to the room. I'll bring you some ice."

So Rex had Greg whip up a roast beef sandwich on sourdough, which he consumed at one of the tables with a bottle of Dos Equis. Then he purchased his JD and a bowl of ice and was shown the way to his quarters for the night. The cottage was about ten yards from the back door of the store. Greg indicated the bathroom, through another door to the left. Greg showed him into the cottage, apologized for the lack of a key, and bid Rex a comfortable night.

Rex surveyed his abode. A double bed with chenille spread, a side table with a dim lamp. A drop-leaf table with a spindle-back chair. A small bureau. A single bulb dropping from the ceiling. A bare wood floor covered only by a small braided rug next to the bed. No TV.

"Clearly not the Mark Hopkins," reflected Rex. "But in fact not that different from my own room on Maple Street, a lot less cluttered, in fact. With Uncle Jack's sibling here, I think it will be a cozy night."

CHAPTER THIRTY-SEVEN

Rex woke up slowly, and it took a few moments for him to realize where he was. There was a bowl next to his bed and it had water in it. It was from the ice Greg had brought him the night before to cool his Jack Daniels. What hadn't gone into his glass for his JD had melted overnight, and now Rex dashed it on his face to get the day started. He wasn't exactly refreshed by his night at San Gregorio Arms, but it was nine o'clock and he figured he'd gotten enough rest.

I've slept in worse places, he thought. Then, I've slept in better ones too. Well, I'd better make my pit stop and haul ass out of here. Come on, JD, there still enough of you left for some additional companionship.

With that, Rex left the cabin and went in the back door of the store, said good morning to Greg and made use of the facilities.

"You can take a shower, if you want," said Greg as Rex came out of the bathroom. "It comes with the room. The towels are clean."

"No thanks. Don't need one exactly. But I do need something to eat."

"What kind of grub do you have a hankerin' for, pod'ner?" said Greg with a grin.

Rex went along with the ribbing and just smiled. Maybe on another day he would have asked for some kind of vittles, but today he was in more or less of a hurry to get on the road. So he just said, "I can smell the coffee. What have you got in the way of donuts?"

"Right there," said Greg, pointing to a glass dome over a raised plate, stacked with about a dozen doughnuts. "What kind and how many?"

"About three of the cake ones. With the white frosting on them. And can you put a large black coffee in a to-go cup and sack it all up for me? I need to get moving."

"I know the feeling," replied Greg enigmatically.

Rex just looked at Greg, shrugged and then, on a hunch, said, "Say, you haven't seen a bunch of hippies riding around in a crazy painted up old school bus, have you?"

"As a matter of fact, I have. They stopped by yesterday, about an hour before you got here. Crazy outfit. We get a lot of hippie types come in here, but this was one strange bunch. Bought a lot of brownie and cookie mix, and almost all the peanut butter I had on the shelves. Lots of giggling goin' on. The called each other names from the "Peanuts" comic strip. The oldest seemed to be their leader. Shepherd might be a better word. He paid for everything. Weird cat. All beads and robe. Had a funny mark on his head and made signs with his fingers. Wished me peace."

"Well, that sort of shit isn't that unusual, I guess," said Rex. "Not anymore."

"Not around these parts, it isn't," answered Greg.

Rex paid the tab, gathered his things and made his way to the Monza, the screen door announcing his exit with a loud "thwap". Once the top was down and he had arranged access to his coffee in the car's cup holder, an aftermarket accoutrement. With the donuts close at hand, he got back on the road to La Honda.

By the end of his first mile of travel, the donuts were gone, and after the second mile so was the coffee. Just as he tossed the crumpled up cup on the car floor on the passenger side, he caught sight on his left of a sign for Bear Gulch Road.

Recognizing the road to Hillandale Stables, Rex blurted aloud, "Well, now, I sure have been here before. Hell, why didn't I think to look for that punk Jud at the farm. Better late than never. Let's just see what we can see." Rex turned onto Bear Gulch Road and followed it to the horse farm entry. He slowed and drove through the gate marked Hillandale Stables est. 1960.

Rex recalled his last visit to Hillandale Stables and his confrontation with Red Ramsey. "What a schmuck," thought Rex. The pissant from Peoria.

As he pulled off to the side of the road, he could see a wispy cloud of smoke rising behind a psychedelic bus parked in the pasture in front of him and partially hidden behind a sagging shed.

"Well, lo and behold, I hit the jackpot," he marveled.

Rex left his car, this time making sure his .38 special was securely tucked in his belt at the small of his back. Coming to the bus he could hear the quiet chattering of people on the other side of the bus. As he turned to go around the bus, his eye caught sight of Red Ramsey coming from the stables beyond the paddock, just on the other side of the pasture fence. Ramsey was fuming as he stormed toward the school bus. They were separated by about thirty yards, but Rex could clearly see Ramsey's red face and tight jaws.

When Rex rounded the end of the psychedelic bus, he could see what Ramsey could see and where he was headed. About ten feet from the bus was the hippie camp. Sprawled around a small, smoky campfire, they were enjoying a breakfast spread of coffee and exotic teas, smoking pot and munching on brownies and cookies. A Dutch oven, having served its purpose, was next to the glowing coals, on its side and empty, and a teapot was suspended on a tripod above the smoldering fire.

"Jud, you little shit!" screamed Red as he reached the group. "I told you no friggin' fire. What the hell are you doing? Get the hell off of this property."

Red walked to the campfire and was about to kick over the teapot and tripod when he spied Rex standing next to the bus. He stopped in midstride, and the two men locked gazes. Rex pulled his jacket back with his right hand and tucked his fingers into his belt next to the .38 at the small of his back. Red got the message and took a step backward. The air, full of insouciance five minutes before, was now full of tension. Nothing moved except the wandering smoke of the fire.

The Saint broke the silence when he carefully stood up, raised his arm and made his strange sign with his hand. "Peace, all," he intoned, as if he were Jesus addressing the multitudes.

Then Frodo giggled. Someone else followed, and soon everyone was laughing, some even rolling on the ground. Red turned one way, then another, totally nonplussed. A smile came to Rex's face as he watched Red's discomfort grow.

Finally Rex said, "All right. That's enough," his voice carrying an unmistakable tone of authority. "Jud, I think breakfast is over. It's time for your little group to close up shop and move on. You can start by putting out the fire. Mr. Ramsey here and I are going to have a little chat over at the stable. When I come back, I think you folks will be ready to leave. Does everyone understand that?" And he headed for the stable, gesturing for Red Ramsey to follow him.

Rex's manner had a sobering effect that would put most rehab centers to shame with its speed and efficiency, and the Peanuts gang immediately calmed down and began to break camp as instructed. Not surprisingly, it was The Saint who assumed command and called for the group's attention. More surprisingly, he designated Jud as his deputy in charge of the clean-up and retreated to watch from the driver's seat in the bus. He watched with satisfaction and amusement as Jud took over. The others began to treat Jud with a new deference in the process, and he was no longer Pig Pen or even Jud. He was Judson now.

When Rex and Red reached the stable, Rex made sure they were out of sight and whispered menacingly to Red, "Listen up you dumb-ass son of a bitch. I'm going to get that bunch of potheads off of this property, so cool your jets!"

Red bristled and started in, "If you thin... "

But Rex cut him off. "I don't want to hear one fuckin' word out of you, got that? It would just be a waste of time, because

I ain't gonna' believe a word you say anyway. I'm taking Jud with me now, and when he does come back here, I don't want you to lay a hand on him. Understood? Now get out and stay outta' my sight until we are gone." And Rex left Red standing in stunned shock. When he got back to the bus, Rex couldn't help noticing a change in the Jud's bearing and the regard shown for him by his peers.

"Son," he said to Jud, "let's go over there on the other side of the bus. We need to chat." To the others he said, "Just wait, this won't take long."

When they looked at him, Jud said to them, "Go on. Finish packing and get in the bus. I'll be right back." They did as he instructed.

When they were alone, Rex told Jud that he needed to get back together with Kay.

"But I don't want to. I want to be with my friends and be free."

"But you need to get back. People that care about you want you to be safe."

"I'm safe here with The Saint and everyone. We're having a good time."

"But everyone is looking for you. If the cops get you first, you could be in deep shit. Don't you get that?" Rex pleaded with Jud. "And your grandmother says 'hello', by the way."

Jud sort of smiled, "Tell her I'm having a great time."

"You can tell her yourself. I want you to come with me." Rex became more firm, and it was obvious he wasn't going to let Jud stay with the hippies. "Now. Or you can stay here with Red and answer to the fuzz when they show up looking for you. That circus bus you want to ride in isn't too hard to spot, you know."

Jud thought for a moment, then his face fell and he sighed heavily. "It looks like I don't have much of a choice."

"No, you don't. Now you go over to my car there and wait for me. I will tell the others," Rex said.

"Can't I go say goodbye?" Jud was plaintive.

"No. I will tell them for you. You can wave from the Monza. The top is down."

Rex went to the school bus and stepped up so his head was inside. "Jud will see you later. He has some business to take care of," he said, and left without waiting for a reply, not even The Saint's benediction of "Peace". He joined Jud in the car and started the engine. As they were leaving, Jud waved at the bus, which honked in reply. They headed south on Bear Gulch Road and then east for La Honda.

As they cruised down the road toward La Honda, Rex glanced at the rearview mirror and saw the school bus in the distance, following the same path. He sped up.

CHAPTER THIRTY-EIGHT

Going up La Honda Road, Rex could see in the rear-view mirror that the painted bus was keeping pace. He wanted to shake the Peanuts gang, but the putt-putt air-cooled engine of the Monza gasped, telling him, "I'm doing all I can, Boss—I'm just not built for speed in these damn hills."

I'll grant you that, Rex thought. And not fit for tight handling on the curves, either. Rex found the Monza the only willing listener, as Jud, slumped in the seat next to him, was in a sulk and so far had rejected Rex's somewhat awkward overtures toward conversation. When the Monza reached La Honda the bus that had been behind them was out of sight at last. "They must have ventured onto a side road somewhere back. And good riddance," Rex said softly to no one in particular.

With the distraction of the Peanuts gang out of the way, Rex had a little time to collect his thoughts as the two of them cruised along. He was pretty certain now that Jud had not killed his father. He didn't know when it was exactly that he decided that Jud was probably not a suspect. Maybe it was on the way to Half Moon Bay or maybe it was on the trip down the coast to San Gregorio. He really couldn't put his finger on exactly where along the way it was, not that it mattered, he thought. He left Redwood City feeling one way about Jud, and got to where they were on the road past La Honda feeling another. In working with the pieces of the puzzle he knew about, Jud's being the killer simply didn't emerge. One thing that didn't make sense was why Jud was on the run if he didn't do it. Another thing—why or how did he go from being a caged animal at Sheila's to a happy-go-lucky flake with his hippie friends? That part Rex just couldn't rationalize. Sensing that this was all too "thinky-thinky", he decided to accept things as they were. He glanced at this long-haired hippie that he had taken under his wing and shook his head with a little private tsk, tsk. Rex, be careful about jumping to conclusions, he said to himself. Don't go and get paternal now.

His introspection ended as he reached the crossroads at Skylonda. He pulled off the road at Alice's Cafe, looked over at Jud and said simply, "Donuts and coffee—that's what we need before we can carry on with this journey. It won't hurt to give the Monza a little rest, too."

Jud just grunted and followed Rex into the cafe.

Once inside, Rex ordered black coffee and two glazed donuts. Jud, spying strawberry-rhubarb pie on the counter, ordered a slice, with herbal tea. Jud lit a cigarette. Rex noted that Jud's face was drawn and pale and when he took the cigarette from his mouth and exhaled, his fingers were shaking.

"You look as nervous as a whore in church. What's the matter, my friend?" said Rex.

"What if you are just giving me a line of crap and are really going to turn me over to the cops?"

"If I were going to do that, I would have called them from Sheila's. Before you escaped. Think about it. And what are you afraid of? You haven't done anything, have you? Other than the grass?"

Jud offered a quick, slight smile in acknowledgement. Rex sensed an opening.

"Come on, what is it?"

"It's about Earnest, my friend. He's dead," and Jud began to tear up.

"You mean Earnest Kayne, your father, don't you?" said Rex softly.

"You mean you know?" Jud's head was down but he cut his eyes directly at Rex.

"Yeah, I know. I know that he was your dad and that Kay is your aunt and that Hulda Stern Franken is your grandmother. I know a lot, kid."

"But I think I hurt Daddy. I may have...you know...Kay and I were there and we tried to help bu...," Jud whispered hoarsely, a tear rolling down his cheek. "I may be a murderer."

"If you thought that, why the hell didn't you stay hidden at Sheila's house instead of jumping out a window and stealing a car?"

"I just wanted to get away. I was all mixed up. There was just too much. I couldn't handle it. I needed to be alone. By myself, with some grass. To escape from the world. Then I ran into my friends with the bus and they asked me to go with them. It seemed like a good place to escape to, so I went."

"Didn't it occur to you that that a psychedelic bus is about the easiest thing to spot this side of the moon? That being with those people is the opposite of hiding?"

"I just wasn't thinking. A gang of bikers was after me. I didn't care how I got away from them. There was the bus and The Saint and I just went for it."

Rex thought about this response for a minute and then decided not to pursue the issue.

"I'm going out on a limb with this, kid, but I don't think that you are a murderer. Or that Kay is either. I don't know exactly what happened at that cemetery, but my gut tells me you didn't kill Kayne. I know your Aunt Kay pretty damn well, and I don't think she is capable of killing someone. I could be really wrong about all of this, and my ass is going to be in a sling if I am. But for now, that is the way I see it," Rex said, expressing more conviction than he really felt.

"Then why are you and everyone chasing me?"

"Because your aunt asked me to find you. She wants to protect you while all of this business is sorted out."

"But the police. They're after me. You said they would get me if I stayed at the farm," Jud offered.

"Maybe I exaggerated a bit. I needed to get you out of there. The cops are looking for you because you are missing and because Mrs. William Dale showed up missing at the same time and because that damn bus is something to look for. Along with the Cadillac. I don't think anyone is looking for you because of the dead guy in the cemetery. I mean your father, that is. No one has made that connection," said Rex, and then to himself ironically, not yet, anyway. No one except maybe me and Abel and Wunderlich.

"So just relax for now. Do you like your pie? Want some more when you finish that?" Rex asked for lack of anything else to say. The pie looked awfully good to Rex.

"Yes and no. No thanks," replied Jud.

There was an awkward silence then, and neither knew what to say. Both concentrated on the food they had been served and avoided each other's eyes. Donuts never tasted better to Rex, and he had consumed many in his time. When the donuts were gone, he finally had to break the tension.

"Say, kid, I hate to admit this, but I was mighty impressed by your behavior back there. You really seemed to be comfortable taking charge of those kids. You ought to be proud of yourself. I think you might have some backbone I hadn't seen. I really have to give you credit for what you did. You know, if you show more of that kind of grit, I think you may have a future that's worth a shit."

Jud showed his embarrassment with a dismissive gesture of his right hand, the one with the cigarette, from which some ash fell onto the table. But Rex could see that the boy was pleased by the compliment.

Jud looked Rex in the eyes and began, "Oh, well, you know... maybe I just all of a sudden, like, felt, like, the kids were beginning to pay some attention to me, and give me some, you know, respect. And The Saint has really been nice to me. He treats me like a real person, like I was an adult. And, you know, I was really surprised that you were willing to trust me to get things together. And, I'll tell you, I didn't mind kinda showing off in front of Red Ramsey. He's such a prick, always on my case, like he didn't ever notice that I broke my butt working those horses."

Rex caught Jud's eye and held it with his own gaze. "Let me ask you something. If you were at the cemetery that night, maybe you know something about how the lipstick got on the raincoat?"

"Well...ah...I wrote on the coat. It was a saying from a plaque in Grandma Rosebud's house."

"A saying?"

"Yes," said Jud, "it says 'If you seek forgiveness, start with yourself'." I got as far as the end of 'seek' and Aunt Kay stopped me."

"Did you get the lipstick from Kay?"

"Yeah," Jud started, then said in a low voice, "...er, well, no, I mean...not directly. When Kay and I were driving over to the cemetery, a tube of lipstick was on the seat when I got in her car. I picked it up and was sorta playing with it in my hand...I dunno...I was nervous about everything. When we got out of the car, I just dropped the tube in my shirt pocket. Then a little later I got a kind of...impulse, I guess...to pull out the lipstick and write the letters on the raincoat. Then Kay stopped me, and when we left I put the lipstick back in my pocket. After that, I kinda held on to it as, I dunno...what ya call it...a memento."

"Oh, I see...," Rex said gently, so as not to break the tempo, and he waited for Jud to continue.

Looking away from Rex, Jud said, "I gotta tell you something else. People are gonna find out anyway, they always do." He paused and sighed. "Sometimes I just like to dress up, you know, put on a skirt and just dance and let myself go. I like the way it makes me feel—like I am floating in the wind. It has always been that way, since I was a little kid. Funny, it doesn't mean I'm gay or anything. I do like girls. I'm not attracted to guys. I don't understand it, but I just like to dress up and dance around. That's why I was in the cemetery in the first place."

"Thanks for telling me all that. It clears up a lot," said Rex and he smiled and placed his fist on the table with a pudgy finger pointed at Jud. "When we get back to town, I'm going to give a very good report to your Aunt Kay and your grandmother. And don't worry, I think what you just told me can stay between the two of us. Okay?"

On the downhill run from Skyline Boulevard through Woodside and into Redwood City, Jud opened up. He became a chatterbox, telling Rex how he wanted to be more grown-up, how he loved working with horses, and more on how he despised Ramsey. He said he didn't want to go back to Stockton, that maybe he could get work on another horse setup here on the Peninsula and eventually become a trainer.

As they approached Sheila's place, Rex said to Jud, "Look, you should realize there are people, like your mother and The Saint, who care about you and what happens to you. In particular there are people like Kay and Bill and your grandmother, and hell, maybe even me and Sheila, who can help you out with contacts and maybe a little money now and then. I think if you begin to show them some respect, you'll find that they're going to pay you respect in return and give you support. I understand you are in a rough position right now on account of the circumstances of Earnest's death. But look, we're going to work that out. I just want you to be patient. You and Kay still need to lay low for now, but I really believe we're going to get to the truth very soon. I'm asking you to just calm down, be cool, and practice being your best self, okay?"

Jud brightened up with the closest thing to a real smile that Rex had ever seen from him.

"Yes, sir," he said. "I'm sure going to try!"

Rex pulled into Sheila's driveway and asked Jud to stay in the car for a couple of minutes while he went in the house. Rex pressed the button beside the front door, and chimes sounded the first line of the theme from "Love Story." Sheila opened the door, and Rex could see Kay sitting in a living room chair, looking expectantly toward the front door.

Rex gave them a big smile. "I have a surprise for you!" and he turned to Jud and motioned him to follow as he went into the house.

What ensued after that could best be described as a love fest. Even Sheila herself seemed to be softened, and was finally treating Jud as a fellow human being, offering to make his room more comfortable. "I have a little mini-fridge in the garage that we could move into your room," she suggested.

With a sigh of satisfaction and relief, Rex left the three of them to their newfound bliss and departed. When he arrived home, he went directly to the telephone and dialed Hulda's number in Pleasanton.

Her machine came on and he left a message. "Hulda, I've retrieved your grandson. He needs to be kept under wraps for a while yet, but he's in good hands and I'm confident that he's going to stay put and cooperate with us. If you want to drive over to Redwood City, I can arrange for you to visit with him. I think a little 'Gramma love' would do him a world of good about now. Plus, I wouldn't overlook the therapeutic values of your favorite natural substance."

CHAPTER THIRTY-NINE

On Friday morning at nine fifteen, Captain Wunderlich was at his desk reviewing budget proposals sent over from the chief's office. He stifled a yawn as the phone rang.

"Wunderlich."

"It's Nick. The examiner's report is done. I was going to walk it over to review with you, but I was thinking, we could meet halfway and get coffee at the Break-Thyme. I'm buying—are you in?"

"About time! I'll see you there in ten minutes."

Wunderlich arrived at the cafe at nine twenty five and grabbed a table with a view of the door. He had learned long ago that a cop is always watchful, even at the Break-Thyme. County Medical Examiner Nicholas Nakamura strolled in two minutes later, signaled the waitress and joined Wunderlich at his table.

Rhonda, the ever present waitress, brought coffee and offered menus. She left while the two men considered what to order.

Nakamura pushed a half-inch thick blue-covered report along with a thinner yellow folder across the table.

Wunderlich thumbed through both documents, stopping occasionally to scan a page.

"You expect me to read this stuff? It might as well be in Japanese," grumbled Wunderlich. "Gimme the 'Cliff Notes' version."

"Oh come on, Captain. How many of these things have you seen in your lifetime? Don't tell me you can't read them. Hell, if they were in Japanese, I couldn't read them at all."

Wunderlich gave him a stare of non-cooperation, saying nothing.

Finally, Nakamura gave in. "Okay, let's see if I can dumb this down for you, Einstein. Hand them back to me and I will translate."

Nakamura opened the blue report, reading quickly. He earmarked a couple of pages and then began dispassionately. "This is what I believe to be the pertinent stuff:

Section 412.BAC—Blood Alcohol Content: Point one five. Well above the legal limit of point one zero for motor vehicle operation. Seems as if our friend was pretty well stewed when he checked out. And I don't think he drove himself to the cemetery.

Section 513. Hematology: Non naturally-occurring substances. Now here's something that will tickle your frontal lobes. Chloral hydrate and phosgene. Chloroform in other words."

"Chloral hydrate I recognize. Another name for a Mickey Finn. Someone slipped our victim a Mickey. I'll be damned. Kind of an old stunt. We used to see more of it than we do now," said Wunderlich. "So Kayne was fed a knockout cocktail?" he queried. "But that shouldn't kill a guy—not under normal circumstances."

Nick smiled. "When did you ever see normal circumstances? Not in your job. You're right, a Mickey Finn, even on top of a load of liquor, wouldn't be deadly. It would put a healthy guy out of commission for a good while, but he would eventually come to."

"But phosgene? I thought that was a gas that was outlawed in World War I."

"That is correct, Sherlock. But when non-medical chloroform, that is chloroform without ether in it, enters the body, it decomposes into phosgene, a fatal substance."

"So you are telling me this guy was gassed? He didn't drink it, I assume, so how did it get in his body?"

"I don't know exactly. I am just reading the lab report. The phosgene was in his lungs. But traces of chloroform were found on his face, all around his mouth, in a way that indicates it had been smeared on, maybe with a cloth."

"Like I said, people used to get knocked out with chloroform all the time. Then Mickey Finns kind of replaced it, as I recall. I didn't know you could even buy it anymore," said Wunderlich.

"You can, but it is regulated. But it is easy to make, particularly in this day of amateur chemists. Some of these idiots are sniffing it for a cheap high."

"Really?" Wunderlich was surprised.

"Yep. All you need is bleach and acetone and some ice to keep it from turning into phosgene gas. Like it did in Mr. Kayne's lungs. So, the secret ingredient here, the catalyst you might say, was chloroform—seemingly, a relatively innocuous substance."

Nakamura continued. "Here is another interesting tidbit that I remember from my days in medical school. For what it is worth. At one time chloroform was used by vets to anesthetize large animals for surgery. In the right quantities in the hands of a professional, it worked quite well. It was eventually replaced with more modern drugs, like everything else in medicine."

"Yeah, that's no surprise. Guess it's a matter of chemistry and progress, huh?"

Rhonda came back for their orders. Nick declined to order while Wunderlich requested two donuts.

Nick went on. "Not necessarily chemistry alone. Do you remember that a feather was found in one of the victim's nostrils?"

Wunderlich chuckled. "Are you pulling that gag on me again? That the death was caused by a bird?"

"Before I answer that, let me finish up with the report. The last item is probably the most important that I have to tell you. It is the C.O.D. *Item 971-1A—The Cause of Death*. In this report, it leads us to a possible answer."

"And...?" Nakamura had Wunderlich's full attention.

"*Item 971-1A, Cause of Death:....Suffocation and phosgene poisoning are main causes with high levels of chloral hydrate and alcohol as contributing factors. Method of administering not definitive.* In other words, this report tells us what but not how."

"Look, Nick. No joking around, OK? What's with the feather?"

"That's what this is for," said Nakamura, and replaced the blue-covered report with the thin yellow one.

Rhonda arrived with Wunderlich's donuts and refilled their coffee cups. She hesitated, trying to see the report and snapping her gum, until Wunderlich waved her away. Nakamura opened the yellow folder.

"This, my friend, is something you may have forgotten about. It is a report from Pauline Esters, the ornithologist San Mateo County has on retainer. After the lab people were done with the deceased, the nose feather was extracted and sent to her for analysis and identification," Nakamura explained as he placed his hand flat on the open yellow folder. "What this says is that the feather is from an owl and that it is, or was, saturated with chloroform at one time. That is based on the amount of residue left and the rate of off-gassing for the compounds in chloroform."

"Oh, really?" said Wunderlich with a small smirk. "And the owl? What kind is it? Or do we give a hoot?" and he chuckled at his own little joke.

Nakamura dead-panned his response as he opened the report and read, " 'The feather is from the barred owl—*Strix varia*, more commonly known as the hoot owl. It is a nocturnal bird, not uncommon to this region. It has recently been declared a candidate for the endangered species list because of the popularity of the owl's soft and fluffy chest feathers for use in pillows and comforters and the potential for over-harvesting the bird's feathers for commercial purposes.' So—there you have it. Here, these are for you to read or not. My job is to see that you get them and to see that you understand the contents." And he pushed the reports toward Wunderlich.

"Thanks, Doc. Now that we have the facts, do you want to venture an opinion as to what actually took place?"

"Only very indirectly. I think the feather is indicative of how the chloroform may have been delivered. This is purely speculation, not science, so it's not written up in the medical report. This is for a detective to deduce. The feather could be one dropped from a resident bird like an owl. You might also want to think about pillows, and how feathers have a way of escaping from the pillow casings. Someone just might have spread chloroform on a feather pillow and applied the pillow to a drugged but still-alive victim, as a coup de grace. Whatever happened, it seems to have been drawn out in stages, maybe even in different places. The large amount of alcohol, capped by a Mickey Finn—maybe in a bar or a living room, then finally the chloroform, maybe in the cemetery. But why not do something quicker if the murder was premeditated? But all that's your business. I'm just the doc—I'll leave that to the master."

Wunderlich gazed at Nakamura for a moment. "There are a couple of things that you haven't mentioned yet. The blue lips that you had a fancy name for, to start with."

"Oh yes," and Nick smiled slightly, remembering. "You must be referring to the azure orbicular oculi discoloration on the victim's face."

"If you say so. Why was he blue in the face? Tell me in English, please."

"Windex. Or more precisely, Windex residue. Not significant medically, so it's not that important."

"Well, it is important to me. I have a crime to solve. What the hell was Windex doing on the guy's kisser? Any theories?"

"The only thing I can come up with is that Windex has a lot of ammonia in it and maybe someone tried to revive him, thinking of smelling salts, which are almost entirely ammonia. They were too late. It was in the mouth too, but not in his breathing passages. He was dead before someone tried to clean his windows."

"And the lipstick?"

"Oh, yeah. I forgot about that. I did have that analyzed. Here. Give me back that blue one." And Nick leafed through the report to the next to last page. "Here it is. *Section 999.0B. Non-medical extraneous material. The red graphic material found on the subject's plastic rain coat was determined to be lipstick, manufactured by Avon Corporation. Color: Petit-Scarlett Pandora Tara."*

"I knew it. I just knew it," laughed Wunderlich and Nakamura joined him as they got up to leave.

"Me too," said Nick.

CHAPTER FORTY

Rex slept late for a Friday morning, and suddenly his snoring startled him awake. Actually it was a big snort rather than a full snore, and he wondered momentarily where it came from before he realized that it came from him. He added a satisfying belch. He was hungry, and when he saw the clock said ten forty five, he got hungrier.

"Ah, crap," Rex moaned aloud. "It's too late for breakfast and too early for lunch. And I'm out of coffee and sweet rolls. I was goin' to the 7-Eleven this morning for groceries, and now I'm out of time. I'll do it later."

A quick armpit check told him Right Guard was no longer an option and that it was bath time. He wished again that he had a shower and didn't have to go to the trouble of filling the tub. But fill it he did, and without Mr. Bullwinkle's bubbles this time. His hunger drove him to quick and efficient bathing and by the time he was out of the tub and dressed it was after eleven.

Still a little early for lunch, he thought. Hmmm...well, if I walk, by the time I get to the Break-Thyme, it will be time for lunch. And Rex set out for Broadway, his stomach growling and his thoughts collecting on the case. When he got to the cafe, he was tempted to step next door and go up to his office to check the mail and the phone messages.

Nope, he thought, no more checking messages, not yet any-way. Every time I check my answering machines, it is a woman with a damn problem. It's already eleven fifteen. Right now I need to solve my own problem, hunger. And Rex went into the Break-Thyme Cafe for something to eat.

"I'll have," he told Rhonda the waitress with the timeless 50's bee-hive hair-do, "a couple of eggs over-easy, an English muffin, and a cup of java, no sugar, no cream."

"Will that be all, Mr. Nickel-dime?" Rhonda moved her gum to one side of her mouth and spoke from the other.

"For breakfast, yeah. For lunch I'd like some chili and some hash browns."

"Breakfast and lunch? At the same time?" she asked.

"We only go around once, sweetheart, and I don't want to miss anything. Especially lunch," Rex said with a grin.

Rhonda finished writing on her order pad and as she walked back to the kitchen she said quietly, "It doesn't look like you missed very many."

"What was that?" called Rex.

She turned her head and said, "I said, did you want the Chili Three Ways? Like yesterday?" anticipating a smart-ass answer.

"No, one-way is enough. Just chili. I am watching the waist-line, you know. And hold the crackers, too."

"Yes, Mr. Nickel-dime," said Rhonda and she rolled her eyes as she did every time she had to wait on him.

After Rex had polished off the last of his hash browns and Rhonda had filled his cup for the third time, he stirred the coffee out of habit and sat motionless for a time, sorting through the loose ends of the case in his head. He had touched most the bases, but one thing stood out that seemed to need his attention. It was Abel Willing.

Abel N. Willing, he mused. So he's with the State Horse Racing Board, is he? A buddy of Wunderlich. Hmmm. And he snoops the Budner section of the library looking for the skinny on Earnest Kayne and William Dale II.

He reached for his wallet and retrieved the page from the notebook he had written Willing's phone number on at the library.

He unfolded and smoothed it out on the turquoise Formica table top in front of him. "Abel N. Willing Sales (415) 633-2468", it read.

I don't know what he is selling at the State Racing Board, but I think I will find out. Rex heaved himself out of the booth and headed for the pay phone next to the restrooms. Before he did, he left a tip on the table for Rhonda. As usual, it was whatever pocket change he had on him, less the quarter he needed for the call to Willing.

He dialed the number and watched Rhonda clearing off the table, counting his tip as he waited for an answer. When she turned and gave him a small smile, he realized he had probably over-tipped and said to himself, Damn. Next time I'll count it.

"Hello. Willing here," came a voice on the phone. "How can I help you?"

"I need to speak to Abel Willing. He is in sales, I believe." Rex said sarcastically.

"This is Abe Willing. Who are you?"

"I am Rex Nickels. I'm a private investigator. Fred Wunderlich told me about you."

"Well, I am a public investigator, and Captain Wunderlich told me about you too. What is this about sales?"

"Oh, I'm just giggin' you a little. I got your number from the card you left with Rosie over at the library. The card said you were in sales. Not that I believed it. Maybe Rosie did. Probably better if she did."

"So why are you calling?" asked Willing patiently.

"I'd like for us to get together and talk about some recent events here in Red City."

"Like what recent events?"

"Like a naked body in a cemetery and some peculiar goin's on at a certain horse farm. Maybe we could talk and exchange some information concerning those events." Rex spoke in a way that wouldn't get him in trouble if someone were listening in on the conversation. Over his career Rex had learned that being a little paranoid was not a bad thing.

"All right. I will meet with you. Where?" asked Willing.

"Let's say my office, right after lunch, tomorrow. That would give you time to get down from San Francisco and have a bite beforehand."

"Well, tomorrow at your office about one fifteen would be fine, but I have an office here in Redwood City." replied Abe. "I'm about a block from the library."

"Oh, I didn't know that. I thought the offices of the Racing Board were in San Francisco."

"Well, technically, that is true. Let's just say I am TDY here for a while."

Rex knew from the military that TDY meant "temporary duty", and hearing the term took him back to his "duty" at the dance at Stanford and... . "I guess you can explain sometime," said Rex, bringing himself quickly to the present. "I don't suppose you can make it here today, could you?"

"I don't see why not. Could we do lunch?" asked Willing.

"Sorry, I just had a snack to tide me over. Maybe another time for lunch. As for meeting, want to make it about two, two fifteen? That'll give you time to eat and get over here. I'm on Broadway in the Young's Drug Building, second floor at the back." Rex was relieved he didn't have to travel for this meeting, just make the stairs. His feet and legs were about traveled out. And two o'clock would give him time for a catnap.

●●●

At a little after two a rap on the office door quickly wakened Rex from his feet-on-the-desk after-lunch snooze.

"Come in, come in," called Rex, and he went to the opening door to greet the visitor he knew would be Abel Willing.

"I'm Willing. Abel Willing," said the short, compact, well-dressed man as he came into Rex's office.

"Nickels, here. Rex Nickels."

"Private Eye," continued Willing with a smile.

"Agent Willing. Would that be 'secret agent'?"

"Ah, I see we like the same flicks."

"Come on in and sit," said Rex. "Seen the latest?" Rex warmed to Abe at once.

"If you mean 'On Her Majesty's Secret Service' that came out last year, yes."

"But it didn't have Connery in it. I didn't care much for the new guy," Rex opined.

"Me neither. I don't know why they got him instead of Connery. Connery's done all the other ones."

There was an awkward lull as both men realized they were probably enjoying their newly found mutual fascination with James Bond movies too much. Finally, Willing broke the silence.

"So, what do we want to meet about, Agent Rex?" and he wasn't being sarcastic.

"Before we start, do I have your understanding that anything I might tell is for you only?" Rex was all business, though friendlier than usual.

"To the extent that it is on the right side of the law, yes. And as long as you understand that I will inform the authorities of any wrong-doing we may discuss, sooner or later," said Willing,

Rex thought to himself, that is a bunch of twisted cover-my-ass baloney if I ever heard it. But it is about what I have told other people in this thing, so I'll go along. I sense I can trust the little snoop.

"Same here," responded Rex. "Now, here is the deal. As you know, this is about one Earnest Kayne, the dead guy found in Union Cemetery on the sixteenth of this month."

"Of course. I know about it," said Abe.

"What you don't know, at least I hope you don't, is that I have been hired by his mother to find the killer." Rex studied Abel's eyes and face for verification that this was new news to Abel. He saw that Abel didn't know.

"His mother?" Willing was a tad incredulous.

"Yep. Earnest's mother, Hulda Stern-Franken. Pick a name. She came here and told me all about her background and about Earnest.

Said she wanted me to find his killer. I said I would if she paid me, and that it all had to be legal. I am on the payroll as we speak."

"If I'd known that, I wouldn't have had lunch alone. And it would have been on your expense account."

"Next time we will plan for that. Just how much do you know about the Kayne case?" Rex was all business now.

"Allow me to start from the side of this that has my interest, and tell you what I know from that angle. We, that is the Racing Board, get interested in any race track, or owner or horse that has winnings above or below the norm. Over the past several years, three to be exact, since I have held this investigative position, Bay Meadows Race Track in San Mateo has been showing a pattern, an admittedly hard to discern pattern, but still a pattern, of being above the average in winnings for certain horses one year followed two years later by the same horses, or their stable mates, showing up consistently out of the money."

"And you are saying that there is someone out there who consistently finishes in the money," pondered Rex.

"I'm saying that there is someone out there who loses enough not to stand out from the crowd, and wins big without the public realizing it. Someone who is very cagey and clever. The someone I have in mind may just be too clever for his own good."

Rex was impressed, and said, "It sounds to me like you are pretty far down the road with this. How does it tie in with a naked guy in a cemetery?"

"You mean how does this tie in with a naked pharmacist in a cemetery, don't you?" Able was enjoying the repartee.

"Drugs! Damn I knew it," said Rex. "Drugs and horses and pharmacists and hippies and horse farms and rich owners and races and trainers, and now money, big money apparently. All in the same pot. You know Mr. Willing, I think we are both stirring the same soup with different spoons. You have the illegitimate racing spoon and I have the murder spoon. The question is what or who is the secret ingredient? Have you got someone in mind?" asked Rex, with a small, knowing grin.

"Indeed I do. But, before I tell you, I'd like to hear what things you have an interest in, in this soup of ours." Abel said with a coy smirk.

Coy, Rex was not. "Like I said, I'm in this to find the guy that likes cemeteries but doesn't care much for pharmacists. From what I've been able to figure out, Earnest Kayne was doin' something a little off the record with Red Ramsey, the horse trainer. You know about him by now I assume."

"Yes. Him and his boss Owen Owens, with whom I had a very interesting conversation not too long ago. Mainly I know them from our file on them that goes way back. But, please go on."

"Well, there was a negotiation one evening, between Kayne and Ramsey that started at a motel and went from bar to bar and ended up with an argument that was settled in a parking lot. My source says that Ramsey punched Kayne out with one swing and then put him in a car and drove off," Rex reported.

"Who told you that?" asked Abel.

"A guy named Jimson. Arthur Jimson."

"Never heard of him."

"Me neither. Before or since. I met him at a place called El Flamingo Real. It's a bar and restaurant. Jimson is a regular there. Older guy. He and some of his cronies were there having some drinks and dinner two Sundays ago, and were just witnesses. I'm sure we could find him again if we had to. He said the car's license plate had an 'RX' on it. That tells me it was probably Kayne's car. Where they went after that, I don't know. I'm pretty certain it was Union Cemetery because that's where Kayne ended up. But I haven't talked to anyone who actually saw them or the car there."

"It's beginning to sound like we have both stirred up the same number one ingredient. Namely, one Red Ramsey," Abel concluded.

"That is who I put at the top of my list, too. Red Ramsey," Rex confirmed.

"List? You have a list? Can I ask who else was on it?" Abel was a little more than curious.

"There were seven to start with. I called them my 'Magnificent Seven'. Loved that movie. Let me see. Owen and Ramsey were on it. And the son, Judson Kayne, who is sometimes calls himself Periwinkle, was there. But after getting to know him a little, I don't think he is a consideration anymore. Kayne's ex-wife was on the list, but she has an air-tight alibi. William Dale II was a consideration, because he has known Owens all his life. His father went to college with Owens. But Dale has enough money that could take care of Earnest in a more, shall we say, sophisticated way. And he has a reputation for being very cool and never losing his temper. Kay Dale, his wife, was listed until I thought about it. I have a personal history with her that goes way back, and I decided that unless something blatant cropped up that pointed to her, she wasn't going to be a suspect. Not for murder anyway." Rex paused long enough to indicate he was finished.

"That is only six. You said seven. 'Magnificent Seven', I believe you said." Able was polite but sharp.

"It was you, my friend. Abel N. Willing. At the start, I didn't rule anyone out. You were on it for a while, because you visited Rosie Budner right after the murder. But I was covering all my bases when I made the list, and later when I talked to Fred Wunderlich and found out who you were, of course, you were off the list."

"That is reassuring. At least it convinces me you are thorough. And that we have similar taste in movies. So, if you eliminated five of us, that leaves Owens and Ramsey. And the Bobbsey twin that got your nod for Number One suspect was Ramsey," said Abel.

"Rod 'Red' Ramsey. He was at the top of my list anyway, along with a note to find out his real name. And your selection was the same?" asked Nickels.

"Well, Ramsey, yes. His full name is Rodney Kilmer Ramsey. Actually his legal name is Ramsy, spelled without the 'e'. By adding that one letter to his name he's made it a little bit harder for anyone to trace his history. But I have connections and resources, and I found out about him and his record."

"And...?"

"Let's just say he isn't in line to be named Pope very soon. Did time in Iowa State Prison for a variety of things. Assault with a deadly weapon and illegal gambling top the list. Paroled about twenty years ago and has been off the radar screen since. Goes by 'Red' Ramsey. Pretty tough customer."

"At least he thinks he's tough. I'm not so sure he is. He's the kind that doesn't know the difference between mean and tough. He's a mean bastard all right. Maybe not so tough. But smart," Rex reflected.

"So you've met him?"

"Yeah. I told you that Earnest's mother hired me to find his killer. What I didn't tell you is that Kay Dale, Mrs. William Dale II that is, also asked me to help her and Judson Kayne in this matter. Judson works for Red Ramsey at the horse farm owned by Owen Owens and..."

"...William Dale II and his wife Kay," Abel finished the sentence.

And Rex and Abel spent the next twenty minutes going over their notes and comparing what they concluded were the facts. Finally, Rex leaned back in his chair and said, "I think we are pretty solid with Rod 'Red' Ramsey being the killer."

"Only we can't prove it. Not enough for a conviction," sighed Abel.

"Are we at the point where we need to sit down and confess our sins to Father Wunderlich? Isn't this his dance now?" asked Rex.

"From your side of the kitchen, I think we should. Probably they will be able to convict him of something eventually. But it is not clear cut, legally. Obvious, but not open and shut. From my side, there is a problem with nailing Ramsey and not getting Owens at the same time. Once Owens knows that we have Red, he will cover his tracks as fast as he can and we may never get him. And Owens is my real target," said Abel.

"You are convinced of that?"

"After our discussion here today, I am. There is much more in his file that will fill in the blanks of what we said, and I think we've just about got him. We have the coffin and all the nails but one." Abel was up and pacing the room.

Rex said, "These guys are very, very smart. But they had to have slipped up somewhere. My view is that if we can get Ramsey where we have him dead to rights, and when he knows he is going to be found guilty of murder, we can get him to rat on Owens for some special considerations."

"Well, that would be between the police and the prosecutors. We can go only so far without telling what we know. And we can't wait too long or we will both be in trouble."

"Yeah, there is room for a couple of investigators in that soup of trouble," quipped Rex.

"You know, I think maybe we need to talk to Fred now, not later. He's a good cop but maybe he hasn't told us everything. Let's play it on the safe side and try to get him to hold up on arresting Ramsey until we have enough to get Owens at the same time," Willing pressed.

"Yeah. I agree. Let the chips fall where they may and the shit fall on someone else but us truly."

"Well, you called this pow-wow, Mr. Nickels. I think it is now time for us to sit down with Captain Wunderlich. Shall I set up such a meeting? It's still a little before three o'clock. With luck maybe we can go over and see him this afternoon."

"By all means, Mr. Willing. By all means."

CHAPTER FORTY-ONE

Rex and Abel arrived at police headquarters at three thirty on Friday afternoon and were shown into Captain Wunderlich's office. Fred Wunderlich stood, came around his desk and gave hearty handshakes to his two visitors.

"Welcome, gentlemen. So you two seem to have become acquainted! Well, it's a pretty small town, and I guess you could call us all colleagues in one way or another. Here, have seats," Wunderlich indicated two chairs fronting his desk, and returned to his own. "Abe's call indicated you two wanted to talk to me about the naked guy in the cemetery."

"Thank you, Captain, for being available on such short notice," Abel said. "Rex and I met earlier today. He contacted me because he's been thinking about possible connections between Earnest Kayne and the good folks at Hillandale and the racing world. To cut to the chase, or better said, the home stretch, both of us can give you two words: 'Red Ramsey'."

Wunderlich had been distractedly perusing papers on his desk. At mention of Ramsey he looked up with surprise, first at Willing, then, shifting his gaze, focused on Rex. "So, Nickels...I've talked before to Abel here about the possible involvement of Ramsey. I had to think that he tends to view everything through a filter of horse racing. But tell me, how did you come around to seeing Red Ramsey as a suspect?"

Rex recounted his investigations of the Catalina motel, the Woodside Road bars, and the El Flamingo, reporting the interview with Arthur Jimson, and how he had systematically evaluated a number of suspects. Rex told how he and Willing had come to the same conclusion from different perspectives, one looking at violations of racing regulations, the other looking at murder. But mostly what brought them to Ramsey was evidence of association with Earnest Kayne.

"So that's pretty much how we got where we are, and how Abel and I realized that we needed to check in with you, to give you the benefit of our thinking," Rex concluded.

Wunderlich broke into a broad grin. "Well, well. Good work, gentlemen. Our shop has gone through most of the same processes and I'm happy that we agree. And Rex, I must admit that you've found one piece that we didn't know about. We never heard of Arthur Jimson. I'm glad you have come forward with that, just in time to keep you out of trouble. We'll have to get a statement from him right away. Now, what else do you know that we don't?"

Rex gave the captain a gaze of round-eyed innocence. "How could you imagine that I wouldn't come clean with you in such a serious matter as this?"

The captain replied, "Well, just be sure you let us know if there's anything you've overlooked."

"We're both happy to be of service," said Abel. "We hope we're helping the case along. We both have some doubts, though, about how an air-tight case is going to be made against Ramsey. We strongly feel Owens himself is involved, though maybe not in the killing of Kayne. But we know that Owens carries a lot of clout around these parts, and is sure to provide a strong defense for Ramsey if he's accused. I have an interest in seeing Owens brought to justice with respect to his numerous racing violations. A premature move on Ramsey might let Owens slip the net. I hope all of this can be paced so that both Ramsey and Owens get their desserts."

"I thoroughly agree with that," Wunderlich responded. "We have to be careful with Owens. Look, I think the next thing for me to do is talk with the Chief and the D.A., and begin to frame some prosecution strategy. Owens has many friends in this county, but I'm confident that the D.A. isn't one of them. And I don't think he can be bought. Meanwhile we'll continue to develop the evidence, specifically including Jimson's testimony, for which we can thank Mr. Nickels."

"One other thing," Rex inquired. "What about the actual cause of Kayne's death? You must have gotten a report from the medical examiner by now?"

"In good time," Wunderlich replied. "All in good time. You'll know soon."

Wunderlich was acting on his own little agenda. After Rex and Abel left his office, the captain made quick calls to the police chief and the mayor to give them a heads-up about the medical report. Then he called a press briefing to announce the findings on the cause of death. No harm in a little TV time, Wunderlich said to himself. And I don't mind that the city council will be pleased to hear of positive movement in the naked body case.

CHAPTER FORTY-TWO

Rex let his full weight fall onto the couch, and the force of gravity flattened the cushions. He was entirely drained after an intense day. After his meetings with Willing and Wunderlich, he had gone back to his office to figure out his income tax for the year. This year, I am gonna' get this sucker in on time, no extensions, no penalties and no more tax than I can help, he vowed as he sat down at his desk, figuring that if he set aside a few hours just for doing his taxes, he would be ahead of the game for a change. After battling the forms and trying to organize his deductions and locating his receipts in the piles of partially filed papers, he was on the verge of defeat. Six hours into it, he closed up the office, new stacks of papers replacing and outnumbering the old ones, and went home.

All he wanted was to mindlessly watch television with a cold Acme beer and something to eat. He clicked on the TV with his remote, took a big swallow of beer, and arranged his sandwich plate on the arm of the couch while he waited for the picture to come up. When he saw it was the evening news, he wasn't really interested, but changing the station would mean putting down either the beer or his freshly made sandwich, neither of which he was willing to do. So he just relaxed and lay back, ate, drank, and watched.

*"Good evening and welcome to "Seven at Eleven"
brought to you tonight by Seven Continents Market, your
neighborhood source for natural foods. I'm Norbert Swisher.
On the local front, there are some new developments in the
Redwood City naked body case. From a police briefing we
have learned that the medical examiner's report appears to
confirm earlier accounts of the death of Stockton pharmacist Earnest Kayne as having been caused by suffocation. A
Channel 7 source has revealed that chloroform was found
in the victim, and what may be a feather from an owl was
found in his nose. Our source told us that owl feathers are
often used in pillows..."*

Rex had watched with full attention as he restored himself
with beer and food. He stopped in mid-bite when he heard *"...
death of Earnest Kayne as having been caused by suffocation..."*

Well thanks a freaking lot, Fred, you sneaky shit! Why the hell
didn't you tell us that this afternoon? Okay, then. Now, I won't
feel so bad about not telling you and Abel everything, you political
bastard!

Rex's train of thought was interrupted again when he heard,
*"... feather was from the barred owl, or hoot owl. These feathers are
often used in pillows..."* A bell went off in his head and he knew he
had heard that before. He resumed chewing, but slowly and with
deliberation as he racked his brain for the connection. Finally, he
had it. The newspaper! The article in the paper while I was waiting for Hulda Stern Franken Stern! he exclaimed, almost aloud.
The professor from Foothill College that got the big grant to
study owls because they are becoming endangered. Endangered
because their feathers are used in pillows. He's the guy that discovered the body. What was his name? Oh, yeah, Crow. Earl T.
Crow. Professor Earl T. Crow. Didn't want to talk about his award
if I remember right. Well guess what, Mr. Crow, I think you need
to do some talking, and certainly about more than your award,
and a little more than you have stated to Captain Wunderlich.

After he finished his small repast, Rex arose from the couch and with a loud and satisfying belch went to the kitchen where he kept the phone book. His finger ran down the C's in the directory. "C...Ca...Cl...Co...Cr...here we go. Cramer...Crenson...Crind...Crow. Okay, now where are you, Earl? No Earls, but here is an E.T. Crow. Gotcha. As he was jotting down the number, the phone, which was just out of reach, rang. Well, you'll just have to wait, whoever you are. Leave a message; I'm not looking up this number again.

As he was writing down E.T.'s number and street address, the answering machine recorded a message. "Hello there, Mr. Private Eye. This is Abe Willing. Give me a call at..."

Him I do want to talk to. He needs to hear from Mr. Crow too, Rex thought. He tried to reach the phone before Abe hung up, then stopped himself. No, wait a minute, Rexy. It's okay to share, but he doesn't have to know everything I do. Not just yet, anyway.

CHAPTER FORTY-THREE

WHAT THE OWL SAW

I come frequently to the Union cemetery, for the bucolic soli-
tude and the safety a burial ground affords, and of course the
food. That is mainly why I come. The food. I come on nights that
are still, when the dark lavender sky is pierced by the moon and
stars, and on stormy nights when the celestial lights are doused
by dense pillows of clouds. Weather doesn't intimidate me. Not
much does when I am hungry. Hunger has a way of taking away
my fear and, since I am hungry always, I am afraid never. For I am
an owl. Those who know me well call me *Strix varia*.

That particular night in mid-March was lighted by a full
moon. I had flown to a perch in a great live-oak tree where I had
a clear view of the entrance to the cemetery. From that vantage
point I could see any unwise mouse or other creature that might
foolishly venture out after dark. As I was scanning the scene in
search of an entree for the evening, a car drove into the cemetery.
That was unusual for that hour, and I followed the course of the
car until it stopped near the stone base that had held the old soldier statue back when I was a young bird.

A man got out of the car. He looked all around, as if he, too,
were on the lookout for something to eat. Then he opened a door
on the other side of the car where another man was all slumped
over and not moving. The first man pulled the slumped man from
the car and dragged him to the old monument base and propped
him up against the stone surface.

The first man proceeded to remove all the clothing from the other man. He wadded the clothes into a ball and turned to stuff them into the car The naked one then began to move, and I thought the first man should know about that that, so I called to him, "Hoot/hoo, hoo, too-HOO; hoo, hoo, too-HOO, ooo."

The man by the car jumped and looked terrified, so I tried to reassure him that it was just me, a bird, wise but not a threat.

"Hoot/hoo, hoo, too-HOO; hoo, hoo, too-HOO, ooo," I called again softly.

When he figured out what the sound was, he cursed me. "A goddamned owl!" he cried.

"Well same to you, dumbbell! Am I not one of God's creatures too? Who are you to damn me?" I furiously hooted back at him. With that off my breast, there wasn't much for me to do other than to watch, which I did with both eyes.

The naked man then began to moan and tried to move his arms. The rude man became agitated and yelled, "Shit and double shit. Haven't you had enough, you money-grubbing druggist son of a bitch? Well, let's see how you like this!"

And he went to over the car and grabbed a pillow and a dark colored bottle. He put the pillow over the naked man's face and held it as his victim struggled weakly, moving his head back and forth, trying for air. The angry man put the bottle between his knees, removed the stopper, and poured the contents onto the pillow, every last drop. After several minutes, the naked man became still, and the angry man pressed the pillow harder against the man's face, holding it tight for a long while. Then he took the pillow away from the face and moved away. As I saw him putting the pillow and the empty bottle in the car, he seemed to be looking for something in the back of the car. He slammed the car door and turned back to the naked man.

"You dirty bastard, you said there were two bottles of the stuff, and there was just that one. And I wasted it killing your ass. You shit-faced cheatin' son of a...," and he angrily hit the naked man's face several times with the pillow. Feathers flew on a gust of the night breeze and some landed on the naked man. I sincerely hoped that no one would think they came from an owl, for I didn't want to be involved in whatever was going on. The angry man carefully picked the feathers off of the naked man and put them in his pocket. But, probably because I can see so well in the dark, I noticed that he had missed one feather. It had lodged in the naked man's nose. The angry man took the pillow with him as he got back in the car and drove off.

I said goodbye, even though he probably didn't hear me in his haste. "Too-HOO, ooo," I said, "too-HOO, ooo."

● ● ●

Alone at last, I sighed with pleasure. Now it's just me and my quarry—no humans. But, just then, another man appeared from behind the trees and approached the monument. I had seen him on other nights. I recognized from the boxes on his back and the pipe he used to look at me. He knelt down beside the naked man and was touching his wrist when the sound of crunching gravel and the staccato rumble of a motorcycle could be heard from the direction of the cemetery entrance. The sounds were accompanied by a beam of light. The man jumped up and ran back to his hiding place behind the trees.

The rider of the motorcycle was also one I had seen before and often. He had long hair and his clothes were a bit ragged. On his frequent visits he would always set a fire to stuff in a little tube of paper and then lean back against the monument's plinth and suck on the smoke from the burning stuff. Then he would sleep. More than once I was close enough to smell the smoke, and I have to admit it was sweet and seemed to make the night go better. Sometimes he put on a skirt like I see the females wear, and he would dance around and sing. But not on this night. This time, he got off his bike and slowly approached the monument where the naked man was propped. He looked closely at the man and then yelled out into the night.

"It's you! Oh my God, it's you. How did you get here? You are alive, aren't you? You can't be dead. I don't know what to do. You're naked. Oh, this is awful. You must be cold. Where are your clothes? Are you stoned? Oh, God, what am I supposed to do? Help. I need to go for help. But you look so cold. Here, let me get something. Hold on."

And the long-haired man took an item out of a pouch attached to his motorcycle. The item was a folded-up shiny coat you could see through. With a considerable struggle he got the coat onto to the naked man. Then he stood up, but didn't move, he just stared down at the wrapped man. I could see he was crying. Then he said, "I'll be right back. Just wait. I'll get help," and he raced away on the motorcycle. The man with the tube and boxes was still there among the trees. I looked very closely at him. He seemed frozen in place. A woeful foghorn sounded far off and it was answered by the ever lonely whistle from a train at some distant crossing. The sounds did not seem to affect the man. Thinking he may have fallen asleep, I called out to him, "Hoot hoo, hoo, too-HOO." When he finally came out of his trance, I flew straight up as fast and as high as I could and circled the cemetery. I watched him as he gathered his equipment and took his leave, looping back toward the front of the cemetery. I could see a bicycle hidden in the bushes near the entry. The man got on the bicycle peddled out the gate. I wanted to give him a good bye hoot, but we were too far apart. I am sure I will see him again, however, when things calm down here.

I returned to my treetop vantage point to see what would happen next. Hardly had the man on the bicycle left when another car raced into cemetery, barely slowing as it made its way among the gravesites. This was a really big car, long and square, like the one that bring the big boxes that people place into the ground. The car pulled up next to the soldier monument in a rush, barely missing two old headstones. The long-haired man bolted out of the door and rushed to the raincoat-clad body. The young man was joined by the other person from the car, a woman, dressed in exercise clothes with a scarf tied over her head

"Wake up," he pleaded, "Wake up." And he grabbed the raincoat and began to shake the man, slowly at first, and then harder and harder. I could see the naked man's head was flopping back and forth, not unlike the way the heads of my dinners flop as I carry them away to eat.

Then the woman hissed, "Stop! You'll hurt him. You can break his neck that way. Just calm down. Move over," and she knelt beside the naked man in the coat.

After a few moments she turned to the young and said, "Quick, there's a bottle of Windex in the car. Get it! It's under the passenger seat!"

He came back with a bottle with blue liquid in it and gave it to the woman. She tilted the man's head back, squeezed open his mouth and pushed on the top of the bottle with her finger. A spray came out but the man did not react. Then she slapped him lightly on the cheek and his head flopped to one side. Again I thought of my dinner flopping around, and my stomach told me I should find some food before it got much later.

"You killed him!" exclaimed the young man, now acting panicky.

The woman touched the man's chest and then sat back on the ground. "No, I don't think so."

"But he was alive," cried the young man.

"He's dead, son. All that shaking, I told you to stop."

"It was the Windex. That's poison. And you slapped him, too."

"No, it is not. I think it has ammonia in it like smelling salts and should wake him if he's alive. But he's dead. At least I'm pretty sure. Whatever the case, we need to get out of here," she said as she rose and moved toward the car.

When she looked back to summon the young man, he was bent over the body, writing with a red stick on the front of the raincoat.

"What in the hell are you doing?" the woman cried.

"I'm writing something for him."

"You must be out of your mind!" the woman yelled in a mad voice, grabbing him by the back of his shirt and pulling him toward the car. "For the love of God, what were you writing on that raincoat?"

The young man, the red stick still in his hand answered her. "It is a saying that Grandma has on a plaque in her house. It says 'If you seek forgiveness, start with yourself.' But you didn't let me finish it."

Then the two people got in the big long car and went away. And I got down to the business of finding something to eat, while there was a lull in the happenings of this busy and memorable spring night.

CHAPTER FORTY-FOUR

Rex brushed off the top of the old foot locker with the back of his hand, filling the air in the attic with dust that made him sneeze and curse. The stenciled black lettering on the olive drab locker read "NICKELS, REX R/23574597".

It's been a while...twenty years...since everything in this trunk was all I owned, and the Army owned me. He pulled himself back from remembering his G.I. days and opened the lid. Here was his uniform, which he, like many others before him, had kept and would never wear again, even if he could get into it. There were pictures and other things from childhood that he kept for no logical reason. Near the bottom he found what he was looking for, the merit badge sash from his Boy Scout uniform. Sewn onto it were twenty one merit badges and pinned to it were the badges of rank he had earned as a Scout. He rubbed a thumb over the silver eagle on his Eagle Scout badge, remembering how his father pushed him to earn it. "Someday, if not now, this will mean something to you and other people," his father, Rufus, had said.

"I guess you were finally right, Dad," muttered Rex as he took the sash from the footlocker and closed the lid. He made his way to the hatch in the attic floor and down the folding ladder into the house.

Finishing breakfast with a second cup of coffee and a blueberry muffin, he reviewed his plan for the tenth time and called the number he had found for E.T. Crow. "Hello?" a voice answered cautiously.

"May I speak to Earl Crow, please?" said Rex.

"What is this about? Who's calling?"

"My name is Forrest Curtiss. I am a Boy Scout merit badge counselor for the Bird Watching Merit Badge, and I need some help. Are you Mr. Crow?"

"Oh, yes. I am he. What kind of help do you need, and why call me?" Crow was thawing out a bit, but still wary.

"I read about you in the Trib and the medal for your work with the owls. Congratulations. I'm an amateur bird watcher and when my son became a Scout they needed a counselor for the merit badge. It looked like a simple job at first, but it seems it may be a little more than I am qualified for. Owls are my son's favorite bird. He has pictures of them all over his room. He keeps asking me questions I can't answer. I thought maybe you could give me some tips or tell me where to read up on the birds that the Scouts might be able to locate and study."

"Well, sure, I guess that would be all right. I was a Scout myself once. That merit badge is how I started to get interested in birds, as a matter of fact," said Crow, now warm to the idea.

Bingo! Rex said to himself. I've hit the mother lode. Then aloud, "Oh, what a relief. I thought you might not be interested or not have enough time, what with your teaching and all. I don't suppose you could see me today, could you? I know it is short notice and all, but the Court of Review for Troop 73 is coming up week after next, and some of these kids need my help before that. But you probably are too busy."

"Actually, Mr. Curtiss, today is the only day that I do have time. It is Saturday and I don't have any Saturday classes this semester. So, I can talk to you today, if you like. I'm leaving shortly for my office. I plan on being there for the rest of the morning. Is that too soon for you?"

"Not at all. My son and I were going to the museum sometime today, but we can do it in the afternoon. Where is your office? I can meet you there."

Crow told Rex to go to the college and park in the public lot next to the bookstore. He would meet him there and they could walk to the office he shared with two other adjunct professors, an office hard to find at the other end of the campus. They agreed on ten o'clock. He decided to take his merit badge sash with him for support.

Rex was surprised that Crow's office was spare and undecorated. Hardly anything on the walls except his degrees, which were hard for Rex to read without being obvious. There was a pile of what looked like hiking equipment in one corner: a knapsack, a telescope, binoculars and some other items in leather cases with straps. There was nothing at all on Crow's desk, and seeing an uncluttered desk told Rex that he and Crow were probably different in more than one way. Rex had not seen his own desk top since he bought the desk. When they were seated, Rex placed the merit badge sash on the desk, and unfolded it. Then he looked Crow directly in the eye.

"These merit badges, are all mine, including the one for Bird Watching. This is it, here," and Rex placed his pudgy index finger on the medallion embroidered with the red figure of a cardinal. "And this, my Eagle badge. And this sash. At one time it fit over my shoulder and around my body. All that is true. Some of the other things I told you are not entirely so."

"What do you mean?" said Crow, at once cautious. "What is not true?"

"I am not Forrest Curtiss. I don't have a son, and I am not connected in any way to the Boy Scouts, other than having been one once. My name is Rex Nickels and I am a private investigator."

"I thought that Boy Scouts always told the truth, if I recall my Scout oath correctly," retorted Crow. It wasn't surprising to Rex, perhaps because Crow was on his own academic turf. He turned aggressive. "It is hypocritical, or outright dishonest of you to come here under the guise of being with the Boy Scouts and talk about 'truth'."

Rex countered. "Professor, may I point out to you that there is nothing in the Boy Scout oath about telling the truth. Or in the Boy Scout Law, for that matter. Your memory could use a refresher course. But there is mention of being 'trustworthy' and being 'helpful'."

"What am I supposed to derive from that comment? Why are you here?"

"I'm helping in the investigation of the dead man you discovered in Union Cemetery."

"I reported all that to the police." Crow became defensive.

"Yeah, sure you did. But here is where 'trustworthy' and 'helpful' come in. You were neither, were you? You told just enough to cover yourself. There is more to tell, isn't there, Professor? Maybe, even, a lot more?"

There was a moment of silence marked by unwavering eye contact between the two. When Crow finally looked away, Rex decided it was time to take the gloves off.

"Let's cut the crap, Crow. Something happened at the cemetery that night and you know what it is. You are going to tell me. Now."

"You are not the police. I don't have to tell you a thing. Now get out of my office." Crow had become defiant.

"No, you don't have to tell me anything. But you may want to. But if you don't talk to me today, and I find out there is more to tell, then I will use this. I promise you." And Rex pulled an envelope from his jacket pocket.

"What is that?"

"This, my owl-watching friend, is an envelope addressed to Mr. Robert Strouse, President, Allday Avian Conservatory, 1411 Mockingbird Lane, Maycomb, Alabama. You don't believe The Conservatory would want someone who told less than the truth wearing their esteemed Gold Medal, now, do you? If something comes out later that should come out now, all I have to do is tell Mr. Strouse that in a letter, put the letter in this envelope, put a stamp on the envelope and mail it."

The veins in Crow's neck became visible and his face reddened. He turned to Rex and hissed in a low voice. "Let me tell you something, you lying pseudo detective. I am E. T. Crow, and I'm highly recognized in my field. I'm the Chairman of the Northern California Professional Ornithologists Association. I study creatures to learn about them for whatever good I can find. I'm not like your kind who spy on people so you can find out whatever bad you can. Letter? You are threatening me with a letter? There is nothing you could possibly tell Strouse or the Allday Avian Conservancy that isn't pure conjecture. You are trying to blackmail me Mr. Nickels, and you need to leave before I call the police."

"Before you get yourself too far out on a limb," Rex said calmly, "it might be good for you to know that withholding information is obstruction of justice which is a crime punishable by ten to fifteen years in jail."

"So?"

"So, if you know something that you aren't telling, you could end up with a lot bigger problem than your standing in the bird world. All you have learned and know about owls won't mean shit if you are locked up. All that work, all those years will be wasted. No one will ever have heard of you. And this isn't the only envelope. I have another one with the same information ready to be delivered to Captain Wunderlich at the Redwood City Police Department."

Crow's body sagged as he took a deep breath and let out a long sigh. He let a minute pass without moving or saying anything. Finally, his eyes became a little watery, and he turned to look out of the window, saying softly, "I just didn't want to get involved, that's all."

"Well, you are. This isn't bird watching. Talk to me."

With quiet resignation and the deliberate academic attitude worthy of an adjunct professor, Earl T. Crow described what he saw on the night of March 15th. He told of his purpose to locate *Strix varia* and record its sound, of seeing a car containing two men drive up to the monument and of one man taking the other from the car and placing him against the monument. He revealed that he watched as one man removed the other's clothing, and how, when the naked man began to move and moan, the first man got a pillow and a bottle of something from the car, emptied the bottle onto the pillow and put it on the naked man's face. He told of the first man returning to the car and yelling at the naked man and then hitting him in the face with the pillow, and then driving off.

"As soon as he was gone I came out of the trees where I was hiding and went to check on the man at the monument. I was looking for a pulse when some kid came into the cemetery on a motorcycle and I went back into the trees to watch."

Crow continued his narrative, relating how the motorcycle kid yelled, "It's you! Oh my God." He related that the kid was crying and talking to the naked man and had gotten a plastic raincoat and put it on him and then left to get help.

"I decided I didn't want to see anymore and I gathered my gear and headed back into the cemetery to get as far away as I could. I was shocked at what I had seen and very upset. I really wanted to get away. After walking a bit, I circled back along the edge of the property that borders Woodside, found my bike in the bushes and got the hell out of there."

"What time was this?" asked Rex.

"It must have been about four in the morning. I got back to my apartment at four thirty. I tried to sleep and couldn't. I tossed and turned for an hour or so and finally decided to get in touch with the authorities. I called them from my place and then rode back over to the cemetery."

"So, the business about calling from a pay phone wasn't..."

"Exactly accurate," finished Crow. "I didn't want to explain to policeman all the details of why I was out there in the middle of the night studying owls, so I simplified things by telling them that I was bird watching just before dawn. I figured they would understand that and not question me any further. My account of what happened wasn't..."

"Exactly accurate," said Rex sarcastically.

"Look, I had nothing to do with the murder. I didn't even know he was dead, for sure. I don't take pulses for a living. I study birds. Owls in particular. I just didn't want to get involved. And I still don't."

"Whether you like it or not, you are, Professor. Thanks for the information. I believe what you've told me, and if you want it, here's some free advice. Tell all of this to the police. As soon as possible. You probably aren't in too much trouble if you come forward now. If you wait, it can only get worse for you."

Rex stood up to leave and turned back as he reached the door and said, "And you might want to talk to a lawyer before you go in. Just to be on the safe side."

He took a step back to Crow's desk and put the envelope on it. As the door closed behind Rex, Crow looked at the envelope. It was blank.

CHAPTER FORTY-FIVE

On Monday morning Earl T. Crow made his way to the address he had been given on Hamilton Street behind the Courthouse in Redwood City. When he found a tidy Victorian house at the designated location, he was a bit confused, having expected an office building of some sort. Instead he found a surprisingly well-preserved old house with a gingerbread-trimmed front porch. Attached to the porch railing was a modest sign that proclaimed: "Alan Meade Poole-Gass, Consultant".

Okay. That's the name of the man Nickels told me about, so here goes, Crow thought as he ascended the six steps to the porch. Next to the door was a brass doorbell, activated by a twist lever, which he turned. He could hear the 'brr..ringg' inside and shortly the door was opened by a young woman in a very, very short skirt. Crow blurted, "Mr. Poole, uh, Gass?"

"Yes, this is the right place," the woman said. "Are you Mr. Crow? I'm Daphne Priestly, Mr. Poole-Gass's assistant. Please come in."

"Uh, yes," Crow blurted, struggling to keep his eyes on Daphne's face, in order to avoid staring at her legs. "I think Rex Nickels arranged an appointment for me?"

"Oh, yes, Mr. Poole-Gass is expecting you," Daphne gestured through an open door.

"Please have a seat here in his office. He'll be right with you."

Crow took a chair by the desk and surveyed the room. Dark paneling, books, heavy drapes. Some framed diplomas and awards. A lot of photos of people posing with each other. Nothing of real interest to him like stuffed birds or avian figurines. Not even an Audubon print. After a minute a door behind the desk opened, and a large figure entered the room and extended his hand in greeting. "Mr. Crow! How do you do? I'm Al Poole."

Crow took the offered hand. He was somewhat stunned. He immediately saw that Poole-Gass was the image of Rod Taylor, the star of Hitchcock's *The Birds*, Crow's all-time favorite movie. Older, somewhat heavier, but tall, same sandy hair, square jaw, blue eyes.

"Uh, oh, well, thanks for seeing me. Rex Nickels said you could arrange for me to consult with an attorney? He believes I need some help in, uh, in clarifying some matters with the police. Uh, I'm not sure I understand why he sent me to you. Are you an attorney yourself?"

Poole-Gass smiled. "Oh, I did spend some time studying the law in London, but I got interested in other things and was never admitted to the bar. I manage some investments and do a lot of, let's say 'coordinating'—putting people together. I've known Rex from around town, and his father before him. And I pretty well know all of the attorneys in San Mateo County, including the prosecutors and most of the law enforcement officers for that matter. So that's why Rex sent you my way. I do, in fact, have someone in mind. I've taken the liberty of discussing your situation with a smart young lawyer who is interested in advising you. In fact, she happens to be here in my chambers right now, and I would like to introduce you if I may?"

Crow responded, "Oh! I didn't expect things to move so fast. Well, sure, yes, of course!"

Poole-Gass pressed a button on his phone, and almost immediately a female figure stepped through the door from the reception area. Crow twisted around to see her and stumbled to his feet. Yikes! he thought to himself. Can this be Tippi Hedren, or am I losing my mind?

Poole-Gass said, "My dear, may I present Earl T. Crow? Mr. Crow, this is Willa Peale, Esquire, one of my favorite advocates."

"Mr. Crow, I'm so happy to meet you. Mr. Poole-Gass has described your unusual situation to me, and I've also spoken briefly to Mr. Nickels. I feel confident that we can get things worked out."

Willa shook Crow's hand, and at her touch he could only mumble a barely adequate response. He thought, I am going crazy. The lips. And look at those big eyes, the arched eyebrows. And blonde hair piled up all soft like the rump of a swan. It is Tippi, my dream! Crow smiled to himself and felt giddy.

Poole-Gass said, "Well, Mr. Crow, I take it by your smile that you're receptive to Willa's services. If you like, the two of you can confer here, in the next room just through that door. Daphne will be available to provide tea or whatever else you may need."

"Shall we, Mr. Crow?" Willa said in her most professional sexy voice, opened the adjacent conference room door and went in.

Unable to speak coherently, Crow could only obey, and puppy-like, followed Willa into the room.

CHAPTER FORTY-SIX

"Just remember, Mr. Crow, you are a scientist. A good scientist. A scientist is objective. Remain objective and deliberate when you talk to the police captain," Willa Peale reminded Earl as they approached the entrance to Police Headquarters.

"Except a good scientist doesn't lie. I lied," Crow responded glumly.

She stopped them both and took his shoulders, looking him straight in the eye. Their faces were very close. Geeze, thought Crow, how can I be objective when I am this close to Tippi Hendren? His keen scientific mind fuzzed over for a minute, and he looked away from her gaze.

"Remember what we said at our meeting this morning in Poole-Gass's office. You have done nothing wrong. You may not have done all you could, but you did nothing overtly wrong."

•••

At that initial meeting with Peale, Crow had asked, "Isn't it a crime to withhold evidence?"

"In the first place, you didn't withhold evidence. Information, maybe, but not evidence. What you did may have been wrong, but it wasn't a crime. And it wasn't that intentional."

"Isn't that splitting hairs, Miss Attorney Peale?" Earl had said somewhat sarcastically.

"That's what I do, Professor Crow. Split hairs. That is why I am here," she had said in a low and determined voice that would put any man off-center.

And in a far off corner of his mind he had wanted to say, "I thought what you do was to act in movies." But he had snapped out of it and said to Willa, "Yeah, I understand. I guess it is all in the definitions, isn't it? 'Overtly', 'all I could', 'withhold', 'wrong', 'crime', 'intentional'. My world is more cut and dried than that."

"Right now, your world is a little upside down, and my job is to put it back right side up. So, you tell me what you told the police, and what you didn't tell them. We will talk about what your problems are and what can and can't be done. After this meeting you will call the police station and make an appointment to visit with Captain Wunderlich. It won't be necessary to tell him on the phone that I will be accompanying you."

Crow had told her everything he had done and seen that night, and his account was detailed and concise. This was a relief to Willa, as she had not expected such focus from someone as addled and withdrawn as Crow had appeared. She reminded herself that he was, after all, a scientist and an academic.

When he had finished, she had pointedly moved the telephone right in front of him with a piece of paper and a phone number. "I will wait outside." And then she had left, closing the door to the conference room behind her.

Feeling somewhat like an elementary student that had been sent to the principal's office, Earle Crow had made the call and set up the meeting they were about to have with Wunderlich.

•••

Willa released her grip on Earl's shoulders, and they continued into Police Headquarters where they sought out Fred Wunderlich's office. The receptionist asked them to have a seat while she notified the Captain of their presence.

"Remember," Willa said in a low voice, "be honest and straight-forward and keep your composure. I won't say anything unless I have to. But if I interrupt, let me speak. Okay?"

Crow, sitting hunched over with his forearms on his legs and his head down, turned to Peale and simply said "Yes," trying not to look at her as a woman, but as his lawyer who was here to get him out of a jam. It wasn't easy.

After five minutes they were shown into Wunderlich's office, and when the Captain saw there were two visitors and that one was a woman, he stood up and came around the desk.

"You, I take it, are Earl T. Crow?" he looked at Crow. And then to Peale. "And you? Are you Mrs. Crow?" he said, keeping his composure. Surprises he didn't like. Women he did. So he struggled inside to be Captain Wunderlich and not Fred.

"How do you do," said Willa, offering her hand to Wunderlich. "I'm Willa Peale. I am Mr. Crow's counsel."

Any problem that Wunderlich may have had with which hat to wear was quickly dispensed with that revelation, and after a perfunctory handshake he returned to his chair. A lawyer was a lawyer, no matter what he, or even she, looked like. As he sat, he put his hands together behind his head, lacing his fingers and leaned back in his chair, not speaking, and studied the two people standing in front of him. He allowed the awkward silence that followed to grow and work to his advantage until he finally said, mockingly, "Please take a seat, Miss *Beale*, and you, Mister Crow." Wunderlich radiated all-cop mode.

"When you set this up, you told my assistant that you had something to tell me about the murder in Union Cemetery. Since you are the one who called us to report discovery of the body, I assume something has come to memory that you want to relate. Would that be correct? And why would you need an attorney to tell me that?"

Crow cleared his throat, glanced at Willa and said apologetically, "When I talked to the officer that morning..."

"That would be Sergeant Rooney," Wunderlich interrupted and picked up his phone and punched the intercom button.

"Doris, have Bud Rooney come in please." And to the two in front of him he said, "I want Bud to hear this, so we all have our stories straight."

The door opened and a burly young cop with pink cheeks came in. He nodded shyly to all, found a chair and awkwardly took a seat.

"Sergeant Rooney, this, as you know, is Mr. Earl T. Crow. And with him is his lawyer, a Wilma Pearl, I think you said."

"That would be Willa Peale," she said sharply, but with a smile. "Here is my card in case you need help in remembering the name correctly," and she gave cards to both policemen.

"I think the person with the remembering problem is Mr. Crow," countered Wunderlich. "Please continue, Mr. Crow. And Bud, I want you to listen carefully and speak up if he tells a different story from what he told you when you were at the cemetery. I know you aren't used to meetings with lawyers present, but don't hesitate to speak up. Now, Mr. Crow, go ahead."

"As I was saying...uh...when I talked to this officer that morning, I told him that I discovered the body when I was out bird watching and that I was calling from a pay phone to report it to the police..."

"The report I have here on my desk says that you called right after you discovered the body. At six thirty in the morning. Right, Bud?"

"It was exactly zero six hundred hours, twenty-three minutes. Yes, that's right, Sir," said Rooney.

Almost in a trance, Crow cleared his throat again, continuing, "...to report it to the police and that I would be returning to the cemetery. What I really did..." and Crow looked at Willa for support. She gave him a tiny smile of encouragement and nodded for him to continue, "...was to call from my house, not a pay phone. After I called, I rode back to the cemetery on my bicycle to meet the officer. When I met him there, I told him what he told you, I guess. That I found the body when I was on an early morning bird watching trip. Which was sort of true."

239

"So what you told the officer was not entirely true?" Wunderlich said, trying to intimidate Crow.

Willa spoke up in that low and powerful voice, "I am disturbed by your adversarial tone, Captain. Please remember that Mr. Crow is here by his own volition and that he is free to leave if he is not treated with respect."

Wunderlich realized he had underestimated her and pulled back. "What do you mean by 'sort of true,' Mr. Crow?"

"Well, it was just before six thirty when I called. And I did find the body when I was in the cemetery. But it wasn't exactly bird watching I was doing. Well, it was, but it wasn't..."

Wunderlich saw an opening to exploit Crow's searching for words and rattle him, but one glance at Willa's steely gaze made him think otherwise. He remained silent.

"...wasn't just birds I was watching, it was *Strix varia*. Owls to you, hoot owls. I teach ornithology at Foothill College and am doing a research project on *Strix varia*. They are entirely nocturnal and the Union Cemetery is one of their main habitats. So, every night for the last month I have been taking my recording equipment and night glasses out there to record their movements and the sounds they make. In the middle of all the confusion with the police cars and the blinking red lights and all, I just didn't want to try to explain all of that. So I just said that I was bird watching."

"I never really think of owls as birds," observed Wunderlich.

Crow raised his eyebrows as college professors often do when exposed to another's lack of knowledge and continued. "Well, they are, complete with feathers and wings," Crow said with veiled irritation. "So, to go on, it wasn't six thirty in the morning when I discovered the man, it was more like one thirty or two. And I saw more than just him sitting there. A lot more."

"What do you mean, 'a lot more'?" asked Wunderlich.

Crow then proceeded to repeat what he had told Rex Nickels previously. About seeing the two men drive up in a car, of one putting the other against the monument and removing his clothes, then putting a pillow over his head and pouring something into it and then hitting the naked man with the pillow. Crow told about trying to take the man's pulse and being interrupted by the hippie on the motorcycle and how he had hidden and watched the hippie and then fled, returned for his bicycle and gone home.

"And what time was it when you saw all this? When you went home?"

"It must have been about four in the morning, because I got home around four thirty."

"Why didn't you call us then?"

"I was shocked and upset by what I saw and my first reaction was to stay out of it. I really didn't want to get involved. I realized when I got home that my sound recorder for the owl calls was on when I was watching the hippie talk to the naked man. I played it, and it was frightening. I tried to sleep but it haunted me and I couldn't. Finally I got up, called you and rode my bike back to the cemetery. You know the rest." Crow sank back in his chair, his shoulders slumped, and looked at Wunderlich, wondering what was next.

Actually, Captain Wunderlich himself was also wondering what was next. The ball was in his court and he had several choices. He could believe the guy, or not. Crow may be the killer and this could all be an elaborate fabrication. God knows he had heard some doozies in his day. How hard should he question Crow? Should he charge him with false statement to law enforcement? Or obstruction? All of these were options for Wunderlich. But then there was this woman lawyer. How does she fit in? How would an egghead like Crow come up with this knock-out looker with a razor brain? There is something here he should know before he went on.

"I would like to ask a question of your client, Miss Peale. He doesn't have to answer. It is mere curiosity on my part. Off the record."

"You can ask, but he doesn't have to answer unless he wants to and unless I say he can. Off the record or not." Peale answered evenly.

"How did you come to hire Miss Peale here as your attorney?"

Crow looked at Peale for guidance. She nodded for him to answer.

"I had talked to Rex Nickels, and he suggested that I come to you and bring a lawyer. He put me in touch with Mr. Alan Poole-Gass who linked me up with Miss Peale."

"Oh ho," said Wunderlich, as a light came on in his head. "The English guy with two or three names who knows everyone. I see." He now knew which of his options was the best, and, outside of Crow being the killer, which wasn't likely, there wasn't any option that didn't let Crow off the hook easily. He thought to himself, if Alan Meade Poole-Gass is involved, that means this guy is probably connected.

Wunderlich announced to all, "Okay. Thanks. Now we are back on the record. Mr. Crow, I am going to believe your story, because I don't believe you killed anyone and because I need your cooperation to find who the real killer is."

"He has told you all he knows. That was his obligation as a citizen. Exactly what do you mean by cooperation? What else can he tell you?" Peale wanted to know.

"Ease up young lady, let me explain. And don't forget that Mr. Crow here still has to answer to the fact that he didn't tell us all of this in the beginning. But let's hold that till later. What I mean by cooperation is that I want to show him some pictures of people. Maybe he can identify someone as being at the scene. Certainly that can't be incriminating, now can it?"

Wunderlich took a manila folder containing photographs from a drawer in his desk and opened the folder, turning it so Crow could see the pictures right side up. First in the stack was the picture of the victim's car.

"Recognize that?" asked Wunderlich?

"Yes, I think so. It was dark, but I think that is the car the two men arrived in. Everything I saw, I saw with a naked eye and then I used my night scope to check if I could see better. It didn't help. It gives a strange image sometimes. It is made for watching owls, not people. But, yes, I'm pretty sure that's the car I saw." Wunderlich put the photo to one side, and Crow looked at the next one.

"I'll tell you what," said Wunderlich. "You just go through the pictures and make three piles. One for those you can identify, one for those you can't and a third pile for ones you aren't sure about. And feel free to change your mind."

The file contained a random stack of photographs, some-times more than one of the same subject and of different quality. It included pictures of Earnest Kayne, Kay Dale, Kay Dale's car, William Dale, Judson Kayne, Red Ramsey, Owen Owens and sev-eral of people and cars not connected to the case.

They waited while Crow studied each image carefully, sort-ing and stacking as instructed. When he finished, Wunderlich removed the pile of pictures that Crow didn't recognize at all, and put them to one side.

"Now that you have been through them once, look through the pile that's left and see if anything new comes to mind."

When the photographs were finally sorted out, seven of them had been put at the top of the pile. Crow was pretty sure that the young man he had seen at the cemetery was in two of them, but couldn't be absolutely sure. The person in the next two photos Crow thought that he recognized as the one who took the unconscious man from the car, but wasn't 100 percent sure, because it was dark in the cemetery when he saw them and the car. Then there was a picture of the deceased, and of course he recognized him.

Crow then hesitated and put his hands over the pictures that were left and closed his eyes in frustration.

"Only two more, Mr. Crow. Let's finish this up," encouraged Wunderlich.

Of the two photos left to see, one appeared to be of a Cadillac station wagon, and the other had nothing to do with the case so far as Crow could tell. When he looked again and refocused, he was confident in saying that he couldn't identify either for sure.

Wunderlich made notations on his yellow pad and turned it face down on the desk. As he gathered up all the photos and put them back in the file folder, he stood up and said, "That about wraps it up for now. What you have told us will be very helpful, very helpful indeed. Thank you for your cooperation, Mr. Crow. And yours, Miss Peale."

"You are welcome, Captain. And may I ask what cooperation we can expect from you regarding my client's less than timely reporting of the details in this incident?" Willa turned on just enough charm to be effective without losing her no-nonsense demeanor.

"Well, he did apparently witness a crime being committed, and we will want him in town and available until the matter is resolved. Please advise him of that. And if you would be so kind, have him bring us the recording tape he made that night. Please don't make me go to the trouble to get it with a subpoena. As far as what he reported earlier and what he just told me, I can't make any promises, you know that. But I'm sure that leniency will be the first thing that comes to the D.A.'s mind when I tell him how helpful you have been," said Wunderlich with a slight smirk. "I'll let you know."

"I hope you do...soon. Goodbye, Captain. And give the district attorney my best. Let's Go, Mr. Crow. The meeting is over." And a slightly bewildered client and his attorney left the captain's office.

After their departure, Wunderlich turned over his yellow pad and said aloud to Rooney, who was still there. "He identified the car positively and Judson Kayne and Red Ramsey pretty much for sure. And of course, the victim. He didn't recognize either of the Dales or their car. And he didn't identify Owen Owens at all, dammit! You can go now Bud."

Wunderlich pushed the red button on his phone and picked up the receiver. After two rings a voice came on and said, "Olson here. What do you need, Fred?" It was Wilber Olson, the Chief of Police.

"Chief, I need your go-ahead on something. I just had a very interesting conversation with a Mr. Earl T. Crow and his attorney, and he seems to have been an eyewitness to the murder over at Union Cemetery. I think we are about to close this thing out."

"Good job, Fred. Who is the bad guy?"

"It isn't a hundred percent lock yet, so I'd rather not say. But we are close," said Wunderlich. "Since we have a 'person of interest' in mind, I thought you might want to call a press conference and let the public know where we are."

"You said Crow had an attorney with him. Who?"

"A broad named Willa Peale. Know her?"

"No, but I have heard about her. I had a call this morning from my friend Al Poole-Gass, who does know her. I am really busy right now, and since you don't have a suspect to name, I think I will pass on the press conference. Why don't you handle it for me? Just be the spokesman for the department and say I asked you to call the conference. Get the mayor in on it too so he doesn't get his nose out of joint for being kept in the dark. And smooth sailing, Captain." With that, Chief Olson hung up. He was a good cop, and not a bad politician either.

"Thank you, sir. I'll give it my best," Wunderlich replied before Olson signed off. Then he punched the button for his assistant and told her to get the mayor on the line.

"Mayor De La Rossa ? This is Fred Wunderlich over at police headquarters...I'm fine, yes...Dorothea is fine and so are the kids. Thanks for asking...well, I just got off the phone with Chief Olson and we were talking about the Union Cemetery murder. There has been a break in the case and he thinks we should call a press conference with you and release the information...yes...in the public interest. What do you think of the idea?"

Wunderlich waited while the Mayor hemmed and hawed, as he expected he would, and finally the Mayor apparently saw the public relations value in it and agreed.

"Do you want to call the media or should I?" asked Wunderlich. When he got a reply he said, "Yes, I think you should too. Your staff is used to that sort of thing and I am not. I can meet you in your office about a half hour ahead of time and brief you on what I know. I'm free all afternoon so I can be with you at the conference as spokesman for the Department, and help with any questions that may come up...yeah, you are right about that...there are going to be questions. Those guys don't ever let up. Okay, I will wait to hear from your office about time and everything, and thanks, Sir. Goodbye."

Wunderlich leaned back in his chair and assumed his favorite position with his head back and his fingers laced together behind his head. "I love this job," he said.

CHAPTER FORTY-SEVEN

Monday afternoon Rex was in his office, distractedly sort-
ing through junk mail. Earlier he had been alerted by Alan
Mead Poole-Gass to expect a "most interesting" phone call. Just
as Rex was feeling most itchy, thinking about going home to consult with Uncle Jack Daniels, the phone rang.

"Rex, it's Al Poole. Got some jolly news for you. I just heard
from Willa Peale. She and Crow met with Wunderlich this afternoon. Appears it all came down rather well. Crow gave a full
description of what he witnessed at the graveyard. He was shown
some photos, without knowing who he was looking at, and apparently was able to identify photos of Red Ramsey as one of the
guys, and his car as one he saw at the scene. He also ID'd a couple
pictures of Judson Kayne. The kid had shown up, it would seem,
after Earnest Kayne was already dead. Wunderlich seemed to
believe Crow's story, which would mean that he wasn't interested
in Jud. That is the impression that Willa got. And by the way, Kay
Dale's photo went unrecognized when it was shown to Crow. So it
looks rather as though your people are in the clear. Willa had the
feeling that Wunderlich was not terribly anxious to keep all this
under wraps, so you might want to see what turns up on the news
at eleven tonight."

Rex enthusiastically thanked Poole-Gass for the report. After
hanging up, he immediately rang Sheila's number.

"Sheila, listen. I've received a tip that there may be some important news on Channel 7 at eleven tonight. I want you to make sure you and your house guests are tuned in. I'm going to come over to your place just before eleven to check it out with you. Can't say more. See you then."

Sheila and Kay had just been cleaning up after dinner. Jud had gone off to his room to watch TV. It was only nine o'clock, a long wait for Rex's arrival. The women chatted about what news could be coming, and finished a bottle of chardonnay they had started with dinner.

Restless, Sheila said, "Oh, what the hell, here's another one just like that one, all chilled and ready to go. What do you say, Kay?"

Kay smiled and nodded with enthusiasm. Sheila uncorked the bottle and topped up their glasses. Meanwhile, Jud had thrown open the windows in his room and was relaxing with a joint as he enjoyed *The Brady Bunch*.

So it was that, once Rex arrived, having made his own consultation with Uncle Jack, an exceedingly merry group assembled before the TV in Sheila's living room. They didn't know whether they were prepared to celebrate good news, or fortified against bad news. They were at the point that they didn't really care too much, one way or another.

By the time Rex and the two women slumped into Sheila's long couch, while Jud sat cross-legged in front of them on the floor, the newscast had already begun.

"*...still the best. I'm Nan Ebu in tonight for Norbert Swisher, who is ill. Let's get right to the latest from down in Redwood City. About the naked bodies, or body, whatever. Mayor De La Rossa announced today that the local police have identified an 'interested person' oops make that 'person of interest' and there may be one or more persons...or is that people?...all of whom were not identified. When asked by our reporter about the cause of death, information was withheld, was not forthcoming, uh, the last time, where was*

I? Oh well, they still don't know who killed him, or won't tell us, so we can't tell you. But they said a bird, or an owl, was involved, and someone was studying sex variations of owls that hoot. He may have seen something interesting. I've heard they have good eyes. And there was a feather pillow... Oh! Swish! How are you? We thought you were..."

"Sick! I am sick! But not that sick. Ladies and gentlemen, I'll return—alone—after these announcements."

Kay looked at Sheila, Jud looked at Kay, they all turned to Rex, who shrugged and said, "It's just local TV, not Walter Cronkite! Well, here's the latest skinny. My sources tell me that the real story is that a witness named Earl T. Crow has identified Red Ramsey as the person seen dragging Earnest's body to the war monument and applying some kind of liquid and finally smothering him with a pillow."

"Oh my God! No sheeut? It wasn't us?!" Jud cried out.

"Tell us more! What's next?" Kay said.

Jud jumped in, "Now can we get outta' here?"

Rex raised both hands above his head. "I know it's hard, but try to be calm. It's wonderful news, but there's a lot that still needs to play out. I don't want to be a party pooper, but we need to have some serious talk. I don't think any of us is in any condition tonight to focus on hard issues. Wait till tomorrow morning. I'll come back and we'll work on our next moves. But tonight we can all just relax and enjoy the moment. Is there any more of that chardonnay?"

CHAPTER FORTY-EIGHT

Nine o'clock in the morning seemed awfully early to Rex as he maneuvered his way back to Sheila's house. He resented not being at home and on his own time. But, as always, when he drove the twisting, unfettered streets around Vista Drive, he began to feel refreshed and free, as he did with Sheila when they were first married. "You know the way, Monza," he said to his car, "this little bit of fog won't stop us, will it?" Rex was glad he had the top down as he drove though whips of grey-white mist and smelled the morning air.

The job Rex faced this morning was to get Kay and Jud to focus seriously on things that needed to be resolved before they could get back into the public eye. First he would talk to Kay and then Jud. Not exactly saving the best till last, he thought as he parked and went into Sheila's house for the second time in twelve hours.

Sheila and Kay were there when Rex came into the living room, but Jud was nowhere in sight. Rex froze and had an "Oh no, not again" moment that must have shown, because Sheila laughed and said, "Ease up Rexy, he's still here. He's in the john, and the window in there doesn't open up far enough for him to get out. I don't think he wants to go anywhere now, at any rate."

"Not and miss *Days of Our Lives,* which is about to start," smiled Kay.

"Want to join us?" asked Sheila, knowing how much Rex hated soap operas.

"I told you both last night that we needed some serious discussion, and that's what I'm here for. Not for any mushy soap opera crap."

"Oh, I thought it was because you just couldn't stay away," said Sheila, fluttering her eyes. She knew how to get to Rex, particularly in the morning.

"Cut it, Sheila. Kay, I'd like to speak to you. Out on the porch, if you don't mind, privately. And Sheila, you could keep your eye on our friend in there, just to make sure he stays here and stays grown up," Rex instructed as he held the front door for Kay.

When they were settled in the cheap plastic chairs Sheila kept on the porch, Rex got right to the point. "Kay, I think it is okay now for you and Jud to come out of hiding and quit dodging the cops. They aren't interested in you as suspects any longer. And I'm sure that Bill will want to hear from you in person, not just from a pay phone. You will still have some issues to resolve with the police about what transpired with you and Jud at the cemetery, even if they know you are innocent of any crime."

"More important, I would think, is that now Jud and I know that we are innocent of any crime," Kay said. "I honestly thought we might have killed him, Rex."

"Well, you didn't. But you still need to have an attorney to get you all the way out of this. Do you have one?"

"Bill has a firm he uses for business, Mason, Newburg, Frazier, & Payne. But we use Coddington and Wilkins for our personal affairs. I would think they would be the ones to help us with this."

"This is pretty nitty-gritty stuff, Kay. Messy things, like murder, nudity, feathers and pillows, that may not be what Coddington and Wilkins are used to dealing with. Aren't they more into codicils and wills and that stuff?" Rex asked.

"Wilkins may have gotten successful in the law business because of his smarts and his wealthy connections, but Tom Coddington came up the hard way. First he was a cop, then a prosecutor and then went into private practice. He is a hard boiled old coot who takes a little getting used to, maybe, but he knows his stuff. He and Wilkins make a great team. They are tough and smart. I'll talk it over with Bill, but I'm sure he will agree they are what we need."

Rex looked down at the old wood boards of the porch floor for a moment, then spoke without raising his head. "And Jud? He will have his own legal complications. Who helps him out?"

"I'm sure Coddington and Wilkins will take Jud under their wing too. We need to be sure that Jud behaves himself until this all blows over. You can play a part in that."

"Sounds like a good deal to me. Thanks. You talk to Bill, have him contact the lawyers, and then go home, for cryin' out loud. And take that Cadillac of yours with you."

"Too bad there isn't a bus to take," Kay said seductively, wedging Rex into a different frame of mind.

Rex did turn his head then, looked into her eyes and said, "I don't think I could afford the fare anymore." He squeezed her hand.

Kay whispered, "You'll always be in my heart."

Rex gently nudged Kay away and said, "Now, if you don't mind, would you go back in and send young Mr. Judson Kayne out here, so I can give him some of my priestly council?"

Kay reached out and gave Rex a peck on the cheek and did as asked. Soon Jud came out and stood awkwardly in front of Rex.

"Sit down, son. We have some things to get straight."

"I thought I was out of trouble. They know I didn't kill my dad," said Jud and took a seat in one of the plastic porch chairs where Rex indicated.

"You are out of the deep shit, but there is still some on you. Like, explaining what you were doing in the cemetery in the first place, and what you did to Earnest and why. All those explanations can't just float off into the universe you know. These are real-life cops you have to deal with, not The Saint."

Jud stared off to the hills and said in a dreamy voice, "I wonder what my friends are doing now. I wonder if they are listening to The Saint."

Rex snapped his fingers as loud as he could. "Hey! Don't go off into la la land, now. That is the old Jud. Be the new Jud. Focus. Okay?"

And Jud did snap out of it and looked at Rex seriously. "What do I need to do?" he asked, his new maturity emerging at last.

"For right now, don't go anywhere. Stay here with Sheila until I tell you to leave. Be thinking about where you will go eventually and we can talk about it when the time comes. But for now, just stay here. Understand? You will probably be asked to talk to the police and I want you to have a lawyer with you when you do. I am arranging with Kay to have her firm represent you as well. And if the press shows up, don't talk to them under any circumstances. Do only what the lawyers tell you."

"How do I pay them? I can't afford a lawyer"

"Kay is taking care of that. And when this is all over, you may inherit some money, who knows. What is important is that you stay here and keep your mouth shut. No one but Kay, Sheila and I know where you are. Don't answer the phone and don't talk on the phone unless Sheila says you can. Got it?

"And please do all you can to get along with Sheila," Rex continued. "That is not an easy assignment, I should know. But you have to do as I say if you want out of this. Remember, you are the new Jud. You have a future. Don't screw it up." The way Rex said it left no doubt in Jud's mind that it wasn't a mere request.

Rex got up abruptly and went to his car, leaving Jud sitting on the porch. As he pulled out of the driveway, he checked in his mirror to see if Jud went back in the house. He did.

CHAPTER FORTY-NINE

From Sheila's kitchen Kay dialed Bill's private office line, the one to by-pass his secretary. When he answered, it was the first time she had heard his voice in what seemed like a month.

"Bill! Oh, it's so wonderful to hear you...I...I..." said Kay, struggling to maintain her composure.

"Kay! Oh my God, Kay! Where are you? Are you all right? Oh I'm so happy! Are you coming home? Tell me where you are, I'll be right there."

"Oh, Bill. Yes, yes, I'm perfectly all right. Actually I'm not far away, a few minutes. Just in Redwood City, up above the Alameda. I've been staying with, uh, a friend. I'll tell you all about it. I have my car here and I'm just going to drive right home, just as soon as I gather up the few things I have with me and say some goodbyes. Oh how I'm looking forward to my own bathtub and a change of clothes! And to see you, my dearest. Don't ask me any questions right now. Wait till I'm home. Can you get away and meet me at the house?"

"I'm out the door. I'll be there before you, and have your bath drawn!"

After hanging up, Kay looked out to the porch and saw Rex and Jud in a serious talk. She was pleased to see that Jud was engaged and looking Rex in the eye. She packed her small bag and grabbed her car keys.

She found Sheila sitting quietly at the dining room table, leafing through the morning paper, over a cup of coffee.

"Sheila, I hate to run out on you after all you've done..."

Sheila interrupted her. "Kay, I know, I know. Don't waste your time on the niceties. Just go and enjoy your freedom and get back with your husband, fer chrissake."

Kay reached out and embraced Sheila. "You'll always be my friend. In a few days, I'll call and have you come over, for lunch, maybe a swim. How's that sound?"

"Just super," answered Sheila, planting a big smack on Kay's cheek.

Jud came in from the porch. Kay turned to him and said, "Jud, dear, I know Rex wants you to hang on here for a while. I know it will be hard, but please keep cool, do what Rex says, and be really nice to Sheila. You're still going to have a place in my life and we'll be together again soon." She gave Jud a warm hug. He only squirmed a little bit, and rewarded her with a smile.

At last in her car, and headed out of Sheila's driveway, Kay felt herself luxuriating in her plush vehicle, fully appreciating the life that had been interrupted, however briefly, and realizing how eager she was to make up for lost time. She even had a sensuous rush thinking of good, dull old Bill, and what kind of reunion they would enjoy.

Kay piloted her Eldorado wagon down the Alameda de las Pulgas, past the Menlo Country Club, found her regular short-cut to Shelby Lane, and then to her own remote-controlled gate, home at last. Not too surprisingly there was Bill's car in the drive-way, and she found him as promised, in her bathroom beside a full, warm bathtub. They embraced lustily, and to her immense pleasure, Bill joined her in the tub.

Later, on the poolside patio, over salmon sandwiches and a pitcher of sangria, Kay reviewed her adventures of the past ten days, providing only a vague sketch of how Rex Nickels had happened into the picture. Clearly Bill had never imagined anything like the situations, the places, or the people she was describing, but he listened sympathetically. Kay described her growing affection for Jud and her pleasure at how he had seemed to be turning, in recent days, into a grownup. And reluctantly she pointed out that there was still a legal cloud about her behavior "that night" and in following days, and that she would need legal protection.

Bill assured Kay that he would put the whole thing in the hands of Coddington and Wilkins that very day, and that there would be nothing for her to worry about. As for Jud, "Let's see what we can do to help the lad. He probably shouldn't be back at our farm, under the circumstances. Maybe we can find other work for him in the horse business around here. And until he's better settled, what do you say we put him up here in the downstairs bedroom, next to the pool? He could have his privacy, we could have ours. We'd have to agree on some rules, of course."

"Perfect, darling," Kay purred. "Oh Bill, it's so marvelous to be back home with you. You do everything for me. Never let me stray again."

CHAPTER FIFTY

The Break-Thyme Cafe's lunch crowd had just about dispersed when Abel Willing and Rex Nickels sat down for a late lunch and some serious conversation.

Rhonda was still on duty and flounced her way to their table. As she handed them menus she said, snapping her gum, "Good afternoon, gentlemen. What would you like today?" And glancing at Rex, she said, "Besides the entire lunch menu?"

"You mean you aren't serving breakfast? Hell, it's only a little after noon," complained Rex.

"We have 'Chili Three Ways-Peoria Style'," said Rhonda with resignation, rolling her eyes and looking out of the window. "We always have Chili Three Ways-Peoria Style. And for your information, noon was over an hour and a half ago."

"How about donuts?"

"We always have donuts."

"Well, then, you really are still serving breakfast, now, aren't you?" Rex smirked up at Rhonda, who just crossed her arms and waited.

"I will have the famous Chili Three Ways-Peoria Style. It's been on my mind a lot, recently. Peoria, that is," put forth Abel.

"I guess I will go light and just have Chili Two Ways-Redwood City Style," Rex decided, and after a pause added, "and of course three frosted donuts. Don't want to miss breakfast, you know." Rex always enjoyed irritating Rhonda.

As she wrote out the order, she read it aloud. "That's two Chili Three Ways, hold the cheddar on one, and three white wall spare tires. That it?"

"Coffee for me," said Rex. "You too?" he asked Abel, who nodded yes.

As Rhonda repeated her saucy flounce on her way back to the kitchen, Rex and Abel got down to brass tacks.

"Abel, we just about have Ramsey, that son of a bitch. We are almost home. All we need is a clincher."

"Yeah, I know," said Willing, "The captain and I had one of those little professional exchanges of information that cooperating enforcement agencies have from time-to-time. The guilty guy is our old friend Red Ramsey, and Wunderlich is ready to bring him in. Fred knows that I have had my eye on both Ramsey and Owens, and he wanted to make sure the timing was right to nab Ramsey. I mentioned to him before that I wanted to catch Owens in the same net if possible. He's the one I'm after. The captain may have Ramsey dead to rights, but I'm still missing the final piece I need to get Owens."

"I guess you know as much as I do about how the murder took place and the positive I.D. of Ramsey at the scene and doing the deed," said Rex.

"Yes, but from what Wunderlich told me, they still need for Crow to identify Ramsey in person, and not just as someone in a photograph. Fred is really anxious for that to take place."

"And I imagine you really worked on old Fred to hold off until you can get them both at the same time?"

"Yes, and I was successful," Abel smiled faintly.

"Perhaps there were debts out there...inter-agency debts, and one came due?" suggested Rex.

"I think you could say that, yes. And now we are even for a while. It cost me in that regard, but I am determined to get that sly bastard Owens. And part of the deal now is that Ramsey and Owens come in under the same arrest."

"I get the impression that you have something brewing in your head as to how this can be done." Rex offered as he pushed back from the table to make room for Rhonda and her tray.

"I have something in mind, but it's not entirely put together yet. I thought that we might brainstorm and see what we can come up with."

Rex nodded and gave an affirmative thumbs up, being unable to use words because his mouth was already full of chili. By the time he finished that first mouthful, he had a full grip on a frosted donut, which he used as a pointer. With his free hand he pulled a folded paper from his pocket and placed it on the table so Abel could read it. It was the latest copy of the racing newspaper, *The Bay Meadows Bugle*. Using his donut, he pointed to an article circled in red.

Bay Meadows Handicap To Be Run On Saturday
Bay Meadows Race Track posted the latest list of entries for the 37th running of the 'Bay Meadows Handicap' on this coming Saturday. Among the horses scheduled to run are:

Awesome Dancer (Whispering Oaks)	*2-1*
Boaster (Dublin Glen)	*3-1*
Golden Times (Coventry Lane Farm)	*5-2*
Dare To Go (Maplewood Place)	*6-1*
Globetrotter (Meadowlark Acres)	*6-5*
Alimaya (Windfall Acres)	*10-1*
Roman Night (Meadows Green)	*20-1*
Peoria Heights (Hillandale Stables)	*30-1*

Odds makers are awaiting the news out of Hillandale Stables concerning Princess Khey. As late as Monday night, Red Ramsey, the trainer at Hillandale, declined to confirm if the horse will be in the race. The owners, William and Kay Dale and Owen Owens, could not be reached for comment. It was, however, confirmed that Princess Khey's stable mate, Peoria Heights, would be running.

"Being the sleuth that you are, I'm sure you know about this," said Rex.

"Oh, yeah. Of course. Other people get to read the comics and the obituaries when they get up in the morning. In my business, the first thing is the *B.M. Bugle*. It looks to me like Owens and Ramsey are up to their old tricks, keeping the betting world guessing until the last minute. The horse will run, believe me. He knows it. But they will wait to announce that until right before the deadline for setting the odds, which will change with Princess Khey in the race, and the odds against the long shot wining will skyrocket. Before most of the rest of the betting world can react, Owens will place a lot of moderate bets all over the map and clean up when the long odds horse wins."

"But how does he know which horse will win?" asked Rex, fascinated by the scheme.

Abel answered quickly. "He doesn't, not for absolute sure. But he has the raced rigged nonetheless."

"But how is it rigged? And which horse is it?"

"The how and the which are tied up together. The horse is going to be, I'm damned sure, Peoria Heights".

"But that is a horse from Hillandale Stables. She is the slowest plug on the lot, from what I've heard."

"That is what you have been supposed to hear. All year, she has finished last or nearly last, and nobody pays any attention to her. The horse from the next stall, Princess Khey, wins about as much as Peoria Heights loses, and everyone knows her name and her record."

"What prevents Khey from winning, and screwing up the curve, so to speak?" Rex had actually stopped eating and, sat motionless, holding a half-eaten frosted donut in mid-air, his elbow on the table. "Is Ramsey going to drug the horses? Is that what this is all about? Drugs, horses and a dead pharmacist all point a finger at horse doping it seems to me. How do you know all this?"

"A little scholarship, my friend. A little scholarly research. I went back and studied the races these horses had been in and their performance. Then I did the same for all the other horses in the races. And what I discovered is that even though Princess Khey wins most of the time, she beats inferior horses. She's a great horse, don't mistake that, but what they have been doing is carefully putting her up against horses that are slightly slower, but have respectable times at other tracks. And they let her lose or place once in a while. But the main thing is that they have created an image of a horse that is almost unbeatable.

"And as far as Peoria Heights is concerned, this is where it gets interesting. It seems that before Hillandale bought this horse, she was one of the most promising young fillies in all of Ireland. The owner went broke, and the Dales and Owens got the horse for a song. They kept the whole thing under wraps as much as possible. When they started racing her, somehow, Ramsey got her to not do so well. Some of our surveillance out there at the farm saw her doing incredible times that she has never come close to in actual races. And when they had her working out with Princess Khey, Peoria Heights never lost."

"What do you mean, exactly, by your 'surveillance'?" Rex asked.

"This is off the record, because all of the legal back up may not be in place yet, so I'll have to trust you to forget I ever told you any of this. Okay? For some time now, we've had a hidden camera out at Hillandale, trained on their workout track. It's concealed in an old tree at the edge of the track, and has an electric eye that controls it. It works great, but changing the film and batteries is not easy. Our staff has a couple of pretty sneaky guys who handle that sort of thing. So far, they haven't been spotted."

Rex said nothing, but was attentive and deep in thought, awaiting the next piece of scholarly research.

"And how do you suppose Ramsey got her to 'not do so well'? Hmm? My private detective friend?" Abel queried when he realized Rex was not going to speak.

Then Rex pounced, slamming his fist down on the counter, scattering bits of doughnut frosting everywhere. "He was drugging the dam nag, that is what he was doing! He was drugging

Peoria Heights while everyone was watching Princess Khey. He was drugging her to slow down, to lose. To build a record as a loser! So eventually she could win as a surprise against tough odds and pay big. But what drug? Is that the connection with Kayne? And I thought they could test for that, that they did test for that."

"This is where the scholastic research really paid off," Abel explained. "It seems as if chloroform was used as a veterinary anesthetic early in this century. It fell into disuse as time and medicine progressed. It used to be pretty prevalent as a knock-out drug, but not anymore. It's still around, and would you believe, it is relatively easy to make if you have the right ingredients and know how to mix them. Using a small amount on an animal as large a horse slows the animal's reflexes enough to just take the edge off his or her performance. And the amount is small and metabolized very quickly. An examiner would have to really be looking hard to find it, and it isn't even on most of their radars. I checked with our guys and they said it isn't something they would be looking for on a regular check-up. Bear in mind that it is still a regulated substance."

"Aha, but someone working in a pharmacy would have access to it or its ingredients and the equipment and know-how to mix it. Enter Earnest Kayne, pharmacist. He must have been supplying it to Red Ramsey. Something went wrong and Ramsey killed him. Sucker probably raised his prices once too often, and Ramsey lost patience," offered Rex.

"Or Kayne figured out the betting scheme that Owens was up to and tried to blackmail them both. Either way, Kayne is dead, Ramsey killed him and Owens is part of the whole mess. He might steer clear of the murder part, but he can't get out of the race fixing and betting part. He is my target for that," Abel was raising his voice.

"You really hate that guy don't you?" said Rex. "Well, rest assured he won't be able to wash his hands of what happened to Kayne. They'll get him. But right now they want to nail Ramsey more than Owens and you want Owens more than Ramsey. How nice," he observed sarcastically. "So now I understand your strategy. We need to come up with something where they get Ramsey solid, and gather in Owens at the same time."

"They could take care of Ramsey with a line-up. Crow can make a positive ID," Abel noted. "But there is no probable cause at this point to bring Owens in for a line-up, and the minute they arrest Ramsey, he will disappear, I can guarantee. He's a slippery customer. And as much as I hate to admit it, an extremely smart one too."

Rex had finished his chili and all but half of the last donut, and signaled Rhonda for a coffee refill. He tapped the *Bay Meadows Bugle* headline with the donut fragment, sprinkling it with another shower of frosting bits and donut crumbs. "I think there is your answer, if we can get Wunderlich to go along with it," he said.

"I think I know where you are headed, but go on."

"This is one of the biggest races of the season at Bay Meadows, so I'm sure that everyone and his brother will be there, including Ramsey and Owens. And all of the other people involved in this, like the Dales and Jud and Sheila. Sheila's my ex. It is at her place that Kay and Jud have been staying, in case you didn't know. Their being there would not alert Owens or Ramsey to anything going on nor would Wunderlich and Nakamura's presence. After all, just because they are with law enforcement doesn't mean they wouldn't follow horse racing. And remember, Ramsey will be back in the barns with the horses. It is Owens who will be in the stands and the public areas. The one person that would look out of place around the barns would be Crow, but it sure would be a good time for him to be there and identify Ramsey and avoid a line-up."

"What about you and me? Wouldn't Owens see us there with these other people and get suspicious? And certainly if he or Ramsey spots Crow, the alarm bells will go off. Like I say, he is sharp. That's why he has stayed out of jail this long."

"In the first place, all of these people shouldn't be in one group at the track," Rex responded. "We don't have to give everyone the details, but just ask them to cooperate by being in certain specific locations. In the second place, your being there would be normal, since you are with the Racing Board. Just be sure some of your agents who Owens would recognize are there with you, as they would be if nothing was up. We need to give him a 'business as usual' impression. Third, I think I can convince Jud and Sheila to go along with me and not raise too much hell. A little for effect, maybe. She and I used to love going to the races together. The big hickey is Crow. With the publicity he's had recently in the papers, either Owens or Ramsey might wonder why a guy connected with birds and feathers would be at a horserace," said Rex while finishing off the final half donut.

"Can't we get Crow back in the paddock before the race, when there are a crowd of onlookers seeing the animals up close? I don't know if Owens will be there with the horses, but Ramsey is sure to be."

Rhonda had re-filled the men's coffee cups and was headed back to the kitchen when Rex called, "Say hon, I think my friend here needs more donuts. Be a sweetie and bring him a couple. Just glazed this time. And two clean plates." Rhonda gave him a desultory nod as he continued with Abel. "That's what I was thinking. Of course he might need a disguise of some sort, at least so he would blend in with the crowd. The big thing is who is with him to witness the identification? Have you thought of that?"

"Well, no. What about Bud Rooney. Sergeant Bud Rooney? He was at the scene when Crow reported the crime and was in on the interview Wunderlich had with Crow. He is pretty innocuous looking in plain clothes, but he is a big guy and tough. He could handle Ramsey well enough if there is trouble."

"If you say so. We can put that up to Wunderlich. He'll have to agree to it," answered Rex.

Abel continued. "And another question is when do we do all this? Before the race? After? Have you thought of that?"

"I would suggest that it be Ramsey before the race, and Owens after" said Rex. "Before, all parties will be at the track proper, and

Ramsey should be there in the paddock with Peoria Heights and Princess Khey. Owens is bound to be in the stands glad-handing and showing off. After the race, Owens will be by the stands, maybe even in the winner's circle, if you have this pegged right. And Wunderlich can have his people around and briefed. Owens won't know we already have Ramsey, and we can get him by surprise. That is pretty much a slam dunk."

"It is Owens that I'm still not too sure about. Since he is almost certain of the outcome of the race, he may leave as soon as he sees that Peoria Heights is winning, and slip away while everyone is standing and yelling at the finish," Abel said. "And, it may dawn on him that Ramsey is nowhere to be seen. Let's just hope his bimbos and the crowd keep him distracted."

"There is just one thing we haven't thought about," said Rex.

"And that would be?"

"Jurisdiction! Ramsey killed Kayne in Redwood City. Owens did all his shit at the farm and God knows where else. We are talking about arresting these guys in San Mateo, a separate city from everything except the track." Rex got a sinking feeling that things might not be as simple as they were planning.

"No problem." said Abel, "Look at it this way. All of those places may be in separate cities, but they are all in San Mateo County. Even the horse farm. My agency has authority statewide, so for any of the malfeasance of a racing nature, I can file charges. And I am sure that Captain Wunderlich has a long-standing relationship with San Mateo County Sheriff Ware that can put anyone in jail any time they want to. But you bring up a good point about making it all legal. I have known Avery Ware a long time, and I will get with him and Fred and make sure we have this set up with all the legal details zipped up ahead of time."

"All of that coffee is making me think it's time I made use of my zipper," said Rex as he headed for the restroom and let Abel pay the bill. "I think we are done here. I'll call you if you don't call me."

CHAPTER FIFTY-ONE

"**O**h, Bill, darling," Kay Dale trilled as her husband inched the Cadillac toward valet parking, "I'm just so happy that you bought this wonderful car for me. What fun to arrive with such a splash. The perfect chariot for a sporting event, don't you think? It's my favorite event of the year." Kay looked around at the festive banners lining the roadway and the colorfully-dressed crowd hurrying toward the entrance gates. "Oh, Bill, what fun we're going to have! And I'm so goddamned happy to have all that murder stuff behind us. Well, almost behind. At least for me and Jud, and you too. All we have to think of is the horses, and seeing friends and having a really grand time today."

Bill agreed. "I'm thankful we can celebrate getting back to normal. I don't mind telling you how hard all that was on me. But of course that would sound selfish compared to what you've been through. Okay, here we are."

Red-coated valets helped them out of the car as they arrived at the entrance to the Club House at Bay Meadows. Both valets waved a thumbs-up admiration of the custom Eldorado station wagon.

It was April 4, 1970, the first Saturday in April and the traditional date of the running of the Bay Meadows Handicap. A Bay Area-perfect early spring day. Sunny, but cool enough that fine fabrics, including light woolens and heavy silks, and even modest furs, could be displayed without fear of perspiring. Expensive

266

hats were in order for all. By consensus, the better established men eschewed straw hats this early—Memorial Day would be the time for that.

The Dales proceeded through the club house, amidst a gaggle of on-lookers, including friends and acquaintances, with whom they exchanged smiles, nods, waves and air-kisses, as was appropriate to each individual's status. They were recognized by most of the people present, not just for the notoriety of the recent unpleasantness, but for their position as owners of not one, but two, entrants on today's card for the Handicap. Bill and Kay made their way out to the bright sunlight of the grandstand and down to the family box, their Ray-Bans and smiles suitably in place.

With almost prescient timing, a number of favored guests and family relations were already assembled. Sheila was present at Kay's insistence. Rex had indicated that he would join them later. Jud was with his grandmother Hulda (the object of many pairs of binoculars in surrounding boxes, near and far.) Both enjoyed being included in such select company. Bill's children, William and Alexis, were in the Dale box, Alexis being briefly home from Pomona, where she was at college. Also there were a smattering of Atherton neighbors and business associates of Bill's.

Two boxes to the left of the Dales' box were Owen Owens and his entourage, conspicuously including Amber and Twilee, his two "secretarial associates." Owens was in his element, holding court with his own guests of horse owners, trainers and political connections, and heartily waving at owners, trainers and pols in other boxes nearby. Owens saw the Dales arriving and vied for their attention, but Kay was distracted, and Bill appeared to be giving him a cold shoulder.

Well, another time, Owens thought, yes sir, another time.

Of course Handicap Day at Bay Meadows would never be complete without Alan Meade Poole-Gass. Al was making the rounds of the better-class of boxes, carrying an aura of Edwardian grandeur. After hob-knobbing with Owens, Poole-Gass arrived at the Dale box where Kay greeted him warmly and thanked him for helping bring to light Crow's testimony. She introduced Poole-Gass to the other members of her party, including Hulda and Jud.

Poole-Gass was stunned by the sight of Hulda. Statuesque, chic, dewy complexioned, a brilliant, slightly wry smile, and an intriguing hint of a European accent. He kissed her hand, and listened distractedly as Kay introduced Jud. Not quite moving his eyes, or hand, away from Hulda, Poole-Gass said. "Ah yes! The young stable boy. We've heard good things about him. I think my cousin Murky may need some help at his horse set-up in Woodside. I'll put in a word for the young chap."

"Murky?" said Hulda with her best wide-eyed doe smile. "My, what a strange name."

"Sorry about the use of his nickname. How crass of me. I am referring to my cousin John Murchison Poole. His horsey friends call him 'Murky'."

"Fascinating," cooed Hulda.

As Poole-Gass continued his overtures to Hulda, the rest of the people in the box focused on the track, where the contenders in one of the preliminary races had just burst out of the gate.

●●●

While the party in the Dale's box urged their favorites to victory in the sixth race, Rex's party of himself, Captain Wunderlich, Abel Willing and Earl Crow were in the paddock area, observing Red Ramsey from a discreet distance.

Moss green painted barns and sheds formed a subdued background for the vivid colors of the jockeys' silks, and the shiny blacks, caramels, creams and mahoganies of the horses. A dull murmur of race track talk among track stewards, workers and visitors was punctuated by the whinnying, gentle snorting and occasional stomping of the horses. The jockeys had begun to mount their rides, as had the outriders, who, with their side-kick horses, would help calm the racers and guide them to the starting gate.

To avoid notice by Ramsey, Rex was wearing a dark fedora with the brim pulled low over his eyes, which were veiled by dark glasses. The rest of his attire on this occasion was very unlike Rex's daily norm of khakis and plaid shirt, which Ramsey might recognize from prior encounters. Today Rex was wearing his respectable, court appearance suit and his green tie appliquéd with running horses, the better to blend with dressy horse own-ers, track officials and others who had special-guest access to the paddock.

Captain Wunderlich had managed to secure official badges for Rex and Earl Crow to be admitted to the paddock. As a peace officer, Wunderlich's presence, and that of his men, would not seem remarkable, and they wore civilian clothes instead of their police uniforms. Abel had permanent entrée as a state official, and was well-known by many at the track, including Ramsey. He made a point of greeting Ramsey initially, then taking care not to let Ramsey see who else he might be talking to. As for Crow, it was assumed that, with sunglasses and his hair combed differ-ently from his usual coif, he wouldn't stand out in the crowd, and he didn't.

Rex's little band milled about individually, careful not to look like a group with a purpose. They mostly communicated with small hand signals. Their mission today was to get Crow close enough to Ramsey for Crow to positively identify Ramsey as the man he saw suffocating Earnest Kayne that night in the cemetery.

Rex took a few steps to join Crow, and with his hand on the younger man's back, nodded in the direction of Ramsey, who was standing near Princess Khey's stall. Ramsey was in deep con-versation with a groom. Other onlookers were milling about the line of stalls, so it seemed possible for Crow to walk casually past Ramsey for a close look without drawing Ramsey's notice.

Crow could see Ramsey's bright red hair as he approached nervously, hoping he looked as though he belonged in this setting although it was completely foreign to his own experience. Coming abreast of Ramsey, Crow steeled his courage and looked directly into the redhead's face. At that very moment Ramsey looked up and caught Crow's eye. To Crow it seemed the eye-contact lasted for minutes. He felt the blood drain from his face and knew he was caught. What excuse could he make?

Rex hadn't told him what to do if he was challenged. He managed to turn his face to avert Red's eyes, but was immediately, compulsively, drawn to look back at Ramsey's face. Ramsey was again engaged with the groom, not seeming to pay attention to Crow. Crow swung around and rushed back in Rex's direction.

Rex saw Crow coming but stepped to the side, out of the line of sight with Ramsey. Crow joined Rex, let out his breath in a whoosh, and stammered, "Y-y-esss! My God, yes, that's him. I'm sure. I thought he was going to recognize me and come after me! It's him, the guy from the cemetery."

Wunderlich, standing a few yards away, talking to Abel Willing, was able to catch the gist of Crow's reaction. He joined Crow and Rex and said, "It's him? You're sure?"

"Yes!" responded Crow. "Without a doubt! That's the man I saw that night."

"That's all I need!' Wunderlich said, with a broad grin. "Good work, Professor Crow. I'll take it from here. Rooney, you are on."

There was a rustle as the call went out to form up for the post parade for the Handicap. Red Ramsey was standing next to Princess Khey, wishing good luck to horse and jockey. He straightened the saddle cloth which bore Khey's position number, helped the jockey mount up and gave the horse a pat on the rear as it headed out of the paddock. He was about to follow when he felt a presence next to him. He turned and saw a large man displaying a police badge.

"Rodney Ramsey? I am Sergeant Rooney of the Redwood City PD, and that man over there is Captain Wunderlich. We are placing you under arrest for the murder of Earnest Kayne on March 15, 1970. You have the right to remain silent." His admonition was heard only by Ramsey, and Rooney firmly guided him away from the crowd.

CHAPTER FIFTY-TWO

A bugle sounds "To The Post", announcing the post parade for the day's seventh race, the thirty-seventh annual running of the Bay Meadows Handicap. A momentary, expectant hush falls over the stands, followed by applause and polite cheering.

The field of nine contenders begins filing past the stands at a walk, each entrant accompanied by a companion horse and rider. The bright colors of the silks out-dazzle even the spring finery of the spectators, and the stands begin to erupt with partisan cheers for the favorites and the rest of the field. Princess Khey has drawn the number 4 post position. Her stable-mate, Peoria Heights, will be in stall 9 of the gate.

"There she is!" Kay calls out, "There's our big girl, Princess Khey!" Her bay coat glistening in the sun, Princess Khey passes by, carrying Mike Jimenez in the green and gold colors of Hillandale Farms.

After what must feel like an hour to the horses, the jockeys and the spectators, the last mount is packed into the starting gate. The finish line is six furlongs away, a mile and a quarter down the track. The bells ring and the gates spring open. A huge noise, combining the sound of thirty-six hoofs pounding the dirt with the great, pent-up roar of the crowd, fills the Bay Meadows track.

Kay, glued to her binoculars, sees green and gold. "Here she comes! Oh!" She grabs Bill's elbow, "A great, smooth start. Mike's taking it easy with her."

The announcer calls,

Alimaya, with 10-1 odds, takes an early lead, closely followed by Awesome Dancer, the 2-1 favorite and Princess Khey at 8-1.

"Okay, Khey, Okay, Khey!" chant Kay and Bill in unison, a call quickly taken up by the guests in the Dale box.

In the middle of the back stretch, it's Awesome Dancer, Princess Khey and Golden Times, 5-2.

"She's right up there! Oh I hope he's not pushing her too hard!" Kay frets.

Coming out of the first turn, Princess Khey has taken the lead and is hugging the inside fence. Awesome Dancer has dropped back. Alimaya is coming up, trying to reclaim the early advantage. Golden Times is holding on at fourth. Dare To Go, 6-1, is coming up on the outside.

Meanwhile, after finishing their work at the paddock, Rex, Able and Wunderlich have made their way to the grandstand. Abel and Wunderlich are careful to mix with the crowd so that Owens won't see them, but they can keep an eye on him and his "associates."

Rex enters the Dale's box, gives Sheila a hug, and at once is taken up by the excitement as Princess Khey takes the lead of the pack into the stretch turn. As the runners complete the turn and enter the home stretch, they are a thundering, tight-packed mass of sweating, panting horse flesh.

Princess Khey maintains a slim lead, followed by Dare To Go, Golden Times, Awesome Dancer and Alimaya. The rest, including Peoria Heights, trail further back.

"Oh my God!" Kay cries. "Bill! Do you think she could actually win?"

Coming down the home stretch, past the stands, Paco Lopez has urged Golden Times into the lead. Dare To Go, with Jack Riley aboard, runs second, with Awesome Dancer close behind carrying Pete Schmidt. Princess Khey has fallen back into the pack.

Bill puts an arm around Kay's shoulder. "Looks like our girl's not going to place, but she's done well and made us proud."

Through tears, Kay answers, "Yes, darling, very proud indeed."

Nearing the finish line, Golden Times and Dare To Go are running neck and neck. Awesome Dancer is half a length behind. Princess Khey struggles to stay in the elite group. They cross the finish line, and the winner is...DareToGo! Golden Times places, and Awesome Dancer shows. Princess Khey takes fourth, missing out by just a length behind the winner. Among the other also-rans is Peoria Heights, in eighth place, a bit ahead of Roman Night.

Earlier, while driving up to Bay Meadows, Kay and Bill had agreed with resignation that a win by Princess Khey might not be the best outcome, considering the cloud of suspicion brought on by Ramsey and Owens and the murder of Earnest. So now, putting on their happiest faces, the Dales join their guests to celebrate Khey's brave effort, and acknowledge that Peoria Heights could have done worse and with good training may be a future winner.

●●●

While Dare To Go, in his necklace of flowers, and his owners with their silver trophy, posed for pictures in the winner's circle, the rest of the horses, their jockeys relaxed now on their tiny saddles, slowly walk back to the paddock.

Suddenly, a young reporter—not a regular member of the racing press—broke from the crowd around Dare To Go and chased after Princess Khey.

When he caught up with her, he yelled to the jockey in a rude voice, "Hey, hold up a minute, will you? How come this horse didn't win?" The reporter reached out and patted Princess Khey on the rump.

Princess Khey was a skittish horse under the best of circumstances, and with the racing blinders on did not see the reporter's approach from the rear. She jumped and then reared up, sending the jockey flying. Luckily, he kept his hold on the reins and managed to get to his feet, dazed, barely controlling Princess Khey, who was getting wilder and wilder.

Jud Kayne saw all this, and without any prompting, jumped the front rail of the box and sprinted to the troubled horse and rider. Taking the reins from the jockey, he pulled Princess Khey's head toward his, talking to her and calming her.

"Easy now, girl, easy," he said. "We will get you back to the stall, cool you down and then something to munch on. OK? Yeah, you do like to munch, don't you?"

Princess Khey seemed to recognize his voice. She tossed her head and looked around at him. She flexed her nostrils and snorted and seemed to relax. After a few moments of having her nose stroked, she settled down and Jud led her back to the paddock, talking to and patting her. A small group of onlookers gave them a scattered round of applause.

Jud's actions did not go unnoticed in the Dale box. Poole-Gass turned to Hulda and with a warmer than necessary smile, said, "Well, Madam Stern-Franken, it seems as if your grandson has his wits about him. He saw what transpired with that out-of-control horse and he just stepped in and took charge. I'm sure that Murky could use a lad like that. Yes, I think he could."

"Oh, I hope so," said Hulda. "I think Jud needs to get away from Hillandale for a while. And as you can see, he knows how to handle horses."

Rex had been taken up with the thrill of the finish, and snapped out of it with Jud's vault over the rail. He quickly looked around for Owens. Rex had not been concentrating on Owens in those last charged moments of the race. Now, Owens was nowhere to be seen, nor were his "associates," Amber and Twilee.

"That son of a bitch!" cried Rex, and headed for the VIP parking lot. Owens' Mercedes sedan was nowhere to be seen. He spied Able and Wunderlich coming from the grandstand and waved at them. "He's not here," Rex yelled, gathering strange looks from others who were getting to their cars.

Abel and Wunderlich came as fast as they could, without running, to Rex.

"Where..." Abel started to ask.

"Vanished!" said Rex. "That slimy, two bit hustler is gone. One minute he was fifteen feet from me and the next...poof! He's gone, his bimbos are gone and his car is gone. Like farts in the wind. I thought you guys were watching him?" Rex was incredulous.

"We were, we were," said Wunderlich. "At the finish, everyone started waving their arms and moving around. By the time we got to his box, he and the ladies were gone. Shit. We fucked it up."

"Well, you got that part right, sir!" Rex cut Wunderlich short and turned away, headed to his Monza.

Unlike Rex, Abel was not given to overt demonstrations of his feelings. He made the effort to direct his thoughts to solving this new problem. "We could check out his home but something tells me he's not there. And he would probably be long gone before anyone could get out there. SFO is not a good bet. My guess he's on his way to some private airport. I don't think Owens is a guy who operates without a contingency plan."

CHAPTER FIFTY-THREE

After all of the excitement of the weekend, William Dale was relieved to get back to the normal work week on Monday. His desk was clear, save one sheet on paper carefully centered there. Everything in its place and the faint odor of cleaning fluids and vacuumed carpets signaled a new start. At his large rosewood desk, he reveled that he was back where he belonged, in control, where he was the boss.

Ah, it is good to be chief and not an Indian, he thought with a sigh, and began to review the week's appointment schedule on his desk. He got as far as Wednesday before the feeling of power faded. He remembered the immediate need to secure some legal distance for Kay and himself from all that had gone on with the dead man in the cemetery and the ensuing brouhaha. To say nothing of the situation at Hillandale Stables in the absence of Ramsey.

He called to his secretary through the open door, "Linda, will you get the lawyer on the phone. I need to talk with him, now. And then shut the door."

Linda came to the doorway and asked, "Do you want someone from Mason, Newburg, Frazier & Payne or someone from Coddington and Wilkins? And who from which? Is this for business or pleasure?" Linda, like any good executive secretary, put up with the boss's ego. But she had her limits, and had just about reached them with William Dale's royal attitude that morning.

He had barely said hello to her when he came in and, turned away her positive comments about the results of Saturday's race.

"It is not for pleasure, but it is personal. So get ahold of Coddington and Wilkins. Either Tom Coddington or Percy Wilkins will do, although I prefer Tom. Either way, I need to speak with one of them right away. And in case I forgot the 'please' in my door request, please."

She shut the door between their offices, and within five minutes his intercom buzzed.

"I have Mr. Coddington waiting on line 2, Mr. Dale," said Linda crisply.

"Thank you, Miss Lewis," said Dale. "I'll take it."

"Tom, this is Bill Dale. Good morning to you too. Here's why I'm calling." Dale proceeded to review the situation with Kay's involvement in the murder case with Judson Kayne, and the problems with Ramsey and Owens at the track, and Hillandale, the news of Ramsey's arrest, and what Rex Nickels had done, and so more.

When Dale finished his point-by-point outline, Coddington said, "Well, Bill, from what you just told me, it looks to me that you are basically okay, but there may be some issues of complicity here. And I can imagine some elements of exposure that may need to be nailed down to be sure there is nothing unseen now or down the line that could cause problems."

"And that means?"

"That means I think we need to have a sit-down with my friend, San Mateo County District Attorney Waldemar Booker, and get something clear, and in writing, that absolves you and your family of any wrong-doing."

"How do we do this meeting, and when?"

"I'll set it up with him and I think we should do it as soon as possible, while all the publicity in the news media is positive toward you and before we get some snoopy reporter stirring up any unwelcome public interest. What is your schedule like?"

"You are making this sound urgent. Let me check the agenda here. Ummm. Not anything here that can't be moved, if we can do it this week. Set it up and let me or Linda know. Uh, Tom, uh, do you think that the DA is going to make any waves?"

"Let me put it this way, Bill. If you recall in the election that kept Waldemar 'Wally' Booker in office four years ago, there was a lot of advertising touting 'Waldemar Is Best By Far', and 'Wally Will Do It!' and 'Keep Booker', etc. Yours truly paid for a great deal of that stuff. Not the firm, but me personally. It was all above board and on the up-and-up, mind you, but it isn't something I want Wally to forget. If you get my drift. And there is another election coming up at the end of this year."

"The hint of future contributions sounds a little like bribery to me." Dale was skeptical.

"Leverage. A fine line there is between leverage and bribery, my friend. That line is what we lawyers are good at finding. Finding lines is what we lawyers do. Now, let me think about the best place to have this meeting and get busy contacting Wonderful Wally. I'll let you know when and where by the end of the day."

"Tom, don't forget that there are other people involved in this that need some absolution too. Like Judson Kayne, and...well, write these names down, so you don't forget. Sheila Sneaker, Earl T. Crow, and Rex Nickels."

"Oh, so you're upping the ante."

"That's what businessmen do. Goodbye, Tom."

●●●

At eleven, Dale's phone rang. "It's Mr. Coddington on line 1, Mr. Dale," Linda's intercom voice was cold and mechanical.

"Thanks, Linda," said Bill, trying to make it up to her.

"Bill? Tom Coddington here. There's been a little change in plans. Not to worry. I talked to Booker and although his manner was conciliatory, his guard was up and he wants to talk to some people before we get together."

"Some people?"

"Namely, Fred Wunderlich, Abel Willing and San Mateo County Sheriff Avery Ware. He wants to check with each of them, separately and collectively to be sure none of them have any outstanding complaints against any of these people. As much of a good old boy the D.A. is, he is keen on upholding the law. He gave me a little lecture on the difference between eye-wink leniency and the benefit of the doubt. So far he is willing to believe me and I am willing to believe you that none of the people in question have broken the law, or at least not bent it no more than it can be straightened out. In other words, Wally is covering his ass. If these guys sign off, then we will meet with him and get a deal in writing."

"How long will this take? It seems to be getting complicated," said Bill flatly.

"Long enough for the ink to dry on my check contributing to his re-election campaign fund, but not too long. He's the big duck in the pond on this one, and when he quacks, the rest paddle. He was meeting with the sheriff this morning anyway about something else, and he probably will see the others tomorrow. He said to set up it with you and the rest for Thursday morning at 11:30. He was confident he would have his information and a decision by then."

"Why does he want to meet everyone? I thought this was a lawyer-only deal."

"Wally is big on sermons, and this is an opportunity to preach a little and collect a few votes at the same time. There will be legal issues involved, and he said to be sure all of the people involved had their attorneys present," said Coddington. "I am representing you and Kay. Who have you got lined up for the other four?"

"You, if that is okay. Sheila and Judson aren't in any position to pay for a lawyer and Nickels and Crow aren't either. So, put it on my tab. I'll check with them to see if it's all right, but I'm sure it will be. Hell, it's free."

"To them. Not you," said Coddington with an unseen smirk on his face. "And of course, you know, if there is any conflict of interest, I can only serve one party."

CHAPTER FIFTY-FOUR

Nine people were in the small conference room at the court-house when the DA arrived. Rex Nickels, Sheila Sneaker and Judson Kayne were on one side of the long table while Earl Crow, Bill Dale and Kay Dale sat across from them. Tom Coddington was at the far end of the table. Hulda Stern-Franken and Alan Meade Poole-Gass were seated in chairs against the back wall. Waldemar Booker made his well-practiced entrance into the room, carrying a legal folder under his arm. The studied aura of importance, the all-business and time-efficient charm that he had observed and copied, early in his career from people of prominence, was very valuable at times like this. Coddington began to rise, but Booker motioned him down and took a seat at the head of the table.

Smiling his best business smile Waldemar Booker began the meeting. "Looks as if we are all here. Let me guess who is who." Starting at the far end of the table he pointed and named the visitors. "You, Counselor, of course I know. Good morning to you Mr. Coddington. And to your right I see Mr. & Mrs. Dale. I believe we have met at the fund-raiser for orphans my wife is involved with. From pictures in the paper I see we have Professor Crow, our famous owl expert. Congratulations on your grant, Professor." Booker removed his glasses, gave them a quick wipe with a hand-kerchief, replaced his glasses and gazed across the table. "And coming around on the other side you must be Judson Kayne.

I am so sorry about your father, young man. Ma'am," addressing Sheila, "We haven't met, but I would surmise that you are Sheila Sneaker and next to you must be the eminent private investigator, Rex Nickels. Our paths have crossed before, haven't they Rex?"

Rex had been briefed on the importance of keeping his counsel at this meeting, and reluctantly chose not to engage the DA in any repartee. He didn't like the guy and resented having to sit there and listen to his bullshit, but he remained still, putting on his best Mona Lisa smile just for the hell of it. Let Wonderful Wally do the talking. One of Rex's gifts was being surly and not letting it show.

Pointing over Coddington's head, he singled out Poole-Gass, calling him by his first name. "Alan, so glad to have you with us. I don't know why you are here or who your lovely companion is. Perhaps you can enlighten me on both counts."

"This, Mr. District Attorney, is Madam Hulda Stern-Franken, and I am here as her escort today. She is the mother of the deceased, and young Judson there is her grandson. She wanted to be here for him."

Getting to his feet, Booker gave a slight bow (influenced no doubt by Poole-Gass's English mannerisms) and said to Hulda, "It is a pleasure to meet you, Madam Franken. I wish it were under other circumstances. You have my condolences for the loss of your son." Hulda gave him one of her beatific smiles, and he practically melted back into his chair.

"Let's make this short," he began. "A man is dead. It has been determined that he was murdered. His alleged murderer, based on an eyewitness to the crime, has been arrested and is in custody. It is suspected that the deceased was involved with his killer in doping horses at the Hillandale horse farm. Simply stated, Professor Crow here saw an employee of Hillandale Stables kill Mr. Kayne. Hillandale Stables is owned by the Dales along with Mr. Owen Owens, who is nowhere to be found. Judson, you worked at the farm, and you know Mrs. Dale quite well. At one time, you and Mrs. Dale thought you had a part in Mr. Kayne's death and became fugitives from the police. Miss Sneaker, you and Mr. Nickels were complicit in hiding them from the authorities. If it would serve justice, I could find some law that each of you, except Mr. Dale, may have broken." Booker once again paused to wipe his glasses, letting his ominous summary soak in. He continued, "After consulting the County Sheriff, Special Racing Board Investigator Abel Willing and Captain Fred Wunderlich of the Redwood City Police Department, however, in light of how each of you contributed to bringing the alleged killer to justice, I have decided not to pursue any charges against any of you in this room. I must add that this does not apply to Owen Owens, who of course is not here and who is considered a wanted man. It is my understanding that Mr. Thomas Coddington of Coddington and Wilkins represents each of you. Speak up if this is not true. I take your silence as agreement. It will take a week or so to get all of this in writing, and when that is done Mr. Coddington will have papers for you to sign and some for you to keep. If there are no questions, this meeting is adjourned. You are all free to go."

Waldemar Booker dramatically arose from his chair at the head of the table and left the room, as he had seen others do when he was young—hurriedly, not shutting the door as he sped off to his next appointment, which was lunch.

•••

Coddington left his group of clients talking in a small circle outside of the courthouse. They were pleased with the outcome of the meeting and glad it was behind them, and enjoyed just being social.

"Jud," said Kay, "Do you have any plans? You may not want to stay at the farm anymore. Are you thinking of moving in with your grandmother now? Maybe your mother?"

Before he could answer. Hulda spoke up. "You know, you are always welcome in my home, Judson. Would you like to come live with me?"

The way she said it, and the way that Hulda and Poole-Glass had been looking at each other all day told Kay that Hulda's was an obligatory invitation, not a sincere one. She could tell that Hulda had another roommate in mind and was wishing like hell that Jud would say "no".

Jud didn't know what to say. He didn't want to go back to his old way of life and his dead father's house. But he knew his grand-mother well enough to know her invitation was at best lukewarm. And he didn't relish going back to live with his mother.

Kay got them all off the hook when she said, "Jud, Here's an idea! Come and live with Bill and me. There are plenty of rooms in our house and you can have your own space. You told me you wanted to get a fresh start, and a new place to live would help immensely. You would need to get a job of course, and we could probably help you find something. Couldn't we Bill?"

"Yes, of course," Dale responded. "We'd love to have you and we think it best if you are employed. We can help with contacts."

Jud was very excited and accepted the invitation at once. "I am a little worried about the job thing. Now that Ramsey and Owens aren't at the farm anymore, there's no one in charge. And I don't think I'm capable of running a place that big."

Alan Meade Poole-Gass cleared his throat and stepped in. "I have a bonny idea, Judson. I saw what you did at the race track Saturday when Princess Khey was frightened by that crass reporter. It was right on as far as clear headed action is concerned. They said you were good with horses, and you're quick too. I believe it now from seeing it with my own eyes. I had told your grandmother that my cousin, Murky Poole, might need some help at his horse place in Woodside. It is called Murchison Stables. Someone to care for the horses and be a general caretaker of the place. Murky's not able to spend much time there. After what I saw at the track on Saturday, I talked to Murky and it seems as if he is looking for a lad just like you. Are you interested?"

"Am I interested? You bet your last joint I am!" Jud was exuberant, and let slip a little his interest in exploring his inner self. "Oh, I mean, yeah sure." His face flushed. He feared he had screwed up.

"Not to worry, old chap," said Poole-Gass, "Murky has interests similar to yours when it comes to gardening. I think you will enjoy tending to the patch behind his barn."

"I don't want to know any more," said Dale. "You are welcome at our house. Do I call you Jud or Judson."

"Call me Judson"

As everyone but Sheila and Rex found their way to their cars, the two of them stood awkwardly in front of the courthouse, by themselves, searching for something to say. There was no more business between them and there was no good reason to say anything other than a simple "Goodbye." They sensed an old magic, and that, mixed with the successful outcome of the events of the past three weeks, gave them a shared sense of excitement and exuberance.

"I let Jud take my car to get his things at my house," said Sheila.

"I have the Monza, and it's not far to my place. Shall we?" said Rex.

"Why the hell not?" said Sheila, and she took Rex's arm, on their way to his car.

● ● ●

As Jud drove up the hill to Sheila's house, he thought about his future at Murchison Stables. Not the least of his musings was about the freedom he would have to just let loose out in the pasture, all alone, dancing in his Periwinkle skirt, whenever desire called. For the first time in a very long time Jud's face broke into a big smile.

CHAPTER FIFTY-FIVE

Thundering hoofs were stirring a cloud of dust, no, make that snow, and the horses, or were they running leopards, attired in rich Ralph Lauren colors leapt over white fences. A bugle sounded the first two notes of "Hey Jude"...Sheila reluctantly drifted out of her dream state, wiggled her hips, rolled onto her right side and opened one eye.

She awakened to find the sun, casting a bright yellow shaft through a bent venetian blind slat onto a patch of never-cleaned, chartreuse carpet, and a pile of clothing on the floor near the bed.

Sheila opened the other eye. My God! she thought. Those clothes are mine!...And that carpet could only be Rex's!

She rolled over and looked to her left. Beyond the rumpled valleys and crests of the thin, never-again-to-be-"Rinso-White" sheets, she saw the pudgy folds of a man's back. Oh yeah, that can only be Rex's too. Memory of the hours before came flooding back, and Sheila smiled. She reached out with a sculptured scarlet nail and gave the back a gentle, scratching tickle.

Rex turned onto his back and focused a sleepy but contented gaze on Sheila, who quickly and demurely wrapped her body in the sheets. All of it, that is, but one fulsome breast.

"Rex, you son of a bitch! Now I know why you never invited me to see this place of yours! As Bette Davis once said, 'whatta dump!'"

"Well, Sheila my dear, I wouldn't know about Big Eyes Bette. I was always more of a Jane Russell fan, who you strongly resemble. And the top o' the mornin' to you too! Hold that thought while I make a trip to the john, okay?"

While Rex made a bee line to the bathroom, Sheila decided to tidy the bed a bit. She smoothed out the sheets and fluffed the pillows. When she did, a feather escaped from one of them and she caught it in mid-air. She was rubbing it against her cheek when Rex returned to the freshened bed, the final sounds of a just-flushed toilet fading in the background.

Sheila reached over and patted his soft, exposed tummy. "You win. Good morning yourself. Rex, I must admit it. Last night I got that 'ooollld feeelin.' There really is something still there. You know, these last few weeks have been some kind of hell for me, but I've gotten used to having you around. That's made it all kind of worthwhile. And I never thought I'd say this, after our alimony wars and all, and, let's face it, our various other interests and attachments, but you've really shown yourself to be a good man, Sexy Rexy." She giggled, "And I don't just mean in the bedding department. You've really handled the whole business with Kay and Jud and Ramsey...I don't know...like a real pro. You recognized strengths in Jud that no one else saw, and you gave him a real push into adulthood. Hell, I even think you did the same for yourself. You finally grew up, you bastard!"

Rex pulled himself to a sitting position and inched over to get an arm around Sheila's shoulders. "Well, will you listen to the new Miss Congeniality! I had forgotten how nice you can be before you get out of bed! Seriously though, I've kind of enjoyed it too. The case, that is. Not just the business of it, though I guess I would call the whole thing a career highlight of sorts. I do have real regrets that Owens gave us the slip. I blamed the other guys, but I was right there on the scene. I should have been more on my toes. Ramsey may have been the bad guy, but Owens was the master villain. I'll always wonder where the son of a bitch went... and if he will come back to haunt us? But let's forget about the bad part for now. The good part wouldn't ever have happened without your hospitality to Kay and Jud and your patience with all the mayhem. Hell, the truth of it all is, it was just damn nice having you around. Made me remember the old days. Those didn't last very long, but we did have some happy times, didn't we?"

Sheila shifted so that they were in a full embrace, face-to-face. She rubbed the feather across Rex's forehead. "Do you think we can keep this love-fest going? I'd be willing to give it a serious try." She gazed over Rex's shoulder, and around the bedroom. "Of course, I couldn't stay in this pigsty. But we could be happy in our old dream house up in the hills. Could we make a go of it? Are we ready?"

"I did enjoy spending time up on Vista Drive." Rex responded, stroking Sheila's hair, and gently taking the feather from her fingers. "Nice and quiet, everything in such good order, so clean! But how long would I be able to keep it that way? Remember our squabbles over where I left my socks, how I stacked beer cans, the clutter in the garage?

"What you like is tooling your little Corona up and down the Alameda, shopping and lunching in Palo Alto and San Mateo, keeping your house and your garden tidy. I, on the other hand, enjoy living here on Maple Street near downtown in funky old Redwood City, near the courthouse and all its political shenanigans. I really like walking to the 7-Eleven instead of driving two miles, and walking to my office. I like seeing what's going on at the Hotel Sequoia and the Break-Thyme. I like running into folks at the post office and the library, stopping in one of the bars on my way home. And I like not having to do any of those things if that's my choice. And not having to pick up clothes, wash dishes, or pull weeds in the yard."

Sheila listened, eyes downcast. She had pulled the feather back and twirled it between her thumb and forefinger. When he finished, she looked up with a small smile. "Okay. I get your point. We are two different people, with two very different lives. I guess that's why it didn't work the first time around. Maybe we could talk about some new way to add all of it up to four—two people, two lives. Or maybe five. Two people, three lives—adding a new shared life that we can live when it suits us? What if we separated ourselves from our individual styles, say four times a month? I could go for a plan like that."

Rex got up on his knees and leaned down and gave Sheila a lingering kiss. He said with a grin, "I think we may be close to a deal. Our own lives, and a shared life. And whatever works or doesn't work, we'll always have good times at the races. And now, could I have that feather? I want to show you something that I think you will really enjoy."

"I thought you hated feathers?" whispered Sheila, as she complied.

"Not anymore."

CHAPTER FIFTY-SIX

At ten o'clock on Friday morning, April 24, 1970, William Dale was at his office in Palo Alto, reviewing a prospectus on a cherry orchard in Cupertino. Not that he had any interest in growing fruit. That part of the Santa Clara Valley was getting hot for industrial development and he wanted to be in on it. Something about semi-conductors. Dale didn't know what they were, exactly (he wouldn't know a semi-conductor from a Southern Pacific conductor), but he understood from conversations with Dave Packard and Bill Hewlett, as well as Professor Fred Terman at Stanford, that this new industry was going to mean big things for the Peninsula and the Valley.

His telephone buzzed. It was the private line, seldom used by anyone except his wife, Kay. He pressed the speaker phone button, and said, "Good morning again, dear. What's up?"

"This is Ned," announced a voice that Dale recognized immediately.

"Yes, the code name. I'd almost forgotten. Where in hell are you?"

"Somewhere near the northern coast of South America, to be non-specific. I'm sure you know where I'm talking about. It should be sufficient for you to know that it is very comfortable here for me and my associates."

"If you are where I think you are, you should be comfortable physically. Do I assume you have access to sufficient financial resources?

"Enough for now. You're aware of how I've stashed some nest eggs in various banana republics and tropical paradises, just for contingencies such as this."

"Yes. So why call me?"

"You and I need to come to terms on liquidating some assets that we share interests in. Looks like I'll be away from the States for a good while, so it's probably not a good business climate for me. I'm calling to tell you that nestled in my basket of tropical eggs is a packet of certain documents and photographs, a tidy little library which I've amassed over the years. As a hobby, one might say."

Dale responded, feigning disinterest. "I'm glad you have something to amuse you in your golden years. From what you say and for reasons of my own, I am not opposed to liquidation. I suggest putting that in the hands of Mason, Newburg, Frazier, & Payne. They've handled all of our business together for years, and they understand discretion."

Ned interjected, "You don't get it, do you? I'm feathering my retirement nest. I need funding for that, and you are going to help. You see, I have untapped assets in the form of certain information that you might not want others, including your lovely wife, to get wind of. Exactly how I use those particular assets is up to you. I'd like to think you'll want them to serve our mutual benefit, as we part ways and move into a bright future."

"Look here, *Colonel*," Dale said forcefully, "don't think you can put the squeeze on me with anything you've kept in a dossier. You've known me all my life. I know I have no secrets as far as you're concerned. But let's just remember, it's a two-way street and your side has a lot more traffic than mine."

"Fairly stated. But there's more cross-over on that street than I expect you would like the world to be aware of. Need I make reference to circumstances regarding a druggist? Now, who has more to lose, a septuagenarian exile with a sequestered pile of assets that you'll never find, or a well-established, still-young player with a good rep and a nice family, with nowhere to go but up, as long as a few, dark, inconvenient secrets remain in the tropics?"

A very brief silence ensued.

Ned did not wait for a response from Dale. "Let that marinate for a while. A settlement is not all I called about. We need to talk about our friend Red. I've arranged, with help from our friends back east, for counsel for the worthy trainer. Fellow named Radolfo Nardoni. He works out of Peoria but is a member of the California Bar. I've agreed to take care of all expenses. Nardoni will put up a good defense, or a good show of one, but between you and me, he doesn't expect to see any result short of a murder one conviction, most likely life. In any case, after a discreet period, we can expect news of a brutal prison incident, courtesy of our boys back east."

At this new twist, Dale paled momentarily. He could defend himself against blackmail, but a "brutal prison incident" was something else. Then he considered how one word from Ramsey could scuttle his future plans. "Whatever it takes for him to be out of my life for good. That is your side of the street, not mine. I never heard you say what you just said."

"Now," Dale continued in a subdued tone, "as to the business at hand. I understand what you want to do, but I really don't know what would satisfy you. Why don't I take a stab at an offer? First off, I would give you the stable operation. I've got some temporary people at Hillandale for now, thanks to help from Murky Poole. He found a live-in couple to keep the farm running, till things are settled. I've decided I don't want any further connection with racing. I want to split-off my house site, so Kay can still enjoy it, and I want to retain the right for her to keep up to three horses there. Otherwise it's all yours to dispose of as you please. Secondly, I could agree to a division of all other shared assets, so that you would net sixty percent. In consideration of that, you will turn over your 'collection', and any facsimiles, to our attorneys for conveyance to me, along with any affidavits they may require for my protection."

After a pause Ned responded, "Seventy percent and it's a done deal!"

Dale, with his eye on the investment potential for Santa Clara County, which was beginning to be called "Silicon Valley", and for San Mateo County as well, knew a sacrifice short term could help him play a big role long term. "Why the hell not! Then we're agreed?"

"Send in Mason, Newburg, Frazier, &..." Ned replied with a chuckle. "Who's the other one?"

"Payne, Colonel. Payne. Payne is always involved in a deal like this. I'll call them this morning. Oh, one more thing. Don't ever call this line again. In fact I'm going to change the number today."

"No kind parting words for your father's oldest friend?"

"None other than this. When you are enjoying those feathers in your nest, Colonel, remember, they have quills on the other end. Goodbye. *Ned*."

END

AUTHOR BIOGRAPHY

An architect and a city planner walked into a bar. The bartender said, "We don't serve your kind—only writers and birds here."

The two old friends, both seventy something, said in unison, "We know how to write," and they sat down at the bar and began to collaborate on a detective novel. Art the architect lived in Dallas, Texas, and Ed the planner lived in Oakland, California, but no problem, they could exchange their jottings via e-mail.

And so over the next five years, chapters multiplied and flew back and forth through cyberspace, until one day, from the end of the bar, an Owl said, "Enough already, let me tell what really happened."

Besides age, long friendship, and longterm marriages, Arthur Rogers and Edward Phillips have something else in common: writing. But while Rogers has penned poetry, short stories, and plays, Phillips has crafted plan documents, as well as policy positions and regulations.

Rogers and Phillips are currently writing the second Rex Nickels mystery.

CPSIA information can be obtained at www.ICGtesting.com
Printed in the USA
LVOW10s1756050516

486866LV00020B/976/P